PUFFIN BOOKS

THE GREENWICH CHRONICLES

THE TIME APPRENTICE

Books by Val Tyler

THE TIME WRECCAS
THE TIME APPRENTICE

THE GREENWICH CHRONICLES

THE TIME APPRENTICE

VAL TYLER

PUFFIN

PUFFIN BOOKS

Published by the Penguin Group
Penguin Books Ltd, 80 Strand, London WC2R ORL, England
Penguin Group (USA) Inc., 375 Hudson Street, New York, New York 10014, USA
Penguin Group (Canada), 90 Eglinton Avenue East, Suite 700, Toronto, Ontario, Canada M4P 2Y3
(a division of Pearson Penguin Canada Inc.)
Penguin Ireland, 25 St Stephen's Green, Dublin 2, Ireland (a division of Penguin Books Ltd)
Penguin Group (Australia), 250 Camberwell Road, Camberwell, Victoria 3124, Australia
(a division of Pearson Australia Group Pty Ltd)
Penguin Books India Pvt Ltd, 11 Community Centre, Panchsheel Park, New Delhi – 110 017, India
Penguin Group (NZ), cnr Airborne and Rosedale Roads, Albany, Auckland 1310, New Zealand
(a division of Pearson New Zealand Ltd)
Penguin Books (South Africa) (Pty) Ltd, 24 Sturdee Avenue, Rosebank, Johannesburg 2196, South Africa

Penguin Books Ltd, Registered Offices: 80 Strand, London WC2R ORL, England

www.penguin.com

First published 2006
1

Copyright © Val Tyler, 2006

The moral right of the author has been asserted

Set in Monotype Baskerville
Typeset by Palimpsest Book Production Limited, Polmont, Stirlingshire
Made and printed in England by Clays Ltd, St Ives plc

British Library Cataloguing in Publication Data
A CIP catalogue record for this book is available from the British Library

978-0-141-38244-9
0-141-38244-9

www.valtyler.co.uk

For Mum and Dad

I would like to thank Dr Nicholas Perkins at St Hugh's College, Oxford, for the Old English translations, Bethia Tyler for reading the manuscript at an early stage, Kelly Tung for the Cantonese translation, and Yu Yul Tsang for lending me her name.

Author's Note

Vremya, Wakaa, Zeit, Seegan and Aleyesu all mean 'time' in the language of each Guardian.

Old English

The Old English in this book is as accurate as I can make it while leaving it readable.

Tid means 'time'.

Wrecca comes from 'wrӕcca', which means 'wretch', 'exile', 'outcast'.

'Gemet' means 'measure' and 'bur' means 'chamber', and so a 'Gemetbur' is a 'measuring chamber or room'.

'in me bewreoh' means 'conceal inside me' and is pronounced 'in me be-rayoh'. The 'me' is like 'met' without the 't'.

'opena ond me cyth' means 'open up and reveal me' and is pronounced as you would expect except that 'cyth' is 'cuth'.

'geweald of lyfte' means 'power from the air' and is pronounced 'ye-wayald of lufte'; the final 'e' would be pronounced but not stressed.

'endebyrdnes is geniwad' means 'old order is restored' and is pronounced 'enderbeardness is ye-newad'.

'tide healdath, ealle brucath' means 'we guard/keep time; everyone uses/enjoys it'. The final 'e' in 'tide' would be pronounced but not stressed and so the pronunciation is verging on 'teeda haldath, alla brucath'.

Contents

The Wobble

Offa Scratch's eyes ran up the tunnel wall, across the ceiling and down the other side.

The Wreccas stood and watched in fearful anticipation. Would he approve?

'Good, isn't it?' Sniff volunteered hopefully.

'Good?' Offa Scratch asked menacingly.

'Well,' Sniff realized his leader was not as happy as Sniff had hoped, 'it seems to be in the right place.'

'Seems?' Offa Scratch snarled.

More than a year of being the Wrecca leader's second-in-command had taught Sniff a great deal about how to keep out of trouble. Offa Scratch had shown them where to dig and so, of course, they had to be in exactly the right place.

'I's a bit slow sometimes, Your Almightiness,' Sniff grovelled, bowing to his leader. 'I know you told us right. You thought up the plan . . . the brilliant plan,' he quickly corrected himself. 'You's a mighty brain.'

Slightly soothed, Offa Scratch paced the tunnel, watched by his men.

Wreccas are dirty, stupid, miserable beings. They have

stooping shoulders because they spend most of their time in tunnels, and matted hair because they do not use brushes. They live under ground in a series of dark, damp, dingy tunnels called the Underneath, and most of the time they are in mortal fear of their ferocious leader.

Offa Scratch now turned to Scamp, who stood apart from the others. He was covered from head to toe in soil. Scamp was the lead digger. Although no longer a youth, Scamp was considered young to hold such a position.

'How long till it's finished?' Offa Scratch demanded.

Scamp leant on a battered old shovel that was the mark of his trade. He scratched his head, dislodging the earth that was caught in his shaggy mane of tangled hair. 'Hard to say,' he mumbled.

'Hard to say?' Offa Scratch spat. 'It's your job to say!'

Scamp shook his head and a shower of loose soil cascaded to the ground. He looked up without fear. For some strange reason, Scamp was the only Wrecca who was not absolutely terrified of their ferocious leader. 'It's a long way to dig,' he said, violently thumping his temple with the heel of his hand, trying to empty the soil out of his ear.

'Scamp don't have your quick brain, Your Greatness,' Sniff interjected, seeing his leader's temper beginning to flare. Offa Scratch found Scamp's casual attitude infuriating. If he had not been so good at digging, Offa Scratch would have delivered Scamp up to the Ruckus long ago.

'It's ages,' Sniff said, expertly diverting the subject away from Scamp, 'since I heared the story of how you saved us all from the terrible danger down by the roaring river.'

Offa Scratch's chest swelled at the thought. This was a story he loved to tell. He had been the hero that day and always enjoyed boasting about it. 'I'll tell everyone!'

'Wonderful idea, Your Masterfulness,' Sniff grovelled, guiding his leader away. The Wreccas would not object to hearing the story again if it kept their leader happy.

Scamp remained where he was, still thumping his head, blissfully unaware just how close he had been to danger.

The hot summer sun baked Greenwich Park. The usually lush grass was brown. Those who sat in the park kept to the protective shade of the majestic trees. Chattering groups of summer visitors, each with a rucksack strapped to his or her back, sauntered down the hill. They might have been forgiven for thinking that whatever they were doing or saying was nothing to do with you, me or anyone else. But they would be wrong. Even our smallest actions can have powerful consequences.

A boy carrying a rucksack walked alone through the park. His shoulders were hunched and his hands were thrust deep into his pockets. His dark eyes glowered at the ground just in front of his feet.

Seth watched this boy.

Seth had been born a Wrecca but now lived above

ground with the Guardian People. Living Topside, as the Wreccas called it, was totally different from the wretched misery of the Underneath, but Seth had found the change bewildering. As a result, he withdrew into himself and could not make friends. Perhaps that was why he noticed this particular boy. There was something in the way he walked that made Seth understand that he, too, felt alone. He watched as the boy took off his rucksack and flung it to the ground. A schoolbook fell out. The boy did not seem to notice.

Seth found himself watching with increasing interest. Leaning forward, he made no attempt to conceal his curiosity. He looked straight at the boy without any concern that he might be noticed. This boy would not be annoyed that a stranger was watching him so closely because he could not see Seth. The boy was Human.

The lad now trudged up and down, a short distance from Seth, repeatedly covering the same patch of ground, mumbling to himself. Seth tipped his head to one side to try and hear what he was saying, but could not. He moved closer to catch the boy's words but found it difficult to understand because the boy was speaking in an unfamiliar accent.

'Stupid name!' the boy was grumbling with growing ferocity. 'I hate them! I hate Greenwich! I hate Dad!' Suddenly he swung his leg back and savagely kicked a large stone that shot off across the park and thudded into one of the trees.

Seth could almost hear the tree groan as the stone bit cruelly into the bark and chipped a chunk of it away.

By the time Seth looked back, the boy had stuffed his book back into his bag and was grumpily striding off with shoulders hunched and hands deep in his pockets.

Seth walked over to the tree and picked up the chunk of bark that lay on the ground. 'Poor old tree,' he said, running his hand tenderly over the wound.

'Hello, Grandfather!' Tid and Sofi called out cheerfully as they arrived home from school.

Old Father Tim bent down and kissed Sofi on the head and ruffled Tid's hair. 'Did you have a good day?' he asked.

'All right,' they answered, noticing a sticky chocolate cake that was on the table. The kettle started whistling and the old man began making the tea.

Old Father Tim was the powerful leader of the Guardian People. Some found him rather frightening, but Sofi and Tid knew him to be kind and loving. There was, however, something mysteriously marvellous about the old man. Like all Guardians, Old Father Tim wore a full-length tunic under a long outer coat, but his was dark blue and it sparkled with a hint of sapphire and starlight. His shoulder-length hair and short beard hinted silver and, on occasions, his usually kind eyes had a glint of steel.

The Guardian People are wise and noble. They guard time for everyone, live in tidy, well-kept cottages, value learning and respect one another. They inhabit the same places that we Humans do, except we cannot see them or any part of their world. Humans and Guardian

People can even walk straight through one another with no reaction other than a strange feeling.

Tid and Sofi washed their hands at the kitchen sink before Sofi cut each of them a large piece of cake. The chocolate stuck to her fingers as she put a slice on to plates for Tid and herself. They were both licking their lips appreciatively when Old Father Tim and Tid suddenly stopped still. They looked at each other questioningly.

'Did you feel that?' Old Father Tim asked.

Tid nodded.

Sofi looked from Tid to her grandfather. She had no idea what they were talking about.

'Feel what?' she asked.

'The wobble.'

'I very much doubt that Sofi could have felt it,' Old Father Tim said.

Sofi looked at him indignantly. She was about to say that she was just as likely to feel a wobble (whatever a wobble was) as Tid when Old Father Tim said, 'Wipe your fingers, my boy. I must go to the Meridian Line, and I think it would be fitting for you to come too.'

Sofi looked at him expectantly.

'I am sorry, Sofi,' Old Father Tim said, not wanting to disappoint her but knowing that he must. 'As the Old Father Grandson and possible future leader, there are certain things that Tid needs to know. I cannot ask you to accompany us. Will you be all right on your own or shall I ask Enderell to come over?'

Mortified as she was at being left out, Sofi did not

want to suffer the indignity of a babysitter while it was still daylight. She was too old for that.

'I shall be fine,' she said, forcing a smile. 'I've loads of work to do.'

Tid gulped down the last of his cake and quickly wiped his mouth and fingers on the damp cloth that Old Father Tim held out to him. Giving Sofi an apologetic smile, he followed his grandfather out of the cottage.

Sofi put down what remained of her piece of cake and pouted. She had been born a Wrecca, living in the Underneath until eighteen months before, when she and Seth had come to live Topside. She now felt that her transformation from Wrecca to one of the Guardian People was complete. Not only did she dress, speak and think like them, she usually forgot that she had ever been anything else. It hurt that there was something that Tid was allowed to do because he had had the good fortune to be born one of the Guardian People, while she was not because she had had a wretched beginning as a Wrecca.

Grumpily, she sat down, banging her elbows on to the table and thumping her chin into her hands.

She opened her one of her schoolbooks, supposing she must do her homework, but she did not want to. Why should she work while Tid was off having fun? Instead, she slammed the book shut and pulled *Tempus and the Gemetbur* out of her bag. It had been her turn to take her favourite storybook into school to show the class. *Tempus and the Gemetbur* was about the very first

Guardian, Tempus. Sofi had learnt to read since coming Topside. It proved she was now one of the Guardians. Wreccas could not read. She settled back in her chair and idly flipped through the pages until Tid and Old Father Tim returned from the Line.

Tid burst through the door, excitedly exclaiming that there had been a wobble in time. 'Humans will have to repeat a day. Just think, Sofi,' he said enthusiastically, 'all day tomorrow they will do exactly the same as they did today, and they won't know anything about it!'

Sofi had a hundred questions, but pretended not to be interested. 'I'm busy,' she lied, closing her storybook and starting to do her homework.

Seth's Big Mistake

Seth was alone, as usual. Just as he had done the previous day, he sat and watched the Human boy stomping through the park.

The Greenwich Guardian, who was Seth's adoptive grandmother, had warned him to keep away from Humans. 'They will be repeating their day,' she had explained at breakfast.

'Will our day repeat as well?' Seth had asked.

'No, our time will continue as normal.' Then she had added very seriously, 'But if Human time is to return to what it should be, you must be very careful to keep out of their way. Did you pass through any of them yesterday?'

'No,' Seth had said.

'Good, then make sure you stay away from them today as well. To pass through one of them at the same time as changing anything they do could be disastrous.'

'All right.'

'Are you sure you understand?' his grandmother had persisted. 'Repeating days can be a little tricky.'

'I didn't pass through anyone yesterday and I'm not

going to pass through anyone today,' Seth assured her, trying to hide his irritation. 'I'll keep out of their way, like always.'

'Good boy,' the Greenwich Guardian had said, taking some more toast.

Seth had nodded. The time wobble sounded boring, anyway. He still did not feel part of the Guardian world, nor did he understand it yet. Nevertheless, Seth had been careful to do as his grandmother had asked, and had kept away from the Humans all day. It had been easy at school, but now something had drawn him back to the place where he had been yesterday. He sat and idly watched this boy, knowing exactly what he was about to do.

The boy was trudging up and down, repeatedly covering the same patch of ground. Hands deep in his pockets, he mumbled to himself. Seth tried to hear if he was saying exactly the same as yesterday and moved closer to catch the boy's words.

'Stupid name!' he was grumbling with growing anger. 'I hate them! I hate Greenwich! I hate Dad!' Suddenly Seth remembered what the boy was about to do. He was going to kick that stone and it would hurtle into the tree and damage it as it had done yesterday.

Seth should not have done it, and if he had realized just how much trouble his action was going to cause, he probably would not, but he did not stop to think. As the boy swung his leg, Seth stooped down and grabbed the stone away. The boy seemed to lose his balance as he missed it. His foot followed through, but Seth was not bothered. He knew that the boy's foot would swing right through his hand. That was the way it was: Humans and Guardian People passed right through one another. And so it was with considerable surprise that Seth felt a scorching blow on his hand as the boy's foot smartly collided with it.

'Ouch!' Seth cried, falling over backwards, clutching his injured hand. The ground trembled beneath him, but Seth was too shocked to notice.

The boy jumped back, staring at Seth in amazement. 'Where did you come from?' he asked. Seth had appeared from nowhere.

Seth looked about him. This boy could not be talking to him. A Human could not possibly see him.

'You,' the boy said, pushing him with his foot. 'I'm talking to you.'

Seth swallowed hard. He did not know what to say. This could not be happening.

'How dumb are you?' the boy asked. When Seth did not answer, the boy tried again. 'Look, I'm sorry I kicked you.' He did not sound sorry, but appeared to think this was something he was meant to say. 'But you shouldn't creep up on people. I didn't see you.'

Seth still said nothing. This Human spoke in a way that Seth had never heard before.

The boy seemed unsure what to say next. He hesitated for a moment before asking, 'You're not going to tell on me, are you? Cos if you are, I'll tell Miss Carter that you sneaked up on me and it wasn't my fault.'

Still Seth did not answer. The boy looked puzzled. 'You *do* go to my school, don't you?'

Seth shook his head.

The boy looked relieved. 'That's all right then.' Dad had said if there were any more problems at school then he would be in serious trouble.

Seth was still holding his injured hand.

'Is it all right?' the boy asked.

Seth nodded.

'What's your name?'

Seth knew he should not be speaking to a Human, but then a Human should not be able to see him. What else could he do?

'Seth.'

'I'm Baz.' There was a moment's silence while Baz bent down to retrieve his schoolbook and stuff it back into his bag. 'Where do you go to school?'

Seth did not think he should be naming his school to a Human, and so he said vaguely, 'Down the hill.'

'Funny uniform,' Baz commented, nodding towards Seth's short tunic worn over trousers. 'I like the belt. Where did you get it?'

Like all Guardian boys, Seth wore a heavy belt round his waist. His was particularly fine, with intricate patterns deeply scored into the leather.

'My grandmother gave it to me.'

'I wish my grandma would get me something real cool like that,' Baz said. 'Isn't it great weather! Don't you just love it when it's hot? Which team do you support?'

Seth was dazed by Baz's ability to dodge rapidly from one subject to another.

'I know,' Baz said, misunderstanding Seth's silence, 'soccer, football you call it, is a bit lame, isn't it. No one ever scores! Dad takes me to see Charlton when they're at home. I watch basketball in New York. It's a much better game. I support the Knicks.' He paused, as an unpleasant thought from the past clouded his mind, but he immediately discarded it. 'Is your hand OK?'

Seth looked dumbly at his hand and nodded.

'You copped it all right!' Baz said, rather impressed. 'I have to go.' He stood up and hoisted his rucksack on to his back. 'I'll see you around,' he said hopefully.

'All right.'

With a cheery wave of the hand, Baz turned and walked off. He no longer hung his head or looked grumpy.

Elsewhere in the park, Sofi and Tid were returning home from school.

'You must have felt that one!' Tid exclaimed to Sofi as they turned into the gate of their cottage. 'That wobble was enormous!'

'I don't know,' Sofi said, unsure of herself. 'I think I did.'

'It was the biggest ever!'

Old Father Tim appeared at the front door.

'Are you going to the Meridian Line?' Tid asked hopefully.

Old Father Tim did not seem to hear him. 'Very strange,' he muttered. 'Very strange indeed.'

'Can I come too?' Tid asked, surprised that his grandfather had bypassed the usual Guardian greetings. He passed his school-bag to Sofi with an apologetic smile and followed Old Father Tim out of the gate.

Sofi watched them go in silence.

The Meridian Line in Greenwich Park is the most sacred place to the Guardian People. This is where the impressive Timepiece stands, looking like a very ornate clock that you and I would call a grandfather clock. It is the heartbeat of time. Without it, time would stop forever. Eighteen months before, Sofi had helped the Wreccas to steal part of it. As soon as she had understood the danger, she had taken many risks to restore it. If it had not been for her, Sofi thought bitterly, everything would have ended then and there, and yet Tid was allowed to accompany his grandfather and she was not.

She wandered into the cottage and flopped into a chair, shoving their school-bags on to the kitchen table and nearly hitting a newly baked banana cake. She almost wished she had sent it crashing to the floor. Well, one thing was certain: she was not going to do homework while Tid was off with Grandfather having fun!

She stood up, pushing her chair away with the back of her legs so that it screeched on the shiny tiled floor. With a grumble of frustration, she stomped out of the cottage.

In the gloom of the Underneath, Offa Scratch edged silently towards the end of the newly excavated tunnel. Sniff held a flaming torch high above their heads. They both peered into the shadows.

'It stops there,' Sniff whispered. Offa Scratch continued moving forward until the flat of his hand touched the rough wall where the tunnel ended. Leaning forward, he pressed his ear to it, trying to listen to anything that might be happening on the other side.

Anxious to assist, Sniff held the flame high above Offa Scratch's head so that he might have more light. A lick of flame dripped on to his cheek.

'Arrgghhh!' Offa Scratch yelled, swiping at Sniff with his dangerously sharp nails and forgetting to be quiet. 'You stupid dung-brain!' he snarled. 'Is you trying to set I on fire?'

Sniff expertly ducked out of the way. This was something he had learnt to do since becoming second-in-command. Whenever angry, his leader would lash out, and Sniff had learnt the hard way that quick reactions were important if he wanted to avoid serious injury.

'I's sorry, Your Wonderfulness,' Sniff said quietly, anxious that they should not be heard by those on the other side of the wall.

Offa Scratch instantly remembered that they were supposed to be quiet. 'Stupid dung-head!' he hissed. 'You's making a noise when us is supposed to be quiet!'

'I's sorry,' Sniff said again, not at all bothered about apologizing for something he had not done.

Offa Scratch returned his ear to the wall and listened once more.

'I can't hear nothing,' he said irritably. 'Is you sure they's digged in the right place?'

'Yer,' Sniff said, deciding it was best not to point out that they had dug where Offa Scratch had told them to.

'They hasn't gone far enough.'

'The problem, Your Grandness,' Sniff continued, bowing low, 'is that now they's hit rock, it's much harder. It'll be all right,' he added quickly, anxious not to irritate again. 'Scamp is sorting out the pointy hammers that they need for rock. There isn't much further to go.'

'And them on the other side doesn't have no idea what us is doing?'

'Ner.'

Offa Scratch nodded sagely. 'You listen to I,' he said. 'I's the one who knows how things need to be done.' He was always reminding the other Wreccas that they were stupid compared to him, and not without justification. Offa Scratch did have more brain than the others, but that did not make him clever, just cleverer than anyone else in the Underneath.

Lost in thought as she strode across the park, Sofi did not immediately notice when her name was called.

'Sofi.'

She continued walking.

'Sofi!'

This time, she heard. Turning round, she saw a fair teenage girl, standing some distance away.

The girl was wearing a long, faded, leaf-green dress that flared below the waist down to the ground. The sleeves were fitted to the elbow but wide at the wrist.

The girl had blonde hair and was a stranger to Sofi.

Knowing that she should not talk to people who were unknown to her, Sofi turned away, but the girl ran after her, calling her name once more.

'Do I know you?' Sofi asked as the girl drew level.

'You doesn't remember.'

Sofi stared at the girl. There was something familiar in the way that she spoke.

'I's Scaggy.'

Sofi's eyes opened wide in surprise. Scaggy! She was a Wrecca whom Sofi had known when she had lived in the Underneath. One day Scaggy had abruptly disappeared, like all the girls did eventually. Sofi had assumed that she had gone to live with the women. 'I'm not supposed to talk to Wreccas,' Sofi said bluntly, moving away.

'Why not? You's a Wrecca yourself.'

Sofi stopped dead in her tracks. 'No, I'm not,' she said indignantly.

'Of course you is.'

The words had not been spoken unkindly, but they hurt Sofi nonetheless. She had worked long and hard to change. Of course she was no longer a Wrecca. She did not even talk like them any more.

'Do it matter so very much?' Scaggy asked gently, quite unlike the way Sofi remembered Wreccas speaking.

'I's not a Wrecca no more!' Sofi blurted out and then winced because for the first time in ages she had spoken like one.

17

'Not all Wreccas is bad,' Scaggy said, not noticing.

'Oh yeah?' Sofi said hostilely. 'Name me one that isn't!'

'You,' Scaggy said simply.

Sofi suddenly felt ashamed. Scaggy had never behaved unkindly towards her when they had both lived in the Underneath. In fact, she had often helped feed Sofi when she had been too little to fend for herself.

When Sofi spoke again, it was in a much softer voice. 'How do you know my name is Sofi?' In the Underneath she had been called Snot.

'Us all knows.'

This made Sofi feel very strange. She did not want the Wreccas to know anything about her.

Scaggy was looking at her curiously.

'I like your dress,' Sofi said, in an attempt to change the subject.

Guardian girls do not wear dresses. They wear tunics and trousers, like the boys. Sofi's tunic was blue and, because it was summer, the sleeves were short.

Scaggy smiled, obviously delighted. 'I maked it,' she said with pride.

'Do all Wrecca women dress like that?'

'Ner. Us sort of dresses how us likes.'

When Sofi had lived in the Underneath, there were no teenage girls or women, only children and men. Sofi knew the women must live somewhere, and yet she had never known where. This was her chance to find out.

'Where do you live now?'

'In the Labyrinth.'

'What's that?'

'The women's tunnels,' Scaggy explained.

'Where are they?'

'Way over the other side of Blackheath. I'll show you if you like.'

Sofi stepped back, instantly distrustful.

Scaggy understood. 'You doesn't have to come. But you'd be safe if you did.'

'No thanks,' Sofi said, backing away.

'Look, Sofi.' A note of urgency had crept into Scaggy's voice. 'There's something strange going on at the edge of the Labyrinth. There's all sorts of bangings and rumblings. It sounds as if someone is digging really close to us. I was thinking . . .' she hesitated, 'I was thinking that maybe . . . perhaps . . . I mean . . . you'll let me talk to Old Father Tim about it.'

'Grandfather?' Sofi asked suspiciously. 'Why?'

'Him can help.'

'No,' Sofi said, immediately certain that this was some sort of a trap.

'I'd not take much of his time.'

'No.'

'Us needs help.'

'Not from him. Sort it out yourselves. Grandfather doesn't know anything about what goes on below ground.'

'Us can't do it alone without magic. Perhaps you can talk to Old Father Tim and ask him if . . .'

'No,' Sofi said stubbornly, and then she added, more mildly, 'I can't.'

'Yer you can,' Scaggy said encouragingly, gently laying her hand on Sofi's arm.

'No I can't!' Sofi exclaimed, throwing off Scaggy's hand. 'I'm not a Wrecca no more! I'm one of the Guardian People and I don't talk to Wreccas!' Without pausing, she turned and ran away.

The forcefulness of Sofi's rejection surprised Scaggy. She stood and watched until Sofi was out of sight. It had been her idea to ask for help. Now she would have to go back and admit to the others that she had been wrong.

Somehow, they would have to work this one out by themselves.

3

The Time Bounce

Bryn Brownal was at the Line when Old Father Tim and Tid arrived.

'What happened this time?' Old Father Tim asked.

'There has been the most enormous confabulation in the meteoric constrictions of earth's illuminal cords.'

'What's a confab . . .' but Tid not have time to complete his question. Old Father Tim and Bryn Brownal seemed to have forgotten he was there.

'I thought it must be something like that,' Old Father Tim said.

'Exactly how bad do you think it is?'

Old Father Tim rubbed his chin through his short beard. 'Hard to tell without careful calculations.'

'You must have some sort of idea,' Bryn continued. As one of the Elders of the Park, Bryn was considered wise but, as the leader of the Guardians, Old Father Tim was wiser still.

'It will take a while to be certain,' Old Father Tim said thoughtfully, 'but it seems to me that something has happened to bounce time well and truly out of alignment.'

Although he had been listening carefully, Tid had not understood what they were talking about. 'What's happened?'

His grandfather, still deep in thought, spoke only to Bryn. 'The longer we wait, the harder it will be to put things right. Let me think. The apprentices are arriving shortly, are they not, for the final selection process?'

'They are due in a couple of days,' Bryn said.

'Excellent,' Old Father Tim said. 'They can help with this. It will be much better to judge their abilities by seeing them working on a real problem. Who is coming?'

'Wakaa is bringing an apprentice called Kanika.'

'Good, we will need deep magic.'

'Vremya is coming with two apprentices.'

'Two? He must have a very good crop coming through. Vremya understands Guardian history. That will be useful.'

'And Seegan is bringing a young apprentice who he esteems very highly.'

'Excellent; he understands calculations. Is there anyone else?'

'No, that is all.'

'What about ancient laws; we will need someone who understands the law . . . er . . . do you think Zeit is the man for that?'

'He is a bit of a hothead.'

'I know, I know,' Old Father Tim said, 'but his heart is in the right place.'

'And he has an excellent brain.'

'Send for Zeit.'

Bryn wrote it down.

Old Father Tim rubbed his chin again, concentrating deeply. 'Translations will be vital. We shall need . . .' He thought for a moment. 'I know he is newly come as a Guardian, but Aleyesu shows advanced wisdom. I think he is the one we should ask to translate for us.'

'Very well.' Bryn waited to see if Old Father Tim needed anyone else.

'I think that will be all.'

'Then I shall make the arrangements.'

Bryn hurried off.

Tid knew most of these Guardians a little. They had been in Greenwich when Old Father Tim had summoned the Great Gathering of the Guardians during the last emergency. 'Will you summon another Gathering?' he asked hopefully. Gatherings were exciting because it brought Guardians to Greenwich from all over the world.

'No, not this time. We are only summoning those we need. In fact, some of the Guardians will be arriving soon, anyway.'

'I heard Pa Brownal say they were bringing apprentices. Why?'

'So that we can choose the new Time Apprentice.'

'What's that?'

'I suppose,' Old Father Tim said, sitting down on a wooden bench, 'the Time Apprentice could be considered the best apprentice. Instead of only working with the one Guardian, he or she will have the opportunity of working with several. It gives them a head start in their studies.'

'Were you the Time Apprentice when you were young?'

'No, that was the Greenwich Guardian. I was the Old Father Grandson.'

'Will I be able to meet some of the apprentices when they arrive?'

'There will be no time for socializing, because of these wobbles.'

Tid frowned. He was disappointed.

Old Father Tim patted the bench next to him. 'Sit down, my boy.'

Tid sat down.

'Do you understand the importance of these wobbles?'

'Not really.'

'Well,' the old man took a deep breath, 'the first wobble in time was just one of those things. They can happen for no reason. It meant nothing. But this second one is completely different. Something momentous has happened to cause this second wobble. It was quite the biggest I have ever felt. I suspect it has bounced time out of alignment.'

'I heard you tell Pa Brownal that, but what does it mean?'

'It means, my boy, that Human and Guardian times have split away from each other. While our time will continue as normal, Humans will repeat the same day over and over until we can bounce their time back into line with ours.'

It did not sound so bad. Tid had lived through worse. 'So, while Humans repeat the same day,' he said logically, 'we shall live our lives normally, won't we?'

'Yes.'

'Then, how can it affect us?'

Old Father Tim paused for a moment, trying to think how he could possibly make this easy for his grandson to understand. 'Supposing you and I were walking together across Greenwich to the Hither House.'

Tid nodded.

'Well, imagine that, instead of walking side by side, we were walking on opposite sides of the road. We would start together, follow exactly the same route, remain parallel the whole way and eventually arrive at the Hither House at exactly same time.'

'But the route would be slightly different, wouldn't it?' Tid asked, picturing the scene in his head. 'I might have to cross a road when you didn't.'

'Precisely so, my boy,' Old Father Tim said enthusiastically. 'Those are very minor wobbles that happen from time to time. The Timepiece has been designed to take account of such things, and we hardly notice them. But supposing on my side of the road I am diverted and have to go round a roundabout.'

'Then I would have to slow down until you caught up.'

'But what if I got stuck on that roundabout and kept going round and round? What would happen then?'

'Well, if we wanted to arrive at the Hither House together, then I suppose I would have to stand still until you got off the roundabout.'

'But you can't stand still, Tid. Time cannot stand still. You would go on and I would keep going round and round.'

'Then I suppose I would arrive without you.'

Old Father Tim nodded. 'Exactly, and unless someone did something spectacular to get me off the roundabout and helped me catch up with you, we would never meet up again.'

'How spectacular would it have to be?'

Old Father Tim looked very grave. 'Pretty spectacular, my boy. You see, Guardian and Human times are designed to work side by side. If one permanently breaks away from the other, we would be thrown into turmoil. Law and order would break down. We would return to the utter chaos of ancient times.'

'What does that mean?'

'There would be no order. Humans and the Guardian People would inhabit the same world.'

Tid was appalled. 'Do you mean they would see us?'

'I'm afraid they would do more than see us. They would be our close neighbours. In the past, that has led to war.'

'War? But the Guardian People are no good at fighting.'

'That is true. We would have to use our magic against them.'

'That would be a bit one-sided, wouldn't it?'

'Not necessarily. You must remember that once Humans start fighting they will not stop, even when they are beaten. They can also be very cunning and quite clever. There is a very real danger, young Tid, that each would destroy the other.'

'Do you mean we would all die?' Tid asked, horrified.

'We would.'

Tid's heart began to thud in his chest. 'Then we have to get you off the roundabout.'

'Yes,' Old Father Tim said, trying to sound brighter. 'That is what we shall be trying to do, with the help of the Guardians.'

'And their apprentices?'

'Yes.'

Tid took hold of his grandfather's hand.

'I have told you,' Old Father Tim continued, 'because as the Old Father Grandson you need to know. But it is best not to burden anyone else with this.'

'You mean Sofi?'

'I mean anyone.'

Tid nodded. 'All right. I won't breathe a word. How long have we got?'

'No one can know for certain. It could be a month or two.'

'That would give us time,' Tid said, feeling slightly better.

'Or it could happen tomorrow.'

Scaggy knocked at the door of the Labyrinth and waited for Falryd to open up. There was no handle on the outside of the door and so Scaggy had to wait. As usual, Falryd took her time. Eventually she dragged open the door and Scaggy entered without saying a word. Her mind was on the forthcoming interview with Berwyth. She was not looking forward to it.

Just like the Underneath, the Labyrinth was under ground but, unlike the men, the women had not built these tunnels themselves. Many years before, when the men had thrown the women out of the Underneath, they had had to find somewhere safe to live. Below ground was all they had ever known and so this was where they looked. On the other side of Blackheath, one of them had happened upon an opening. It revealed a maze of dry and relatively warm tunnels that ran for miles. They had been carved out of the rock by Humans thousands of years before. This was where the women had made their home.

Berwyth and the members of her Committee occupied the best accommodation. Their walls were decorated with pictures that had been scavenged from above ground, and they had beds with sheets and blankets, not as clean or as fine as you or I would expect, but certainly many times better than anything in the Underneath. The majority of Wrecca women did not have beds or pictures on the wall. Some had managed to screen off private alcoves with faded pieces of material or scraps of wood, and the rest slept in a shared tunnel.

All the tunnels were dry and, with so many living there, they remained reasonably warm. All except Berwyth and her Committee ate in the kitchen. The food was often stale but was reasonably well cooked. The women had fashioned a large oven and there were several fires where different pots could be boiled and stale bread toasted. The kitchen had been decked out with tables, chairs and benches, each one scavenged from rubbish dumps on the Topside. The Wrecca women kept them almost clean, but much of the furniture was in a very poor state of repair.

Scaggy walked through the tunnels towards the Committee Chamber. The Committee was the council that organized the Labyrinth. There were six members. Each had been personally appointed by Berwyth. Consequently, if anyone wanted to be on the Committee, she would have to grovel to Berwyth for years until there was an opening.

It had taken a while, but Scaggy had been the one to persuade the Committee to ask Old Father Tim for help. No one had thought it a good idea. Berwyth had only agreed because she had no other plan. Scaggy now dreaded the reaction when they learnt that she had failed. It was a pity she had even tried.

Yaryth was standing outside the Committee Chamber. 'Well?' she demanded, as soon as she saw Scaggy. 'Him sayed ner, did him?'

'I's here to report to Berwyth,' Scaggy said haughtily.

Yaryth shrugged her shoulders and disappeared behind the long, dark-red, slightly grubby curtain that kept the Committee Chamber private, to announce Scaggy's arrival.

'You can go in,' Yaryth said, as soon as she returned.

Scaggy pushed aside the curtain and entered.

The Committee sat on two long benches, either side of the chamber. Berwyth herself lay on the bed that she called a couch, at the far end of the room.

Like most Wreccas, Berwyth was dark-haired. She had a round face, bulbous eyes and thick, fleshy lips that she liked to daub with bright red juice; her maid, Yaryth, made it from grinding dried berries. This powder was then added to water and smeared on her lips. Berwyth was very large; some called her fat, but only behind her back.

'Well?' she demanded as soon as Scaggy arrived. 'Is Old Father Fat-Nose coming to the rescue?'

Scaggy stood between the two benches. Three members of the Committee sat on each. They watched Scaggy through narrowed eyes, anxious to discover from her manner whether she had succeeded or not. Scaggy ignored them and looked straight at Berwyth, trying to sound more confident than she felt. 'Ner,' she said.

Various comments burst from the women on either side.

'Told you so!'

'You thought you knowed better!'

'Him'll never help us!'

'Learned the hard way, didn't you!'

Scaggy kept her head high and her eyes on Berwyth. 'Sofi isn't going to ask him,' she finished.

'Little cat!' Berwyth spat. 'All the luxury of living Topside and her willn't lift a finger to help her own kind.'

Once again comments bounced around the room.

'Not a finger!'

'Little vixen!'

'Living in luxury!'

'Not help us!'

'You can't really blame her,' Scaggy said loyally.

'Not blame her?'

'Oh can't us?'

'Her don't know that us can be trusted,' Scaggy fought on. 'For all her knows, us could be helping the men nab her back.'

'Us help them foul-smelling pigs?' Berwyth spat in disgust.

'Foul!'

'Pigs!'

'I willn't lift a finger to help them!'

'Sofi doesn't know that,' Scaggy said reasonably.

'Oh listen to Miss High-and-Mighty!' Berwyth sneered, looking around at the others and receiving their approval, as she knew she must. 'Ner good you sucking up to that little prig. I told you her willn't have time for you now. Her thinks her has moved up in the world. The likes of her'll always look down on the likes of you!'

Scaggy said no more. She had said all that she had planned to say and was anxious to be gone.

'Is that all?' she asked.

Berwyth was reluctant to let Scaggy off so lightly. Scaggy had always irritated her. There was something in her manner and the way she dressed that made Berwyth feel that she thought herself superior. This might not have annoyed Berwyth quite so much if she had not secretly believed it to be true. Thus, she took every opportunity to put Scaggy down. One thing was certain: Scaggy would never be a member of the Committee, not as long as Berwyth was in charge.

'So, you'll admit you was wrong?' she asked nastily.

Scaggy lifted her chin and replied, 'It was worth a go.'

'It was worth a go,' Berwyth mimicked Scaggy spitefully. 'You's not as clever as you think, is you?'

'As always, Berwyth, you's absolutely accurate in your analysis.' Scaggy loved using long words. She had learnt a great deal over the years. Much of her time had been spent sitting in a tree, watching and listening to the Guardian People in the park. 'I apologize for failing to understand the enormity of the assignment you's ordered I to execute.'

'Humph!' Berwyth snorted, totally intimidated because she did not understand a word Scaggy was saying. 'You's failed. Get out!'

Gratefully, Scaggy turned on her heels and swept away through the curtain and off down the tunnels. She did not slacken her pace until she was halfway across Blackheath.

4

Proof

Seth gritted his teeth and waited.

Baz was walking towards him, scowling at the ground as usual.

Seth had been worried all day. He knew he should not have moved the stone yesterday. His grandmother would be furious if she ever found out. Now he desperately hoped that everything had somehow been put right in the night.

Baz was getting closer.

Seth waited.

Suddenly, Baz altered direction.

Seth had to be sure. If Baz walked through him, everything would be all right. Stepping to the side, he barred Baz's way once more. Immediately, Baz moved to the other side. Seth moved too.

Baz looked up. 'What's your problem?'

Seth's heart sank. Nothing had changed.

Baz glowered at Seth, but this was not at all unusual. Baz was often grumpy and unsociable. He had not wanted to come to England to live with his father in the first place, arguing that he was perfectly capable of staying at home by himself while his mother was in hospital. When his father had left America, Baz had missed him desperately. Now, he deeply resented being forced to live in England with him. When his mother had finally returned home from hospital, Baz had not been allowed to go back. Instead, he spoke to her on the telephone almost daily, and although she tried to put on a brave voice, Baz could tell that she was desperately tired. Consequently, he worried about her all the time and was sullen and moody.

Maybe this was why his classmates turned against him. They laughed at his accent and made fun of his unpractised football skills. Recently, the taunting had turned to bullying. He thought that this was what Seth was doing now and, because he had learnt that it was a mistake to show fear, Baz jutted out his chin and aggressively demanded, 'Are you dumb or something?'

Surprised, Seth took an involuntary step back.

Baz's stare turned to one of puzzlement. 'I know you, don't I?'

Seth nodded.

Baz was confused. 'But you don't go to my school.'

Seth shook his head.

Baz's face contorted in concentration. 'Your name is . . . er . . . something odd.' He had a dim memory of this boy, but it was foggy.

'Seth.'

'Seth!' Baz blurted out. 'Of course, Seth. I kicked your hand. Is it OK?' Baz was relaxing. He remembered Seth as an odd boy, but not one who would cause trouble.

'What stupid kind of name is Seth, anyway?' he asked.

Of all the things that had happened to him since moving Topside, Seth's name was one of the best. He loved it. In the Underneath he had been called Snivel. Seth was definitely an improvement on that. Baz's scorn hurt Seth's pride, and so he instinctively reverted to normal Wrecca behaviour and hit back. 'What kind of a stupid name is Baz?'

Baz pulled a face, as if conceding that Seth had a point. 'It's better than the alternative.'

'What's that?'

'Sebastian.' Baz spoke the name with loathing. 'Fancy landing your kid with a name like Sebastian!'

'Sebastian's not so bad,' Seth said honestly. He rather liked it.

'That's because it's not yours. What's Seth short for, anyway?'

Seth wasn't aware that it was short for anything. 'Seth,' he said.

Baz put his head to one side and studied Seth carefully. 'How do I know you?'

But Seth was no longer looking at Baz. He seemed to be staring into the distance behind him, and a look of alarm was spreading across his face.

Baz wheeled around and saw two children, dressed just as strangely as Seth, walking across the park. He turned back.

Seth had disappeared.

Baz looked around and found Seth behind a tree, clearly hiding from the two children. Having been bullied

himself, Baz thought that Seth was suffering in a similar
way. He looked over at Tid and Sofi. They did not
appear to be the type who would bully, but then it was
not always easy to tell. He joined Seth behind the tree.

'Give you a hard time, do they?' he asked.

'Only if they see me talking to you,' Seth said, peeping
out from behind the tree as they passed by.

'Why?'

Seth was concentrating on Tid and Sofi, and so when
he spoke he did so without thinking how strange his
words would sound to a Human. 'You're not supposed
to see me.'

'Why not?'

Seth made certain that Tid and Sofi were well out
of sight before he turned back and leant against the
tree. He vaguely remembered that Baz had spoken to
him. 'Why not what?' he asked.

'Why am I not supposed to see you?'

How could Seth answer? He thought about it for a
second and decided that the best option would be to
tell the truth. 'Because you're Human!'

'What?' Baz asked, puzzled.

'You and I are different,' Seth explained.

'That's because I come from the States and you come
from here.'

'What's "the States"?'

Baz gave Seth a questioning look; surely everyone
knew that. 'America,' he said.

Seth shook his head vaguely and shrugged again.

Baz stepped back and looked at this peculiar boy as

if he was seeing him for the first time. His clothes were odd – Baz had never seen a belt like that before – and he spoke differently from the boys at school. There was something exceptionally strange about him.

'Who *are* you?' Baz asked, suddenly not quite sure.

Seth thought about this for a moment.

'My name is Seth, and I'm . . .' He hesitated. What was he? Was he a Wrecca or one of the Guardian People? He did not know, but he did know one thing for certain. 'I'm not Human.'

Sniff stood back and watched as Offa Scratch inspected the troops. Slime had organized them, and so they were not Sniff's responsibility. If Offa Scratch was not impressed, it would be Slime who would suffer, but Sniff still felt nervous. He always did around his leader.

Offa Scratch walked along several ragged rows of scruffy Wreccas who were proudly standing with their chests puffed out. They were dressed in dirty trousers and tunics that were miserable shades of brown. Each held a lump of wood in his hand. No two lumps were the same weight or length. Some were clearly bits of tree, others had been pulled from old fences and one looked like a chipped rounders bat. This was held by Slime. He was a particularly revolting Wrecca who was so named because goo tended to drip from his nose, mouth and ears. He was always wiping it away with an old rag encrusted with dried ooze.

Offa Scratch looked each Wrecca up and down before moving to the next. He was inspecting the troops.

'Not bad,' he said, when he had finished. The Wreccas swelled with pride, puffing out their chests even more. This had the effect of making them top-heavy and in danger of toppling over.

'But can they fight?' Offa Scratch asked.

'Yes, sir!' spat Slime, trying to sound like a soldier. Turning to the troops, he bellowed, 'Weapons at the ready!'

Straight away, but not together, the troops lifted their lumps of wood above their heads as if to attack. Some held their weapons in the right hand and some in the left. It was a ragged display, but Offa Scratch was impressed.

'Forward!' bellowed Slime, and slowly the Wreccas began to advance. Once again, nothing was synchronized. Then, from deep in their throats there arose a low, menacing, monosyllabic, grunting chant that throbbed slowly and rhythmically around the chamber. It echoed threateningly through the tunnels and could not fail to intimidate. The Wrecca band shuffled towards their leader, hoping they were making a good impression.

Offa Scratch instinctively backed away. Ragged and undisciplined though they were, they were a formidable fighting force. Without intending to, they instilled fear rather than admiration in their leader.

Offa Scratch's palms went wet and his mouth became dry. His mind suddenly flashed back to the moment when he had seized the leadership. He had taken his opportunity and had ruthlessly done away with their previous leader, Old Killjoy. Was this what was happening to him now?

Once he had identified the danger, Offa Scratch's reaction was swift and violent. Resolutely deciding not to be defeated without a fight, he sprang towards the nearest Wrecca. With a ferocious roar, he lashed out at the surprised man, who stumbled backwards in shock, blood dripping from his gashed face. He did not dare fight back.

Offa Scratch swooped up the lump of wood that the Wrecca had dropped. Holding it in front of him, ready to pounce, he glanced about warily, trying to work out who would attack first.

The chant faded on the Wreccas' lips and they stood still, jaws hanging open in surprise.

Determined not to be fooled by a bout of play-acting, Offa Scratch growled, 'Come on, then, if you're coming.' He bounced on the balls of his feet, his knuckles white as he gripped the lump of wood in his trembling hand.

The Wreccas stared at their leader. What was he doing?

As second-in-command, Sniff knew his leader better than most. He had quickly worked out what was happening. As usual, he would have to remedy the situation, and he did so by applauding loudly and enthusiastically. It was so unexpected that everyone jumped.

'Congratulations, Oh Powerful One!' Sniff roared. 'You's the mightiest warrior of them all!'

Offa Scratch looked at him distrustfully.

Sniff continued thumping his hands together and looked across at Slime. He lifted his hands and nodded to Slime, trying to encourage him to do the same.

Eventually, Slime understood. He tucked his bat under his arm and clapped.

One by one, the Wreccas joined in.

The ovation grew louder.

'Hurray!' shouted Sniff, and soon everyone was cheering.

Offa Scratch looked about him. At first he thought it was part of the trap, but when no one attacked he began to think that the applause was real. Slowly it dawned on him that he was being honoured. Relaxing just a little, he stood upright.

The cheers became deafening.

Offa Scratch risked a smile.

The celebration became wilder.

He accepted their praise with a bow of the head. If the troops had panicked him, they had to be good.

They were ready.

Baz was sitting under the tree, scratching his head. Seth had explained as best he could about the Guardian world, the repeating day and how they could now see each other because of it. Baz was having difficulty understanding, and so Seth did not point out that talking to each other now could only make matters worse.

'And you live in the park?' Baz asked, more for something to say than because he wanted to know. He was not sure that this boy was sane.

'No, I live on the other side of Greenwich, but lots of us do live in the park.'

Baz seemed to be having trouble taking it in. He

thought carefully. This was the stuff of fairy tales.
'You're crazy,' he finally said, dismissively.

Seth did not blame him. He could see how improbable all this must seem. He looked about, wondering how he could prove it. A group of Human boys were coming along the path. They were a noisy bunch that Seth had often noticed hanging around in the park. He turned to Baz. 'Watch this,' he said. 'Don't take your eyes off me.'

Seth ran over to the path. He cast a look over his shoulder to make sure that Baz was watching. He would let the boys walk right through him. He stood on the path and waited, checking back to make sure that Baz was paying attention.

As they got nearer, Seth's stomach twisted nervously. Supposing the time wobble had affected more than just Baz, and all Human boys could see him? If he stayed where he was, he would be in their way and they did not look the sort of boys he would want to annoy. Well, he had to risk it if he was going to convince Baz of the truth. He held his ground.

Just before impact, Seth closed his eyes and waited for the bump. It did not come; instead there was the odd sensation that he always felt when passing through a Human.

He opened his eyes and cast a look towards Baz, who was staring in dumbfounded amazement. Seth knew he should not do it, but he had to be certain that Baz understood what he had just seen. He turned and ran through another boy.

'I've just had a well-weird feeling,' the boy said.

'Yeah, me too,' said the boy who had walked through Seth first.

'Ooooh!' laughed a third. 'All right, girls?'

This comment brought derisive laughter from the others.

The first boy did not like being on the receiving end of scorn and he scanned the area for a quick change of subject. His eyes lit up as he spied Baz under the tree. 'Looky here, it's the Yank!' he said nastily.

The other boys spun round to look.

Baz's face turned rigid with fear. Slowly he stood up. It was safer to face Cooper and his gang when standing.

The boys intimidatingly clustered around him, barring Seth from his view. Seth understood how Baz must be feeling; he had often felt the same when living in the Underneath.

'Oh, look,' Cooper sneered, 'he's scared!' and he quivered his hands and knees to illustrate how Baz was feeling.

'You wish!' Baz said, trying to sound convincing.

'Oo-er!' Cooper mocked, 'he's shaking in his . . . ouch!' Cooper put his hand to the back of his head and rubbed it. It was wet.

There was blood on Cooper's hand.

'Who did that?' he yelled, wheeling around, furious. But before he could find out, another stone whizzed in and clipped him on the forehead. 'Was that you?' he asked one of the boys, grabbing him by his school tie.

'N . . . n . . . no,' the boy stammered.

Cooper did not believe him.

Seth recognized the thrill of excitement that ran through a Wrecca crowd when a fight was looming. The boys were forming a circle around the two of them.

'Go on, Coop, hit him!'

As the fight loomed, it suddenly occurred to Seth that he had done it again. Picking up the stone in the first place had caused Baz to see him; would hitting Cooper on the head with another stone have the same effect?

He had to know.

Stepping forward, he waved his hands above his head. 'Hey!' he shouted.

Cooper was concentrating on punishing the boy in front of him.

'Coop! Over here!' Seth yelled, waving his hands.

Cooper did not react.

Baz stared in alarm. Was Seth trying to get them both killed? Taking advantage of the mayhem, he skirted round the group and hissed at his friend, 'What are you doing?'

Seth had no desire to hang about, now he was sure that Cooper and his gang could not see him. 'Come on!' he said. 'Let's go!'

Baz grabbed his school-bag and darted off.

The two boys ran, blundering through the park, ducking under low branches and leaping over bushes. They kept going at speed until they were exhausted. Finally they flopped, gasping for breath, on to the sun-baked grass.

'Was that you throwing the stones?' Baz panted.

'Yeah.'

A grin spread across Baz's dark face. 'You caught Cooper a great one on the head! Did you see? He was mad!'

Seth suddenly felt a surge of happiness and started laughing. His laughter was infectious, and Baz started laughing too. The more one laughed, the funnier the other found it. Soon they were rolling about in hysterics. It felt wonderful!

They bellowed with happiness until their faces were wet with tears and their sides ached from the effort. Slowly, their hilarity subsided. Each wiped his eyes.

'Seth,' Baz finally said, 'if I was able to see you because you moved the stone that I was gonna kick, why couldn't Cooper see you when you hit him?'

'Not sure,' Seth said, thinking hard, 'but I changed what you did and at exactly the same moment you touched me. Your foot should have passed through my hand, but it didn't.'

'Would that have made the difference?'

Seth shrugged. He did not know. He thought that his grandmother would, but he was not going to ask her.

An easy silence fell between them.

'What shall we do now?' Baz asked.

'We don't have time to do anything,' Seth said. 'You've got to go home.'

'Why?'

'Because of the day. I told you it's repeating and you're not supposed to change what you do. Today is supposed to be exactly the same as yesterday, and it's not.'

'Yeah, Cooper will give me a kicking tomorrow,' Baz said, suddenly serious.

'He won't remember.'

'Why not?'

'He shouldn't remember anything that happened today,' Seth explained. 'It's the way it works.'

'Really,' Baz said, encouraged.

'In fact, you might not either.'

'I remembered you today.'

'I think that may have been my fault,' Seth admitted. 'I shouldn't really have got in your way, because meeting up and talking and everything might mean that you will be repeating this same day for ages.'

'Great!' Baz said, thrilled.

The corners of Seth's mouth flickered into a smile. It felt good to have a friend. 'If we stay out of Cooper's way,' he reasoned, hoping it to be true, 'it can't cause much more trouble if you're the only one who changes what you do. I mean, how much difference can the two of us make?'

'And so we can meet up tomorrow and do something?'

'Yes!' Seth said, eyes shining. 'But you've got to go home now.'

'I suppose,' Baz said grudgingly. Then he added hopefully, 'Will you be here tomorrow?'

Seth knew he should say no. 'I'll meet you by the gates.'

'And so they are going to choose the best apprentice while they are here?' Sofi asked as she and Tid had been walking home from the school.

45

'Yes, he or she will be called the Time Apprentice and will be able to study with different Guardians, not just the one.'

'Wouldn't that be great,' said Sofi, enthralled by the idea. 'Do you think I could be the Time Apprentice when I'm older?' Then she added dejectedly, 'I suppose you'd get it.'

'No, I can't, because I am the Old Father Grandson, but I don't see why you shouldn't.'

'Really?' Sofi said, delighted. 'Wouldn't that be exciting,' and she drifted off into dreaming about it.

Tid opened the garden gate, relieved that the subject of the Time Apprentice was occupying Sofi's thoughts so that she had not asked more about the time wobbles. He had been tempted to mention them, just to get her opinion, but because he had promised his grandfather, he did not.

'Those anagrams were tough.'

'Yes, they were, weren't they?' Sofi said, shutting the gate and forcing herself to cut short her daydreaming. 'Ma Watten seems to think they're easy. She's a good teacher most of the time, but she doesn't understand how tough it is if you have a tricky name. Sofi Mossel is not right for them. One "s" would be all right, but I've got three! I could only come up with "fool misses", which seemed pretty lame. I wish I had a middle name. That would have helped.'

'I could only get "items sold" out of mine,' Tid complained, as they entered the cottage.

'Cissy Perrafin,' Sofi said wistfully, 'made "Fairy

Princess" out of hers. She's so lucky!'

'Timothy Boar,' Tid started giggling, 'made a great one out of his. Guess what it was?'

Sofi shrugged.

'Hairy bot . . .' But Tid did not finish because Old Father Tim came downstairs.

'Good afternoon,' the old man said.

'Good afternoon,' they replied politely.

'Did you have a good day at school?'

'Yes,' Sofi said as she put down her bag and hugged her grandfather. He kissed the top of her head and then handed her a knife so that she could cut the lemon cake.

'Have there been any more wobbles?' she asked, putting down the knife so that she could wash her hands.

'Not that I have felt.'

'Why are they happening?' she asked.

'It could be one of several reasons,' Old Father Tim said, filling the kettle and putting it on the stove.

'What sort of reasons?

Old Father Tim rubbed his chin through his silvery beard. 'Well, it could be that an outside force has imposed its time value on our time, but that is unlikely. There would be other signs. Is that cake good?'

'What signs?' Tid asked, forgetting his piece.

Sofi was more interested in possible causes. 'What else makes a wobble happen?' she asked quickly, before taking a mouthful of cake.

'It could be,' Old Father Tim said, answering Sofi, 'that there are excavational forces at work below ground, or direct contact between the Human and Guardian worlds would make a wobble, but that is unlikely. No one from our world would be stupid enough to interfere with the Human world.'

Sofi's heart thudded a little faster. 'What forces at work below ground?' she asked, a tinge of worry in her voice.

Old Father Tim started spooning tea into the pot. 'Excavational forces,' he repeated. 'It means that if someone is digging under ground, near the sensitive time locators, then it could result in a wobble.'

'Who would be digging?' asked Tid.

Sofi remembered that Scaggy had said that it sounded like someone was digging near the Labyrinth. Her grandfather was pouring the tea. Tid was talking enthusiastically to him. She knew she should say something but she did not want to tell them she had been talking to a Wrecca.

She took another bite of cake.

5

The Apprentices

Old Father Tim spent the following day in the library at the Hither House, which was the home of the Greenwich Guardian as well as a meeting place for all the Guardian People. The library was a particularly splendid room, being very tall. The walls were lined with dark, wooden shelves filled with books of every size and age. Each book was bound in dark leather, with gold writing on the spine. The newer books were dark and crisp, while the ancient ones were faded and slightly shabby from centuries of use. In order to reach the shelves at the top, two walkways at different levels had been built right around the room. Beautifully carved steps, worn from centuries of use, were needed to reach the balconies. The ceiling was heavily vaulted. There were no windows. The books had been enchanted to glow, and because of this the room was infused with a warm light.

Seegan and his apprentice were already there, having travelled from Guangdong in China. Although dressed like the other Guardians, with a long robe worn under an outer coat, Seegan's coat was richly decorated with a colourful ceremonial dragon. His young apprentice was a shy girl called Yu Yul. She worked closely with Seegan, constantly consulting the manuscripts and books from the library and the ancient scrolls that they had brought with them. Seegan consulted Yu Yul in low tones, and she scribbled away on a parchment.

Vremya was a very old Guardian who came from the Ural Mountains in Russia. He was a little deaf and cupped his hand to his ear in order to hear. His deep voice resonated through his thick Russian accent. Tid liked Vremya because he looked as if he was smiling, even when he wasn't. He was the expert on ancient histories. His finger would touch a specific word in the ancient volume he was studying and Pasha, one of his young apprentices, would note it in a large journal. Sasha, Vremya's second apprentice, who was shorter and stockier that Pasha, hovered nearby. He was always ready to run nimbly up the steps to the balconies and search for the next volume. The knees of his trousers were scuffed from crawling on the floor, trying to find books on the lower shelves.

Wakaa, a very stern-looking Guardian from the Great Riff Valley in Kenya, stood at a lectern, studying a large open book with heavy pages. Kanika was his apprentice. She wore a brightly patterned tunic with wide sleeves. Occasionally Wakaa would mutter a word, incomprehensible to anyone but Kanika. She would then rummage in a carved wooden trunk and bring out a dark powder in a pottery flask or a richly decorated pebble. Each article was carefully placed on a shallow dish.

Old Father Tim sat in a big armchair with an ancient volume on his lap. He was studying star charts. The Greenwich Guardian sat by his side in another armchair. She was also studying large books. Every now and then her young secretary, Joss, would bring her another.

When the door opened, the Greenwich Guardian lifted her head and exclaimed, 'Zeit, it's good to see you.'

Old Father Tim looked up and smiled. He leant heavily on the arms of his chair and levered himself up. Crossing to Zeit, he took his hand and shook it warmly. 'Welcome,' Old Father Tim said with a smile; then, looking towards Zeit's apprentice, who was almost completely obscured behind a pile of leather-bound volumes, he said, 'I see you come well prepared.'

Zeit nodded and greeted the other Guardians. Zeit came from Neidersachsen in Germany. He was the expert in Guardian law. The Greenwich Guardian showed him where he would be working. His apprentice, staggering under the weight of the books he was carrying, was glad to put them down.

'I have brought the books you suggested,' Zeit said to Old Father Tim. 'Although, I do not know what use they will be.'

'On their own, none at all,' Old Father Tim agreed, 'but Grenya,' he nodded towards the Greenwich Guardian, 'found something in the Chronicles that may be relevant.' He crossed to yet another table, where a large, faded, leather tome lay. He lifted the heavy cover and turned to the appropriate page.

Zeit leant over it. 'Very interesting,' he murmured, 'very interesting indeed.' Then, without looking up, he called to his apprentice, 'Sheldon, take this down.'

Old Father Tim and the Greenwich Guardian looked across at the apprentice. 'Sheldon Croe!' Old Father Tim said in amazement.

Sheldon looked up. This was exactly why he had not wanted to come to Greenwich. 'Yes,' he said self-consciously. By now, all other eyes in the library were upon him.

'You have grown, my boy,' Old Father Tim said with grandfatherly pride. 'It warms my heart to see you.'

Zeit looked up, somewhat irritated that Sheldon had taken so long. 'Sheldon!' he snapped.

'Excuse me, Old Father Tim,' Sheldon mumbled and immediately set about doing Zeit's bidding.

Old Father Tim and the Greenwich Guardian exchanged a look of satisfaction. Eighteen months before, Sheldon Croe had been sent away from Greenwich. He had proved himself to be disloyal and wayward, and had been taken, against his will, to Germany, where Zeit ran the Reform School for Guardian boys like Sheldon.

'Ahem,' Seegan cleared his throat as he had done a hundred times already that day. 'Yu Yul, your recalsumation is inaccurate.'

Yu Yul squinted at her working-out and suddenly drew in her breath as she realized her mistake. 'Sorry,' she said.

'You must concentrate *all* the time, not *some* of it.'

Yu Yul blushed in shame at her public reprimand and redoubled her efforts.

The hot summer sun baked Greenwich Park. The usually lush grass was brown. Those who sat in the park kept to the protective shade of the majestic trees. Chattering groups of summer visitors, each with a rucksack strapped to his or her back, sauntered down the hill. Seth was leaning against the tree where he had first met Baz. This had become the place where they met each day after school.

When he saw Baz approaching, Seth walked off, heading towards a quiet part of the park. Once away from prying eyes, they were free to talk. They settled down on the ground.

'Here,' Seth said, holding out a raspberry muffin that Enderell had made for his lunchbox. He had saved it for Baz.

'You try this,' Baz said, handing over an iced cake with a cherry on top that his grandmother had baked.

Seth tasted it. It was interesting, but in no way compared to Enderell's delicious offerings. 'That's nice,' he said politely.

Meanwhile, Baz had sunk his teeth into Enderell's raspberry muffin. He closed his eyes in ecstasy as the delicious taste flooded his senses.

'Who made that?' he asked when he had finished, deeply impressed.

'Enderell,' Seth said rather proudly. 'She works for my grandmother. She's a great cook.'

'You're not kidding. Grandma's cake must taste pretty lame.'

Seth wanted to be polite and deny this, but he could not. Instead, he smiled. 'I'll save you something every day. Sometimes she makes flatjacks.'

'Don't you mean flapjacks?' Baz asked.

'No, flatjacks. They're flat sort of cakes that she makes in the oven with oats and butter and syrup. They're the best, but they're not so good for my teeth, and Grandmother says I can only have them sometimes.'

Baz stretched his legs out. 'Dad goes on about my teeth too, but I still buy these.' He pulled out a tube of sweets and offered it to Seth. He took one and popped it in his mouth.

'I saw your two friends again today,' Baz said. 'It's crazy how I can see everything in your world now. I can't believe it's always been there and I never knew. Would it be the same in New York?'

'Everywhere,' Seth said.

'Wow! I wish I could tell Dad. He'd freak!'

'You can't tell anyone,' Seth said, immediately concerned.

'Don't worry, he'd think I was nuts if I did.' Then Baz suddenly remembered something. 'There was a girl on the way to school today, one of your lot. She must have been late for school or something, because she was running flat out, straight for me. I mean, she didn't try to miss me or anything. Would she have run through me like you did with Cooper, or would she have smacked straight into me?'

'I don't know, best not find out. What did you do?'

'I couldn't dive out of her way cos that would have been pretty obvious.'

'What happened?'

'I sort of froze, not sure what to do, and she suddenly tripped over and fell. Her ponytail bobbed up as she went down,' he chuckled. 'It was real hard not to laugh. I sort of swallowed my tongue and just walked on.'

Seth smiled. Baz was easy to talk to.

'Hey, Seth.'

'Yeah?'

'Would you show me inside one of your houses? They look so cute. Some have thatched roofs.'

'Old Father Tim's does.'

'Wow, could I see it?'

'Of course not. We don't want people to see us together. We have to stay out of sight. That's why we hang around here. No one comes to this part of the park.'

Baz sighed disappointedly.

'Do you play football?' Seth asked.

'I'm not very good,' Baz replied sullenly. 'They make fun of me at school, but they would look just as stupid on a basketball court.'

'I'm not very good either,' Seth said, 'but I've got a ball.' He pulled a football out of his bag. It was a tight fit and took a while. 'No one will ever play with me because I'm so useless.'

'Me too,' Baz said.

'Do you want a game?' Seth asked slightly nervously.

'Oh boy! Yeah!' Baz exclaimed. 'There's this thing that Cooper does.' He stood up. 'He nudges the ball behind him with his foot, sort of like this,' Baz rolled the ball behind him in slow motion, 'and somehow flips it over his head.' Baz tried to do the same, but the ball spun off in the wrong direction. Baz shrugged. 'That always happens, or else I fall over.'

'I know what you mean,' Seth said, running to fetch the ball. 'I've tried to do that too.' He placed his foot on top of the ball and dragged it behind him, turning as he did so, but he lost his balance and fell over.

Baz laughed. It wasn't an unkind laugh, it was the sort of laugh that made Seth want to laugh too.

'I see what you did wrong,' Baz said, putting out his hand and pulling Seth to his feet. 'Try it like this.'

Sofi sat on the wall outside their cottage, watching Tid playing football with Herbie Connal. Sofi was thinking about joining in, but the sun was still hot, even though it was now low in the sky, and she thought she would prefer to be in the shade of the trees. There was one particular tree, not far from the pond, that Sofi preferred to all the others. Its long, low branches almost swept the ground, leaving a cosy place, cool in summer, dry in winter, where she could sit and be completely alone. There were times when Sofi enjoyed being solitary, and this was just such a moment. With a last casual look at the boys, she slipped off the wall and headed towards her tree.

The park's squirrels had been busy because of the

repeating day. They needed to keep Human activity the same. Their leader, Walnut Bushytail, had drawn up plans, lists and rotas so that this could be accomplished. It did not matter if exactly the same Bushytail approached a Human for the food they held out, as long as it was one of them. Humans could not tell one Bushytail from another. Sofi waved at her friend Hazel, but she was too busy taking a nut from a child's outstretched hand to notice.

Stooping low, Sofi crept into her tree and scrambled on to the obliging branch at its heart. She lay along it and stared up at the layers of branches above her. There was a decision she had to make. Should she tell Old Father Tim about her meeting with Scaggy? Thoughts of Scaggy brought with them thoughts of her home. Sofi had always been fascinated by the women's tunnels, which is what she used to call them when she lived in the Underneath, because that would be where her mother should be. Sofi could not remember her mother because she had been taken to the Underneath while still very young. All her life she had longed to know her.

'Hello.'

Sofi turned so quickly that she nearly fell off the branch. Looking across, she saw Scaggy standing at the outer edge of the canopy, bending low so as to avoid the spreading branches.

'Hello,' Sofi replied, looking around to see if Scaggy was alone. She seemed to be.

Sofi swung her legs over the side of the branch and let

her feet drop so that she was now in a sitting position.

'I thought I'd find you here.'

'Why?' Sofi asked distrustfully.

Scaggy shrugged. 'This is your tree. I often see you.'

'Have you been spying on me?' Sofi asked suspiciously.

'Ner, of course not,' Scaggy said, a little hurt. 'I doesn't spy on no one, I just like to watch, that's all. Life's more interesting up here.'

Compared with life below ground, life in the park was very exciting with the Bushytails, Humans and the Guardian People. Sofi remembered that when she was young, Scaggy had often disappeared Topside from the Underneath. It made sense that now she was older she might spend even more time up here.

'Where do you watch from?' Sofi asked.

'I's a favourite tree too,' Scaggy said. 'Not here, but towards the deer park.'

An uneasy silence fell between them. Scaggy moved closer in, so that she could stand up straight.

'Did you solve your problem about the digging?' Sofi asked.

'Ner,' Scaggy said. 'Us is in big trouble.'

'What's happened?'

'The thumpings and bangings is getting louder. It sounds like someone is hitting the walls with hammers.'

'Couldn't it be some of the women building something?'

Scaggy looked at her in surprise. There was obviously a great deal that Sofi did not know about the world that she was from. 'The women doesn't build nothing.'

'Perhaps this someone is doing something in secret.'

'There's no secrets in the Labyrinth,' Scaggy said. Then she added soberly, 'I think that the men's digging their way through. You see,' she leant closer to Sofi and lowered her voice, 'I think that the men want to take us over.'

'Take you over?'

Scaggy nodded.

'Why? They hate women.'

'They say they does and the women is always going on about how horrid them men is, but they get on all right when they want to. I's seed them.'

'And you think the men want to move into the Labyrinth?'

'Why not? It's loads nicer than their tunnels, and us has the little'uns.'

'The men don't like children either.'

'They may not like them, but they does need them,' Scaggy explained.

'Why?'

'Use your brain, Sofi. The men's tunnels will die if they doesn't have the boys to grow up into men.'

'I suppose so, but why does that mean they want to take over the Labyrinth?'

'When you was in the Underneath with the men,' Scaggy said mysteriously, 'hadn't you noticed about the little'uns?'

'What about them?' Sofi thought back. It was not

easy. She had tried so hard to forget her miserable existence below ground that now it was difficult to
remember. 'There weren't any, not after Seth.'

'Yer,' Scaggy said with a satisfied smile. 'I knowed you
spotted it. Snivel . . . I mean Seth . . . was the last. After
he'd been taked, the women stopped letting them go.'

'Stopped?'

'Yer. The men used to walk in whenever they feeled
like it. It getted so that us didn't have nothing nice down
there, cos they just walked in and took whatever they
wanted, including the little'uns. Berwyth says they did
it just to be nasty.'

'Who is Berwyth?'

'She's the leader of the Committee.' Then, before
Sofi could ask, she explained, 'They run the Labyrinth.
In some ways they doesn't do a bad job. In other ways
they's awful. Anyway, they stopped the little'uns being
taked.'

'How?'

'It was easy really,' Scaggy said with slight giggle. 'Us
just telled the men, well, us didn't really tell them, just
sort of gossiped it so that it got back to Old Killjoy,
about Old Father Tim's magic.'

'What about it?'

'Us said that Old Father Tim had put some of his
strongest magic on the Labyrinth door. Us said that the
magic was so strong that anyone who walked through
it without being invited will be turned into a frog!' She
gave a short laugh. 'Silly nut-heads believed it. They's
really stupid.'

Sofi smiled. Scaggy had a lovely laugh.

'They stopped coming after that, and so we get to keep anything nice that us can scavenge, and the little'uns is growing up with their mothers. Thing is,' she looked serious once more, 'Scratch has more brain than Old Killjoy and I think he's up to something. First it was the tremblings, but now there's noises too.'

'What noises?'

'Right by my alcove. I live on the edge of the Labyrinth. I like it there cos it's quiet, or it was. Now there's not only bangings but scratchings too. I think they's digging through. It takes a brain to work that out. They can't use the door and so they'll tunnel their way in.'

'Old Killjoy would never have thought of that.' Sofi remembered too well just how stupid the previous Wrecca leader had been.

'Old Killjoy isn't in charge ner more. He left about the same time you did. Rumour has it that Scratch did away with him. Anyway, Scratch is the leader now. He's even gived himself some daft title. He calls himself Offa Scratch, not sure why.'

Sofi was not really listening. It was difficult to imagine the Underneath without Old Killjoy, but she did not dwell on it. 'Are the Labyrinth and Underneath close to each other?'

'Some say they's connected, but I doesn't see how they can be. I think they's had to dig a long way to get to us, and I know you's going to say that the men can't dig so far, but they's been at it a long time.'

Sofi was thinking carefully. Old Father Tim had said that excavational forces below ground could have caused the wobble.

'What do you want Grandfather to do?'

'I . . . that is us, thinked that if him put a real magic spell on the tunnels, then the men'll never get through.'

'That won't work,' Sofi said. 'Guardians don't have powers below ground.'

'Normal ones doesn't, but Old Father Tim's special. Him's a great Guardian, us all knows that. Him can do it.'

Sofi was doubtful, but she did not say so. 'Would you like to meet him?'

'Yer,' Scaggy said earnestly.

'All right,' Sofi said, jumping down. 'Come home with me now.'

Scaggy suddenly did not look so eager. Speaking to Old Father Tim had been her goal but, faced with the reality, she was suddenly nervous. 'It doesn't have to be straight away.'

Roles were reversed. Sofi was now certain that Scaggy had to meet her grandfather at once. 'Of course it has to be straight away. You say the men have been at it for ages, they could be breaking through at this moment. You have to talk to Grandfather.'

Scaggy was hesitant. 'Old Father Tim willn't want a Wrecca in the house.'

'He won't mind you.'

'But . . .' Scaggy stood her ground. 'Supposing there's magic on the doors. You know,' she said in answer to

Sofi's questioning stare, 'the sort of magic that turns a Wrecca into a frog or something.'

Sofi tried not to laugh. 'Grandfather wouldn't do that.'

Scaggy was not so sure.

'Supposing he met you in the garden,' Sofi suggested.

'Why not here?'

The reason was that Sofi did not want to risk Scaggy running away while she went to fetch her grandfather. She remembered back at how frightened she had been when waiting to meet Old Father Tim for the first time.

'He's an old man,' Sofi said, thinking fast, 'and he shouldn't have to go chasing all round the park after you.'

Scaggy frowned. 'All right, but I isn't going into ner house!'

❀ₒ❀⁕❀ 6 ❀⁕.❀ₒ❀

Sum Choy Day Har

'Excavational forces!' Vremya had spoken so loudly that everyone in the library looked up. He tapped the manuscript he had been studying with his finger. 'In the histories of Vladimir the Valiant there were exceptional excavational forces that coincided with a time bounce.'

'Ah!' Seegan said, sounding excited. 'That might well match with something we have here, at least I think it might.' He looked at Yu Yul. 'How would you translate that?' He pointed to a short passage of ancient script.

Yu Yul's forehead creased as she concentrated on the words. 'Sum choy day har?' she said hesitantly.

'Yes!' Seegan exclaimed, delighted. 'You have it!'

Yu Yul's pretty young face glowed with pleasure.

'Sum choy day har,' Seegan repeated, staring at the manuscript and suddenly becoming lost in it.

The Guardians waited for Seegan to explain. After several moments of silence Old Father Tim mildly said, 'We do not have the least idea what you mean.'

His voice brought Seegan back to reality. 'I am sorry,' he said. 'I forget my manners. "Sum choy day har" means "deep under ground". By these calculations, activity deep under ground can severely disrupt time.'

'That is interesting,' Old Father Tim said, fingering his beard. 'Bryn has noted that there has been underground activity for several months. If it is close to the sensitive time locators, we could have found the reason for the time bounce.'

'It will be looked into,' the Greenwich Guardian said.

'Thank you, Grenya,' Old Father Time smiled, 'and thank you, Seegan, and Vremya too, this is very helpful.' He looked at Zeit, 'What about the ancient laws?'

'Unfortunately, I can find nothing relevant to our situation,' Zeit said.

'Very well, and deep magic?'

Wakaa shook his head.

'Oh. And so excavational forces are the only possible reason we have found.'

'Surely we cannot rule out a cross-over between the Human and our worlds,' the Greenwich Guardian said. 'That could be the reason.'

'Who would do that?' Zeit asked. 'No one would ever do anything so contrary to our laws. Why, we learn about such things from the cradle.'

'Perhaps we should still check it out?' Old Father Tim suggested.

'I'll talk to Bryn,' the Greenwich Guardian said. 'He is in regular contact with the Bushytails. They will be the ones to know if anything of this nature has happened in the park.'

*

Scaggy stood nervously in Old Father Tim's front garden while Sofi ran indoors. Tid and Herbie stopped playing ball and stared at the newcomer.

'Enderell, is Grandfather home?' Sofi called through the open door.

Elegant as always, Enderell looked up from a large book in which she was writing. 'Not yet,' she said serenely.

Enderell was the Guardians' expert on healing herbs. She stayed with Tid and Sofi if Old Father Tim had to be elsewhere for longer than he would like.

'But she's come to see him.'

'Who has?'

'A sort of friend of mine.'

Enderell looked blankly at Sofi.

'Well, actually she's a Wrecca.'

Enderell's eyes popped wide open in amazement.

'But she's not like the others,' Sofi quickly assured her. 'She was always nice to me, and she's got something important to say to Grandfather. It might have something to do with the time wobble, although she doesn't know it. Can you fetch him back? Can you be Mindful all the way to the Hither House?'

Enderell looked out of the window and saw the young Wrecca woman in the garden, nervously twisting her fingers together.

'No, I cannot be Mindful that far.' Enderell closed her eyes for a moment and Sofi knew she was being Mindful to someone. Guardian People can transfer thoughts to each other. Tid and Sofi could both do this, but they were not yet experts and it took a lot of concentration. The grown-ups could manage it more readily.

When Enderell opened her eyes, Sofi asked, 'Who's coming?'

Enderell did not answer but walked out into the garden.

When Scaggy saw Enderell approaching, she straightened her back and self-consciously smoothed the faded skirt of her dress.

'This is Enderell,' Sofi said, feeling it her duty to make the introductions.

'I know,' Scaggy said quietly. She had seen her many times in the park.

Sofi turned to Enderell. It was now time to introduce Scaggy. 'And this is . . .'

'Lorin,' Scaggy interrupted, glancing at Sofi.

Sofi stared at her in surprise.

'When us get back to the Labyrinth after leaving the Underneath,' Lorin explained, 'us takes the name our mothers gived us when us was born, instead of the horrid name the men gived us,' and then she added, 'that's if her's still there and can remember.'

'Welcome, Lorin,' Enderell said, gracefully extending a hand.

Most Wreccas would not have understood the gesture, but Lorin had spent many hours watching and learning. She recognized the Guardian greeting and awkwardly extended her hand, allowing Enderell to shake it.

'Will you come in and take a cup of tea?'

'Go in there?' Lorin asked uneasily.

Enderell smiled. 'Yes.'

'But I's a . . .' Lorin hesitated. 'Surely I's not welcome in . . . in *his* house.'

Enderell's smile widened. 'Any friend of Sofi's is a friend of ours. Please come.'

Sofi encouraged Lorin with a fervent nod of the head.

Nervously gripping the folds of her dress, Lorin followed Enderell. As she drew near the cottage doorway she hung back, wary of crossing the threshold. She was very scared of what she was about to do but knew she had to do it. She bit her bottom lip, closed her eyes and boldly stepped over the doorstep. Once inside, she opened her eyes and stood for a moment, waiting to see if anything terrible had happened. She felt no different. Her heart was still beating. She felt her fingers: they were not webbed. Nothing had altered. She had not been turned into a frog.

Tid and Herbie had given up playing football and had come to the doorway, intrigued by the stranger. Enderell poured hot water into a teapot. Lorin looked about her.

It was a cosy kitchen with brightly coloured curtains at the window and a cheerful rag rug on the tiled floor. Enderell was putting cups and saucers on a round table that was covered by a checked cloth. Sofi pulled out a chair and asked Lorin to sit. A cushion that matched the tablecloth was tied to the back with small bows. Lorin sat down gingerly, never having sat on a chair with a cushion before.

'Would you like some cake?' Sofi asked, putting a

partly cut cake on the table. 'It's strawberry and I made it.'

Lorin nodded vaguely. There was too much to take in. So much luxury. So much splendour.

Sofi understood how she felt; it had been the same for her the first time she had sat at this table and eaten a meal with Tid and Old Father Tim. Sofi remembered that Tid had apologized for it only being pie, and yet it was more delicious than anything Sofi had ever dreamt of. She understood now why Lorin looked at the cake with wide eyes and did not touch it.

Tid and Herbie approached eagerly. Cake was being offered and they always had room for cake, but Sofi shook her head and withdrew the plate once she had given Lorin hers. 'You've had your supper,' she said to the boys, sounding like a grown-up.

Before Enderell could finish pouring the tea, a voice came from the doorway. 'Is everything all right, Enderell?'

Enderell looked up and smiled. 'Bryn. Thank you for coming. Would you like some tea?'

'That would be grand,' said Bryn Brownal.

Sofi realized that Pa Brownal was the one to whom Enderell had been Mindful.

'Hello, lads,' he said jovially, as he squeezed past the boys in the doorway. 'I think it is time you were off home, Herbie. I met your grandfather on my way here. He said you are expected.'

'Oh,' Herbie said, reluctant to leave. It looked as though something interesting was about to happen. He hesitated in the doorway, but Bryn said goodbye and propelled him out with a slight push in the back, before shutting the door.

'Hello, young Sofi.'

'Hello, Pa Brownal,' Sofi said politely. 'This is Lorin.'

Now Bryn Brownal turned his eyes upon the newcomer, although he had noted her carefully the moment he had arrived.

'Good evening, Lorin,' he said formally, holding out his hand.

Lorin extended her trembling hand and allowed him to shake it.

'I have sometimes seen you in the park,' he said, sitting on a chair and reaching for the cup that Enderell was passing.

Lorin was taken aback. She had always thought she was safe from prying eyes when hidden in her tree.

Sofi cut a slice of cake and gave it to Bryn.

He thanked her with a smile but continued talking to Lorin. 'I never thought you would want to talk to us,' he said. He took a large mouthful of cake, declared it to be delicious, congratulated Sofi when he heard she had baked it and urged Lorin to eat her piece.

But Lorin did not. It was all too much. The beauty of the cottage, the smell of the first piece of cake she had ever been offered and the number of eyes fixed on her made her self-conscious. She sat on the edge of her chair in silence.

'My word, this is something of party!'

Everyone jumped and looked towards the door. It

had opened so quietly that no one had heard it. Old Father Tim had arrived home.

'Grandfather!' Sofi exclaimed, running towards him and throwing her arms around his large waist. He hugged her warmly and, bending down, kissed her on the top of her head. Then he rested his hand on Tid's tousled hair as they exchanged a warm smile. 'Hello, Grandfather.'

'Hello, my boy.'

Old Father Tim greeted Enderell and Bryn before finally turning to the newcomer.

'This is Lorin,' Sofi said as she slipped her hand into her grandfather's. 'Do you remember I once told you about a . . .' she hesitated, unwilling to use the word but also needing to explain. She raised herself up on to her toes and he bent a little so that she could speak quietly, '. . . the Wrecca who was nice to me in the Underneath. We used to call her Scaggy but she's called Lorin now.' And then she added in a louder voice, 'She wants to talk to you, Grandfather. There's something important happening.'

Old Father Tim nodded. 'Welcome, young Lorin,' he said warmly. 'I see you have some cake.' And then he added, 'I was hoping for some myself.'

Sofi gave a small yelp as she realized how neglectful she had been and immediately set about putting the last piece of cake on a plate for her grandfather.

Lorin looked at her plate nervously.

Old Father Tim understood. 'Tid, I think it is time for you to have your bath.'

Tid looked at him indignantly. He was too old to be sent away to have a bath, especially in front of a guest, and anyway, it was too early. He drew breath to object, but one look from his grandfather silenced him.

'Sofi,' Tid said, 'you can have the first one.'

'Sofi will stay here,' Old Father Tim said quietly. 'You can have the first bath tonight, my boy.'

Tid was deeply offended that Sofi was allowed to stay while he was being sent away. This was too much! After all, he was the Old Father Grandson. He had a right to stay!

These were the thoughts he wanted to voice, but he knew he must not. Trying not to show his annoyance, he left, gently thumping the door shut behind him.

Sofi felt a twinge of pride because she was allowed to stay.

'Thank you for coming, Bryn,' Old Father Tim said amiably. 'Perhaps you will come back later.'

Bryn understood at once. He gathered the few remaining crumbs up from his plate and popped them in his mouth. He made his farewells to each of them, adding at the end, 'Very nice to have met you, Lorin,' and left.

Having only lived with women in the Labyrinth made it difficult enough for Lorin to talk to one man, let alone two men and a boy. Inwardly she thanked Old Father Tim for sending them away.

With a gesture of his hand, Old Father Tim invited Enderell and Sofi to sit. They did so without speaking.

'What is this "important happening" that you wish to talk to me about?' he asked gently.

Lorin sat for a moment, trying to build up the courage to use her voice. She had practised what to say many times but, now she was faced with the reality, rehearsals were forgotten.

'Perhaps a sip of tea first,' Old Father Tim suggested.

Grateful for the opportunity of delay, Lorin took a gulp, but now new sensations took away all thoughts of anything she might say. The tea was more delicious than anything Lorin had ever tasted. She stared into it. It looked like tea, but it tasted different.

'Yes,' Old Father Tim said with an understanding smile, 'Enderell can make tea taste like nectar. It is her gifting.'

Enderell smiled her thanks.

'It surprises me every time I drink it,' Old Father Tim said, taking a sip, and Lorin was grateful to him for trying to put her at her ease, even if he was failing.

Swallowing one more mouthful, Lorin licked her lips and spoke. Nothing came out, and so she cleared her throat and started again. 'Old Father Tim,' she said, so quietly that each of them had to lean a little closer to catch her words. 'Us . . . that is the women in the Labyrinth need your help.'

There, she had said it. She sat waiting for his reaction, eyes firmly fixed on the tablecloth.

'How might I do that?' Old Father Tim asked kindly.

Lorin took a deep breath, but her courage failed her and she cast a desperate look towards Sofi, who came to her rescue.

'Lorin was telling me earlier . . .' and she quickly explained about the children and the Wreccas and the tunnelling.

Old Father Tim rubbed his chin through his beard.

'How long have they been digging?'

'They started the summer after Sofi comed Topside,' Lorin said, relieved that her voice had returned.

Old Father Tim nodded to himself. That must be the underground vibrations that Bryn had spoken of.

'But they's getting close. I can feel it. Sometimes, I put my hands on the wall by my alcove and it's like the wall is moving.'

Old Father Tim thought for a moment. 'You did right coming to see me,' he said.

'Can you help us?' she asked, looking up at him intently.

Old Father Tim looked deep into her eyes. He was able to read more in people's eyes than anyone and could tell that she was in earnest.

'Yes, I can,' he said.

'Oh!' Lorin exclaimed, very relieved. 'Can you come with I now and tell Berwyth?'

'No.' Old Father Tim spoke gently.

Lorin was crestfallen. 'But you said . . .'

'First, I must consult with the Council.'

'But there's no time, supposing the men is breaking through right now?'

'You have to understand, Lorin,' Old Father Tim spoke kindly but firmly, 'that we are different from Wreccas. We listen, we discuss, and then we plan. It does not suit us to rush off and do something until all the options have been thoroughly thought through. The Wreccas have been digging for a long time, I doubt that one more day will make any difference.'

'But you can do some magic now, just to be safe, and then go away and talk and stuff, and then come back later and do what the Council says. Us doesn't stand a chance if the men break through. They can be rotten vicious. In the past they just taked the children, but the women willn't let them do that ner more and it'll be a blood bath. Us'll never let the littl'uns go easy.'

Old Father Tim looked at her anxious face and wished he could do more. 'I do not have the magic that would work below ground.'

'You has,' Lorin declared obstinately. 'You's the Old Father. You can do anything.'

'No, I cannot,' he said firmly. 'It is true that there is magic that may work below ground. It is the deepest, most ancient magic of all. I know a little of it, but not enough to protect you. I need time.'

'There is no time.'

Old Father Tim was moved by her sincerity. He did not underestimate how hard it must have been for her to seek him out and ask for help. He wished he could do more.

Sofi watched him carefully. She had lived in his home long enough to realize when he was not going to change his mind. He was just trying to think of the best way of saying so. Sofi thought it would be awful if Lorin went away empty-handed, and so she blurted out the first thing that came into her mind. 'Perhaps we could build a wall.'

Everyone was taken aback by her sudden outburst.

'Some of us could go back to the Labyrinth with Lorin,' she said enthusiastically, 'and help them build a wall right against the one they are trying to break through. That would help keep Scratch and the others out until you've organized the magic, Grandfather.' She looked at him hopefully. If he said yes, Sofi planned to go too.

'That willn't work,' Lorin said.

Sofi flashed her a look of annoyance. 'It's a good idea,' she said.

'It's possible Berwyth'll accept Old Father Tim arriving without warning, but a whole bunch of you?' She shook her head. 'Never.'

'You'd tell her it's her best hope,' Sofi persisted. 'She'd listen to you.'

Lorin gave a derisory laugh. 'Sofi, you's lived too long Topside. Boss Wreccas make up their own minds. They doesn't take ner notice of girls like I.'

Sofi thought for a moment. If there was the smallest opportunity of going to the Labyrinth and seeking her mother, she was going to take it. 'I could talk to Berwyth,' she said bravely.

Lorin laughed out loud this time, and it made Sofi feel very young and foolish.

Old Father Tim was unwilling to see Sofi made to look silly. 'I would not let you go, young one,' he said affectionately.

Sofi drew breath to argue but, seeing the look of loving concern yet steely determination in his eyes, she closed her mouth and remained silent.

'Lorin,' he said. 'You must go back to the Labyrinth and talk with Berwyth. Tell her that we are willing to help, but that I must talk with the Council first.'

7

Lorin's Tonic

After she had gone to bed, Sofi sat alone in the bedroom that had been specially built for her when she began living at Old Father Tim's house. Enderell had helped her with the decoration. Sofi had wanted it to be blue, which was her favourite colour, but Enderell had said that blue was a cold colour. Sofi could not understand this. To her, brown was the coldest colour because it was the colour of the Underneath. However, not wanting to offend, she compromised and the walls of her room had been painted in blue and yellow swirls. Enderell said that yellow would stop the blue feeling so cold.

Old Father Tim had made shelves with intricately carved edges that were also blue. She stored her growing collection of books on them. Her bed was covered with a blue-and-yellow patchwork quilt that Ma Brownal had made especially for her; but her favourite thing sat on the small cupboard that her grandfather had made to go next to her bed. It was a glass dome in which floated a model of a fairy. She had long blonde hair and wore a blue dress that, like her hair, was always moving. If

Sofi touched the top of the dome with her finger, it lit up with sparkling lights that flashed around her room.

Sitting on her bed, she looked miserably out of the window. She had desperately wanted to be allowed to go to the Labyrinth with Lorin. It was all so unfair. Tid was allowed to go to the Line because he had been lucky enough to be born the grandson of the Old Father. Well, now it was Sofi's turn. She had been born a Wrecca and so it was her right to go below ground and help.

Sofi sighed. Perhaps she was being selfish. She had been happy living with Old Father Tim and Tid, happier than she could ever have believed possible. The old man had been both grandfather and grandmother to her. In his home, she felt safe. She loved him completely. Deep in her heart she felt that to search for a mother (who might not exist anyway) was somehow a betrayal of all that he had come to mean to her and, maybe more importantly, all that she had come to mean to him. She did not want to disappoint him by implying that he was not enough of a parent for her by searching for her real mother.

Sofi sighed deeply once again and lay down on her bed. She pushed the quilt back with her feet. It was too hot. Sleep seemed far away. Sofi knew it would be a long night.

Offa Scratch sat on his throne, lightly trailing a long nail over his thin lips. He was deep in thought. He had a problem.

It was all very well breaking through into the Labyrinth and attacking the women. This would be relatively easy. Everyone knew that Wrecca men fought like demons. They were brutal, cold and merciless killers. The women would be no match for his fighting force. Offa Scratch knew he would win, but at what cost? The men would break through, and if he was not careful, within a very short time every woman and child in the Labyrinth would be slaughtered. Offa Scratch had no concern for the women or their children, but he did care about himself.

The filth and squalor of the Underneath was getting worse with every passing year. Offa Scratch wanted to live in the Labyrinth, where he knew conditions were much better. He knew that the men could never keep it comfortable. That was where the women would be useful. They were good at that sort of thing and would leave the men to do the really important work, like thinking, talking and fighting, but how could he get the women to cooperate?

This was why Offa Scratch was deep in thought. His brow furrowed as he absent-mindedly trailed a nail along his cheekbone. How could he make the women work for him?

Lorin knocked on the Labyrinth door and waited. 'Get a move on!' she muttered under her breath. Falwyth, who shared door-keeping duties with her sister Falryd, also liked to keep people waiting.

Eventually, the door opened.

'You's been a long time,' Falwyth grumbled as Lorin entered. 'What's you been doing?'

'There's no requirement for you to be concerned,' Lorin said, deliberately using words Falwyth would not understand.

Falwyth snorted. 'Ner good you getting all hoity-toity. Herself wants to see you.'

'Berwyth?' Lorin asked. 'Why?'

Falwyth smirked. 'Too often Topside, I reckon.'

Lorin did not believe that. She had always spent much of her time Topside. Berwyth had never bothered about it before.

'You better not keep her waiting,' Falwyth said, relishing the thought that Lorin might be in trouble.

Lorin stalked off.

'Lorin!'

Her friend, Morlenni, was hurrying towards her. She was a young Wrecca, not much older than Lorin, and a little shorter. Her mousey-coloured hair was worn in long dreadlocks. She wore baggy trousers and a well-worn, loose-fitting jumper. Morlenni was easy-going and never questioned things but accepted life as it was and tried to make the best of it. Today, she was wearing a frown. She had been suffering from headaches of late and, from the way she winced as she moved, this one was bad. 'They's at it again,' she said as soon as she had caught up with Lorin. 'The rumblings is worse! Everyone is worried now.'

Ah, so this was it. Berwyth wanted to talk to Lorin about the men and their tunnelling. 'Us is doing every-thing us can,' Lorin said.

'My alcove is right on that wall,' Morlenni moaned. 'I can almost hear them talking.'

'Really?' They had never heard talking before.

'Ner,' Morlenni said honestly, 'not really, but they's close. Them's bashing away all the time. I doesn't get a minute's sleep ner more. It does my head in.'

'All right,' Lorin said. 'I's off to see Berwyth about it now. Don't worry, us is working on it.'

'You's better work fast.'

'Yer. How's your head?'

Morlenni pulled a face. 'Ner good. Has you any more of that tonic?'

'Ner, I'm out of the soil I need for heads. I'll collect some more as soon as I's talked to Berwyth. Once I's got it, it won't take long to mix it up. All right?'

Morlenni winced. Recently, her headaches had been getting worse. 'I'll tell you what,' she said. 'I know where you get it. I'll nip Topside and collect some while you's talking to Berwyth. Then you can mix it up as soon as you's done.'

'Is you sure? It's big up there,' Lorin said doubtfully. Like the other women, Morlenni was used to the confines of the Labyrinth. The wide open spaces Topside were unnerving.

'I's doing no good hanging around here with my head hurting. It'll be easier if I's doing something,' and then she added, 'I know where it is. I comed with you last time. I'll fill a tub.'

'A small tub,' Lorin said, 'and don't forget to use the flat scraper. It's easier.'

'All right,' Morlenni agreed. 'I willn't be long.'

Lorin watched her leave. She felt strangely nervous about letting her friend go. Unlike the men, women were never stopped from going above ground if they wanted to; but few did, as the world frightened them. Morlenni might be older than Lorin, but she was less confident. Momentarily, Lorin thought she should run after her friend, but it would be more trouble than it was worth to keep Berwyth waiting.

With one last look over her shoulder, Lorin walked on. It would be best to get this interview with Berwyth over and done with. She quickened her step and soon arrived at the Committee Chamber. Yaryth was lounging, as usual, by the faded red curtain.

'Where's you been?' she demanded.

Lorin ignored the question and instead asked, 'Is you going to hang around or is you going to tell them I's here?'

'Keep your hair on!' Yaryth pushed the curtain aside and entered.

Lorin stood alone, trying to calm herself. She hated the fact that she always felt nervous before going before the Committee.

'You's to go in,' Yaryth said as she reappeared.

Lorin lifted her chin and squared her shoulders before entering.

There were two Committee members on one bench and one on the other. Lorin immediately suspected she had been summoned for nothing important, or all six would have been there.

'You wanted to see I, Berwyth?' she asked.

'Harfed needs you,' Berwyth said in a bored voice.

Lorin turned to the lone Committee member sitting on her left. She was a middle-aged, slightly bent woman with very curly hair that was dyed jet black. Her eyes were small and fierce. 'That tonic did ner good,' she moaned miserably in her unnaturally high voice.

So, this was what it was all about. Harfed had stomach ache!

'I telled you that it does no good to eat all day and night,' Lorin said.

Harfed was a new Committee member, having been approved only a few days earlier. With her new-found status, she had found it impossible to resist all the best food that the kitchen had to offer. Consequently, she had stuffed herself for four days. It was not surprising that her stomach now hurt.

Lorin was the acknowledged Tonic-Maker in the Labyrinth. She had a certain amount of knowledge about healing soils that she mixed to give medical help to those suffering from mild ailments. The day before, Lorin had given Harfed a tonic made from some of this healing soil. However, eating less food would help more.

'I shall make some more up. It'll be stronger this time. In fact, it's so strong,' she tried to sound dramatic, 'that your stomach will explode if you eat anything for two whole days and nights.' She held up two fingers to stress the point.

Harfed believed her without question. Her eyes grew huge with fear, but she did not protest. Even going without food would be worth it if only her stomach stopped hurting.

'I'll go and mix it as soon as I's finished talking with Berwyth.'

'For the sake of my poor head, do it now,' Berwyth grumbled. 'I can't stand another moment of her blubbing.'

At this Harfed groaned even louder.

'And if you doesn't shut your gob, I'll chuck you off the Committee before you's properly fixed in!' Berwyth snapped.

Harfed shut her mouth so quickly that Lorin heard a slight pop.

'There is just one thing,' Lorin said.

'Shove off, you worm!' Berwyth growled.

Lorin did not move but said quietly, 'I's been talking with Old Father Tim.'

Suddenly she had everyone's attention. Even Harfed looked as if her stomach was forgotten.

Berwyth narrowed her eyes. 'You what?'

'I's just been sitting in Old Father Tim's kitchen, drinking tea and eating cake.' She said this as casually as she could, remembering with regret that she had not actually tasted the strawberry cake.

'Is you turning traitor?' Berwyth asked nastily.

'Of course not! You telled I to talk to him, and so I has.'

'That little cat, Sofi, sayed ner.'

'Well, today her sayed yer, and I haved tea with them.'

'What did it taste like?' Harfed asked, drooling.

Lorin ignored her and kept her eyes on Berwyth. 'Him says him'll help us.'

For a moment Berwyth said nothing. Her bulbous eyes bored into Lorin. Then she snapped, 'Us doesn't need no help from a fat-nose like him!'

This was typical of Berwyth. She was always cantankerous.

'I talked with Morlenni when I comed in,' Lorin persevered. 'She says the knocking sound's getting louder. What's going to happen if the men break right through? You know us doesn't stand a chance against them.'

Berwyth said nothing. She knew that Lorin was right, but she was not going to admit it.

'Get the tonic,' she said icily.

Lorin bit her lip. It would be a waste of time to press the matter further. When Berwyth was in this sort of mood, nothing moved her. She would make Harfed's tonic and then go Topside to help Morlenni with the soil. She would have to speak to Berwyth again in the morning.

Old Father Tim returned to the Hither House after Tid and Sofi had gone to bed. He sat with the other Guardians and talked through all that Lorin had told him.

'Ancient magic?' Wakaa asked. 'Have you any idea how difficult that is?'

'I know,' Old Father Tim said, 'but we must do something, partly because we cannot stand by and allow the

Wrecca men to attack the women without trying to help.'

'I agree,' Wakaa said.

'And partly, if Seegan is right,' Old Father Tim continued, 'then these might be the excavational forces that bounced time out of alignment.'

'We must find out more,' Wakaa said. 'When will we know if the digging has caused this?'

'When the time locators have all been checked. The Park Council has already started, but it will take a while.'

'I suppose,' Zeit said, 'we could try to explain the situation to the Wreccas and ask them to stop.'

'I tried that once before,' Old Father Tim said, remembering back. 'It did not work then, and I doubt it will work now. Wreccas are not bred for listening.'

'Whatever we do, we must do it quickly,' Zeit continued. 'We do not have much time.'

'We do not know how much time there is,' Old Father Tim corrected him.

'We could all wake up tomorrow and discover that the time zones have spun out of control,' Zeit continued, without realizing that his voice was rising. 'It could be chaos by lunchtime. Tempus pulled the world out of chaos once before. Who is there to do it again?' He looked around, hoping that someone else would show a similar sense of urgency.

'Does anyone have any other ideas?' Old Father Tim said calmly 'We must explore all possibilities.'

No one spoke.

Zeit clenched his teeth, trying not to allow his intense irritation to show.

Sheldon, sitting in the shadows with the other apprentices, smirked. Back in Germany, Zeit's word was never opposed. It was very entertaining to see him being thwarted by older, more experienced Guardians.

'Grenya,' Old Father Tim addressed the Greenwich Guardian, 'has Bryn heard of any cross-overs between the Human and Guardian worlds?'

'There are rumours, but, apart from the time wobbles, there is no evidence. Bryn had hoped that the Bushytails, who are normally our eyes and ears, might be able to help, but they are so busy keeping Human activity exactly the same each day that few of them can be spared to keep lookout. He is still investigating.'

'Then, for the moment, we shall concentrate on the ancient magic. That will help the Wrecca women, if nothing else.'

'What about the Gemetbur?' Vremya asked quietly.

They looked at him in surprise. 'The Gemetbur?'

Vremya nodded.

'Are you trying to tell us,' Zeit asked disbelievingly, 'that you believe the Gemetbur to be real?'

'I do,' Vremya replied softly.

'You might as well believe in the shadows that lurk in the Guardian tunnels,' Zeit snorted. 'I remember being rather frightened of them when I was a boy!'

'Zeit,' Old Father Tim said sternly, 'it is Guardian practice to discuss and consider using all facts and theories before we dismiss anything out of hand.'

Zeit shut his mouth. How many times had he told

the boys in his care that self-respect depended directly upon the amount of respect they showed to others? He was setting a poor example, and yet it was very hard to show respect when someone said something so totally absurd.

'Forgive me, Vremya,' he said. 'Sometimes I speak out of turn.'

Vremya graciously inclined his head and accepted the apology.

'Do you really think that the Gemetbur could exist?' Old Father Tim asked.

'I do,' Vremya confirmed.

Zeit sat back in his chair and said, as respectfully as possible, 'I always believed it to be a fairy tale.'

'That does not mean that it cannot be true,' Old Father Tim said. He looked towards Vremya. 'Tell us.'

Vremya cleared his throat. 'It is written in the ancient histories that when Tempus walked the earth . . .'

Each Guardian knew that Vremya was talking of the earliest days, many thousands of years before, when the first Guardian, Tempus, worked his own unsurpassed magic upon the earth.

'. . . his concern was what would happen to time after his death. He had saved the world from chaos, but the laws of time had not yet been established,' and Vremya looked at Zeit, who understood these laws better than anyone. 'There was no Guardian network in existence and no way that he could be sure that the time zones he had worked so diligently to separate would remain harmonized.'

Each Guardian nodded. They knew these things.

'If it had been you,' Vremya said, looking at the Old Father, 'what would you have done?'

'I would have put something in place that would keep time safe until the structure of Guardian authority had been established.'

'And what better way,' Vremya said with a smile, 'than with a Gemetbur?'

'But where?' Wakaa asked.

'Sum choy day har,' Seegan said. 'Deep under ground.'

'Is that possible? Old Father Tim asked.

Seegan nodded. 'Perfectly possible.'

No one spoke. It seemed strange that Vremya should believe a story they had been told at their grandmother's knee. Could it be true?

'In my storybook, if I remember correctly,' the Greenwich Guardian said, 'it was a room full of mechanisms. What do you think?'

'That sounds about right.'

'My book showed it to be a cave,' Wakaa said.

'Cave, room, whatever,' Vremya continued. 'It does not matter; but it is my guess that it will be below ground.'

'And this Gemetbur of yours,' Zeit said, 'has gone wrong?'

'The Gemetbur is not mine,' Vremya said mildly. 'It was made by the Great Tempus and so I am certain that it would not have failed, but a time bounce may well have interfered with the way it works.'

'So,' Old Father Tim said, 'to sum up, the time

locators are being checked by the Park Council. These will show us if the Wreccas' digging is causing the problem. Bryn is looking for possible cross-overs, although he is hampered in this by the extremely heavy workload of the Bushytails. Wakaa will research the deep magic so that we can offer some protection to the Wrecca women, and someone will try to discover where the Gemetbur might be located if, indeed, it does exist.'

'Are you suggesting that we search children's story-books in an attempt to locate the Gemetbur?' Zeit asked incredulously. 'And then send someone to fiddle about with it?'

'I am not sure "fiddling" is in order,' Old Father Tim said, briefly smiling, 'and I am sure that the Guardian Chronicles will be far more informative than a children's book, but, yes, I think we should be prepared to correct any fault that the time bounce may have caused to the Gemetbur, if indeed it does exist.'

'Might I suggest,' Zeit said, 'that we do all of these very quickly.'

'Yes,' Old Father Tim replied, 'I understand the urgency. We shall begin at once.'

Lorin quickly mixed up the tonic for Harfed and left it with Yaryth to give to her. Then she checked Morlenni's alcove, just in case her friend had taken fright and returned early. She was aware just how frightened Wrecca women were of the vast space above ground. When she found Morlenni's alcove empty, Lorin hurried off to find her friend.

'Morlenni!' she called at the spot where she usually collected the healing soil for heads. 'Where are you?'

Morlenni did not emerge from the shadows. Lorin was not surprised, expecting her friend to be hiding somewhere, too frightened to find her way home. Lorin smiled as she started searching. In many ways Morlenni was like a child.

The more Lorin searched, the more worried she became. She began crossing the park in an organized fashion, so that no part was left unsearched. Lorin even checked around the buildings at the Line, although she did not expect to find her friend near any Guardian landmarks. She searched around the pond and in the deer park. Finally, she looked up into trees, in case a terrified Morlenni had taken refuge up one of them and was now too scared to come down.

Morlenni had disappeared.

8

A Blood-curdling Cry

Lorin searched all night. As soon as the Wrecca women began to wake up in the morning, she systematically searched the Labyrinth, asking everyone if they had seen her friend.

Finally she returned to Berwyth, who was lying on her couch, dozing, waiting for breakfast. 'Get out, worm!' she snapped, not appreciating being disturbed so early.

'But I's come to . . .'

A blood-curdling cry split the air. It was a long, terrifying scream. Everyone, in all parts of the Labyrinth, froze in terror. Then, even as the scream drew to a close it grew in resonance as the sound bounced from rock to rock, and echoes magnified and merged in the maze of tunnels until the walls throbbed with an eeriness that pierced their ears and petrified their hearts.

Berwyth and Lorin looked at each other, neither daring to speak.

Lorin forgot that Morlenni was missing.

Everyone forgot everything.

The sound rumbled on, lower and lower, until it finally subsided.

Silence hung on the air as threatening as the terrible noise.

Finally Berwyth spoke in a barely controlled whisper. 'Go get Old Father Fat-Nose.'

'Aaggghhhhh!'

The blood-chilling shriek echoed through the tunnels. Wreccas, used to hearing any number of ghastly cries in the Underneath, hesitated, wondering who or what could have made such a horrifying sound. Some paused with a beaker halfway to their lips; others stopped in the middle of a conversation. Still more flinched, fearful of what such a scream might signify. A few, sleeping in disorganized heaps, opened their eyes. Only the oldest and deafest continued their slumbers undisturbed.

Scamp turned, not knowing what to expect, but knowing that it must be bad. It was worse that he could have imagined. Scamp gawped in horror.

Work at the tunnel face was more difficult now that they were chiselling their way through rock, but the work had been steady. They made do with a strange collection of tools that had been scavenged from the Topside. Apart from Scamp's shovel, which was old but in one piece, everything else had been discarded by its Human owner because it was broken. There was an odd assortment of pickaxes, spades, forks, trowels and even spoons or knives roughly tied to pieces of wood. Wreccas, who were not normally known for their enthusiasm when it came to hard physical labour, worked hard for Scamp. He had a way of inspiring them.

The only problem was their lack of discipline. However much Scamp tried to arrange them into some sort of working unit, they soon fell into disorganized groups. Pickaxes and garden forks flailed the air as they cut and chipped their way through the rock. Rubble was dumped into large bins that were haphazardly dragged away.

Recently, there had been a rush to complete the job and receive the rewards that Offa Scratch had promised. Because of this, the work had become wilder, and consequently the tunnel face even more dangerous.

The sight that met Scamp's eyes turned his stomach cold. Slob had been wielding a pickaxe and, unbeknown to him, Stench had moved to the tunnel face to gather up the smaller rocks that littered the area. Slob had not expected him to be there. He had raised the pickaxe high above his head and brought it down with all his strength, realizing his mistake too late. Vainly he had tried to change the direction of his plummeting pickaxe, but to no avail. The blade kept its course and plunged its way towards the rock face. However, it was not the hard rock that it sank into.

It was Stench's head.

The carnage was horrific. The blood-chilling cry had come from Stench, and it was the last sound he was ever to utter. By the time Scamp had scrambled to his side, he was silent, with eyes wide open and blood pouring from his head.

Stench was stone dead.

Kneeling by his side, Scamp tried to stem the flow of blood, without success.

Slob was appalled, not so much by the blood, although that was gruesome; no, Slob was mainly concerned for himself. He did not want even to imagine the trouble he was going to be in. With a stifled cry of terror, he dropped his pickaxe and took off.

The Wreccas stood in stunned silence. Scamp wiped his brow with the back of his hand, leaving Stench's blood smeared across it. 'Best get Sniff,' he said.

Sheldon sat dozing in the library. He could not have been more bored. There was nothing for him to do. He had never wanted to accompany Zeit to Greenwich and it was quite clear that Zeit did not need his help.

Sheldon disliked Greenwich and resented everyone who lived there. His childhood had been very lonely; he had had no friends. He envied people like Tid, who seemed to have so much. It had been easy for envy to turn to hate. He blamed Sofi for all his troubles. He loathed Bryn Brownal for telling him off every time he had broken one of the park rules. He had detested school and all his teachers. Most of all, he hated the way he had felt when he had lived there. Why had Zeit made him come back and remind himself of all the things he had most particularly wanted to forget? Greenwich was the last place he wanted to be.

'Sheldon,' Zeit called.

Sheldon jumped. Zeit was pointing to Yu Yul, who was on the top balcony, straining to reach a book that was out of her reach.

'Careful,' Seegan called up to her.

Sheldon sighed. He understood what he was to do and lazily climbed the ladders. He joined Yu Yul on the top balcony. She looked up at him with her dark slanting eyes, the glow from the books shining off her jet-black hair. She was pointing to a faded brown-leather volume. Reaching up, he tried to read the title, but the language was strange.

'What is it called?' Old Father Tim asked.

'I can't read it.'

'That sounds about right!' Old Father Tim exclaimed brightly. 'Bring it down.'

Sheldon levered the ancient volume from its shelf but, once it was in his hands, he almost dropped it. It was the heaviest book he had ever handled, and during his time with Zeit he had handled many.

'Take care now,' Old Father Tim warned as Sheldon made his way down the well-worn steps, followed by Yu Yul. A space was cleared on one of the tables. Sheldon tried to place the book gently on to it, but it was so heavy that it landed with a loud thud.

'My word!' Old Father Tim exclaimed, running his hand reverently over it. 'This is a volume of the Chronicles that I never really believed existed. To think it has been up there all this time!'

'It is in the histories,' Vremya said.

They watched intently as Old Father Tim lifted the weighty leather-bound cover and opened the book. He started turning the thick, heavy pages. Each was covered in intricate and strangely mysterious writing, bold and black. Most of the symbols were similar to the Guardian alphabet, but some letters were missing and new ones had been added. Some looked as if two letters had been joined together, but not as Guardians do it. The whole thing was impossible to read.

'Does this make sense to anyone?' Old Father Tim asked.

They shook their heads.

Old Father Tim looked at Wakaa. 'Not even you?'

'No, Old Father. This is totally beyond my learning.'

'We need Aleyesu.'

'No!' Zeit blurted out.

The others looked at him, and in their stare he felt uncomfortable.

'I know I am always the one to voice the opposite point of view,' he said, 'but this time I am right. Aleyesu has been a Guardian for too short a time. How can he possibly have the experience to instruct us in such an important issue? Time is too short.'

'Precisely so,' Old Father Tim said. 'We have no time for instruction. This is a case of translation and interpretation, and I can think of none better than Aleyesu. He has already been summoned.'

Zeit sighed. Sometimes he wondered why he bothered opening his mouth.

In the quiet that followed the accident, the Wrecca women stood vigil by the walls in the Labyrinth. Berwyth was convinced that this was a prelude to the invasion. No one slept. No one ate. No one spoke. Harfed forgot that she felt ill and Berwyth forgot that

Old Father Tim was her sworn enemy. She paced up and down the Committee Chamber as she waited for Lorin to return.

Lorin ran Topside and rushed to Old Father Tim's house, pummelling on the front door as soon as she arrived.

'What is the matter?' Enderell asked as she opened it.

'I need to speak to Old Father Tim,' Lorin gasped breathlessly.

'He is not here.'

'I has to see him now,' Lorin panted. 'I think the men's breaking through,' and she quickly described what had happened.

'We must tell the Old Father,' Enderell said.

The quickest way to do this was to go to the Hither House, where the Guardians were working. It was too far to be Mindful. They set off at once.

Lorin found herself running to keep up with the ever graceful Enderell. Never having been in Greenwich before, Lorin might have enjoyed the sights, but there was no time to take them in.

Eventually, Lorin found herself following Enderell up the worn and misshapen steps that led to the Hither House's cracked old front door. Lorin had not seen this crooked old house with sleepy windows when they had first arrived. In fact, she could have sworn it had not been there, but as they crossed the road it appeared as if from nowhere.

From the outside it looked like a tumbledown building

of moderate size, but as she crossed the threshold Lorin discovered she was very much mistaken. The hallway alone seemed to be twice the size of the entire house and there were several doors leading off it. The tall ceiling was heavily decorated in ornate white plaster and was held in place by enormous marble pillars.

To her right was a large fireplace, but as it was summer there was no fire. Instead, the hearth was filled by a pottery vase, overflowing with wild flowers and herbs. In front of the fireplace was a table laden with food.

Lorin had never seen such a spread of pies, fruit, tarts and cakes. She was mesmerized by it all. Enderell was not impressed. She shook her head as she surveyed the feast and clicked her tongue disapprovingly, but there was no time to correct whatever mistake she had noticed. Instead, she walked through a door at the far end of the hall, beckoning Lorin to follow.

Lorin gazed, open-mouthed, at the grandeur of her surroundings as she followed Enderell through one door after another, until they finally entered a small room where a tall young man was looking through papers on a desk.

'Joss, we need to see Old Father Tim,' Enderell said.

He smiled warmly and disappeared through yet another door.

Lorin had often seen Joss in the park and thought him very handsome. His black lashes framed deep-brown eyes that, until now, she had only seen from a distance. It felt very strange to be so near to him and, to her embarrassment, she felt her face becoming very warm. It suddenly occurred to her that she looked shabby, especially compared with the lovely Enderell. Self-consciously she ran a hand over her ruffled hair and tried to smooth her faded dress, but she had little time to worry as Old Father Tim quickly appeared at the door.

'Old Father,' Enderell said, 'Lorin needs to speak with you. I think it may be urgent.'

'My dear young woman,' Old Father Tim said to Lorin, 'has anyone offered you any refreshment?'

Lorin shook her head vaguely. She did not want to be sidetracked by food.

'Berwyth telled I to come and get you,' she blurted out.

'Did she indeed?' the old man said. 'Has something happened?'

Lorin hesitated. How could she explain that terrifying noise? She could not put into words how frightening it had been. 'There was this noise, in the Labyrinth. It sort of comed from where the rumblings and bangings is coming from. It wasn't just any noise. It was like . . .' What was it like? 'It was like . . . nothing I's ever heared before. It was . . .' she shuddered. 'It sounded like a war cry. Berwyth telled I to come and get you straight away.' She looked up into his comfortable, old face. 'The men's about to break through, I's sure of it. Us need your magic, Old Father Tim, and us need it now.'

Lorin's anxiety was clear. Old Father Tim told her

to stay and eat while he went and discussed all she had said with the Guardians. Enderell organized food for Lorin and then disappeared to the kitchens to supervise the correction of whatever mistake she had noticed on the table full of food in the main hall. Joss returned to the papers on his desk.

Lorin felt very self-conscious, sitting in the same room as the person she had most often enjoyed watching from the safety of her tree. It was a relief when Enderell finally returned.

'Old Father Tim will see you now,' she said as she led Lorin to a room that was smaller that any she had previously come across. The walls were wood-lined and gave off their own restful, heartening glow. The floor space was completely filled with a circle of seven armchairs. Each one was different in size and colour and each fitted the occupant perfectly.

Seegan's chair was compact and highly decorated with bright colours. Vremya's was dark and comfortable. Wakaa's was not padded at all, but was made of heavily carved wood and should have been most uncomfortable except that it was perfectly moulded to his body. Zeit's chair was tall and angular and covered in dark leather, and Old Father Tim's padded armchair was covered in a bright checked material with matching cushions.

The Greenwich Guardian rose from her neat and comfortable-looking chair as Lorin entered. 'I hope that you are properly refreshed.'

Lorin assured her in mumbling fashion that she was,

even though she had been far too anxious to touch a morsel of the delicious-looking food Enderell had placed in front of her.

'Please sit down.' Enderell indicated the seventh and unoccupied chair. It was small and made of wicker. The back and sides were lined with fitted patchwork cushions. Lorin thought it the prettiest thing she had ever seen. It seemed too good to sit on, but she had been invited to sit and so she did, very carefully and on the edge of the seat. The Greenwich Guardian sat too.

'Lorin.' It was Old Father Tim who spoke now.

She turned to face him.

'My colleagues and I have discussed your problem and we think we have come up with a solution.'

Strangely enough, in all this luxury, Lorin had forgotten the reason why she had sought out Old Father Tim in the first place. Suddenly the plight of the Labyrinth and all who lived there returned to her. She looked directly at the old man.

Looking into her eyes, he discovered that he liked what he saw. Lorin was earnest and honest. It struck the Old Father how very like Sofi she was.

'Lorin,' he began, 'my fellow Guardians and I have agreed that in order to protect the women in the Labyrinth we shall have to use magic.'

Lorin gasped with relief.

'But,' Old Father Tim continued quickly, 'such magic is very difficult to invoke. In order to produce charms strong enough to work below ground and fend off a fighting force like the Wreccas, it needs to be deep and powerful. Wakaa has agreed to work on this, but it will take time.'

'How much time?' Lorin asked, forgetting to be nervous.

'Several days.'

'Several days?' Lorin repeated in dismay. 'They's about to break through.'

'Some things cannot be rushed. We plan to use a magic that will divert the Wreccas' attention away from digging. You must understand that the magic has to be powerful and precise. To work too quickly would slow down the entire process.'

'But us is in danger *now*,' Lorin stressed.

'That is why,' Old Father Tim continued in a comforting voice, 'we have decided it would be best for the women to move.'

'Move?'

'Only temporarily,' he assured her. 'I understand that the women only use a small part of the cave system. You must move deeper into it.'

'Berwyth'll never do that. Us did it before, when Humans moved into some of the caves. It was awful. Us lost most of our things. Her'll not agree to that again.'

'But it would only be for a short time. Surely that is better than being there when the men attack.'

'What does you think the men'll do, once they get into our Labyrinth?' Lorin asked bluntly. 'It's ever so much nicer than the Underneath. Does you think they'll walk in, see us is not there and go away again?'

'What do you want us to do?' the old man asked.

'Help us fight them at the very least.'

'The Guardian People cannot fight,' Old Father Tim explained. 'We use our wit, wisdom and magic, and that takes time.'

'What wit and wisdom?' she asked disrespectfully.

Old Father Tim smiled indulgently. 'I rather thought we were using the wisdom when we suggested that you moved.'

'If us moves, us'll lose our home forever,' Lorin said. 'How can that be wisdom?'

Zeit tutted and Wakaa shook his head. They were not used to such rudeness.

Lorin did not understand that she was being bad-mannered; she was just stating the truth as she saw it.

Old Father Tim was not offended. Instead, he appreciated her frankness. 'I do not think there is anything else we can do,' he said regretfully. 'I wish there was. You must be very brave, my dear, and lead your people to safety. Would it help if I came with you to the Labyrinth to explain?'

'Ner,' Lorin said bitterly.

Old Father Tim settled back in his chair. It was clear that he thought the interview was over.

The Greenwich Guardian stood. 'Joss will walk you back to the park.'

'I doesn't need that,' Lorin said, her thoughts still on how she could possibly tell Berwyth that Old Father Tim had failed them once again.

'You might need help across Greenwich,' the Greenwich Guardian persisted.

Suddenly, Joss was at Lorin's side. His closeness confused her and she could not argue. With a nod to the Greenwich Guardian, she left the room, closely followed by Joss.

As they crossed Greenwich he tried to talk, but Lorin's answers were brief, and Joss quickly realized that she did not want to. Lorin kept the pace brisk, wishing he would leave her alone as soon as possible. It was not too long before they were walking through the park gates and up the hill. When they passed the Line, Lorin said, 'I know my way from here.'

'The Greenwich Guardian told me to take you home,' Joss said, keeping close to her side.

'Ner!' she said, alarmed. 'She sayed to take I back to the park. It'll be quicker on my own.'

Joss seemed to waver. 'I was told . . .'

'There may be Wreccas on Blackheath,' she persisted. 'No offence, but I doesn't want to be seed with you. It'll cause all sorts of trouble. The Greenwich Guardian only sayed for you to take I across Greenwich.'

'Well . . .' Joss said, uncertainly. 'I could walk some distance behind you, just to make sure . . .'

'Ner!' Lorin cried. To have him tracking her all the way home would be just awful. 'It'll be all right. My tree is just across the park. I know my way from there. I come this way almost every day. Thank you, but I'll be fine.'

'If you are certain?'

'I is.'

'Very well. Goodbye, Lorin.' Joss held his hand out. Trying not to look self-conscious, she extended her own and allowed him to shake it. She felt her face burn as he held her hand. Embarrassed by her reaction, she turned and left at speed. She blundered blindly through the park, trying to lose the feeling that she had behaved very stupidly.

'Miss Scaggy.'

Lorin froze. Only one group of people ever called her Scaggy.

9

Aleyesu

Lorin's heart thumped heavily in her chest as she turned. Sure enough, there stood a Wrecca, but not just any Wrecca. There stood Scratch himself. Why was he calling her 'Miss'?

'What you want?' Lorin asked distrustfully.

'I want to talk to you,' he said in a reasonable voice.

'I doesn't want to listen,' she said, turning to leave.

'That's what Miss Simple sayed.'

Lorin spun back. In the Underneath, Morlenni had been called Simple.

'What's you talking about?'

'Us was able to change *her* mind,' he said with a nasty smile.

'What has you done to her?'

'Nothing, Miss, nothing at all.' He spoke with mock concern. 'Her's perfectly happy in the Underneath with us, 'cept . . .'

''Cept what?'

'. . . 'cept,' Offa Scratch continued as if he had never been interrupted, 'that her's a bit lonely. I suppose it's only natural, with all them rough men around. It's enough to upset any girl.'

'If you hurt . . .'

'Hurt?' Offa Scratch spoke as if such a suggestion was an insult. He played his sharp nails down his cheekbone. 'I's not going to hurt no one . . . not, that is, if someone else does as I tell her.'

Lorin suddenly felt very sick. She tried to remain calm. 'How does I know you really has her?' she asked, playing for time, realizing that this must be why she had been unable to find Morlenni the previous night.

'Come and see for yourself.'

Lorin gave a scornful half-laugh. 'You doesn't get I into the Underneath that easy.'

'Very well. Go back to the Labyrinth and ask around.' Offa Scratch's voice was oily sweet. 'You'll soon discover that Miss Simple isn't there. Someone'll be waiting for you at the Lower Topside door when you's ready.'

'I's not coming to the Underneath,' Lorin said, jutting out her chin obstinately.

'Oh dear.' Offa Scratch pretended to be distressed. 'Miss Simple will be sorry, and so'll the men. I's sure they willn't mean to hurt her, but some of them find it hard to be nice when they's disappointed.' An evil smile played across his thin lips.

'If you dare hurt her!' Lorin snarled, squaring up to him.

It amused Scratch that a mere girl could imagine she could intimidate him. 'Oh we willn't, we willn't,' he said theatrically. 'But you'll want to come and see that for yourself.'

'I's going to check you's telling the truth.'

'Very wise, Miss Scaggy, very wise.' He played a nail across his lips, which were no longer smiling. 'But don't be too long. It'll be a shame if Miss Simple is . . . how do I say this? . . . injured in some way, because you's late.'

Lorin's throat was dry and her hands clammy. What should she do? Morlenni would never be able to cope with Scratch and his men in the Underneath. But how could Lorin be sure she was really there? Her friend might be home by now. Lorin could not take Scratch's word for it. She had to check it out.

All this passed through her mind in an instant.

'I'll be quick,' she said.

Offa Scratch shrugged his shoulders. 'You's better be,' he said and sauntered off.

Lorin watched him go. For a moment her mind was numb, then questions burst through it. Why was he goading her into the Underneath? Why did he not just nab her? How must Morlenni be feeling? Where was she? Did he really have her? What should she do?

Time was short. She knew that Scratch was capable of great cruelty and so she had to be fast. She looked around frantically. Had Joss followed her as he had suggested? 'Joss!' she hissed, not daring to yell too loudly in case Scratch heard her. There was no answer. Why had she sent him away?

For a moment she was unsure what to do. She wanted to tell the Greenwich Guardian or Enderell what was happening, but they were all the way across Greenwich.

Suddenly she made up her mind and, hitching up her dress, she started running as fast as she could towards the Labyrinth.

Back at the Hither House, Old Father Tim was reporting to the other Guardians all that Bryn had told him.

'He has found no evidence of a cross-over, but it is difficult to be certain. The Council has also found nothing to suggest that the time locators have been affected. Of course, both Bryn and the Council will keep investigating.'

'What do we do in the meantime?' Zeit asked.

'I think we need to go in search of the Gemetbur and see if our problem lies there,' Old Father Tim said, and then added, 'and as the most experienced Guardian, I select myself for this.'

'And I shall come with you,' Wakaa said in a manner that would accept no refusal.

'What about the deep magic that we need for the Labyrinth?' Old Father Tim asked.

'I think it is more important that I accompany you,' Wakaa replied.

Zeit loudly agreed. 'And I shall come too.'

'No,' Old Father Tim said. 'You will be more useful up here. We do not need a law expert in the tunnels, but an expert in deep magic might be useful.' He turned to Wakaa. 'But we cannot let Lorin down.'

'She shall get her magic,' Wakaa said. 'Kanika is a very capable apprentice; she shall lead the research. I am sure that the Greenwich Guardian will give her all the resources and help that she needs.'

'Indeed I shall.'

'Then that is settled.'

'How shall you find the Gemetbur?' Zeit asked.

'We shall put ourselves in the hands of Aleyesu,' Old Father Tim said. 'My hope is that he will be able to translate the volume that we could not read.'

'How do you know that it holds the answers?' Zeit questioned.

'Vremya is certain of it.'

'How?'

'A lifetime spent searching the histories.'

Zeit was sceptical.

'Vremya is a very learned and wise Guardian.'

'I know,' Zeit replied, 'and I respect him and his wisdom, but what if he is wrong?'

Before Old Father Tim could answer, his attention was taken by the opening of the door. He turned and saw a tall, grand-looking Guardian standing in the doorway. He had long, dark, glossy hair, part of which was plaited down either side of his head. His nose was long, narrow between the eyes and wide above his full and well-chiselled mouth. He carried a heavily carved staff. This was Aleyesu, the Guardian for Oklahoma in America.

Old Father Tim greeted him warmly. 'Aleyesu! Welcome!' he cried, crossing to him and shaking his hand enthusiastically, before introducing him to the others.

Aleyesu bowed his head respectfully as each was presented to him. Then, without wasting any time, Old Father Tim led him to the library to look at the ancient Chronicle.

Aleyesu studied the symbols and smiled appreciatively. 'These are some of the earliest Guardian writings.'

'Can you read them?' Old Father Tim asked.

Aleyesu then did something strange. He lifted his head, as though extending it as high on his neck as possible, and looked down towards his hand, which he held a few notches above the page, palm down and fingers splayed. Gently, he moved his fingers, staring hard at the space between hand and page. 'It is older than any I have seen.'

'Will you be able to make sense of it?'

'Given time,' he said, letting his hand fall.

'Ah,' Old Father Tim said. 'That is our problem. We have very little of that.'

'Then I will need help.'

'You have not brought an apprentice?'

'No, I left in a hurry.'

'Use Sheldon,' Zeit suggested. 'I do not need him for now.'

Sheldon jumped at the sound of his name. He had been dozing again in the corner.

'Do whatever Aleyesu asks of you,' Zeit told him.

Sheldon nodded, resenting the idea of being at the beck and call of a Guardian he did not know, but there was no arguing with Zeit. Reluctantly, Sheldon took his place at Aleyesu's side.

They worked long into the night. Some of the other Guardians took to their beds but Aleyesu did not, which meant that Sheldon also had to stay. His job was to write down the interpretations as Aleyesu spoke them. It was slow, boring work. Sheldon tried hard to stifle yawns and keep his eyes open. He sometimes stared at the strange symbols as an exercise to try and stay awake, but it was all a jumble and made no sense.

Sometimes Aleyesu would ask Sheldon to look something up in the long leather scrolls he had brought with him. At first, Sheldon found this very difficult and would have gladly handed the task over to Pasha, who stood on the balls of his feet nearby, clearly anxious to become involved. He was eager to demonstrate his ability and willingness, so that he would have a greater chance of being selected as the Time Apprentice. It was probably Sheldon's obstinate desire to thwart Pasha's wishes that made him stick at it. He continued helping Aleyesu resolutely until he found that he was beginning to recognize some of the patterns. 'How do you make a translation?' he asked during a break. 'Does it take long to learn?'

'It takes a lifetime,' Aleyesu replied, but then added, 'except that a lifetime would be too short for most people. These symbols do not only have meanings as they are written, they also have meanings depending on their position on the page, the number of times they are used and the patterns in which they occur.' Seeing that Sheldon did not understand, he added, 'It is almost as if the symbols lift off the page as I read. This one

here and this one and this one down there,' he pointed
to specific symbols, 'shine more brightly than the rest,
and as they shine they lift themselves off the pages and
it looks to me as if they are floating in the air about
here.' He held his hand just above the page. 'Then, if
I contrast their floating positions with the locations on
the page, I can understand their meaning.' Then he
added with a rueful smile, 'Well, I often can. There is
many a time when I cannot.'

Sheldon looked at the page. Nothing was moving. He
squinted at the symbols; none of them was floating.
'They don't move for me.'

Aleyesu nodded. 'It takes a gift to begin and a lifetime to learn.'

Lorin pounded on the door. 'Come on!' she urged under
her breath.

The door was opened much more quickly than usual.
She pushed at it as soon as it was unlatched and a very
startled Falryd almost fell over as it whacked her hard
on the head. 'What d'you think you's doing!' she yelled,
clutching her forehead.

Without a word of explanation, Lorin dashed past and
went straight to Morlenni's alcove and flung back the
threadbare curtain that made her friend's home private.

Morlenni was not there.

Lorin ran to her own alcove, not really expecting her
to be there. She was right. It too was empty.

'Have you seen Morlenni?' she asked everyone she met.
No one had, nor did they seem in the least bothered.

They were still discussing the terrible noise.

Lorin rushed to the Committee Chamber. She had to tell Berwyth.

Yaryth was standing outside as usual. On seeing Lorin, she went inside to announce her. Berwyth wanted to be told the moment Lorin returned.

Lorin walked straight in. 'Berwyth,' she said, forgetting any formality. 'They's taked Morlenni.'

'I knowed it!' Berwyth cried, anger causing a blue vein to stand out and throb in her neck. 'Can't never trust them. Old Father Fat-Nose is a pig. He pretends to be good but –'

'Ner, ner, ner!' Lorin interjected, 'Not Old Father Tim. Him's going to help with magic.'

Lorin vaguely noticed sounds of surprise from the Committee.

'It's Scratch that's got her!'

Berwyth looked confused.

'Scratch taked Morlenni,' Lorin confirmed.

There was a moment's silence and then Berwyth asked, 'What for?'

'Er . . . um . . cos . . . does it matter what for?'

No one answered. Lorin could see that they needed her to give a reason.

'They taked her cos . . . that's what men does!'

'Huh!' Berwyth said dismissively. 'What about the magic?'

'They's taked her to the Underneath,' Lorin persisted, hoping that this would trigger the reaction of outrage she had been expecting.

'Where else is they going to take her? Tell us about the magic!'

Lorin stared at them in confusion. They had missed the point. She was going to have to spell it out to them. 'They's *kidnapped* Morlenni.'

'Better her than I,' Berwyth said. 'What sort of magic is they going to use?'

Lorin knew Berwyth to be an unpleasant shrew of a woman, but her lack of concern for Morlenni was staggering. Lorin glowered at the Committee, who did not seem to notice. They were too busy discussing Old Father Tim and his magic.

Lorin was temporarily lost for words. When she finally found some, she spoke them slowly and deliberately, in a voice dripping with cold fury. Facing one bench of women, she snarled, 'You ugly, cold-hearted,' and then she turned to the other bench, 'stupid old bats!'

Momentarily stunned, their mouths fell open as they gaped at her.

Then a low chuckle bubbled from the end of the chamber.

Berwyth was laughing.

Her mirth became more exaggerated as she clasped her hands around her bulging stomach and roared with laughter. 'Oh my!' she gasped. 'That's a good one! Ugly! Her's not wrong there!' and another roar of laughter ripped from her and echoed around the chamber.

Lorin's fury burned deep inside, but she did not let it show. Instead, she appeared cool and calm. Slowly she approached her leader.

Berwyth was still laughing.

'It wasn't long ago,' Lorin said quietly, 'that you was scared to death at the thought of the men breaking into the Labyrinth.'

Her change of manner steadied Berwyth's laughter, although she still held her copious stomach.

'Terrified, you was,' Lorin continued, advancing. 'You telled I to,' and here her voice changed into a scornful mimic of Berwyth, 'run and fetch Old Father Fat-Nose.'

Berwyth closed her mouth with a snap. It was unthinkable that someone should dare take such liberties. Sparks of fury flecked her eyes. 'How dare you . . .' she snarled.

'You was scared stiff,' Lorin interrupted, still quiet, still fuming. 'But now look at you, all excited at the thought of magic and not giving a rat's tail for Morlenni. You's useless!' She lingered over her words, delivering them straight into Berwyth's reddening face. 'You's a selfish, big-headed, lazy, fat old hag!'

As each insult punctured the air, so Berwyth responded as if she had been stabbed with a needle. Lorin's words hit her hard and the shock rendered her silent. By the time she was able to respond, Lorin had turned on her heels and stormed out of the chamber.

'Her willn't get away with that!' Berwyth said in a rusty-nail sort of voice. 'Stop her!'

The members of the Committee looked at each other apprehensively. Yaryth blinked at Berwyth.

'Bring that sour-faced vixen back!'

No one moved.

Berwyth pushed Yaryth hard in the chest. 'Get her!' she fumed.

'I?' Yaryth asked, clearly not feeling up to the task.

'Who else?' Berwyth yelled, pushing her harder so that she stumbled back and fell against the wall. 'NOW!'

Yaryth staggered to her feet. She was doubtful whether she could catch Lorin, but Berwyth wanted her out, and for once she agreed with her.

10

Tempus and the Gemetbur

Aleyesu put his hand to the back of his neck and rubbed it. He had been working all night.

Old Father Tim was handing him a cup of strong black coffee. 'Drink up.' He handed another cup to Sheldon, who had also been sleeping.

'I must have fallen asleep.'

'It will do you good.'

Aleyesu put the drink to his lips, more because he had been told to than because he wanted anything to drink just yet, but as soon as the liquid touched them, he appreciated its restorative qualities. This was no ordinary coffee. He drank the black liquid down in one.

Old Father Tim smiled. 'One of Enderell's blends,' he said. 'It works for me every time.'

'I must take time to talk with this Enderell,' Aleyesu said appreciatively.

Feeling very much awake now, he looked at the manuscript he had been working on the night before. 'Shoot!' he exclaimed in his American drawl. 'I haven't finished! I thought I had. I must have been dreaming.'

'How much more is there to translate?'

Aleyesu checked. 'Two pages.'

'Does it tell us what we need to know?'

'It tells us where the Guardian tunnels begin, but then I kind of lose the plot.'

'Does it tell us how to get into the Gemetbur?' Old Father Tim asked eagerly.

'If it's anywhere, it's going to be here; it will just take a while.'

'But Wakaa and I are anxious to leave.'

'Then I shall have to come with you.'

'What good will that do?'

'I shall translate as we go.'

'You cannot take such an enormous volume on this sort of journey.'

Aleyesu nodded his head. 'You are right,' he said. 'It is far too bulky.' Then, to Old Father Tim's horror, Aleyesu gripped the two pages and neatly tore them from the ancient Chronicle.

'You cannot do that!' Old Father Tim said, deeply shocked.

'There are some things more important than old books,' Aleyesu said. 'If I have judged it correctly, you will need me and my two pages on this journey with you.'

Sofi and Tid had gone to school as usual, although it was Enderell who had made them their breakfast because Old Father Tim was at the Hither House.

On the way to school, they saw Seth behaving very strangely. He was looking over his shoulder in a secretive sort of way and then ran off when he saw them. It looked as if he was avoiding them.

'He's strange, that friend of yours,' Tid said. He always called Seth 'Sofi's friend' because they had both once lived in the Underneath.

When they arrived home at the end of the day, their grandfather was there. They sat around the table. Instead of the usual cake, Enderell had baked spiced biscuits; they were delicious. Old Father Tim told them about his forthcoming journey to find the Gemetbur.

'You always say that story was made up,' Sofi said.

'I know,' the old man agreed. 'I thought so myself, but Vremya says he has found reference to it in the Guardian History, which means it must be true.'

'How are you going to find it?'

'The Chronicles will tell us how.'

'Does it tell you how to get into the Gemetbur, once you've found it?' Sofi asked.

'Aleyesu is confident that it will. He is coming with us and will translate as he goes.'

'Where are you going to start?' Tid asked.

'That piece of information I shall keep to myself,' the old man said. 'The fewer people who know, the better.' He stood up. 'And now I must go.'

Old Father Tim then kissed Sofi on her head, ruffled Tid's hair and smiled at Enderell. He picked up his staff, lifted the bag that Enderell had packed with sandwiches for the journey and left.

Sofi and Tid stood at the gate and waved. Sofi bit her lip until it hurt, in an attempt to hold back the tears that were pricking her eyes. Although he had made light of it, she knew that her grandfather was walking into potential danger without much in the way of magic to protect him. She wanted to ask if Tid was as worried as she but dared not speak in case her voice betrayed her tears; but from the whiteness of Tid's knuckles as he gripped the garden gate, she suspected he felt the same.

Sheldon Croe leant against a tree. He had not been told that he could leave, but after Aleyesu had gone Sheldon had taken the opportunity of slipping quietly out of the Hither House. Now he was back in the park, he looked about him. He should have been glad to be home, but he was not. Home brought with it all the emotions he had felt when he lived here: loneliness, rejection and resentment.

Life in Germany with Zeit had been strange. At first he had been bitter about being uprooted and forced to leave his home. He had blamed everyone: Sofi, Tid, Old Father Tim, the Greenwich Guardian and even Pa Brownal. After a while, he had started blaming his grandmother for providing such a poor home, then he blamed his father for deserting him and, finally, his mother. Where had she gone?

Over the years Sheldon had spent many hours trying to remember his mother. Why had she left without a word of farewell? He knew that she had been unhappy. Night after night he had lain with his pillow over his head, trying to drown out the arguments between her and his father. And then there was the crying. Of course, his mother tried to hide the tears when he was there, but he could always tell when she had been weeping.

Finally, she had disappeared. One morning, she was not at breakfast. He had asked his father where she was and had received a sharp blow round the head in answer. He soon learnt not to ask.

There was talk, of course. Some of the children at school had said that his father had killed his mother. At the time Sheldon had dismissed this thought. His father was a disagreeable, lazy sort of man who preferred to answer a question by lashing out rather than explaining; but kill his mother? No, he would not believe that.

Then his father had left, not to go with the other parents to study the ways of the Guardian People. If he had done that, Sheldon would have felt some pride. No, his father had 'gone to make his fortune', leaving Sheldon alone with his inept grandmother. The other boys had taunted him, telling him that his father had left because Sheldon was useless.

It was strange how the pain of it all had not diminished over the years. As he stood at the gate of his old home, he felt it now, deep in his stomach. Angrily, he kicked the gate that hung on one hinge. He had last walked through that gate with Sofi under his arm. He had been taking her to the Wreccas at the time. How she had fought him! Thoughts of Sofi turned to thoughts of Tid. He resented Tid more than any other living soul. Tid was clever and popular; but, to make matters worse, he was also the Old Father Grandson and respected by everyone. Sheldon was too blinded by his hatred to see that it was Tid's qualities that earned him respect, not his position as their leader's grandson.

Sheldon ground his teeth. There were a lot of scores he had to settle.

Sofi knew it would be a long night; she was too worried about her grandfather to sleep. Instead, she took a storybook off her bookshelf and settled down on her bed to read. Lightly, she touched her globe that held the fairy, and a sparkling light lit up her blue-and-yellow room.

Sofi read *Tempus and the Gemetbur* by Thadius Thead.

In the beginning there was chaos. The world churned in confusion. There was no order. The Guardian, Tempus, was very worried by this and dedicated his life to changing it. Those around him did not understand what he was doing and became suspicious, trying to destroy his work. To protect it, Tempus hid his workshop below ground and planted a tree above it.

Out of the chaos he created order.

The Guardian People understood the world and used their magic to conserve it. They lived alongside the Humans, who were mostly hardworking and caring. However, some were selfish and greedy, wanting to control everything around them. They looked for ways to make their lives easier and thought that Guardian magic would help. Some of the Guardian People tried to share their magic, but the Humans could not learn how to use it. This made them angry. Their anger soon became hatred. Their hatred turned to war.

It is a terrible thing when hatred and magic collide.

The war caused unspeakable destruction in the world and time itself was in danger. Tempus realized that he could not create harmony unless he separated Humans from the Guardian People. For many years Tempus studied the deepest magic until he finally discovered how to divide time. He then placed the Guardian People in one time and Humans in another. He gave the task of controlling time to the Guardians and made them invisible to the Humans so that time would be safe forever.

The world became more peaceful and better organized but, even so, there were problems. Creatures occasionally crossed between the two worlds because there is always someone who will move a stone at the wrong time or climb a beanstalk.

Some of the Guardian People became jealous and uncaring. They lived apart and did everything they could to make trouble, trying to wreck the structure that Tempus had created.

The Timepiece, which was the heartbeat of time, could not be hidden, because the Tick had to be renewed every thousand years, but the Time-Regulating Chamber, the Gemetbur, needed no attention. Thus, Tempus hid it away and surrounded it with a magic so strong that it could be opened only in one special way. If anyone tried to open it without the true key, then they would never again see the light of day. The true secrets of the Gemetbur were not written in the Chronicles but were passed by word of mouth for centuries until the knowledge was lost.

Yet the secret of the Gemetbur is still with us, hidden somewhere. Only those with deep insight will ever be able to recognize it, find the key and use it

Sofi's eyes began to droop. She turned the page and looked at the drawings of Tempus as an old and grand-looking Guardian. He bore a striking resemblance to

Old Father Tim, standing as he was in a room filled to bursting with mechanisms and wheels covered in cogs.

The borders of each page were coloured purple and gold and were decorated with strange symbols. Sofi had always assumed this was some sort of ancient alphabet, as many letters were similar to the alphabet she used for writing, but some were quite different. When she had once asked Old Father Tim, he had said that they were not real, but he thought they had just been invented from symbols used long ago. Sometimes, she liked to pretend that she could read them, but Old Father Tim said it was only a game. He explained that, although Tempus had been a real Guardian, many myths had grown up around him that were just for fun.

Sofi closed her eyes, but she was not ready for sleep just yet. Opening them a little, she allowed them to travel along the text. Idly, she read a passage she had read many times before. It was one of the baffling aspects of the book. It had strange puzzles that no one understood.

> *Four has the compass,*
> *Beneath me three;*
> *Orb though I am,*
> *Beneath is the key.*

Sofi's eyes closed and she found herself drifting into sleep.

She was unaware how long she had slept, but suddenly she found herself totally awake. It was as though she had never been asleep, except that she knew she had been. The words from the story were pounding in her head. She picked up the book that had slipped from her lap and read: '. . . it could be opened only in one special way. If anyone tried to open it without the true key, then they would never again see the light of day. The true secrets of the Gemetbur were not written in the Chronicles . . .'

Sofi's heart began thumping. She knew this story well, but the last part was new to her. She spoke the words out loud. 'The true secrets of the Gemetbur were not written in the Chronicles.' She was sure she had never read that before. Was it possible to read a story many times and just not notice some of it, or had it not been there? If it had not, where had it come from?

She turned the book over in her hand to see if anything else was different. She studied the pages. Had the borders always been that bright? Had the writing always been so strange?

She turned back to the text and read it again. If the special way of opening the Gemetbur had never been written down in the Chronicles, Aleyesu would not be able to read it there. Perhaps he knew this already, or maybe he had not got that far; but if he could not read it, how could he know the right way to enter the Gemetbur? If they enter the wrong way . . . she placed her hand over her opened mouth as the enormity of this realization dawned on her . . . they would never see the light of day again.

Grandfather was in terrible danger!

Clutching the book, she quietly slipped out of bed

and padded through to Old Father Tim's bedroom. She did not expect to see him there; it was Enderell she was searching for.

Sofi gently tapped on the door. No answer came. Tentatively, she pushed it open. She could not see much, but she could hear Enderell's regular breathing. Silently, she crossed the rag rug and, putting her face down to Enderell's ear, she whispered her name.

Enderell did not stir.

Sofi poked her shoulder with a finger. Enderell opened her eyes. 'Yes?' she said blearily. She lifted her head from the pillow and screwed up her face, as if trying to focus clearly.

'It's me,' Sofi said, trying to be helpful.

'Is there something the matter?' Enderell asked.

'I don't know,' Sofi confessed. 'It's just that I was reading this book,' she held it out so that Enderell could see it, 'and it says that Tempus did not write in the Chronicles how to get into the Gemetbur. It says that if anyone tries to do it the wrong way, they will never see the light of day again.'

Enderell looked puzzled for a minute, as if trying to take in what Sofi had said, and then she smiled re-assuringly. 'That's a children's book, Sofi. The person who wrote it made most of it up.'

'Perhaps this is the bit they didn't make up.'

'Who wrote it?' Enderell asked, trying not to show her sleepiness.

'Thadius Thead,' Sofi said, reading his name.

'Oh that's Thadius Plemet-Thead,' Enderell said,

remembering back to her own childhood. 'He's good. I loved reading his stories when I was young.'

'It only says Thadius Thead here.'

Enderell looked at the cover of the book. 'That's a new edition,' she said. 'He must be long dead by now. He was called Thadius Plemet-Thead when I was a girl. They probably thought that was too much of a mouthful.'

'But Grandfather thinks that the Gemetbur is real, and so does Thadius Thead. If he got that bit right, then maybe he got the rest right too.'

'Look, Sofi,' Enderell sat up and rubbed her eyes, 'Old Father Tim and the other Guardians are very wise. They would notice if anything in the Chronicles was not exactly right.'

Sofi thought about that. 'Maybe.'

'And if the great Tempus wanted to keep how to enter the Gemetbur secret, how would Thadius Plemet-Thead know about it?'

That made sense. 'I suppose so,' Sofi said reluctantly.

Enderell smiled. 'I think you should go back to bed.'

'All right,' Sofi said, unable to disguise her disappointment.

'Don't wake Tid up.'

Sofi nodded and went back to bed, but she did not settle down. She wanted to read the story again.

She had not got far when her bedroom door opened. Tid peered around it.

'What's up?' he whispered. 'Why were you walking around?'

'Look at this,' she said, handing him the book.

Tid sat on the bed and read the passage Sofi indicated.

'What do you think?' she asked.

'I'm not sure,' he said. 'Grandfather knows about this book. He's read it to us enough times.'

'But I don't remember that bit about it not being in the Chronicles. Do you?'

Tid shook his head.

'And look at the borders.'

Tid looked at them.

'Don't they look different?'

Tid could not see a difference. 'What are you trying to say?'

She wanted to tell him that she thought the book had changed somehow, but that was too fanciful for anyone to believe. 'Enderell says it is just a story and I shouldn't take it seriously.'

Tid pulled a face. 'Grown-ups can be like that.'

'And you think that because Grandfather has read the book to us, he knows all about it.'

'Not necessarily,' Tid said, crinkling his brow. 'Grown-ups don't always take much notice of what they read out loud to children, and he hasn't read it to us for ages. Perhaps he's forgotten.'

'What shall we do?'

Tid thought for a moment. He was already burdened by the knowledge that the world might descend into chaos at any time, and now this! He needed help. 'Get a second opinion,' he suggested.

Sofi thought this was a good idea. 'We ought to do it quickly,' she said. 'Grandfather left hours ago. We can't wait until morning.'

Although it was dark outside, Tid and Sofi dressed and slipped silently out of Sofi's window, dropping on to the grass below. Quietly, they ran off.

Being Elder of the Park, Pa Brownal was their first choice, but if Enderell had said they were being silly, perhaps he would too. Anyway, grown-ups were funny about children being out at night. Tid and Sofi had to talk to someone who would not throw a fit just because they were out late without permission.

Suddenly Tid had an idea. 'We'll ask Herbie!'

Sofi thought about Tid's schoolfriend. He might be good at football, but she doubted he would be any help in this matter. 'What would he know about it?' she asked, not at all impressed.

'He might see something that we've missed.'

'Like what?'

'How would I know,' Tid asked impatiently, 'when I've already missed it?'

Sofi gave him a withering look. In her opinion, Herbie was a crazy choice. He would not know any more about this than they did. She would have preferred to have asked Lorin but did not know where to find her. She doubted Lorin would be in her tree in the middle of the night.

'I don't see the point of talking to Herbie, and anyway, how would we manage it without waking his grand-parents?'

'That's easy,' Tid said. 'There's a tree outside his house and the branches go all the way up to his window. If I . . .' He stopped suddenly. He had heard something.

Somcone was coming.

In Search of the Gemetbur

Suddenly it did not seem such a good idea to be out in the night. Tid and Sofi looked around anxiously. They knew that Wreccas came above ground when it was dark. Tid looked for cover. 'Come on!' he hissed.

He started running towards a tree, but stopped almost as soon as he had begun because Sofi was not following him. She was standing still, looking into the gloom of the night. Tid followed the direction of her gaze. There was definitely someone there!

'Come on!' he whispered.

But Sofi did not. Instead, she stepped towards the approaching figure. 'Sheldon, is that you?'

Sheldon Croe jumped as if he had been caught doing something illegal. 'Who's that?' he asked.

'It *is* you,' Sofi said, walking towards him. 'It's me, Sofi!'

She declared herself with such open friendliness that Sheldon felt immediately distrustful.

'Huh,' he said, looking about to see who was with her.

'Tid,' Sofi called behind her, 'it's Sheldon!'

Tid had learnt at an early age not trust the older boy.

In the past, Sheldon had never missed an opportunity to bully. Tid remembered countless knocks and bruises he had received from Sheldon, as well as endless taunts and name-calling. He was not about to drop his guard because Sofi was glad to see him. Warily, Tid walked towards them and stood beside Sofi.

Sheldon eyed him cautiously. He too had memories. He had hated Tid. As the older boy, Sheldon felt that Tid should have respected him, but he never had. Tid had always been a pampered boy who was liked by everyone but, worst of all, he was the grandson of a great man. This was something Sheldon found hard to forgive. Sheldon's own family had been a disaster.

Sheldon did not feel shame at the fact that he bullied Tid. He felt that Tid had deserved everything he had got. In truth, he should have felt far more shame seeing Sofi. Eighteen months before, he had kidnapped her and tried to give her to the Wreccas. If anyone should bear him any resentment, it should have been her, but she seemed genuinely pleased to see him.

'Wow!' she said, smiling up at him. 'You are even taller than you were.' Seeing Sheldon in his Guardian clothes, Sofi found it hard to remember him as the unpleasant youth who had been so unkind to her. Instead, she now saw him as one of the Guardian People and was genuinely happy to see him. 'Did you have a nice time in Germany?'

Sheldon hardly thought that the words 'nice time' adequately summed up all the hard work and self-discovery that had gone on there, but he nodded vaguely.

'When did you get back?'

'A couple of days ago,' he said and then added with just a twinge of pride, 'I came with Zeit as his apprentice.'

'Gosh, you must be doing really well,' Sofi said, suitably impressed, and then added soberly, 'I'm sorry about your grandmother. It must have been hard not seeing her before she died.'

Zeit had offered Sheldon a journey back to see her at the end, but he had refused, not wanting to return to Greenwich.

Anxious to steer the conversation away from himself, Sheldon asked, 'What on earth are you two doing out at this time of night?' It made him sound much older than he felt.

Tid drew breath to say something vague. He had never trusted Sheldon and was not about to start now. He did not, however, get the chance. Much to Tid's irritation, Sofi launched into the real reason why they were there. Clearly she valued Sheldon's opinion more than Herbie's.

She opened the book and, with the help of a torch that Sheldon pulled from his pocket, started showing him the story. Much to Sheldon's amusement, this seemed to irritate Tid, so he made a great show of studying Sofi's book carefully.

'It's hard to see,' she said, directing the narrow beam from Sheldon's torch on to the text she wanted him to look at.

'We should get going,' Tid said.

They did not seem to hear him.

'Sofi!'

She looked up.

'We don't have time for this.'

'Don't be silly,' she said in the schoolteacher manner that Tid usually did not mind. This time it annoyed him. 'We wanted a second opinion, and Sheldon is giving it to us.'

By now, Sheldon was sitting on the grass, book in lap, torch in hand. He was thoroughly enjoying Tid's anger. Just to prolong it, Sheldon ran his finger over the pages and muttered importantly to himself.

'Grandfather, Wakaa and Aleyesu have gone in search of the Gemetbur,' Sofi told him, not realizing that he already knew. 'This here,' she pointed to the correct passage, 'is where I read about how . . .' but her voice trailed off.

Sheldon's finger was tracing not the words but the symbols in the border. They looked a bit like the symbols Aleyesu had been translating. He ran his finger over a sign that looked like a 'd' with two slashes across the upright. There was another, and another. Sheldon remembered Aleyesu's manner and imitated it as he concentrated. He held his hand a little above the page and allowed it to tremble.

Sofi was deeply impressed.

Tid raised his eyes heavenwards.

'Where's the entrance?' Sheldon asked.

'We don't have much time,' Tid snapped.

'We don't know,' Sofi said, answering Sheldon.

'The Old Father's workshop.'

'What?'

Sheldon looked at Sofi. 'In Old Father Tim's work-shop,' he repeated.

Sofi and Tid stared at him.

'How do you know?' Sofi asked.

Sheldon pointed to three symbols on different parts of the page. 'These symbols here,' he said with a quick glance at Tid to make sure that he was still annoyed, 'sort of join together when I move my hand like this.' He trembled his hand above the page and tried to remember what Aleyesu had said.

'And you think they mean workshop?' Sofi asked.

'Yes I do.'

'How do you know?' Sofi asked again.

'Oh, for heaven's sake!' Tid exploded. 'He's making it up!'

'No he's not,' Sofi declared defensively.

'He's trying to make himself look important, as always!' Tid continued.

Sofi got up and quickly crossed to Tid, pulling him roughly to one side. She spoke in a tense whisper, although Sheldon could hear every word.

'Stop it, Tid. You're just being mean.'

'You don't know him like I do.'

'Of course I do.'

'Then you know what he's like.'

'Well,' she conceded, 'I know he hasn't always been good.'

'He was *never* good!'

'But he's been away for nearly two years! He could have changed.'

'It's been little more than a year, and you have no proof that he has changed at all.'

'And you have no proof that he hasn't.'

'Oh, don't be ridiculous!'

'Ridiculous, am I?' she asked testily. Giving him a superior look, she marched back to Sheldon. 'Do you want to help us?' she asked bluntly.

Sheldon had no desire to help anyone, but he did enjoy annoying Tid. 'Yes,' he said.

'Thank you,' Sofi said to Sheldon. Then, turning to Tid, she announced, 'It's up to you whether you help or not.'

'Are you dumping me in favour of him?' Tid asked, deeply offended.

That was not what Sofi had meant, but pride stopped her from saying so. 'I'm just saying it's your choice,' she said haughtily.

Stung though he was by her words, Tid could not leave her in the hands of someone like Sheldon. 'We started this together,' he said, 'and we'll finish it together.'

Sofi was relieved but took care not to show it. 'Very well,' she said. 'Let's go.'

'Where?' Tid asked.

'To Grandfather's workshop, of course,' she said, striding off.

Fighting an impulse to drag her to the ground, sit on her and force her to reconsider, Tid gritted his teeth and followed.

Sheldon followed too, making no attempt to hide from Tid a smile of triumph.

Lorin sat on the mucky floor of a chamber in the Underneath, cradling Morlenni's head in her lap. Morlenni was crying softly. To be back in the Underneath was bringing back all sorts of stressful memories that she had spent years trying to forget.

Tiredness was making Lorin feel like crying too. She had reluctantly come below ground only after searching for her friend for as long as she dared. She would have felt safer now if one of the Guardian People had known where she was, but in her haste she had failed to find any. Now she sat in the place she least wanted to be, trying to keep her breath steady so as not to give in to the tears that threatened.

'Stop your snivelling,' Offa Scratch told Morlenni. 'If you does what you's telled, you'll both be out of here in a couple of days.'

'What does you want us to do?' Lorin asked, keeping her voice even.

Offa Scratch said nothing, but took a beaker of water from a wobbly table and handed it to her. This outward show of kindness frightened Lorin more than anything else he could have done. Wreccas were never kind.

She took the beaker, noticing with disgust how dirty it was.

'You doesn't have to worry,' Offa Scratch said smoothly. 'You'll be home in no time.'

These words should have been comforting, but they sounded more like a threat.

Sofi stood in front of the tree that concealed Old Father Tim's workshop, thinking carefully. She was trying to remember the entry code. Her grandfather had changed it after she had helped some Wreccas break in to steal the Tick, the winter before last. Since then, she and Tid had accompanied their grandfather there many times. Although he had never actually shown them the code, they had often seen him do it.

Stubbornly, Tid refused to offer any help and watched as Sofi stepped forward. She raised her hand towards the knot in the gnarled bark meaning to begin the opening process. Tid roughly pulled it back. 'Not in front of *him*,' he said, jerking his head towards Sheldon.

Sofi thought Tid was being very rude, but she was also aware that the fewer people who knew how to gain access to the Old Father's workshop the better. Feeling very awkward, she turned to Sheldon and asked, 'Would you mind so very much if I asked you to turn around?' Sheldon felt a stab of resentment. So, she did not trust him either.

Something of his thought must have shown on his face because Sofi said, 'It's not that I don't trust you, it's just that,' she lowered her voice, 'Tid's being difficult.'

Sheldon cast an aggrieved look at Tid before doing as he was asked.

Tid glared at Sofi. How like a girl to put the blame on him!

She placed her fingers on the appropriate knots in the gnarled bark and started whispering the code.

'You're doing it wrong.' Tid felt a twinge of pleasure at showing his superior knowledge. 'You have to be holding on to me.'

Sofi felt very silly. She turned to Sheldon and said, 'I'm sorry but you'll have to hold on to Tid. Tid, you hold me.'

Sheldon eyed Tid suspiciously and reluctantly took hold of his arm.

'Keep looking the other way,' Tid hissed unpleasantly.

'You'll have to stand closer,' Sofi said briskly.

They shuffled together.

Sofi took Tid's hand. Stretching up, she placed her thumb and little finger back on the knots in the bark and carefully whispered into the tree's trunk, 'In me bewreoh.'

Instantly, without feeling anything more than a slight jolt of the stomach, they were inside the tree, squashed on to the top step on the other side of what used to be the door.

Sofi and Tid were used to this and immediately descended the familiar, worn old steps.

Sheldon blinked. He had expected a door to open. He had no idea that the spell would transport them inside the tree. He tried to remember the words Sofi had used and muttered them under his breath. It might be useful to know them one day.

He watched the other two as they clambered down steep steps that had been deeply worn by years of use.

Sheldon took his time, ducking at the bottom to avoid a low beam.

The room was lit by a warm glow that radiated from the walls, floor and even the large oak workbench that took up most of the floor space. The walls were lined with shelves neatly stacked with measures, drills, screwdrivers, fine yarns, tins of stardust and shimmering pebbles.

'Let's look at the book again,' Sofi was saying.

It took a moment for Sheldon to remember that he was holding it. He sat on the raised platform at one end of the workshop.

Tid leant back against the workbench, watching. 'We shouldn't even be here,' he grumbled.

They ignored him.

'Grandfather will be furious,' he persisted.

'Not when he knows why,' Sofi said, without looking up.

'Suppose he's tricking us,' Tid said, jerking his head towards Sheldon, 'just to find out where this is.'

'He isn't.'

'How do you know?'

Sofi turned to Sheldon. 'Are you?' she asked directly.

'He's hardly likely to admit it,' Tid snorted.

'I've known where the workshop is for ages,' Sheldon said.

'What?' Sofi asked in surprise.

'You haven't!' Tid responded nastily.

'I saw it on the map,' Sheldon said to Sofi. 'You remember that awful map of the park that Scratch drew. It was on the table when you came in with the drinks.' He guessed it would annoy Tid that he and Sofi shared a memory that Tid knew nothing about.

Sofi thought back to the time when Sheldon had briefly been in the Underneath. She had brought some refreshments into Old Killjoy's chamber, and Sheldon had been sitting at a table with the map. She had not recognized it as a map at that time because she had never done geography, but looking back, she could see that was what it must have been. She remembered it as a very bad map.

'No Wrecca could draw a map,' Tid said.

'Scratch did,' Sofi confirmed.

'And he'd marked on this workshop,' Sheldon said, enjoying being right when Tid was wrong.

'How would a Wrecca know where it was?' Tid asked.

Sofi resented the question but answered it frankly, taking care not to show any of the shame she felt. 'Because I showed him.'

Tid put his lips together and said nothing. He had forgotten that.

'And who showed me?' Sofi asked defiantly.

Tid had been the one to show her, and he burned with bitterness that she had brought this up in front of Sheldon.

Sheldon thoroughly enjoyed their angry exchange.

Tid turned and started poking at a deep cut in the workbench with his finger.

'Can you see anything else in the book?' Sofi asked Sheldon, trying to get back to the reason why they were there.

'The symbols,' Sheldon said, trying to sound important, 'are floating again.' It was true, much to Sheldon's surprise: they actually seemed to be floating.

'What do you mean, floating?' she asked.

'Just here.' He waved his hand a few notches above the page like Aleyesu had done. 'Can't you see it?' he asked, knowing that she did not. 'It says, cl . . .' sounding as if he was struggling to read it, '. . . cl . . . clock.'

'What's a clock?' Sofi asked.

Sheldon shrugged and concentrated on the words once more. 'No, it's not just "clock",' he muttered. 'It says something about being under or behind it.' He scratched his head. 'I don't know.'

Tid knew what a clock was, because his grandfather had once told him. 'A clock is a timepiece,' he said, happy to be able to show off his superior knowledge. 'And when Grandfather was building the new Timepiece, it stood on that platform.'

Sofi and Sheldon turned around and stared behind them. The platform stood against an oak-lined wall. It was the only one in the workshop that had no shelves.

'Behind the Timepiece,' Sofi said to herself as she stepped on to the platform and ran her hands over the panelling that covered the wall. There was no sign of any kind of door. She stepped back and stared at it.

'Are you sure the Timepiece was here?' she asked Tid.

'Absolutely,' he said.

'Are you sure it says *behind* the Timepiece?' she asked Sheldon.

'No.' He was not sure of anything.

'If you're saying it has to be behind the Timepiece,' Tid said, with a note of triumph in his voice, 'then that is the only place it could mean, and there's clearly nothing there. You must have got it wrong.'

Sofi did not want Sheldon to be wrong. If he was wrong, then perhaps she was wrong about the story in her book. She knelt next to Sheldon and leant against his shoulder in order to try and see the page in a way that might make some of the symbols float as Sheldon had said.

It is a sad but true fact that when no one likes you no one touches you. Sheldon had lived an isolated life. Even after transferring to Reform School in Germany, the emphasis was on learning and discipline. No one hugged him. The only time he touched anyone was when he shook a newcomer's hand. It was very strange to have Sofi leaning against him now.

'Three!' he blurted out, feeling the need to say something to cover his awkwardness. He looked at the book. How had he come up with three? He was not sure.

Sofi looked at him in surprise. 'Three what?' she asked.

He shook his head, 'I don't know,' but he had a vague feeling that there was something about three. All this was getting out of hand and it made Sheldon feel uneasy. Was he making this up, or had he actually been translating these symbols all along?

Tid made another contemptuous noise.

Sofi ignored him. 'There's something in the book

about three.' She turned the pages. 'Yes, look,' and she read,

> *Four has the compass,*
> *Beneath me three;*
> *Orb though I am,*
> *Beneath is the key.*

She looked up, 'Beneath me three,' she repeated. 'Sheldon, didn't you say that the book said something about being beneath as well as behind.'

Tid had had enough. 'This is ridiculous!' he declared. 'He's making it up. He hasn't the faintest idea what any of this means. He's just messing about. We're wasting our time. We shouldn't even be here. Let's go.'

'Oh, do shut up, Tid!' Sofi exclaimed, exasperated. 'I'm trying to think.' She stood up and paced up and down with her brow furrowed. 'Three beneath or behind the Timepiece,' she said questioningly, and then her expression suddenly changed to one of enlightenment as she exclaimed, 'Three paces behind the Timepiece!'

'It was against the wall,' Tid said. 'There weren't three notches behind it, let alone three paces.'

'No, not here!' Sofi almost shouted in her delight at having worked it out. 'The Timepiece isn't here any more, it's at the Line!'

Once it had been completed, the new Timepiece had been transported to the Meridian Line, where it now stood, proclaiming time for all to see.

'We're in the wrong place!' Sofi exclaimed.

Tid was prepared to go along with anything that would take them out of the workshop. 'Let's try there then.'

'If it's at the Line,' Sheldon said, 'then why does the book say it's in the workshop?'

'Perhaps,' Sofi said, 'it means . . .' but her voice tailed off. She had no idea what it could possibly mean.

'It has to be here,' Sheldon said.

She stood with her hands on her hips, looking at the wall. 'Well, it might not mean exactly behind, perhaps it could mean three paces to the side. She paced them out, taking care to take extra-large steps that would be nearer the stride of a grown-up.

'This story is old, right?' Sheldon asked.

'Thousands of years,' Sofi said.

'And so how could it know where Old Father Tim would put the Timepiece while he was making it, so many years later?'

Tid knew the answer to this. His grandfather had told him the history of his workshop many times. He could not resist showing the others just how much he knew. 'Because that is what that platform was built for. This workshop is ancient. All Timepieces have been made in it. The platform,' he moved to it and touched it with his foot, 'has ancient magic bound into the wooden floor to prevent any bad magic getting through. Grandfather always said . . .'

He stopped abruptly. Sofi and Sheldon looked at him questioningly. Tid was staring at the floor. He had noticed something. He glanced up at Sofi.

Tid was now in something of a dilemma. If he told Sofi and Sheldon what he had just spotted, it might make them want to continue with this foolishness; but if he did not show them, and Sheldon was right, then he would be passing up the chance of helping his grandfather. Tid might have been angry with Sofi and he might not trust Sheldon, but he knew right from wrong.

He knelt on the platform and pointed to a knot on the floor, some distance from where Sofi stood, her pacing not having revealed anything. He placed his thumb upon it and then put his little finger on another knot, a few notches away. Sofi recognized it at once. These knots looked exactly the same as the knots they had used on the bark of the tree outside.

'It has to be a coincidence,' Tid said, removing his hand. 'Before the Tick was stolen, there was a lever to open the door. If this workshop had been built around the magic of two knots, then why has Grandfather only just started using it?'

'Grandfather must have known these knots were here, and when he saw similar ones on the tree outside, it was just too good an idea to pass up,' Sofi suggested, 'but what has three have to do with them?'

They all stared at the knots in the floor.

Almost idly, Sofi placed her little finger on one knot and her thumb on the other and mumbled, 'Opena ond me cyth.'

When nothing happened, Tid suggested, 'Try "Tide healdath".' He was too intrigued by the knots to remember that he was not supposed to be helping.

Keeping her fingers in place, Sofi spoke the familiar Guardian incantation, 'Tide healdath, ealle brucath.'

There was a distant clunking sound. Then Tid suddenly jumped and skidded to one side as the floor moved beneath him.

12

The Caves of Tempus

The three of them stared in surprise as a section of the platform lifted itself up from the rest of the floor and glided back to reveal an opening just big enough for a person to pass through.

The cool air hit her face as Sofi leant over and peered down the hole. Narrow steps disappeared into blackness.

'It's them!' she declared delightedly. 'The Caves of Tempus!'

'They could be Wrecca tunnels for all we know,' Tid said grimly.

Sofi started clambering down the steps.

'What *are* you doing?' Tid demanded.

'We'd better hurry,' she said just before her head disappeared. 'Grandfather left ages ago.'

'Don't be stupid!' Tid exclaimed. 'It could be some sort of trap.'

Sofi's head reappeared. 'What, from here?' she asked. 'How could anyone plan a trap from Grandfather's workshop?' and she disappeared again.

The boys stared at the dark hole. Then, without warning, Sofi reappeared. 'It's dark down here,' she said, clambering out. 'We're going to need some torches.' Sofi began searching Old Father Tim's workshop. 'There has to be something.'

Sheldon held up his torch. 'I've got this.'

'Then find something for me.'

'Don't you dare touch a thing,' Tid snapped before Sheldon could move. He was not going to have Sheldon Croe searching through his grandfather's belongings.

'If you don't want him to look,' Sofi said testily, 'then perhaps you should start looking yourself.'

'Or perhaps we should go home and tell Enderell what's going on.'

'Good idea,' Sofi said sarcastically, 'and she will go to the Hither House and talk to the Greenwich Guardian, who will talk to Vremya, who will talk to Zeit, who will talk with the Council to decide what to do; and by that time Grandfather and the others could be in real trouble!'

'But that's the way it should be done,' Tid said.

'Fine, then *you* do it. Sheldon and I will go and do something useful.'

Tid hesitated. He resented her words but felt that he had little choice because he would never let her walk into Sheldon's trap alone.

'Sofi,' he said, taking her to one side and talking softly so that Sheldon could not hear them. He tried to sound reasonable. 'I know you want to believe Sheldon.' He could see her lips pressing together irritably so quickly added, 'And I understand why; but stop and think for just a moment. You don't know him like I do.'

'He helped me rescue the Tick,' she said stubbornly.

'He only did that so you would show him how to get out of the Underneath. Don't forget that he tried to sell you to the Wreccas.'

'He didn't try to sell me.'

'He tried to take you there against your will.'

Sofi did not respond to this. Kidnapping didn't sound any better than selling.

'Giving someone a second chance is a good thing to do,' Tid continued, 'but supposing that someone doesn't deserve it. This could be an elaborate trick to get the both of us into the Underneath.'

'We're not going to the Underneath.'

'I know,' Tid said, trying to keep his voice reasonable. 'The caves aren't actually the Underneath, but it is possible that they might connect in some way. There could be a band of Wreccas waiting down there for us right now.'

Sofi's lips were still thin, but he could see from her eyes that she was listening. She looked across at Sheldon, who quickly looked away as she caught his eye. She had to admit that he did look shifty.

Tid pressed home his advantage.

'We know that the Wreccas have been tunnelling. Maybe they are not trying to get into the women's tunnels after all. Maybe they are trying to get to us here.'

'All right, you have a point,' she said, keeping her voice low. 'This could be a trap. I think it is unlikely, but it could be. But you have to admit, there is a possibility that Sheldon is right, and if he is, then we shouldn't hang about. The more time we waste, the harder it is going to be to find Grandfather before he tries to get into the Gemetbur with the wrong key.'

'You're right,' Tid said reluctantly. 'I suppose we have to choose which is the lesser risk.'

'Well, going for Enderell is the least risk to us,' Sofi said, 'but following Grandfather is the least risk to him.'

Sofi had put it in the only way that made it impossible for Tid to refuse to go. Did he value his grandfather's safety more than his own? However much he distrusted Sheldon, he would not put himself first. Tid would have to concede, but not everything.

'All right,' he said. 'Sheldon and I will go after Grandfather, but you go back to Enderell and tell her where we have gone.'

'No way!' Sofi exploded with indignant anger. 'You go to Enderell and I'll go with Sheldon.'

'Don't be daft, you're a girl!' Immediately, Tid winced as he realized what he had said.

'Just a girl, am I?' Sofi said angrily. 'Well, you can do what you like, Tid Mossel. I'm going to find Grandfather. You can come or not, it is up to you,' and she turned back to the shelves and started searching through them for anything that might work as a light.

Tid sighed. Why had he said that about girls? Nothing he could say would stop her from going now, and there was absolutely no way he was going to let her go alone with Sheldon. Tid looked across at him angrily. Sheldon returned the look with hostility.

Sofi picked up Old Father Tim's ruler that was chipped and marked from years of use. It was a pity her book had not been enchanted to glow like the ones that her grandfather used. All his possessions glowed. She moved the ruler around to see how much light it would give off. In the brightness of the workshop it was hard to see, but she reasoned it would glow enough to show her the way in the dark.

'Let's get going,' Sofi said, walking towards the trap-door.

'Just a minute!' Tid had pulled some paper and a pencil from the drawer and quickly wrote:

Sofi, Sheldon and Tid have gone down the trapdoor to find Grandfather.

'Hurry up!'

Tid would like to have written more, but he quickly signed the note and left it with the pencil on the work-bench. He needed a light. The pencil would do, but then his eyes fell upon the paperweight. It had always been his favourite thing in the workshop. It was a glass globe attached to a heavy, triangular base. If touched, turquoise lights swirled within. It shone like a beacon. He stretched out his hand towards it.

'Best not take that,' Sofi said from the trapdoor, 'it's too heavy.'

Sofi was right. It was heavy, but Tid was not going to have her tell him what he should take. He picked it up and crossed to the trapdoor.

Sofi was disappearing down the steps.

Sheldon hesitated, not entirely sure whether he wanted to follow.

'After you,' Tid said coldly. He was going to keep Sheldon where he could see him.

Sheldon threw him a look of hatred and started down the steps. Tid followed. He left the trapdoor open, thinking that they could nip back, should there be any sign of danger; and if anyone came looking for them, it would be clear which way they had gone.

The steps were narrow and carved from rock. They must have been very old but were not at all worn. It was obvious that these steps were seldom used. The chilly air became cooler with each step.

When he reached the bottom, Tid heard a gentle clunk from above. His stomach lurched. The trapdoor had closed. If this was a trap, they were well and truly caught in it.

'Come on!' Sofi said.

'We can't get back. The trapdoor has shut.'

'But we don't want to get back,' Sofi said reasonably. 'We want to find Grandfather. Who has the book?'

'I do,' Sheldon said.

'I'll take that, thank you,' Tid said crisply, taking it.

Sheldon's jaw set rigid and resentment flashed in his eyes.

'Which way?' Tid asked Sofi.

The three of them held up their lights and looked around. They were standing on a solid floor that seemed to be covered with a thin layer of loose earth. The walls were of stone. Tid touched them; they were cold but not damp.

Tid held the paperweight in front of him. It gave much more light than either Sheldon's or Sofi's lights, but he still could not see far.

'Hold it by your side,' Sheldon said.

'What gives you the right to tell me what to do?' Tid snapped.

'Because,' Sheldon said irritably,' if you hold it in front of your face you won't see beyond the light. If you hold it down at your side you will see further.'

Tid glared at him.

'Just try it,' Sheldon said.

Tid and Sofi moved their lights and, sure enough, they could see further.

'That's really good,' Sofi said enthusiastically. 'I can see much better. Come on, this way.'

There seemed to be one long tunnel to the front, with numerous openings either side of it.

'Hang on,' Tid said.

'What now?' Sofi asked, a note of irritation in her voice.

'Perhaps we should go this way.'

Turning around, Sofi saw that Tid was pointing down a similar tunnel that ran to the left of the stairs.

'Or here,' Sheldon said, indicating a third.

They looked from one tunnel to the other.

'I suppose we could split up,' Sofi said falteringly.

'No!' It was one word voiced by both boys together.

'We stay together,' Tid said, slightly taken aback that Sheldon should feel the same.

'Give me the book,' Sofi said, taking it. 'It said something about three, and there are three tunnels. What was it?' She thought for a moment, '"Beneath me three."' She suddenly sounded excited. 'Three tunnels beneath the ground!'

'Does it say which way we should go?' Tid asked.

'I don't think so.' She peered at the book. 'Shine your torch on the page,' she told Sheldon. 'I've just thought of something.' Sofi turned the pages and pointed at a passage. 'Look, it says, "Tempus hid it away and surrounded it with a magic so strong that it could only be opened in one special way. If anyone tried to open it without the true key, then they would never again see the light of day." How do we know,' she asked with a puzzled frown, 'whether the key is right or wrong before we try it?'

'Perfect time to think about that!' Tid said sarcastically.

'I suppose we have to stop them using any key at all,' Sofi said.

Tid was suddenly alarmed. 'Are you doing this to stop Grandfather and the others from even trying to get into the Gemetbur?'

'That's the idea, isn't it?'

'I'm not sure that we should,' Tid said, trying not to sound too concerned. 'Grandfather is going there to reverse this time wobble. If he can only do that from inside the Gemetbur, shouldn't we risk everything to do it?'

'Not if it kills Grandfather and the others.'

Tid was not sure how to answer this without revealing

all that he knew, and he had promised his grandfather that he would not. Was the chance of averting utter chaos worth risking three lives, no matter how noble or how much he loved one of them?

'That's the important part, isn't it?' Sofi continued. 'Keeping Grandfather safe, and anyway,' her brow furrowed. She had an idea. 'Perhaps we do have the key!'

'Do we?' Tid asked, mystified.

'Yes,' she said. 'Sheldon! He knows how to read the book. He must be the "true key".'

'Oh yes, right,' Tid said flatly.

Sheldon was not sure he wanted to be the key. It had been a bit of a laugh when they had been above ground, and it had felt good to do something that Tid could not; but now they were in the tunnels, the situation felt more serious. If he was not careful, everything could go horribly wrong.

'Come on, Sheldon,' Sofi said, 'do your hand-wobbling thing.'

'We should go this way,' Tid said, pointing behind him. He decided to say nothing about the inevitability of chaos just yet. Best try to get safely out of the tunnels first.

'Why?' she asked.

Tid shut his eyes and tried to imagine the workshop above them. 'If the workshop is there,' he said, trying to visualize it, 'then so is the tree, and so the Line will be . . . over there!' he exclaimed, opening his eyes. 'I think that the Gemetbur will be near the Line.'

'Why?'

'Because that is where the Timepiece is. It makes sense to keep all the time mechanisms together.'

'But Tid,' Sofi said. 'It's no distance at all to the Line. If this was the way, then Grandfather would have been there ages ago and he will have already tried to get in and . . .' her voice wavered.

'You think we should go the other way?' Tid said quickly, not wanting to dwell on this unpleasant thought. 'It's so clearly wrong,' he continued, 'that it could be right. It is exactly what Tempus might have done.'

'A trick to keep the Gemetbur safe?' she asked.

'Seems logical.' Tid turned to Sheldon. 'Which way do you think?' he asked.

Sheldon looked at Tid in surprise. He had not expected Tid to ask his opinion. 'I think we should go towards the Line.'

That settled it. If Sheldon wanted to go that way, then Tid would go in the other direction.

'I agree with Sofi,' Tid said.

Sheldon smirked. He knew that Tid would never take his advice.

'Perhaps Sheldon should look at the book, just to make sure,' Sofi said, handing it to him.

Sheldon took it reluctantly. They were trapped below ground. He had to stop messing about. Perhaps he should tell them that he was new to all this, but one look at Tid's face stopped him. He was not going to own up to fooling about and give Tid the opportunity to gloat. Holding his hand over the page, he stared at the space between book and hand.

Tid thought he was overdoing it. Sheldon looked ridiculous and he drew breath to say so, but Sofi stopped him with a wave of her hand.

Sheldon was squinting at the page. He was very confused. How was this happening? Aleyesu had said that it took a gift to start translating symbols like these and a lifetime to learn. Well, Sheldon knew he did not have a gift and had only just started looking at them. How could he be translating them properly? But he *had* come up with the tunnel starting in the workshop. That had to be more than a bit of luck, and he had never heard of the word 'clock' before, so that had to have come from somewhere.

After what seemed like a very long time, Sheldon spoke. 'We go that way.' He pointed in the direction that Tid and Sofi had suggested.

'How do you know?' Sofi asked, in an awed voice.

'There's a sort of map,' Sheldon explained, rather surprised that he really could see a map. 'Those symbols, there.' He pointed to a sign that looked like a falling-over 'd' with a couple of slashes across the upright. 'If you put them with these,' he pointed to a sign that looked like an 'o' and an 'e' that had merged together, 'and let them float, then they form a path. Now, if this here is the steps,' he pointed to where the path started, 'and I think it must be because the book told us to start in the workshop, then we must go that way.'

'Wow,' Sofi murmured, very impressed.

Sheldon felt a touch of pride.

'For heaven's sake, Sheldon,' Tid blurted out, 'if

you're going to make it up, at least make it believable.'

Sofi threw him a dirty look.

'Oh, come on,' Tid said defensively.

'You're just jealous,' Sofi said witheringly.

'J . . . jealous?' Tid spluttered. 'Of him?'

'Absolutely,' Sofi said, taking the book and snapping it shut.

'Oh, come off it, Sofi. He's had his joke, but it's gone far enough. Why are you listening to all this twaddle? It's nothing more than a fairy tale.'

Sofi's expression suddenly softened. 'Don't you see,' she said, in a tone that was closer to her usual voice, 'that is why I *am* listening to him. This book,' she tapped it with her forefinger, '*is* a fairy tale. I'm not stupid, I know it's crazy to follow a children's storybook, Enderell said as much, but it got us here, didn't it? You and I couldn't tell from all these symbols where the entrance was, but somehow Sheldon did.'

'It was a lucky guess!'

'Maybe, but we have no choice now. The trapdoor is shut. We have to go on.'

'Maybe we could open it,' Tid said, running up the steps and putting his shoulder to the door. He heaved with all his strength but there was no give in it at all. It was as though it was made out of solid concrete. A door, magically shut like this, would never open. Tid descended the steps and despondently sat on the bottom one.

'It won't budge,' he said miserably. 'At least let's take a different tunnel.'

'But your logic made sense,' Sofi said.

'I was making it up,' Tid said gloomily.

Sofi sat next to him. 'I know,' she said gently, 'but it was still good logic. I think we should go that way.'

Tid dragged his bottom lip through his teeth before saying, 'Well, I suppose one way is as good as another; but Sofi,' he lowered his voice in the hope that Sheldon could not hear him, 'don't take too much notice of him.'

'I think he's telling the truth.'

'And I think he's lying through his teeth.'

They stared into each other's eyes for a moment, each trying to see the truth that lay behind them.

'Let's be careful,' he said.

Sofi nodded.

13

Thus Aid Death

Enderell was breathing heavily as she crossed the road; she was not used to crossing Greenwich at such speed. It was still early and the heat of the day had not yet kicked in, but she was very warm. She climbed the steps up to the worn old front door of the Hither House. Normally, she would have lingered to see if the food that had been set out for visitors was up to standard. Today, she passed by without even looking. She hurried quickly through several more rooms and up two flights of stairs, until she came to a small, dark, wooden door, where she knocked urgently.

The door was opened by the Greenwich Guardian, who was wearing a long dressing gown, and her deep-red, curling hair looked as if it had not yet been brushed. 'What is the matter?' she asked, immediately concerned by Enderell's worried face.

'They've gone!'

'Who?'

'Tid and Sofi. They must have left the house during the night. They were not in their beds when I went to wake them this morning!' Her voice was unusually high and her hand trembled.

'Come in.'

'I searched the park,' Enderell continued as she entered. 'I called on the Brownals and the Loms. No one has seen them.'

They were in the Greenwich Guardian's private apartment. Seth was sitting at the kitchen table, eating egg, bacon, sausage and beans.

'Seth,' the Greenwich Guardian said, 'did Tid and Sofi have any plans for last night?'

'What sort of plans?' he asked through a mouthful of sausage and egg. He was eating quickly because he wanted to leave early. He hoped to speak to Baz before school. Uncle Bryn had been asking unusual questions, and Seth wanted to make quite sure that Baz knew to be extra careful when they met up later.

The Greenwich Guardian refrained from reminding him not to speak with his mouth full. 'Anything that would take them out during the night?'

'They went out during the night!' Seth exclaimed, delighted.

'Do you have any idea where they might have gone?' Enderell asked anxiously.

Seth shook his head.

'Seth,' the Greenwich Guardian said seriously, 'this is important. You must tell us if you know anything.'

'They wouldn't tell me.'

His grandmother was too preoccupied to notice the resentment in his voice.

'I think they've gone after the Old Father,' Enderell

said, wincing as though this thought caused her physical pain.

'Why would they do that?'

'You know what they are like,' Enderell moaned dismally, 'and after that business with the Tick, they think they can solve anything. Sofi woke me in the night with some half-baked idea that one of her storybooks could help the Old Father find the Gemetbur.'

'Which book?'

'Thadius Plemet-Thead's *Tempus and the Gemetbur.*'

The Greenwich Guardian knew it well.

'I pointed out to her the improbability of the idea and went back to sleep.' Then she added miserably, 'I thought she had too.'

'Sit here and have a cup of tea,' the Greenwich Guardian said, taking a cup and saucer from a wooden dresser. 'It is not as splendid as the tea you make, but it will refresh you. Do not worry. They will not be far.'

Tid felt that they had been walking for ages and yet the scenery had not changed one bit. The floor was still the same beneath their feet and the passageways looked exactly as all the other passageways they had passed along.

Occasionally they stopped to give Sheldon time to look at the 'map' in the book. Tid kept silent. He had said all he was going to say on that subject.

'I wish we had marked where we had come from,' Sheldon said. He had not meant to speak out loud and was surprised when Sofi answered.

'It doesn't matter where we've been, just where we end up.'

Tid felt that they were walking in circles.

'Hey, look at this!' Sofi exclaimed, pointing ahead.

The light showed some difference in the layout. The three of them instinctively moved together for safety.

From his greater height, Sheldon said, 'It looks like a pool.'

Once Sheldon had said this, it suddenly became obvious to the others. The pool was as still as glass and black as pitch.

'Is it on the map?' Sofi asked.

'It's a bit vague on landmarks,' Sheldon confessed.

They approached with caution.

'I wonder how deep it is,' Sofi wondered aloud. The pool was so dark it looked as if it might be bottomless.

'I don't care how deep it is,' Sheldon said, falling to his knees. Cupping his hands he dipped them into the pool and drew up some water.

'Don't!' Sofi exclaimed.

Sheldon paused, hand halfway to his mouth. 'Why not?'

'It might be poisoned.'

Sheldon sniffed it. Then he dipped his tongue into the water that was fast dripping through his fingers. It tasted good. Without waiting further, he drank thirstily.

Tid watched. He was still harbouring suspicions that Sheldon knew more about this place than he was admitting. If he was drinking, it must be safe. Kneeling down, Tid started drinking too.

Sofi stared at them for a moment, and then she too took a drink. 'If it's poisoned,' she reasoned, 'I don't want to watch you two die and be left here by myself.'

When she had drunk her fill, she sat back on her heels.

'Sheldon, you should look at the book again,' she said, 'just to make sure we are going in the right direction.'

Sheldon opened the book but, before he could look at it, Tid had slammed it shut. 'Look at this,' he said, pointing to the cover.

Sheldon tried to jerk the book away, but Sofi rested her hand on his arm to stop him. She could see that Tid had found something on the cover that seriously interested him. She leant over and looked. Tid was pointing to the name, Thead.

'What's interesting about that?' Sofi asked.

'Look at it,' Tid said, 'closely.'

Sofi did and repeated, 'Thead,' quietly to herself.

'Can't you see it?' Tid asked. 'It's an anagram.'

'T-head,' Sofi said.

'No,' Tid snapped. Was she being dense on purpose? 'D-E-A-T-H. Death.'

Sofi worked the letters out in her head. Tid was right. The name 'Thead' did spell out 'death'.

'That doesn't mean anything.'

'It could be a warning.'

'And it could be just a name. Cissy's name spelt "Fairy Princess", but she's just a girl.'

'But Cissy didn't write this book, did she? It has to be a warning,' Tid said. 'We should never have come.'

'But his name is Thadius Thead. Surely, for it to work,

it has to be an anagram of his entire name.'

She had a point. Tid reorganized the letters in his head. With a fleeting look of triumph, he announced, 'Said hut,' but his triumph immediately faded as he realized it meant nothing.

'Anagrams are just a game invented by teachers to keep us quiet,' Sofi said.

Tid started drawing in the loose earth on the ground, trying to rearrange the letters of Thadius.

Sofi cupped her hands, filled them with water and started washing her face.

'I'm sorry,' Sofi said, turning and looking at Tid, thinking that he had spoken to her.

'What for?' he asked.

'I didn't hear what you said just then.'

'I didn't say anything.' Tid returned to his anagram.

'Was it you?' she asked Sheldon.

Sheldon looked up from the book. 'No.'

'Well, one of you did,' she said, more than a little exasperated.

'You're hearing things,' Tid said.

Sofi scowled. One of them was playing a trick on her. Sheldon had been busy with the book, and so it had to be Tid.

'Very funny!' she said, turning her back on him.

'Oh my goodness!' It was Tid who spoke, and his voice was tinged with fear.

'What is it?' Sofi asked, slightly alarmed by his tone.

Even Sheldon looked up.

From the glow of his paperweight, Sofi could see that

all the colour had drained from Tid's face. 'What's the matter?' she asked.

Tid pointed to the ground. 'Thadius is an anagram of "thus aid".'

'So what?

'On its own, not much,' Tid admitted, 'but put it in front of Thead and you've got . . .' he waited for her to work it out, but it was Sheldon who gave voice to the words.

 'Thus aid death.'

Joss did not wake up immediately; he was too deeply asleep to be stirred by the noise at the door. Eventually he turned over and half-opened his eyes. In bleary confusion, he stumbled out of bed and lunged for the doorknob.

'Who on earth is making that racket?' he asked as he opened the door, rubbing the sleep from his eyes. He blinked at the sight of the Greenwich Guardian in her dressing gown. Suddenly, aware that he was wearing only baggy trousers, which was not the usual night-time garb of the Guardian People, he nipped behind the door. 'Is there something the matter?' he said, his head poking out at a comical angle.

The Greenwich Guardian did not seem to notice his awkwardness. Quickly she explained that Tid and Sofi were missing. 'I thought you could organize a search party.'

'Of course,' Joss said. 'Right away.'

'Thank you,' the Greenwich Guardian said. 'I knew I could rely on you.'

Joss shut the door and yawned, before wandering back to his bed. 'Kids,' he muttered. It was not so long ago that he and Conrad had been pulling childish pranks like this. He looked longingly at the soft pillows, scratched his head and started to dress.

Sheldon's stomach was rumbling. He was sure that the others could hear it, but no one said anything. They had bypassed the first pool and were continuing their journey along the same unchanging tunnels. Occasionally Sheldon consulted Sofi's book to check their route.

Every now and then, a small piece of darker rock jutted out from the walls.

'It's flint,' Sheldon explained, watching Tid examine one.

'How do you know?'

'I do go to school,' Sheldon replied curtly.

It was on the tip of Tid's tongue to ask what they actually taught in Reform School, but he thought better of it.

They continued in silence. Tid was dwelling on anagrams. He was mulling over possible anagrams of Sheldon's name. He was so deep in thought that he nearly walked straight into another pool.

'Careful!' Sofi warned, grabbing his tunic from behind.

They stared at the tranquil water.

Once more Sofi heard a voice in her ear. 'What?' she asked.

The boys looked at her.

'What do you mean, what?' Tid asked.

'What you said about crossing the water,' Sofi said.

'What are you going on about?'

'One of you said something about crossing the water.'

'No we didn't,' Tid said, exasperated.

Sofi looked at Sheldon as if expecting him to contradict Tid, but he shook his head.

'Look, Sofi,' Tid said, 'if you think we should cross the pool, why don't you just say so?'

'It's not such a bad idea,' Sheldon said.

'Why can't we go around it?' Tid asked.

'How?' Sheldon asked.

Tid looked about in the gloom as best he could. 'There must be a way.'

'I can't see one,' Sheldon said.

'How can you tell?' Tid asked suspiciously. 'You haven't even looked.'

Sheldon stared back at Tid aggressively. 'It's just an opinion.'

'Well, I'm not swimming that!' Tid exclaimed.

'No one asked you to.'

'Yes you did, I heard you.'

'It wasn't me!'

'Well, who was it then?' Tid asked unpleasantly.

'You're round the bend,' Sheldon retorted equally unpleasantly.

'Someone said I should swim across first.' Suddenly Tid felt nervous.

'Well, it definitely wasn't me,' Sheldon said.

They looked at Sofi.

'It wasn't me.'

The three of them gripped their lights a little tighter and edged closer together.

'We're imagining things,' Tid said. 'We were all thinking that we have to cross the pond, and I imagined someone suggesting swimming it.'

Sofi bit her bottom lip. There was something very odd about this place. 'Which way do we go next, Sheldon?'

'Straight across, like Tid suggested,' Sheldon confirmed.

'I didn't suggest anything of the sort.'

'Well, someone did, just then. I heard them. Didn't you?'

They both shook their heads.

An eerie silence hung all around.

Suddenly, it popped into Tid's mind. 'I've got it!' he declared so suddenly that the other two jumped. He had been jostling letters in his head as he walked along, with no result; but now that he was thinking of something else, it had just popped into his head.

'Got what?' Sofi asked.

'The anagram for Sheldon.' Then he added nastily, 'Anagrams do work after all.'

'What are you talking about?' Sofi asked, irritated.

'You said that Thadius Thead's anagram couldn't be true,' Tid continued. 'Well, the anagram for Sheldon Croe is "sold her once".' He stole a triumphant glance towards Sheldon before looking back at Sofi. 'You can't deny that one!'

'Oh, honestly!' she declared contemptuously. 'And so, according to you, Cissy is a fairy princess and Timothy has a hairy bottom, does he?' she snapped. 'It's just for fun, Tid,' she added, a little patronizingly, 'nothing more.'

'Let him have his games,' Sheldon sneered. 'Little boys must be allowed to play.'

Tid glowered darkly and threw Sheldon a furious look. Sheldon stared back at him antagonistically.

Sofi despaired of the pair of them. This was difficult enough, without them always at each other's throats. She sat down and started taking off her shoes. The boys did not notice; each was busy trying to stare down the other.

With the laces tied, she hung her shoes round her neck and stepped into the water.

'It's freezing!' she declared.

This announcement was enough to shake the boys out of their staring match.

'What *are* you doing?' Tid asked.

'If we are going to cross, we might as well start now.'

'But we hadn't decided,' Tid said, and then he added less certainly, 'had we?'

Sofi did not answer, but kept moving.

'We don't know how deep it is,' Tid said anxiously.

'It doesn't seem to be too bad,' Sofi said. 'Look!' Sure enough, she was a couple of paces from the edge and the water was still only halfway up her shins. 'Hurry up,' she told the boys. 'We don't have all day.'

Holding his shoes in one hand and the book in the other, Sheldon started wading after her. Tid watched.

Why was Sheldon so willing to cross the pond? What was on the other side? Reluctant to follow, but knowing he would never allow Sofi to go on alone with Sheldon, Tid sat down and removed his shoes too. Sofi and Sheldon were some distance from the shore by now, and it was still only up to Sofi's knees.

Quickly Tid began wading after them. He gasped at the iciness of the water, but the pebbles were smooth and well rounded beneath his feet and so they did not hurt.

Sofi was making good progress. The water was deeper now, well up her thighs. 'It shouldn't be much further,' she said, dragging her legs one after the other, and holding her glowing ruler up high.

It still seemed a long way to Tid. In fact, it looked much further now than Tid had originally thought. He turned to see how far they had come. It could not be far, but, looking back, his light was not bright enough to shine to the edge of the pool. He strained to reach Sofi. By now the water was waist deep. He had to hold up his shoes in order to keep them dry.

'Can you see how much further it is?' Tid called.

Sofi could no longer feel her feet. When she spoke, her teeth chattered.

'N . . . no,' she said, standing still.

'Don't stop,' Sheldon said gruffly.

'Give her a break,' Tid said. He had almost reached them. 'She needs to catch her breath.'

Ignoring him, Sheldon took Sofi's hand. 'Keep going,' he urged.

Tid wanted to ask why Sheldon was so anxious to keep moving, but it all seemed too much effort. Instead, he grumbled, 'It's all right for you. You're taller than us.'

The water was now halfway up Sofi's chest.

Sheldon lifted his light as high as he could and peered into the distance. 'Hm,' he grunted. 'Keep going.'

'Turn back,' Tid said.

'N . . . no,' Sofi stammered. 'It c . . . c . . . can't be m . . . m . . . much f . . . f . . . further.' The water was now up to her chin.

Tid had lost the feeling in his legs. The water was rising fast. He was finding it difficult to hold his shoes and light above the water. His arms felt very heavy. Suddenly, three words sounded in his head. 'Thus aid death.' This was it. The water was aiding their death. The pool was intending to kill them.

'I'm going back,' he announced.

'Keep going,' Sheldon insisted.

'N . . . no!' Tid said. 'Sofi!' He lunged for her, managing to grab the back of her tunic but losing his shoes in the process. They sank like stones.

'If you want to go back, then go back,' Sheldon snapped angrily, pulling Sofi's hand, 'but we're going on.'

'Once a traitor, always a traitor!' Tid snarled, pulling Sofi sharply. 'Leave her alone!'

Sofi tried to argue. They were driving her crazy. She was so very tired. Her pale lips trembled. She had now lost all sense of feeling.

'Let go of her!' Tid shouted at Sheldon, tugging at her tunic.

Sheldon answered by bending low in the water.

At first Tid thought he was diving into the shadowy depths, but a moment later Sheldon lurched up out of the water again with Sofi over his shoulder. He was soaked from head to toe.

Such was the force of the move that Sofi's tunic was wrenched from Tid's frozen grasp. He knew he could not wrestle her from Sheldon, and yet he also knew he was not going any further. 'Thus aid death' pounded in his brain. Sheldon was leading them into a trap. Why else would he keep going when it made no sense?

'I'll g . . . go and g . . . get help,' he stammered to the silent Sofi.

Turning round, Tid started walking back the way he had come, but there was something wrong. No matter how far back he went, the water grew deeper still. It was now up to his chin and spilling into his mouth. This could not be! He was walking back the way he had come and yet the pool was getting deeper and deeper. The water was seeping into his nostrils. He spluttered, trying to breath. He lifted his head high and took a gasp of air, and then the water covered his face.

He would have to swim. Why had he not done so before? He was cold, so very cold. He needed more air and tried to lift his head high, but only succeeded in gulping down icy water that made him cough and splutter.

He tried to cry out, but there was no sound, only

bubbles of precious air. Thrashing about in the water, he attempted to swim, but his limbs were frozen.

Tid was too cold to panic now, his mind too numb to think as the black, murky waters claimed him.

14

Lost

Like Tid, Sheldon had given up wading. Now he was swimming on his back with Sofi clutched to his chest. His torch was forgotten. Unlike Tid, he had started swimming before the water had frozen all life out of him. He had a chance. At least, he thought he did.

At school he had learnt about murderous waters like these. He knew their only chance was to keep going. Tid was lost, but Sheldon was not prepared to die, not yet.

He was too numb to feel a faint bump on his back and it took a while for him to realize it when his hand collided with the ground. When he finally stopped swimming and yet did not sink, he realized that they had made it to the other side.

He pushed with his feet and manoeuvred himself and Sofi up the shore. Then, holding Sofi with one arm, he rolled on to his front and crawled ashore before collapsing.

Sofi lay beneath him. For a moment neither moved. Sheldon felt strangely peaceful. Perhaps he should close his eyes and allow himself to drift into merciful sleep. He felt his mind drifting, his body floating.

'NO!' his brain screamed. 'WAKE UP!'

His eyes popped open. He had to pull himself together.

'Stay awake,' he told himself out loud. It was too cold. Sleeping would only lead to one thing.

'Thus aid death.' Suddenly Tid's anagram seemed horribly relevant. Well, he was not going to die today!

His torch was missing. It must have slipped from his icy fingers. Sofi was still clutching Old Father Tim's ruler in her frozen hand.

'Sofi!' He shook her. 'Sofi!' He tapped her white face. Then he rubbed his hands briskly up and down her arms, repeatedly calling her name. He stood up, gripping her limp body to him with one arm and rubbing her back with the other hand. He jumped around, trying to restore some sort of feeling into his own limbs, while hoping to jerk Sofi awake.

She opened her eyes and dropped the light.

'Sh . . . Sh . . . Sh . . .' she stammered, failing to get out his name.

Sheldon said nothing, but rubbed harder.

'T . . . T . . . T . . .' she stammered in his ear. 'T . . . T . . . Tid . . .'

Sheldon looked back at the pond, realizing the worst.

'He's drowned.'

'Nooo!' The cry that echoed round the caves was so desperate, so filled with anguish, that it pierced Sheldon's heart. He steadied her on her feet and held her firmly by the shoulders.

'He won't have felt anything,' he said.

'No,' Sofi cried once more. Numb and frozen as she was, she started fighting her way back towards the water.

Sheldon struggled to keep hold of her. 'It's too late,' he yelled.

'I've g . . . g . . . g . . . got to t . . . t . . . t . . . t . . . try!' she stammered.

Sheldon pulled her back. He knew she would not survive long in the icy grip of the water. Still, she fought him.

'I'll go,' he said, to stop her struggling. 'I'll find him.' He had no intention of doing so but would splash about for a few minutes until Sofi saw that it was absolutely hopeless.

Sofi knew she would not have the energy to do anything worthwhile if she returned to the water. 'Th . . . th . . . thank you!' she cried in utter relief, flinging her arms around him. 'You'll f . . . find him,' she added, pulling back and looking into his face. 'I know y . . . you will.'

There was something in her eyes, always so expressive, that warmed his heart, despite being so bitterly cold.

'I'll hold the l . . . light for y . . . you,' she said, scooping up the ruler, 'so that you w . . . won't lose your w . . . way. Once you have him, just head t . . . towards it.'

Sheldon nodded.

He waded back out into the water. Being already frozen, he did not feel the cold as much as before. As soon as it was deep enough, he pushed off. The pebbles shifted beneath his feet as he launched into the depths.

He had intended just to splash around for a short time, but as he swam the expression in Sofi's eyes burned in his mind. What was that expression? Was it fear? Was it hope? It came as something of a shock when Sheldon realized that it was trust.

Sofi trusted him.

This was a new and interesting sensation. Sofi, who had less reason than most to have faith in him, actually did. She believed that he was really going out into the inky blackness to try and rescue Tid.

Tid, of all people! Tid, whom he had resented and hated all his life. But none of that seemed to matter any more. He just knew that he had to try. He was certain he would fail, but he had to try.

It was no good looking for Tid. Everything was pitch black. Once or twice he looked back, just to make sure he could see the light. There Sofi stood, faithfully holding it up high. He did not have to see her face to know the expression that was on it and the trust in her eyes. Taking a deep breath, he dived.

It was then that his fingers touched something; he had no way of knowing what. His hands were dead to any real feeling, but he was sure there was something there.

His hands clutched at it. Wildly kicking, Sheldon pushed upwards. Once he broke the surface, he gasped for air and closed his arms around a body. He had no way of knowing, but he thought it must be Tid.

Looking wildly around him, he strained his eyes towards the light.

The light?

Where was it?

Thrashing with his feet, he turned a complete circle.

There was no light.

Sofi was not there.

They were lost.

With Tid across his chest, he started swimming on his back once more. He had no idea which direction he was taking, he just swam like a madman.

Joss thumped on the Loms' front door and waited. It was still very early. Ma Lom opened the door.

'Sorry to bother you,' Joss said, 'but we're mounting a search party for the Mossel children. We need Conrad.'

'He did not get in until late.'

'I'm sorry, but we still need him.'

'You barely look awake yourself,' Ma Lom said in a grandmotherly way.

Joss gave a rueful smile and ran his hand through his uncombed hair. 'It's my own fault. I should get to bed earlier.'

Ma Lom smiled. 'I will go and wake up Conrad. He will be in no worse state than you.'

Joss walked to the gate, where a couple of his friends were waiting. Joss looked up at the sky. He was still learning how to tell the time this way and so was not yet totally accurate, but he could tell that it was still early.

Conrad finally arrived, with rumpled hair and eyes barely open. Joss explained about the search. There was an audible sigh. None of them believed that Tid and Sofi were really in danger, just playing some childish prank.

'The sooner we start, the sooner we can go back to bed,' Joss said.

They split up, each taking a different section of the park.

Sofi stood on the shore, holding up her light. As Sheldon had swum further and further out, she strained to hold the light higher so that he would have a better chance of seeing it. She was now standing on tiptoe. Her arm was tired and she swapped the ruler to her other hand.

Chilled to the bone and trembling though she was, she waited, faithfully standing her ground. Even when Sheldon dived she did not move, but continued holding up the glowing ruler.

She swapped arms again and again. She strained her eyes to see into the gloom. The more she waited, the more worried she became, but she did not give up. The effort caused her to shake uncontrollably. Fear was twisting deep in her stomach.

All her strength had gone. It was only her willpower that kept her standing. Then suddenly, without warning, she felt a breeze; a shadow passed through her and she was filled with darkness. Her mind was emptied of thought, her hand drooped and her legs crumpled beneath her. Sofi flopped on to the ground, unconscious.

*

Scamp was leaning against the wall, shovel in one hand, cleaning the grit out of his ear with a finger of the other. He looked as relaxed as Slime looked nervous. Slime stood to one side. His troops were ready and waiting. His future would be decided on their ability to carry out Offa Scratch's instructions. He wiped his nose with a filthy rag and continued to wait.

Offa Scratch arrived, with Sniff at his side.

'Well?' Offa Scratch demanded. Slime jumped and tried to stand to attention.

Scamp looked up and casually acknowledged the arrival of his leader and his second-in-command with a faint nod of the head. As usual, his manner infuriated Offa Scratch, but Scamp was too valuable a digger to be punished just yet. That would come later.

'Is everything ready?' Offa Scratch demanded.

'Yer, Your Masterfulness,' Sniff said, bowing ingratiatingly.

Offa Scratch looked at Slime. 'Are the troops ready for action?'

'Yer, Offa Scratch,' Slime said smartly.

Offa Scratch looked at Scamp. 'The diggers?'

Scamp did not immediately respond. He had an itch in the small of his back and all his attention was taken up trying to satisfy it.

'Scamp!' Sniff hissed.

Scamp looked up indifferently.

'Is the diggers standing by?'

Scamp nodded without showing any interest. 'Just about, I reckon.'

Sniff could almost feel his leader's blood pressure rising.

Slime thought Offa Scratch was about to explode.

Only Scamp was totally unconcerned.

Offa Scratch took a deep breath, all the while telling himself that it would not be long. Scamp's day would come.

'Get the girl,' he growled.

No one in the Labyrinth had slept much. Lorin and Morlenni's disappearance had prompted questions, and it was not long before all sorts of rumours were circulating.

In her panic for her friend, Lorin had forgotten to warn the women to leave the Labyrinth, and the idea did not occur to any of them. As the morning dragged on and there had been no digging and no frightening noises for some time, the women pushed unpleasant thoughts to the back of their minds and passed their time gossiping. They speculated on the whereabouts of Morlenni and laughed at the things Lorin had called Berwyth and her Committee. Yaryth had been unable to keep it to herself. Lorin's words became more insulting with each telling.

Berwyth and her Committee were uniformly disliked. For Lorin to have said to their faces what so many women whispered behind their backs made her something of a celebrity. For the first time in her life, Lorin was in danger of becoming popular.

*

Sheldon was swimming on his back, clutching Tid to his chest. He plunged his hand repeatedly into the water and dragged it down to his side, kicking with his feet. He seemed to be moving.

It was enough.

His mind was as numb as the rest of him; his swimming was automatic. He had no hope of ever finding land.

When he finally bumped on to the shore, he opened his eyes in surprise. He lay there in the blackness for a moment, too frozen to feel any emotion. Then he pulled up his legs and pushed with his heels towards the inky water, thus propelling himself and Tid through the shingle, away from its shadowy depths.

Somewhere in the recesses of his mind he knew he had to get warm.

Tid lay heavily on his chest. Sheldon turned over and Tid rolled on to the ground. His face was deathly white and his lips blue, but it was too dark for Sheldon to know.

Leaning over him, Sheldon put his ear to Tid's chest. There was no sound. His heart was not beating. Tid lay, cold and silent.

Sheldon started shaking him. 'Don't you die on me!' he shouted. 'Don't you dare die on me!' He had risked everything to rescue this spoiled brat. He would not let him die. He would not let him! 'You selfish little runt!' Letting out his frustration, he thumped Tid hard on the chest.

Tid's body jolted. Water dribbled from his mouth. Feebly, he coughed.

Sheldon put his head to Tid's chest again. There was a weak throbbing from his heart.

So Tid was not dead. It would now be Sheldon's responsibility to keep him alive. Typical! The last thing Sheldon needed was a dead weight around his neck! They had to warm up or else they might both die.

Sheldon cast his eyes around, but it was so dark, he could see nothing. He knew where the water was and instinctively moved away from it, holding the unconscious Tid in his arms. It would have been easier if he had slung him over his shoulder, but he did not have the energy. Readjusting his hold, he staggered a few paces before reaching a cold, damp wall.

Slowly he shuffled along, feeling with his hand, and, amazingly enough, it felt drier. A few moments later, he sank on to dry ground. He rubbed his brow but was still so numb that he felt nothing.

Under normal circumstances, he would have felt absolutely terrified of the black, lonely tunnels, but his senses as well as his limbs were numbed. Then, as if they were puppies lying down together, he curled his body around Tid's to try to retain any warmth left in their frozen bodies, and attempted to stay awake.

15

Shadows

By mid morning, the park was as busy as usual. The day was repeating itself yet again and Humans were moving exactly as they had done before. The Bushytails, organized by Walnut, were making sure that they kept to the same routine.

Joss found the rest of the search party sitting in the kitchen at Old Father Tim's, having completed their search earlier.

Enderell was pacing the floor. 'Oh dear!' she was murmuring to herself. 'Oh dear!'

The Greenwich Guardian and Enderell looked hopefully at Joss as he entered. He shook his head.

'Oh dear!' Enderell muttered again.

'Other than Plemet-Thead's book,' Conrad asked, stifling a yawn, 'is there anything missing from their rooms?'

'I don't think so,' Enderell said woefully.

'Think logically,' the Greenwich Guardian said. 'We've checked the school and the park. Where else might they go?'

'I don't know,' Enderell almost wailed.

'Calm yourself.'

'But the Old Father put them in my care and I lost them!'

'And so would he if they had decided to run off in the middle of the night.' The Greenwich Guardian spoke sternly, but not unkindly. 'You were here to care for them, not guard them.'

Enderell gulped and made an effort to calm down.

'Have all the houses in the park been checked?' the Greenwich Guardian asked.

'Yes,' Joss said, 'and all the Human buildings. Tid and Sofi aren't anywhere.'

'What about the Labyrinth? Has anyone thought to look there?' Enderell asked.

'Why would they go there?'

'I thought that Sofi seemed keen when the Old Father was talking to Lorin. It is just a thought.'

'I suppose any young girl might want to go and explore her roots,' the Greenwich Guardian said, 'but why would Tid go?'

'I can't see him passing up the chance of an adventure, can you?' Joss asked.

The Greenwich Guardian clasped her hands tightly together as she thought. 'Very well,' she said at length. 'Joss, you go and see if the Wrecca women know anything.'

'Hasn't Lorin told them to evacuate?' he asked. 'They'll be gone by now.'

'Possibly not,' the Greenwich Guardian replied. 'Wreccas are not the most cooperative beings. It may take Lorin some time to persuade them.'

'All right,' Joss said, trying not to sound too fed up. 'I'll give it a go.'

'But be careful,' the Greenwich Guardian warned. 'Only ask at the door. Under no circumstances are you to go inside.'

'No fear of that,' Joss replied.

'And Conrad, go and find Pa Brownal and ask him to join me here.' The Greenwich Guardian unclasped her hands. 'There is nothing the rest of you can do. You might as well go home.'

Joss sighed. He had the worst job, as usual. Putting aside all thought of bed, he trudged off towards the Labyrinth.

Sofi felt strangely warm. She opened her eyes. By the light of the glowing wooden ruler that lay beside her she could see the dangerous water of the pool, glassy-still once more.

Sitting up, she put her hand into the small of her back. It ached, but at least she could feel it. She was no longer numb; in fact she was no longer cold, and her clothes . . . she felt them in surprise: they were dry.

'Are you well?'

The unexpected voice cut through the air so sharply that Sofi flinched. Who was it? It did not sound like one of the boys. Sofi looked about her. There was no one there. She must be hearing things.

'You should be feeling warmer.'

'Who's there?' Sofi's heart was thumping. She picked up the ruler and, scrambling to her feet, swung it around, trying to pick up the person who had spoken in its light. 'Sheldon? Is that you?'

There was a low chuckle. Sofi felt a shiver, not from cold but from fear.

'You may look around as much as you wish, but you will not see me.'

'Who are you?' she asked nervously.

'Who am I? That is a good question. There was a time when I constantly asked it of myself, but I stopped long ago.'

'You must be someone,' Sofi said, frantically looking around.

'Once I was,' came the reply. 'But alas, no longer.'

'What do you mean?' Sofi asked, not sure she really wanted to know. 'You're not,' her voice turned breathy with fear, 'a ghost?'

'I imagined you were far too sensible to believe in ghosts.'

'Then what are you?'

'I am a shadow,' the voice replied, 'nothing more, nothing less.'

'A shadow of what?'

'A shadow of my former self.'

Sofi gripped her ruler more tightly as she peered around, vainly trying to catch sight of it. 'What does *that* mean?'

'It means,' said the voice, 'that once I was a person, at least I think I was. It's hard to remember. It was a long time ago. Perhaps I dug the tunnels.'

'Why?' Sofi asked, not that she was interested in the

answer, but she was anxious to keep the shadow talking; it was the only way of knowing it was there.

'I believe they were a refuge and a hiding place.'

'Who from?'

'Enemies. Never forget that they are all around.' These words sounded like a warning, and Sofi wondered if this shadow was trustworthy. She would have to be cautious.

'Why am I so warm?' she asked. 'When I fell asleep, I was wet and icy cold. Now I'm as warm as toast. How come?'

'That would be me,' the shadow explained rather proudly. 'I wafted through you all the time you slept. I cannot do much, but I can stimulate living matter if I move fast. I invigorated your insides and warmed you up. It also had the effect of drying your clothes.'

'Well, thank you.'

'You are welcome. Would you like me to float through you again?'

'All right,' Sofi said a little nervously. She waited tensely. Suddenly, a shadow passed behind her eyes and warmth flowed through her.

'Is that not good?' the shadow asked.

'Very,' she said with a smile, enjoying the sensation. 'Thank you.'

'My pleasure.'

'How long was I asleep?'

'Time is of no significance to me,' the shadow replied airily.

Sofi looked out across the pool. It was as tranquil and

innocent as when they had first come across it. There was one question she had to ask, but she dreaded the answer. 'Do you know what happened to my friends?'

'Which one? The tall boy or the short one?'

It was something of a relief to know that this shadow knew who she was talking about. 'Both,' she said hopefully.

'I lost sight of them at the same time as you did. I was occupied saving you. You have no idea how close you came to freezing to death.'

Sofi did not mean to feel ungrateful, but she wished the shadow had spent less time on her and more on Tid and Sheldon.

'Few escape the Murky Deep,' the shadow said gravely.

'The Murky Deep?' It sounded much worse now that it had a name. 'You should have told us it was called that before sending us across,' she said.

'That was not I!' the voice said indignantly.

'I heard you,' Sofi said. 'You told me to cross it.'

'No, that was the shadow of the Murky Deep,' the shadow said, his voice trembling slightly. 'Never trust any shadow, but especially never trust the ones who lurk in such dangerous places. They are the ones whose deaths were most horrific and they are the most treacherous.'

It sounded alarming. 'What makes them so bad?'

'The shadow of the Murky Deep calls travellers into its waters and then makes them deep or shallow at will. It matters not which direction you take. When the traveller is too tired to fight, it sucks him down. You should never have tried to cross it.'

'Why didn't you stop us?'

'How was I to do that?'

'You could have said something!'

'It was not my place.'

'Not your place?' Sofi said angrily. 'You let it take them! You're just as bad as it is!' Furiously, she turned away and stomped a few paces away; but it was difficult to stay angry with someone she could not see, especially when it was the only company she had in a dark and lonely place. Slowly she calmed down. 'Did it suck my friends down?' she asked in a small voice, wondering if the shadow was still there.

'It is likely,' the shadow said stiffly. It did not appreciate being told it was as bad as the shadow of the Murky Deep.

Despair filled her heart. 'Then they are drowned!' Sofi exclaimed, and a sob caught in her throat.

'That depends.'

'On what?' she asked, not daring to hope too much.

'The shadow of the Murky Deep is only able to keep what rightfully belongs to it.'

'What's that?'

'Is that not obvious?'

Sofi shook her head.

'It can only keep what is bad, that which is wrong, anything that is evil. Should your friends be good, then it will only keep them for a while. Their goodness will eventually repel it, and it will have to release them.'

'Tid's good!' Sofi cried excitedly, 'and so he must be alive.'

There was a worrying silence from the shadow.

'Mustn't he?' she asked eagerly.

'Possibly not.'

'What do you mean?'

'It will have sucked him down. If it did not occur to him to take a deep breath as he went under, he will not have been alive when released.'

Sofi shivered at the horror of it all. The shadow obligingly wafted through her once more, but she was too distraught at the thought that Tid and Sheldon might be dead to thank him. She knew that if Tid had not survived the shadow of the Murky Deep, then Sheldon would definitely not have done. No matter how much she might trust Sheldon now, he had been bad once. The shadow would have been able to keep him under the water longer.

'It is no use being sad, young lady,' the shadow gently chided her. 'You should walk. I remember how invigorating walking was. It will help to keep you warm.'

Sofi obliged him only because she did not have the will to argue. Slowly, she started walking. It did not matter in which direction nor that she was barefoot.

'Are you coming with me?' she asked, suddenly afraid of being alone.

'If you wish.'

It was a relief to have his company, although Sofi did not feel much like talking.

After some time of silence, the shadow suddenly asked, 'What is this up ahead?'

Sofi squinted through the darkness. There was a glow. Hope flooded her heart. 'Tid!' she cried, as she started running, her heart beating wildly.

The light became brighter as she drew closer. Lying on the shoreline was Tid's paperweight. 'Tid!' she yelled, looking frantically about her. 'Tid! Sheldon!' But even as she called their names, she knew they would not answer. Common sense told her that they would never willingly have been parted from their only source of light.

She had no doubt that the Murky Deep had been unable to retain a paperweight that belonged to Old Father Tim, even though it was heavy enough to sink in normal waters. She picked it up, hoping it would make her feel better to hold something that Tid had so recently held, but it did not.

She stood there, heartbroken. Tid was dead. How would she ever tell her grandfather?

At length, she took the paperweight to the stone wall that bordered the Murky Deep. Carefully, she placed it on a piece of flint jutting out from the wall. It was her way of honouring the place where Tid and Sheldon had been lost.

The shadow kept its silence.

Sofi stood looking at the light with her head bowed and then walked away.

The shadow respected her silence for a while because it did not want to intrude on her obvious sorrow, but it could not keep quiet for very long. Talking was a luxury it did not often have. Eventually, it asked, 'Why did you come into the mines?'

So overwhelmed with misery, Sofi had almost forgotten the shadow's existence and she jumped at the sound of its voice. Its question made her recall how she had bullied Tid into coming with her. It was her fault that the boys were dead. With no heart to talk, but realizing that the shadow might leave her if she did not, she dully replied, 'We came in to find my grandfather.'

'Who is your grandfather?'

'He's the Guardian leader and he came in to find the Gemetbur.' A thought occurred to her. 'I don't suppose you know where it is?'

'I have drifted through these tunnels for thousands of years,' the shadow said indignantly. 'Do you think anywhere is unknown to me?'

'Then you do know where it is?' she said excitedly.

There was a pause. In fact, it was so long a pause that for a moment, Sofi wondered if the shadow had left her.

'Of course I know,' the voice said, not quite as sure of itself as it had been.

'Where?'

The shadow hesitated. 'Er . . . exactly what *is* a Bemetgur?'

Sofi's heart sank. 'You shouldn't say you know things that you don't,' she said reproachfully. 'And it's a Gemetbur.'

'I know everywhere,' the shadow said petulantly, 'though I may not know its Guardian name. What is it?'

'It's a room that was built thousands of years ago to regulate time.'

'Ahh!'

Another pause.

'Well?' Sofi asked expectantly.

The shadow did not speak for some time. When it finally did, it sounded deeply troubled. 'In the same way that some shadows should be ignored, some places may be too dangerous to investigate.'

Joss stood at the Topside door and knocked. He looked about him as he waited and then knocked again. No one answered. He was not sure what to do. Perhaps the women had a spy hole and did not answer to anyone they did not know.

'Excuse me!' he called loudly.

Silence.

'I have come to ask you a question!'

Still no one responded.

Perhaps he should try to open the door himself, but there was no handle. He wondered if he dared put his shoulder to it. Perhaps not.

'This is a waste of time,' he muttered, deciding to leave. He still had some serious sleeping to do. Suddenly he heard the door-latch lift. Joss stood up smartly, waiting for the door to open. It did, just a crack, and Falwyth peered out.

She had not recognized the knock and thus had been nervous of opening up. However, seeing a young Guardian man who was rather good-looking, she opened the door a little wider and smiled uncertainly. 'What can I do for you?' she asked, fluttering her lashes.

Joss felt uncomfortable. 'I . . . I am looking for Lorin.'

Falwyth scowled. It seemed to her that Lorin received far too much attention. 'What does you want her for?' she asked unpleasantly.

'Important business,' Joss said, trying to maintain an outward appearance of composure. These Wrecca women were alarming.

'Well, her isn't here. Her flounced out a while back.' Then Falwyth's manner altered just as quickly as it had before, and once more she fluttered her short, thin lashes. 'Can I help you?'

'I don't think so,' Joss said, but maybe she could. 'Have you seen a couple of young Guardian children called Tid and Sofi?'

Falwyth's face turned sour once more. 'Does you mean that little cat them men called Snot?'

'Er . . . I think so,' Joss said. He did have a vague memory of Sofi having an unfortunate name when she first arrived.

'Has you lost her?' Falwyth asked, curious.

'It would appear so,' Joss said with a weak smile, trying to make light of it.

Falwyth found his smile appealing. She would like to spend a little more time in this young man's company. 'You's welcome to step inside,' she said, trying to flirt.

Joss opened his eyes wide in alarm.

Falwyth was fluffing up the back of her hair, trying to make it look more attractive, and she opened the door wider. 'I'll ask around.'

Joss began to panic. She was scary. 'That is very kind

of you,' he said, taking a step backwards, 'but I am . . .
er . . . needed back at the Hither House.' He took one
more step. 'Um . . . thank you for your . . . er . . . co-
operation.'

Falwyth tried to look as if she understood what 'co-
operation' was. 'Anything I can do to help you,
Handsome,' she said, smiling seductively, only it looked
more like a grimace to Joss.

'Er . . ' Joss said, still backing away, 'thank you very
much,' and he left, tripping in his haste.

16

The Shadow of the Murky Deep

Sheldon was restless. It was not just that he was cold and wet; this total darkness was unnerving. Although he did not want to fall asleep, it made no sense to keep his eyes open when the oppressive blackness was pressing in on him; but when he closed them, he found himself drifting into sleep and this, he knew, was dangerous.

He kept thinking that he heard murmurings, voices overlapping each other and whispering in his ears, telling him to cross the water, or to stay still and sleep, or to go in search of an exit. He kept expecting to find someone standing nearby, but he did not know if anyone was there because he could not see anything.

Finally, his confused brain decided that he should get up. He listened to Tid's breathing. It was shallow and faster than it should have been, but he was alive. Sheldon's legs hurt, tucked up as they were. It was, however, a bonus to feel them at all. He must be thawing, although his fingers still felt like blocks of ice. He needed to move around.

Slowly, he unfurled himself from around Tid. He felt

a little guilty leaving him alone on the ground, but Sheldon needed to stand. He staggered to his feet and leant against the wall. His clothes were still wet. If only he could light a fire and give them a chance to dry out.

'What's that?' he asked. It sounded as if Tid had spoken. 'Tid?' Sheldon leant over the sleeping boy. 'Did you say something?'

Tid's breathing remained regular. He must have been talking in his sleep. If only there was some light. This blinding blackness was unbearable.

Sheldon moved a short distance from Tid so that he would not step on him, and started stamping his feet and rubbing his upper arms with his icy hands, trying to regain some feeling. It helped a little and so he started rubbing his body and legs.

'Ouch!'

Something had stabbed his leg. What was it? He felt with tingling fingers. There was something in his trouser pocket.

It was not easy to squeeze his hand into it, but he wriggled his fingers in and soon found them wrapping themselves around something long, sharp and thin. When he pulled it out, Sheldon gasped in delight. He was holding Aleyesu's pencil. He had not remembered putting it there, but he must have done so when working in the Hither House. There, its brightness would have gone unnoticed, but in Sheldon's inky world it made a light so pure that he had to squint to protect his eyes. Reverently, he held the pencil in front of his face and stared at it.

'Tid!' he said eagerly. 'We've got a light!'

Tid lay still.

'Tid!'

'Ssh, don't wake him!'

'Who's there?' Sheldon said, whirling around, holding out the pencil and backing towards Tid. 'Sofi, is that you?'

'Let him sleep. He needs his strength.'

'Who are you?' Sheldon asked, returning to Tid and kneeling next to him. He put his hand protectively on his shoulder.

'I am nothing more than a shadow,' the voice said. 'I am here to help you.'

'What sort of shadow?' Sheldon asked, suspicious.

'The shadow of one who hid in the mines not so many years ago. I got lost. I roamed for days, searching for the way out. Finally, I ran out of strength. I collapsed and died. Now I hang about in the darkness, helping travellers find their way.'

Sheldon would have been a lot happier if he could have seen this shadow.

'Is that what you are going to do for us?' he asked. 'Help us find our way?'

'Naturally,' said the sweet voice. 'You must walk with me. Come.'

Sheldon shook Tid, but the shadow said, 'Leave the boy alone. He will be all right here.'

'I can't do that,' Sheldon said, trying to think. Without Sofi's book, he did not have the slightest idea where he was or which way he should go. He knew from his experience of being in the Underneath that it was impossible to find a safe way out of dark tunnels without some sort of guide. It seemed that his only hope now was to trust this shadow, but a feeling, deep in his gut, told him this was dangerous.

He shook Tid by the shoulder. 'Wake up!'

Tid groaned, but otherwise did not stir.

'You'll have to leave him.' The shadow sounded perfectly happy at the thought. 'I shall come back and fetch him when he's ready to wake.'

'No,' Sheldon said. He heaved Tid up on to his shoulder. 'Give me a moment.' He held on to the wall for balance as he staggered to his feet. He was more tired that he cared to admit.

'Follow me,' the shadow said.

Enderell, the Greenwich Guardian and Bryn sat round Old Father Tim's kitchen table. Enderell had made the lunch. It was not up to her usual standard; her mind was not on it. All she could think of was what she was going to say to Old Father Tim when he came back and found his grandchildren were missing.

The search had been extended to all of Greenwich. Each member of the search party reported in regularly.

'Their teacher says that there is no trouble at school,' Bryn was explaining. He had just come back from talking with her. 'There is no reason why they should have run away.'

'Run away!' Enderell breathed in horror.

'They have not run away,' the Greenwich Guardian

said firmly. 'They have gone to do something specific. You know what they are like.'

'I think they've gone to help the Old Father.' Bryn said.

'That's ridiculous!' Enderell said. 'I heard him tell them all about it. There is no way they could have thought that there was anything they could do to help.'

'That was before Sofi read the book,' the Greenwich Guardian said.

'Oh yes,' Enderell admitted. 'The book.'

'Did the Old Father tell them where the entrance to the tunnels was?' Bryn asked.

'No.'

'Well, that is one good thing. Do we know where it is?'

'Yes,' the Greenwich Guardian replied.

Bryn sat back in his chair and placed both his hands flat on the table. 'Then I think that is where we should start.'

'Why? If Tid and Sofi do not know about it, why should we start there?'

'They must be somewhere,' Bryn reasoned, 'and if they have gone to help the Old Father, then we know they will be making for the tunnels. They may have found another way in but we have to start at the one place we know. Where is it?'

'Very well,' the Greenwich Guardian said. 'I need not add that this information must go no further.'

Enderell and Bryn nodded their agreement.

'Old Father Tim's journey begins in his workshop.'

'That makes sense,' Bryn said. 'We should check it out.'

'There is one problem.'

They looked at the Greenwich Guardian questioningly.

'I do not know how to enter the workshop.'

'I do,' Bryn said. 'The Old Father showed me in case there was an emergency.'

'I think this can be called an emergency,' the Greenwich Guardian said decisively. 'You and I, Bryn, shall go there together. Enderell, you stay here.'

'Please, no,' Enderell said, preferring to do something useful.

'I know this is difficult,' the Greenwich Guardian said kindly, 'but if the children return, you are the one who should be here. Joss should also be reporting back soon. If he has any useful information, be Mindful to us.'

Enderell agreed, and the Greenwich Guardian and her brother walked briskly to the workshop.

In order to keep herself busy, Enderell started cleaning the kitchen. It did not need cleaning, but even so she scrubbed away enthusiastically. When there was a movement at the door, she jumped, dropping her brush. She had hoped it would be Tid and Sofi. Her heart sank. It was Zeit.

'Good afternoon, Zeit,' she said politely.

'Good afternoon,' he responded. 'I need to see the Greenwich Guardian.'

'She is not here,' Enderell replied, picking up the fallen brush.

'When will she return?'

'I do not know. Can I help?'

Zeit's jaw was tightly set. Why did everyone disappear when he needed them? He was wondering what he should do next when Joss walked in.

'Did they know anything?' Enderell asked Joss anxiously, referring to the Wrecca women.

Joss shook his head and then said to the Guardian respectfully, 'Good day to you, Zeit.'

'Good day to you. I came to see the Greenwich Guardian.'

'Will it wait?' Enderell asked.

'No.'

'Can I be of help?' Joss offered.

Zeit had seen Joss at the Hither House. He thought him a little wet, always doing as he was bidden without a thought of his own. Still, he had to tell someone, and Joss did work directly for the Greenwich Guardian. 'It may be nothing,' he began, 'but it may be significant. I understand that the Old Father Grandson is missing.'

'He is.'

'With that girl, Sofi? The one who was a Wrecca?'

'Yes.'

'Well,' Zeit took a deep breath, 'I thought you ought to know that Sheldon Croe is also missing.'

Enderell gasped in horror.

'After last time,' Zeit continued, remembering the occasion when Sheldon had kidnapped Sofi, 'I thought the Greenwich Guardian should know.'

'Is there any reason for you to think that Sheldon is with the children?' Joss asked.

'None whatsoever.'

'It's a pity you brought him back,' Enderell said bitterly.

'I do not think he will do it again, or anything like it,' Zeit said. 'Sheldon has come a long way since he was last here.' He paused. 'But I may be wrong.'

Now that his eyes were accustomed to the light, Sheldon realized that the pencil did not give off very much. It was better than nothing, but only just.

'Where are you?' he asked the shadow.

'Keep walking.'

Sheldon did not like following something he could not see. Looking a person in the eye meant that you had some idea about that person. A shadow was altogether different.

'Hurry up!' the shadow urged.

'I'm doing the best I can,' Sheldon snapped. 'It's not easy; Tid's heavy and I can't feel my toes.' He tried to adjust his grip on the pencil, but his fingers were icy cold and he dropped it.

'What's keeping you?' the shadow asked irritably.

'I dropped the light.'

'We don't need that.'

'You might be all right in the dark,' Sheldon grumbled, 'but I'm not.' Slowly, he bent his knees to pick it up. Tid slipped precariously on his shoulder. 'Why are we hurrying, anyway?'

'I thought you were cold.'

Sheldon was freezing, but that was no reason to go

at such a pace. There was something strange about this shadow. Might it be playing a trick on him?

'So,' he said, trying to sound casual, 'you reckon that the Gemetbur is this way?'

'Yes.'

Sheldon's step faltered. He had not mentioned the Gemetbur before. The shadow had only promised to show him the way out.

'I'll be leaving you behind if you don't keep up,' the shadow complained.

Wherever the shadow was taking them, Sheldon did not want to go. Silently, he dropped back a few paces, turned and started to run in the opposite direction as fast as his frozen toes and Tid's dead weight would allow.

'Where do you think you're going?' called the shadow.

Sheldon did not answer, but kept running.

'Come back!' wailed the shadow. 'You'll get lost!'

Sheldon took no notice. With one hand gripping the pencil and the other firmly clamped around Tid, he pushed on as hard as he could. Voices kept pounding in his head. How many shadows were there? Sheldon resolutely ignored them.

He ran until he had no breath left. Then he fell against the wall, gasping, and dropped Tid on the ground, where he lay motionless.

Cautiously, Sheldon checked their surroundings. They were back by the pool. The voices had stopped, but Sheldon had no way of knowing whether the shadows had gone or whether they were watching him silently.

He did not think it wise to hang around but did not know which way they should go. Breathing heavily, he took a number of paces in different directions. There were several promising tunnels that needed checking. Sheldon was reluctant to leave Tid alone, but he reassured himself that if he could not rouse Tid, then no shadow would be able to.

'I'm going to check out the lie of the land,' he said out loud. 'I'll be as quick as I can.'

Bryn and the Greenwich Guardian stood in the workshop.

'Have you any idea where the entrance to the Guardian tunnels may be?' Bryn asked.

'No,' she said, picking up the note that Tid had written. She read it and handed it to her brother. 'Sheldon? You don't suppose he means Sheldon Croe?'

Bryn read the note. 'I know of no other. It is a pity Zeit had to bring him back. He was always a trouble-maker.'

'Why is he with Tid and Sofi?' the Greenwich Guardian asked. 'And why does Tid not say where the trapdoor is?'

'Perhaps it is obvious,' Bryn said, looking around.

'If it is obvious, then why can we not see it?'

'Well, if Tid and Sofi worked it out,' Bryn said, 'I think that a Guardian and a Park Elder should be able to have a reasonable stab at it. Now let me see . . .' He started walking around the workshop, looking intently at the floor, the walls and even under the workbench.

'You cannot help but admire them,' he continued. 'I mean, they are still young, and yet they worked out not only where the entrance is, but how to open it.'

'Perhaps they were lucky,' the Greenwich Guardian suggested.

'Maybe,' he agreed, 'because I can see absolutely nothing to indicate where it could possibly be. I wonder why Tid did not write it in his message.'

The Greenwich Guardian shook her head. 'Perhaps it was obvious. It may have been open.'

'Or perhaps he wrote in a hurry,' Bryn said ominously, 'or in secret.'

The Greenwich Guardian looked at her brother, worried by the tone of his voice.

'Maybe Tid wrote this to warn us,' Bryn concluded, 'because Sheldon Croe has kidnapped them both this time.'

Tid had never felt so cold. He opened his eyes, but it was so dark he thought his eyes must still be closed. He shut them and opened them again. Everything was still inky black. Where could he be? Perhaps he was dead at the bottom of the pool. He looked about, hoping to see something on which to focus. He had never been in such blackness.

He held out his hands and felt all around him. He seemed to be by a wall. Nervously, he stumbled to his feet. Every bit of him ached. The fact that he could feel this should have been a comfort, but Tid did not think of that. He stood with his back pressed against the wall, utterly wretched. He was cold and wet, but he was not at the bottom of the pool. He was alive! How had that happened?

'Hello,' he said. His voice did not sound right. He tried again. 'Hello.' It sounded better this time as it bounced gently off the walls. Then there was silence.

'Is there anyone here?' he called. 'Sofi?'

No answer.

He wrapped his arms around himself and rubbed hard. He was not sure what to do. His stomach lurched nervously. It was frightening, being totally alone in such darkness. Should he move or stay put? If Sofi was looking for him, perhaps he should remain where he was so that she could find him. He wondered where Sofi was. He hoped she was all right. This had to be Sheldon's fault!

'You need to cross the pool.'

The voice was quiet, but in the silence of the caves it was distinct.

'Sofi?' Tid's heart raced with hope. 'Where are you?'

'Come across the pool.'

'I cannot see you. Have you lost your light too?'

'I am on the other side of the pool. I have a light, but you cannot see it. I know the way. All you have to do is cross the water and all will be well.'

Delighted though Tid was at the thought of finding Sofi, he did not like the idea of crossing the water once more.

'Isn't there another way?' he asked. 'Perhaps I can walk round.'

'You cannot.' Sofi's voice sounded a little odd, but then everything sounded strange in this place.

Tid hesitated. He was a brave lad but, even so, the thought of subjecting himself to the icy water again filled his heart with dread. He was still cold from his last dipping.

'I have a fire. It will warm you when you arrive.'

The thought of a fire pushed all doubt from his mind. Holding his hands out in front of him so that he would feel anything that might be in his path before he actually hit it, Tid cautiously put one foot in front of the other. Each time, he felt for the ground beneath his feet before transferring his weight.

Suddenly his foot splashed. He had arrived.

'Hurry. Just go straight into the middle and relax. Don't struggle. I am waiting by the fire on the other side.'

Tid squinted through the blackness. 'Where?' he asked. He thought he should be able to see the fire's glow, however far away it was.

'Tid!'

This was a different voice. It seemed to be some distance away and it came from behind him. 'Who's that?' Tid turned. He saw a faint light in the distance. 'Sheldon,' he breathed.

'Don't wait for him. He'll lead you to your death.'

'I knew it!' Tid exclaimed, a note of triumph in his voice. At last Sofi had realized what Sheldon was up to.

Tid strode out into the water.

'Tid, where are you?' Sheldon called.

Tid strode on; now the water was over his knees. He had to hurry; he did not want to wait and be caught by Sheldon.

'Tid!' The light from the pencil now made it possible for Sheldon just to make out Tid striding into the water. 'Stop! What *are* you doing?'

Tid turned once more. The sight of the glow from Aleyesu's pencil was so welcoming that it made him hesitate.

'Hurry!' Sheldon heard a voice urge.

'Who's that?' Sheldon asked. Then realization dawned on him. He should never have left Tid alone. 'Tid, no!'

Tid was waist deep in the pool now.

Sheldon started running. 'Tid, come back! Don't go!'

'Stay away from me!' Tid shouted, moving further into the pool.

Sheldon's long legs quickly brought him to the edge of the pool. His meagre pencil light illuminated enough of the scene for him to understand what was happening.

'It's a trick,' he shouted.

'No it's not,' Tid called, over his shoulder. 'Sofi is on the other side with a fire. You stay away from me.'

'No she's not!' Sheldon shouted. What a fool Tid was! 'It's a shadow and it's luring you to your death!'

17

The Question

'I'm not listening to you,' Tid yelled, chest deep in the water now. 'You must think I'm stupid!'

'Too right!' Sheldon muttered. He knew the voice was not Sofi's; somehow he had to prove it. 'Ask her a question.'

'What?'

'Ask a question that only Sofi would know. If she answers it right, then you'll know it's her.'

'I'm not playing your game,' Tid retorted nastily.

'What harm can it do? If she knows the answer, then you can go on, but she won't because it isn't Sofi. It's a shadow and it wants you dead!'

Tid hesitated. The water was icy cold and his feet and legs were numb again. He really shouldn't be hanging about, but Sheldon had a point. What harm would it do if he asked Sofi one question?

'If I am wrong,' Sheldon continued, 'and she gets the right answer, I won't stop you.'

Tid shivered. It could not do any harm. 'All right, just to prove you wrong.' He thought for a moment. 'Sofi, what colour is your bedroom?'

The voice did not reply.

'You see!' Sheldon said triumphantly. 'It doesn't know because it isn't Sofi. It's a shadow and it wants you dead!'

'C . . . come on Sofi,' Tid encouraged. 'I'm g . . . getting cold.'

'Yellow!' the voice came back.

'She's right!' Tid yelled jubilantly.

'A lucky guess!' Sheldon shouted.

'I'm not wasting any more time,' Tid retorted, remembering what the voice had told him to do and relaxing, allowing himself to float on top of the water. He would not fight it this time.

'It's not Sofi!' Sheldon yelled as he watched Tid immerse himself in the murky depths. 'Oh damn!' he muttered as he stowed his precious pencil in his pocket. He shivered as the icy water splashed up his legs. He could no longer see Tid, but he knew the direction he had taken. Sheldon launched himself into the pool.

Sheldon was in much better condition than Tid and swam strongly. In a few seconds he had caught up with the younger boy and grabbed his sodden tunic, yanking him backwards.

'Get off!' Tid shouted angrily. He was colder, weaker, smaller and no match for Sheldon, who easily wrapped his arm around Tid and started reversing, dragging the struggling lad back towards the shore.

'Fight, Tid!' the voice urged. 'Fight!'

The distance back to dry land was short, but Tid made it as difficult for Sheldon as possible, kicking and twisting his body, trying to thump his clenched fist into any part of Sheldon that he could reach.

Finally, Sheldon felt pebbles beneath his feet. This released the arm he had swum with to pin down Tid's arms. Gripping him tightly and breathing heavily, Sheldon scrambled up the bank on to dry land. Getting to his feet, he trudged on until he blindly bumped into the wall, where he promptly dropped Tid and sat on him, trapping his flailing arms and legs.

'Get off me!' Tid screamed. 'Sofi, he's kidnapping me!'

'It's not Sofi!' Sheldon yelled back.

'She got the question right.'

'Ask her another one.'

'Get off!'

'Ask her another.'

Tid continued struggling.

'If she gets the next one right, I promise I'll let you go,' Sheldon said.

'You said that before.'

'I mean it this time!' And Sheldon did mean it. He was heartily sick of Tid.

Tid remained silent. He was not going to play Sheldon's game.

'All right then,' Sheldon said, '*I'll* ask her one.' He raised his voice and yelled into the blackness, 'Here, you on the other side. Who drew the map in the Underneath?'

There was no answer.

'Sofi?' Tid yelled. 'Who drew the map?'

Nothing.

'Sofi!' he cried again.

Total silence.

A note of panic edged Tid's voice. 'Where are you?'

'She's not there. She was never there,' Sheldon said, exasperated.

'Yes she was. I heard her.'

'The last time I saw Sofi, she was standing this side of the pool,' Sheldon said. 'At least, I think it was this side. Wherever she is, it's not over there.'

'But she said . . .'

'No, she didn't. It was a shadow speaking. The shadows want us dead.'

'Why?'

'How on earth should I know?'

'What are they?'

'I haven't the faintest idea but I think they may be ghosts of some sort, and for some reason they are trying to kill us.'

'But I heard her!' Energy surged within Tid and he started struggling again.

'No you didn't,' Sheldon said angrily, as he tightened his hold.

This last effort drained Tid of his remaining energy. Sheldon felt him slumping.

'But her room *is* yellow,' Tid said, still thinking about her answer. 'She is so proud of it. We all helped. I got so sick of yellow and blue by the time we'd finished.'

'Yellow and blue?' Sheldon asked.

'Yeah.'

'It only said yellow.'

Tid thought about this. Sheldon was right. She had said yellow, and yet Sofi's room was more blue than yellow. Blue was her favourite colour. She always said that she had a blue room. Sometimes she said it had yellow bits, but she always said it was blue. The truth suddenly dawned on him. 'It wasn't her,' he gasped, horrified.

Sheldon relaxed. 'At last!' he said, releasing his grip on Tid. Sheldon shivered. He was wetter and colder than ever.

'Where is she?' Tid asked.

'How am I supposed to know?' Sheldon said irritably. He stood up and wriggled his hand deep into his sodden pocket. He pulled out the pencil. The small amount of light gave shape and form to their surroundings.

'Where did you get that?' Tid asked, relieved to see a light.

'It's Aleyesu's pencil. I must have picked it up when I was working with him, back at the Hither House.'

'I thought you were Zeit's apprentice,' Tid said suspiciously.

'I am,' Sheldon replied, 'but he told me to help Aleyesu.'

'Who's Aleyesu?'

'An American Guardian. I think he's new.'

Tid gave Sheldon an appraising stare. 'Is that true?'

Sheldon returned the stare with loathing. 'Who cares? It doesn't matter what I tell you, because you're never going to believe a word I say, are you?'

Tid did not reply.

'Come on,' Sheldon snapped. 'We'd better get going. It'll help to get the blood circulating.'

'Where to?' Tid asked. He was still a little baffled. It seemed that Sheldon had saved his life.

Sheldon had no idea which direction they should take. His scouting of the tunnels had left him none the wiser. He wished he had the book, for then he could have used the map. 'This way,' he said, thinking it best to sound confident. 'We'll follow the pool for a bit.'

They began walking. The pencil cast enough of a glow to light their way.

Mysterious voices followed them.

'What's that?' Tid asked.

'Don't listen to them!'

'Not the voices.' Tid was pointing into the distance. There was something at the water's edge.

Cautiously, they approached.

It was Sofi's book.

'We could not find the entrance,' the Greenwich Guardian was saying, back at Old Father Tim's cottage.

'What do we do now?' Enderell asked, her voice tinged with panic.

'Keep searching,' the Greenwich Guardian replied.

'I think we should remember that we have no evidence to suggest that Sheldon has taken them against their will,' Zeit said forcefully, 'and in my professional opinion, I think it very unlikely that he has.'

'I think we should plan for the worst,' Bryn said quietly.

'I am not sure that is being fair to Sheldon,' Zeit argued.

'Fair to Sheldon!' Enderell exclaimed, too distressed to remember her manners. 'What about Tid and Sofi? Who is being fair to them?'

'We shall endeavour,' the Greenwich Guardian said, trying to calm Enderell, 'to do what is best for them all. We shall search for all three of them.'

'I know he has had his problems,' Zeit continued, 'but at heart Sheldon is a good lad.'

'He kidnapped Sofi once before!' Enderell said heatedly.

'For heaven's sake!' Zeit exclaimed. 'Is the poor boy never to be allowed to live that down? He was desperately unhappy at the time.'

'I think we are accomplishing nothing with this discussion, my friends,' the Greenwich Guardian said soothingly. 'Let us concentrate on what we do agree, namely that we must find Tid, Sofi *and* Sheldon as quickly as possible.'

Everyone murmured their agreement, although Enderell looked daggers at Zeit.

'As we are unable to find the entrance in the Old Father's workshop, we need to find another way into the Guardian tunnels.' The Greenwich Guardian looked around at them. 'Any ideas?'

'What about the Labyrinth?' Joss suggested.

'I have heard stories that this could be a possibility,' Bryn said. 'Do you think that the women would let us have a look around?'

'The one I spoke to,' Joss said, remembering the woman at the door, 'asked me in.'

The Greenwich Guardian looked shocked.

'But I didn't go,' Joss assured her.

'The Labyrinth is as good a place to start looking as any. I will go right away,' Bryn declared.

The Greenwich Guardian nodded. 'And I with you.'

'No,' Bryn said. 'It would not be safe. I will not draw attention to myself but, as a Guardian, you give off too much light.'

'Don't be ridiculous,' the Greenwich Guardian said dismissively. 'They will have lights down there. I shall not be noticed.'

'But the Old Father left you in charge,' Bryn said. 'You will be needed here.'

'Yes, Old Father Tim did leave me in charge,' the Greenwich Guardian said pointedly, 'and so I shall make the decisions. You cannot go into the Labyrinth alone. I understand that the women do not regard men too highly. You will need me to mediate. Zeit will be here to take care of things.'

'With the greatest respect,' Bryn insisted, 'he does not know the park.'

'I will help him,' Enderell said supportively.

'Then that's settled,' the Greenwich Guardian said before Bryn could answer. 'Bryn and I shall go to the Labyrinth.'

'And me.' It was Joss who had spoken.

'You will be needed here, helping Zeit,' the Greenwich Guardian said.

'Forgive me,' Joss said, 'I know it is not my place, but I don't think that you and Pa Brownal should go into the Labyrinth alone. I should come too.'

Joss knew he was bordering on being disrespectful, and he was sorry for it, but it was right that he should go. He knew he was destined to play an important role in future years. If he was to prove his worth, he had to face his share of dangers, just as the Greenwich Guardian had done in her youth.

'I must be allowed to come,' he said, fixing his eyes on the Greenwich Guardian.

There was a stunned silence. Joss was breaking all the rules, speaking out like this. Bryn was taken aback. Enderell was shocked. Zeit silently rejoiced: Joss must have more gumption than Zeit had suspected.

Joss knew that the Greenwich Guardian was the one he had to convince, which is why he now held her eyes with his own. Through his stare, he was trying to convey his determination to go. 'I will serve you better down there than up here,' he said resolutely. 'If you find a way through, you will need someone below ground who can . . .' how could he put it? '. . . who can stand his own ground if it comes to a conflict.'

'Conflict?' the Greenwich Guardian asked, concerned. 'The Guardian People were not made to fight.'

'No, I do not intend to fight,' Joss said. 'In a physical fight a Wrecca would always win, but conflict comes in many guises. In a mental conflict, I would say, Greenwich Guardian, that you have the upper hand.' Joss was not flattering her. The Greenwich Guardian was well known for her cleverness. 'But faced with a Wrecca who knows only violence, you and Pa Brownal would not stand a chance.'

'What do you intend to do if we are physically threatened?' Bryn asked dubiously.

'I'd be there,' Joss said simply. 'I know that a Wrecca would not be intimidated by my presence, but I am young and strong, and it might make him hesitate, and we could use that to our advantage.' He continued to look fixedly at the Greenwich Guardian.

She stood up. She had made her decision and she knew the others must obey. 'Bryn and I shall go.'

She paused.

'And Joss shall come with us.'

'Which way do we go now?' Sofi asked the shadow.

'Are you still determined to find this room of which you speak?'

'Yes, I am.'

'Are you sure this is wise?' the shadow persisted. 'Some places are best left undisturbed.'

'I don't want to get into the Gemetbur. I just want to stop Grandfather from trying.'

'Yes,' the shadow said, his voice sounding unstable even for a shadow. 'Terrible things can happen if you have the wrong key.'

'Really?' Sofi said eagerly. She had not mentioned a key. 'Do you know about the key?'

'I know nothing,' the shadow snapped. 'I will say no more about it.'

Sofi had the feeling that the shadow was actually frightened of the Gemetbur.

'But will you help me find it?' she asked in a quiet voice, and then quickly added, 'Just to keep Grandfather safe.'

'I have pledged my existence to keeping travellers safe,' the shadow said self-importantly.

'Grandfather and the others are travellers.'

'Then,' the shadow said gravely, 'I will help you.'

Tid and Sheldon hugged the shoreline of the pool. They walked briskly, trying to warm up as best they could. The book was drying out faster than they were. The meagre light from the pencil was not strong enough to examine it closely, but Sheldon could read the floating symbols and they gave him the outline of a route. They kept moving for they were both wet and cold.

After a while Tid spotted a light up ahead. What was it? It was hard to tell. He glanced at Sheldon, wondering if he had seen it too, but Sheldon was looking at the ground in front of his feet as he walked.

Tid stared ahead.

His heart started pounding.

Was this the trap?

18

A Light in the Dark

Were there Wreccas up ahead?

Tid looked at Sheldon once more. If he was expecting Wreccas as part of the trap he was planning, why was he not looking for them?

Tid had to make a decision and he had to make it now. Could he trust Sheldon or not? Undoubtedly Sheldon had saved him from the pool, but he might have done so in order to deliver Tid to the Wreccas, or he might have done it because he was actually trying to help.

In a moment the decision was made.

'Sheldon,' he whispered, grabbing his arm.

Sheldon looked up, immediately worried by Tid's tone. 'What's up?' he hissed back.

'Up ahead.'

Sheldon looked ahead. There was a light! That could only mean one thing.

'Sofi!' Sheldon exclaimed in an excited but quiet voice.

'Do you think?' Tid asked hopefully.

Sheldon nodded and started running towards the

glow. It became brighter and brighter. This light was coming from more than just a pencil.

Tid followed more cautiously.

Sheldon reached the light first. It was sitting on a jutting-out piece of flint, just where Sofi had put it. He took the glass orb in his hand and, lifting it so that it shed as much light as possible, he started peering about. 'Sofi!' he called out. 'Sofi!'

Tid arrived. 'Where was it?' he asked.

'Here,' Sheldon said, pointing to a large flint that stuck out from the wall. 'But she's not here.'

The familiar glow of the paperweight warmed Tid and made him feel more optimistic.

'It proves one thing,' Sheldon said. 'Sofi was this side of the pool, like I said.'

'How do we know it was Sofi who put it here?'

'Who else is in the tunnels? It's not as if the shadows could pick it up.'

'Why didn't she take it with her?'

'Perhaps she left it for us.'

'So why didn't she wait?'

'She probably thinks we're dead,' Sheldon said matter-of-factly.

'Dead? Both of us? Why?'

'Because she was standing on the shore when I went back for you.'

'You came back for me?' Tid was not sure he had heard correctly.

Suddenly Sheldon felt self-conscious. All his life he had craved recognition and attention; he had never really minded how he got it. To be a hero would have been exactly what he had always wanted. However, it felt different, having actually been the hero. With uncharacteristic modesty he said, 'It was Sofi's idea. Trust me, I didn't want to.'

This was the only way of saying it that Tid could believe. If Sheldon had basked in the glory of it all, Tid would have turned against him. Instead, he simply said, 'Thanks.'

Sheldon had not expected to be thanked. In fact, he had been drawing breath to call Tid an ungrateful, spoilt brat, but the words lodged in his throat. Instead, he said, 'That's all right.'

There was a moment's awkwardness.

'I'll take the paperweight.' Tid said.

'It's heavy. You look as if walking is about as much as you can do right now.'

Sheldon was right; Tid found every step a trial. He nodded his agreement and let Sheldon keep hold of the precious paperweight.

'You know,' Sheldon said, holding the paperweight in the palm of his hand as if he was weighing it, 'you couldn't have chosen a heavier light. Why did you?'

'Sofi said I shouldn't bring it, but I didn't see why she should tell me what to do.'

Sheldon smiled. 'She can be a bit of a pain sometimes.'

'You're not kidding.'

Sheldon's brow furrowed as a thought occurred to him. 'I wonder,' he said, looking at the paperweight.

'What?'

'I'm not sure.' He continued thinking, and then shook his head. 'I'd have to check the book to be certain.'

'Certain of what?'

'Nothing.' Sheldon made up his mind to keep this thought to himself. 'It can't help us now, anyway.' He held out the pencil towards Tid. 'Here, you have this, just in case we get separated.'

With a better light it was easier for Sheldon to translate the symbols in the book. Soon he had a route and they started walking once more.

The caves were changing now; the roofs were getting lower. In places they had to crawl on their hands and knees to get through. There was more water too; some of it trickled down the walls. There were pools of all sizes; not black, like the one they had tried to cross, but crystal clear and shallow. The boys could see the rocks beneath and yet they took care always to walk around. They pretended to each other that they did not want to get wet again, for they were beginning to dry out, but in reality they were frightened of encountering another shadow like the one of the Murky Deep.

Sheldon's stomach gave a particularly loud rumble as they stood up after scrambling through another low passageway. He grimaced. 'Are you as hungry as I am?'

Tid nodded. 'I'm starving. We should have brought some food with us.'

'Sofi was in something of a hurry,' Sheldon pointed out.

'It won't do much good if we die of starvation.'

'We're not going to die of starvation,' Sheldon said. He suddenly had a very strong feeling about this. 'We should have drowned, but we didn't. We'll get through.'

Tid looked at Sheldon in surprise. He had not taken him for the sort of lad who would be good in a difficult situation.

Sheldon was equally surprised, not because he was encouraging Tid, but because Tid seemed to believe him.

'It takes ages to die of starvation,' Sheldon added. 'We have plenty of water. That'll be enough.'

As if to prove the point, he went to a glassy pool and took a drink. The water tasted good, even though it was icy cold. Tid did the same. At least there would be something in his stomach.

'You's ready?' Offa Scratch asked, as Lorin stood in the Underneath behind rows of troops. It wasn't a polite enquiry; it was more of a demand.

She nodded weakly. What else could she do? He had already told her what he expected of her. He had tried to wrap it up, saying that he wanted to help the women; but Lorin knew better than that. Scratch was going to take control of the Labyrinth. The women were going to have to work for him. He wanted Lorin to convince them to do this, or Morlenni would suffer the consequences.

Lorin was in an impossible position. She could not give up all who lived in the Labyrinth for the sake of one terrified young woman now trembling in the bowels of the Underneath, but nor could she desert her friend. Lorin needed time. This was why she had agreed to help Scratch. In return for this help, Scratch had promised to keep Morlenni safe. Of course, Lorin knew that Scratch was not to be trusted, but she felt he would keep his word as long as he needed her. Thus, Morlenni was safe for the present. Lorin had bought a little time. She would pretend to cooperate, but was on the lookout for her chance. Offa Scratch was not all that clever. Given an opportunity, Lorin thought she could outsmart him. It was risky, but at least this way they all had a chance. Not much of one, but a chance nevertheless.

'Us is ready!' Offa Scratch hissed at Sniff.

Sniff nodded and passed the message to Slime, who alerted Scamp.

Scamp signalled to his men. 'Begin on my word,' he said. He had prepared them carefully. 'Ready?'

Everyone was poised. All eyes were fixed on him.

Offa Scratch marvelled at the way the diggers listened to Scamp and did what he said without Scamp having to resort to bullying or brutality; and it suddenly occurred to him that Scamp was more than irritating. Scamp was dangerous. He was a good leader, possibly better than Offa Scratch, and that made things very awkward. He could not risk having Scamp around when this was over. Offa Scratch made a mental note to do something about him at the first opportunity.

'Up and in!' Scamp shouted.

He spoke the three words in rhythm, and suddenly

the rock face was alive with activity. Not wanting to risk another accident, the diggers had listened to Scamp and now did as they had been told. Scamp had arranged them into lines. Three of his best workers were at the rock face. They lifted their pickaxes on the word 'up' and on the word 'in' they plunged them into the rock. Three Wreccas behind readied themselves; their job was to clear away the rock as it fell. Three behind them dumped the rock into tubs. Once full, they were dragged away and quickly replaced.

For Wreccas, this was an extremely well-organized affair. Those who could see watched in awe as Scamp kept the rhythm regular.

'Up and in. Up and in,' he chanted, although no one could hear the word 'in' because each time it was drowned by the deafening sound of axe on rock.

Slime waited nervously. This was his moment. He wiped his nose on his ooze-encrusted rag and eyed his troops. He thought they were magnificent, ragged and disorderly though they were. He ran over the plan in his mind. Offa Scratch had told him again and again that their task was to rush the Labyrinth in one mighty force, making a terrible din. The more frightened the women were, the easier they would be to round up. Some would be killed, of course, that was only to be expected, but Offa Scratch had impressed upon him the need to keep as many women alive as possible.

Slime wondered how it would go. In the heat of battle, the Wrecca instinct was to slaughter; could they be disciplined enough not to do this? He knew that Offa Scratch was holding him personally responsible for any mistakes. Only complete success would be acceptable.

There had been a lot of talk in the Labyrinth since Lorin had disappeared. The gossip was that she had been thrown out by Berwyth because of the names she had called her.

Lorin had never been openly admired until now – she was too different for that – but, as Tonic-Maker, she was valued. If her healing soils worked, the women felt favourably towards her, especially if it was one of their children she had helped. When they heard that she had been banished for nothing more than standing up to Berwyth and telling the Committee what everyone thought of them, they became angry.

However, all thought of Lorin disappeared as soon as the din of breaking into the Labyrinth started. Women held on to each other in fright. The sound of pickaxe on rock terrified them. Mothers ran hither and thither, collecting their children. Finally, when the first pickaxe was seen to splinter through the rock and into the Labyrinth, they panicked.

There was no plan, no organization and no chance for Berwyth or her Committee members to get away first. No one stopped to gather possessions; this was a moment for escape. Mothers grabbed the hands of their children and ran.

Offa Scratch, Lorin and Sniff stood at the back of the troops, waiting. The bulk of the force was supposed to enter the Labyrinth in a rush, secure the tunnels and trap the women. The rest would guard Offa Scratch while Lorin took him straight to the Committee Chamber. From there, he would assume command. He bounced on the balls of his feet, eyes blazing with excitement. Offa Scratch had waited a long time for this moment.

Once the diggers' pickaxes broke through, excitement sizzled through the troops. The anticipation was too much to contain. They trembled with eagerness. Palms that were tightly wrapped around their weapons began to sweat.

It seemed to be taking forever. The diggers could not be doing it right. How was it taking so long? Slime looked at his troops nervously. He knew it would be difficult to contain their excitement much longer.

It was not possible to tell who broke ranks first. As soon as one moved, all the Wreccas surged forward. Forgetting all discipline, they started tearing at the rocks with their bare hands, trampling whoever was in their way.

Scamp stood back. The plan had been for the diggers to continue with their pickaxes until the hole was big enough for the troops to pass through in large numbers. The hole was still too small, but the troops had already started pushing their way through. Scamp was unconcerned. He had done his part.

The hole was far too small. What was supposed to be a tidal wave of troops was only a trickle. One by one, men scrambled through and, instead of waiting for the others and attacking as a group, they ran off in all directions.

The slowness of the attack gave the women the opportunity to escape. By the time more troops had seeped through, the Labyrinth was deserted, although the men hardly noticed. They were wild with excitement. Beds, curtains and chairs were new and exciting to most of them and they could not suppress the urge to take whatever they pleased. They began to squabble over the spoils. Those who found themselves passing the kitchens could not resist the smell of cooking food and were soon eating themselves sick.

By the time he realized what was happening, it was too late. Offa Scratch's face turned red with ferocious fury, but being behind the troops he was not well placed to do anything useful to stop the disorderly advance. The clamour of the men as they surged forward, trying to claw their way through, drowned his roars of anger. There was nothing he could do to stop them. He grabbed at some of the nearest soldiers, lashing them with his nails and kicking them hard, but the damage was done. All control was lost.

Trembling with rage, Offa Scratch looked around, desperate to wreak his revenge on anyone. His eyes fell upon Scamp, who was standing to the side, unconcerned, picking at his fingernails.

In that moment, Offa Scratch hated him more than any other living creature. How he longed to wipe that look of calm off Scamp's face. How he ached to see fear in his eyes.

Lorin watched them both. She remembered Scamp from the days when she had lived in the Underneath. He had been different from the others, living in a world of his own and always fiddling with bits and pieces that he had scavenged from somewhere.

The most amazing thing about Scamp, though, was that he seemed totally unaware of some of the basic rules of survival. Most Wreccas, slow as they were, had worked out while still young that their leader was to be feared. Fear was a good thing; it made the leader happy. Although the fear was always genuine, it did no harm to exaggerate it. Scamp failed to understand this. He seemed to fear no one and did not bother to pretend that he did. Lorin had never worked out whether he was stupid or just different.

Right now, looking at Offa Scratch about to burst a blood vessel, Lorin could see that Scamp's nonchalant air was about to get him into serious trouble. It seemed to her that the Wrecca leader wanted to break a head, and it did not much matter whose head it was. He started towards Scamp.

'Scratch!' Lorin cried out, attempting to divert his attention. She had no idea what she was going to say.

Offa Scratch momentarily halted.

Scamp did not notice either of them.

'The women . . .' Lorin started lamely.

Offa Scratched turned to face her.

Her heart started beating wildly. She glanced at Scamp. If only she could catch his eye, but Scamp was now absorbed in biting a broken nail.

Offa Scratch was glaring at Lorin, his anger now concentrated upon her.

'The women'll be running away,' she said stupidly.

'Of course they'll be running away,' Offa Scratch hissed menacingly.

'Yer, and they can run two ways,' she said, thinking fast, trying to calm her trembling voice, 'either Topside or into the caves.'

With a shock, she suddenly realized that this was true. She could not believe that she was betraying the women for the sake of this one stupid Wrecca.

'If they go into the caves, they'll get lost,' she continued. 'They's scared to death of your troops and they willn't take no notice where they's running. They'll get lost and you'll never find them.'

Offa Scratch's expression turned from fury to distrust. What was she up to?

'If they go Topside, then us has got ages. They'll not go far cos they'll be scared of the size of it, and us can round them up later. But if they go deep into the caves, they'll get lost for sure. There's miles of them. The sooner you send someone into the caves to find them, the better.'

She stopped and waited. Would this work, or had she just betrayed the women for nothing? She desperately hoped that they had not gone deeper into the cave system. However scary the Topside appeared to them, it was at least open and therefore a better opportunity for escape.

'What's you saying?' Offa Scratch demanded threateningly.

'Oh, I doesn't know,' Lorin said. It was dangerous to sound too clever. 'I just thinked that you'll want them finded quick.'

Offa Scratch thought for a moment and then declared, 'That *is* what I think!' suddenly certain that it was his idea.

'You's so clever,' Lorin said, hardly daring to believe that she sounded convincing.

'Slime!' Offa Scratch yelled.

Slime had attempted to stop the troops when they first broke through but had been unable to do anything. Now he was trying to creep away and hide before Offa Scratch could punish him for the failure of his troops. On hearing his name, Slime halted. This was it. The end!

Strangely enough, Offa Scratch had momentarily forgotten about the pitiful display of his crack troops.

'Go and search the caves for the women!'

Slime could not believe his good fortune. 'Yer, sir!' he said as smartly as he knew how.

'Take a handful of men and get going!' Offa Scratch bellowed.

Slime bowed.

Lorin had manoeuvred her way nearer to Scamp. She now tugged at his grimy tunic and indicated with her eyes that she thought he should go with Slime.

Scamp could not work out what she wanted him to do.

Exasperated by his lack of understanding, Lorin pushed him after Slime. Scamp staggered in the direction that

Lorin had shoved. Unfortunately, it was not quite the direction that she had intended, and Scamp stumbled clumsily into his leader.

Offa Scratch's face, which had become slightly calmer, once again burned with savage rage. 'You!' he screamed.

'Yer, you lazy oaf!' Lorin started screaming too. She pushed Scamp after Slime. 'Do as your leader tells you and get after them women!'

Scamp was confused. This nice-looking young woman had suddenly turned into an animal and was yelling at him!

Lorin immediately turned her back on him and gazed up into Offa Scratch's livid face. She gave him a look containing as much concern as her racing heart would allow and said, 'Is you all right, Offa Scratch?' using his title for the first time.

Offa Scratch looked confused by her sudden change of manner.

She brushed an imaginary speck of dust off his shoulder and gave him a sweet smile. She just hoped Scamp was worth all this.

Not wanting to hang about, Slime growled, 'C'mon.' Taking hold of Scamp, he dragged him away.

Lorin heard Scamp's lumbering departure and gave an inward sigh of relief. She now waited in awkward silence as she stood in front of Scratch, not sure what to do next. 'I'll take you to the Committee Chamber,' she said at last.

Still perplexed by Lorin's helpfulness, Offa Scratch

agreed. 'The Committee Chamber, yer,' he said, trying to regain his authority.

Lorin's heart was beating furiously and her palms were clammy. She could not believe that Scratch had responded to her softness so readily. She hoped she would not regret what she had just done.

She led him through the Labyrinth, noting with joy that there were no women left to be captured. It seemed that she and Morlenni were the only ones in danger now.

19

In the Labyrinth

The Greenwich Guardian, Bryn and Joss hurried towards the Labyrinth. As they drew close, they heard a commotion up ahead.

Wrecca women were unexpectedly appearing, running wildly about, shielding their eyes from the sun, absolutely terrified. One held the hand of a small boy. He was crying. On seeing the Guardian and her two companions, the Wrecca women let out cries of fright and darted in all directions.

'The men must have broken through,' the Greenwich Guardian said.

'So it would seem,' Bryn agreed, watching yet more women running as if their lives depended upon it.

'What shall we do?' Joss asked as a child ran past him, screaming.

'We should continue,' the Greenwich Guardian said as the child's mother pelted past, sweeping the child up into her arms. 'But not you,' the Greenwich Guardian said to her brother. 'There are too many Wrecca women running all over the place. Some may take refuge in the park. This is going to cause havoc.

You are the park's Elder. You should remain here.'

'No, Grenya,' Bryn said, relieved to be able to stop his sister from accompanying them on the perilous journey below ground. 'There will be terrified women all over the park, and Greenwich too. It is as you said before, they will need a woman to organize them. This is your jurisdiction. You must be the one to stay.'

Lorin watched Scratch as he lay on Berwyth's couch. He was enthralled by what he saw as luxurious splendour. After rolling about for a while, he swung his legs over the edge and sat up, looking at Lorin. She tried to return his stare calmly.

'Supposing the women hasn't runned into the tunnels like you sayed?' he suddenly asked.

'I doesn't know,' she said, trying to keep her voice steady.

In a few short strides he was standing before her.

'You sayed that if they doesn't go into the tunnels, they'll go Topside.'

'I suppose so.'

Offa Scratch stared at her, trying to work out if she was up to something. Lorin was not like the other women; she was nicer than most. 'You's very pretty, you know,' he said in an oily voice.

Lorin had been expecting any manner of things that he might say, but not this.

'You can't be surprised,' he said in a voice that he intended to sound friendly but was, in fact, dangerously sweet. 'I's marked you out as special. You and I can rule this place. What has you to say about that?' He did not really mean it. Offa Scratch was the only one who would ever rule, but he thought it sounded good.

Lorin wanted to tell him exactly what he could do with his offer, but that would not help Morlenni. 'Really?' she asked, trying to sound interested.

Offa Scratch was encouraged. 'Of course,' he said. 'You and I together! What a team us'll make!'

The thought turned Lorin's stomach, but she forced a smile.

'Thing is,' Offa Scratch said, trying to sound thoughtful now, 'the women need to know that they's in no danger from us. You and I'll be good to them.'

Lorin said nothing, but continued to smile. She knew exactly where he was going with this but remained silent. He had to believe she was too stupid to work out what he wanted; this way he would think he could trust her. She waited patiently, trying to look agreeable.

'If they's in the tunnels, then Slime'll round them up,' Offa Scratch explained, 'but if they's Topside, they'll be spread all over. Someone'll need to let them know how good it'll be for them, back here. I wonder who I can ask.' Offa Scratch rolled his eyes upwards, trying to look as if he was thinking hard.

Lorin thought he looked ridiculous, but she waited in silence.

Offa Scratch gasped, as if a wonderful idea had just occurred to him. 'What about . . . no, I doesn't suppose . . . but maybe . . .' He tailed off.

'Yer?' Lorin asked innocently.

'What about you?' he asked.

'I?' Lorin asked, sounding flattered. She was mightily sick of this game, but she had to continue playing it. 'Does you think I's able?'

'Of course you is!' Offa Scratch exclaimed generously. 'And Sniff will go with you.' He wanted someone to keep an eye on her.

Unfortunately, Lorin dropped her guard. 'Sniff?' she said, unable to hide her alarm. She did not want an escort. 'Er . . . no, not Sniff,' she said clumsily.

Offa Scratch was instantly distrustful. 'Why not?'

'Cos . . .' She had to think of something fast. When she did, it was so simple that she almost laughed out loud. 'Cos the women willn't trust a man. I has to go alone or else it willn't work.'

Offa Scratch thought about this. She had a point. 'How does I know I can trust you?' he asked, reaching forward and trailing one of his carefully sharpened nails down her cheekbone.

Every nerve in Lorin's body was revolted, but she remained calm. 'Cos I want to rule with you,' she said simply, trying to look as if he was her hero.

Could he trust her? Offa Scratch did not know. But then, he had made her the most amazing offer of advancement. Who could refuse that?

'Very well,' he said.

She smiled sweetly.

'You's better be off,' he said.

Lorin smiled again and turned around, a little too eagerly.

Offa Scratch kept pace with her as she crossed the chamber. He had to be absolutely certain. 'You's best not forget that I still has Miss Simple. Her willn't want you to do nothing that might upset I.'

'Of course not,' Lorin said. 'Morlenni will be my maid when you and I rule.' She waited a moment. 'Can I leave?'

Offa Scratch looked at her through narrowed eyes. 'All right.'

He watched her push aside the curtain and exit.

'Sniff!' Offa Scratch shouted when he thought she was out of earshot. 'Follow her and report back what her does.'

Bryn and Joss approached the Labyrinth door with caution. It was open. There was no one about.

'It may be a trap,' Bryn warned.

'I'll check it out.'

Joss ran to the Labyrinth entrance and pressed his back against the wall beside the door. Very slowly, he peered inside. There was nobody there.

He beckoned to Bryn. 'All clear,' he said as soon as Bryn had joined him.

Cautiously, the two of them crept through the door and into the Labyrinth.

Bryn knew a little of what to expect. He was the Guardian expert on Wreccas, having studied them for much of his adult life. However, the interior was something of a revelation to Joss. He gawped at the tunnels that seemed to wind on forever. Flaming torches were fixed to the walls at regular intervals. Had Bryn not tugged at his sleeve to remind him that they had to be careful, he would have wasted a lot of time.

As far as they could see, the Labyrinth was deserted, but they could hear all manner of activity going on elsewhere.

'This way,' Bryn said. He had some idea of the layout. He knew nothing for certain, but he could work out the direction he thought they would need to take if the Labyrinth was going to join the Guardian tunnels.

Not only did they have to keep out of sight, they also had to take care that they could not be smelt; just as Wreccas smell to the Guardian People, so the Guardian People have a distinctive aroma that Wreccas notice. Thus Bryn and Joss had to be doubly careful.

They had crept along quietly for some time when Bryn suddenly hissed, 'In here!' and nipped behind a faded curtain. Joss followed, and together they crouched in the darkness, holding their breath.

Some Wreccas were noisily approaching. It sounded as if they were fighting over spoils. There was a lot of bad language, sounds of a struggle and, finally, a heavy thump. Suddenly, much to Bryn and Joss's alarm, a large and very ugly Wrecca burst backwards through the curtain and landed at their feet, unconscious.

The curtain flapped over the prostrate Wrecca. Bryn and Joss pressed themselves to the back of the alcove and waited in horrified astonishment, expecting the other Wreccas to pull the curtain back and check on the Wrecca they had just knocked out. Joss prepared to run for it. Bryn could only stare, wide-eyed, at the unmoving Wrecca, who was lying on his back. It looked as if his nose had been broken.

They listened carefully. An argument continued on the other side of the curtain, but now it was not so volatile. Knocking out one Wrecca had sorted the problem, and soon all was resolved. The other Wreccas made off with their booty. Bryn and Joss exchanged relieved looks. 'I think he's out cold,' Bryn whispered, looking at the fallen Wrecca. Neither had come so close to one before.

Joss lifted his robes so that they would not touch the lifeless man, and stepped over him.

The Wrecca groaned.

'Do you think we should help him?' Bryn asked.

'No,' Joss hissed. 'Hurry!'

Bryn had never before passed by someone who needed help.

'We have to keep moving,' Joss insisted.

Bryn nodded. 'My apologies,' he said to the Wrecca as he stepped over him. 'I hope you feel better soon.'

Joss pulled at Bryn's outer coat, and the two of them hurried down the tunnel towards more sounds of pillaging.

'We seem to be heading towards the worst of it,' Joss whispered.

'This is the way we need to go,' Bryn explained, moving ahead. Then, suddenly, he pulled back and flattened himself against the wall. Someone was coming. Joss immediately did the same. Fortunately, they were in the shadows between two flaming torches. They might be safe, so long as the approaching figure was more interested in his spoils.

Bryn and Joss froze, pressing themselves against the wall. This Wrecca would be able to smell them as well as see them. As soon as he rounded the corner, they would be captured. There was no time to run for it.

As the Wrecca came into view, snuffling and sniffing, they saw that he was carrying an enormous bundle of curtains and clothing in his arms. On his head he wore a saucepan, his hands being too full to carry it the usual way. He was obviously scavenging as much as he could to take back to the Underneath and did not seem to notice Bryn and Joss.

They suddenly realized why. The Wrecca's eyes were tight shut and he was dragging in a long, shuddering breath. Then he unexpectedly threw his head back, causing the saucepan to crash to the ground as an ear-splitting sneeze exploded from him. The sounds bounced off the walls and echoed down the tunnel. Bryn shut his eyes as the sneeze splattered all over him.

Without taking the time to look about him, the Wrecca instantly spun round to retrieve his saucepan while wiping his dripping nose on his filthy sleeve. He dropped his precious bundle as he tried to ram the saucepan once more on to his head. Then he grabbed his scavenged possessions and took off without once looking around.

He had not noticed them.

'He's got a cold!' Joss murmured, amused. He handed

Bryn a handkerchief. There was no way a Wrecca could smell them through a heavy cold. Bryn wiped his face, which wore an expression of utter revulsion.

'Come on,' Joss urged.

Bryn put the handkerchief in one of his many pockets and hurried off.

The further they penetrated the Labyrinth, the worse the disorder and the louder the clamour. Wreccas were in every direction.

'If we get caught now,' Joss said uneasily, 'we shall be no use to Sofi and Tid.'

'We're not going to get caught,' Bryn whispered. 'They're preoccupied with whatever they are fighting over.'

'But they'll smell us.' They could not hope that all Wreccas would have colds.

'No they won't.'

Joss looked confused, but then Bryn sniffed in an exaggerated manner, to give Joss the idea of sniffing.

'Of course!' Joss breathed.

They were approaching the kitchen, where there were open fires over which hung pots of steaming stew. There were also ovens, where potatoes were baking. Although the food did not smell as delicious as Guardian cooking, it smelt mighty fine to a Wrecca. Surely this must mask any Guardian odour.

The shadow was good company. It spoke of the times when it was alive and, although it was inclined to waffle on a bit, much of what it said was interesting. Every now and then it would waft through Sofi to keep her warm. If her heart had not been so weighed down by the loss of Tid and Sheldon, she might almost have enjoyed herself.

They walked for what seemed like miles. The territory was changing: there were more pools and lower ceilings. Sofi had to duck to get through. However, whatever the obstacle, the shadow never stopped chattering. She felt that she must be the first person to have listened to it in centuries. It appeared to be unburdening itself of years of unvoiced thoughts, and so, when it suddenly fell silent, Sofi was not sure what had happened. At first, she thought it had just run out of things to say, but after another moment or two she felt something was wrong.

'What's the matter?'

'I go no further,' the shadow said mysteriously.

'Why?'

'This is as far as we shadows go, if we wish to remain shadows.'

'What do you mean?'

'Exactly what I said,' it retorted a little petulantly. 'I have already come further than I intended. I shall leave you here.'

'How will I know the way without you?' Sofi asked anxiously.

'Just keep walking straight ahead.'

'These mines twist and turn all over the place. I'll never know what is straight ahead.'

'These are not mines,' the shadow replied. 'We have

left the mines behind. These are caves. Ancient caves.'

Sofi was feeling distinctly uneasy. 'And the Gemetbur is up there?' she asked.

'I never said anything about a Bemetgur!' the shadow replied unhelpfully. 'I do not know Guardian names for strange rooms, but there is something up there that needs to be avoided.' It sounded even more concerned. 'You promise me you are not going to try and get into it.'

'No. I just want to stop Grandfather from trying, that's all. Then we go home.'

'Well, if that is what you intend, the Bemet . . . Meget . . .'

'Gemetbur,' Sofi said helpfully.

'Yes, that,' the shadow said, trying to hide its loss of dignity, having got the name wrong, 'may or may not be up there. I know nothing for certain!'

Although Sofi felt this was not the time to be faint-hearted, the thought of continuing alone was very frightening. If only the shadow would be more definite.

It must have sensed her unease. 'Look,' it said in a softer voice, 'I could take you back, if you like. Not to the door where you came in – I know nothing about secret Guardian doors – but I could take you to one of the openings that the Humans use. It might be a long way from your home, but you would be safer above ground.'

Sofi thought for a moment. She was tempted to accept. She had taken so long trying to reach the Gemetbur that she feared she might already be too late.

'What's that?' Sofi suddenly asked, cocking her head to one side and listening. 'I hear talking.'

The shadow was silent for a moment. 'It's up ahead.'

'Grandfather!' Sofi exclaimed in delight.

'Ssh!'

Sofi froze.

'Stay here. Hide the light. I'll be back.'

Sofi tucked the ruler inside her tunic and waited. It did not feel to Sofi that anyone had left her, just as there had never been a proper sense of anyone being with her. Soon it was back.

'There's a group of them,' it whispered, 'back there.'

'That'll be Grandfather and his friends,' Sofi said excitedly.

'What does he look like, this grandfather of yours?'

'He's old, very old, with a short, white, grizzly beard, a long coat that sometimes shimmers blue, and he carries a staff.'

'I did not see anyone like him. All I saw was an unkempt, filthy group of men, carrying shovels and the like.'

'Filthy?' Sofi asked nervously.

'Absolutely! I have never seen any mortals more untidy.'

Sofi felt a chill in her heart. 'Oh no,' she whispered to herself. 'Do they smell?'

'How would I know?' the shadow asked a little indignantly.

'I'm sorry,' Sofi apologized.

'Who are they?'

'The enemy.'

'Not my enemy.'

'But these people are bad.'

'Who is to say who is good or bad?' the shadow asked philosophically.

'We have to go back,' Sofi said, not willing to get into a debate about it. She pulled out the ruler so that she could see where she was going and started jogging the way they had come.

Sofi had been born a Wrecca. When she had run away, she had taken the Tick with her and had returned it to Old Father Tim. If the Wreccas caught her now, she knew she must expect the worst possible treatment. To keep her safe above ground she, like all the other Guardian children, had been taught a Guardian charm for protection. She did not, however, expect it to work if she was caught below ground.

Sofi ducked behind a pillar. 'Are they still coming?' she whispered.

There was moment's silence while the shadow went to find out. It was soon back. 'Yes, but they are so busy arguing that they are not moving very fast.'

Sofi knew they would arrive eventually. She had no choice now but to go straight ahead into the ancient caves.

'Let's keep going.'

The shadow did not answer.

'Aren't you coming with me?'

'I am at the limit now. I can come no further.'

'All right.' Sofi spoke softly. 'Just do one thing for me.'

'Of course.'

'Slow them down if you can.'

'I am a good shadow,' it said indignantly.

'I am not asking you to lure them to their deaths or anything, just slow them down so that I can get away.'

'That I shall do,' the shadow said, sounding as if he was looking forward to the prospect. Good shadows missed out on a lot of entertainment because they did not abuse their invisibility by scaring defenceless travellers. 'Good luck,' it whispered.

'Thank you,' Sofi said. 'I've enjoyed talking to you, and if I get out of this, I'll come and talk to you whenever I can.'

'You must not do that. You would never know if you were talking to me or to one of the other shadows.'

'I won't put myself at risk, I promise. I could come down with my grandfather. He is far too wise to be tricked by a shadow. Do you have a name?'

'I shall not give it to you, because you must not come here again. Have you not realized by now that it is not safe down here for people like you? I would not forgive myself if you came to harm. I will never forget your kindness. Just remember me as your friendly shadow.'

Sofi instinctively knew it was no good pressing him. She felt him wafting through her a couple of times to give her warmth.

'Thank you for everything,' she said.

'It was a pleasure, my friend.'

Sofi waited for a moment and drew breath to speak, but somehow she knew it was no good. The shadow had gone.

With a resigned sigh, she peeped out from behind the pillar. She could hear voices. There was no time to linger. She sprinted off.

Now she was truly on her own. When living in the Underneath she had been used to being by herself; in fact, she had sought solitude. Since moving Topside she had learnt to enjoy company. Now, to find herself completely alone was very frightening.

On she went. The tunnels were getting wetter and lower all the time. She hoped she was keeping straight ahead but, without any specific landmarks, it was hard to tell.

Then suddenly she heard a whoop and some yelling behind her. Wrecca feet were pounding the rough floor. The Wreccas were running. Had they caught sight of her, or had the shadow made a mistake and chased them towards her?

Sofi ran flat out.

She was a fast runner and did not fall into the trap of wasting time by turning around to look. She knew she had to go straight ahead, and this is what she now did. If a pool was in the way, she splashed on through it. She did not think about there being a shadow lurking in the depths. She paid no heed to the noise she was making. Nothing mattered, other than to outrun the Wreccas.

She dashed on, clutching her light, dodging the pillars and ducking under low roofs. She gasped for breath but did not stop. Every last ounce of energy was put into moving fast, straight ahead.

When, finally, she saw a glow in the distance, she took no notice at first. She was exhausted. It was only to be expected that her eyes might play tricks on her. But the glow became stronger and, as it did, she recognized it.

Only one thing glowed like that.

'Grandfather!' she yelled as she splashed through yet another pool.

The Guardians looked up in stunned surprise. Old Father Tim was too astonished to move or say anything. Instead, he stood still as Sofi crashed into him, plunging her face into his robes and flinging her arms round his thick waist.

He hugged her. Wakaa and Aleyesu stared at her in amazement.

'My granddaughter,' Old Father Tim explained to Aleyesu. Then he pulled Sofi away from him and looked into her face. 'What are you doing here?'

Sofi would not be held apart from him. She gripped him all the tighter and pressed the side of her face against him as she gasped for breath.

'How did you get here?' Wakaa asked, perplexed.

Sofi was not really hearing them. All she could think of was that Grandfather had not yet found the Gemetbur. She was in time and no longer alone.

'Sofi.' Her grandfather was talking to her again. 'What are you doing here?'

Sofi dragged her mind back to reality and suddenly remembered the danger. Looking up at him, she gasped, 'We have to go.' She released her grip and started to move.

The Guardians did not follow.

'You have to hurry,' she urged them, taking her grandfather's hand. 'There are Wreccas back there, and they're coming this way.'

'No, my dear,' Old Father Tim said patiently. 'These are Guardian tunnels. We have not come across any sign of Wre–'

'They are coming,' she insisted.

Wakaa looked up. He could hear footsteps. 'I think Sofi may be right.'

'I am!' she declared, pulling at her grandfather's hand. 'Run!'

20

Wreccas Topside, Guardians Below

Lorin walked away from the Labyrinth, trying to resist the urge to pick up her skirts and run. She knew what she was going to do, but she had to do it carefully. Scratch had allowed her to leave the Labyrinth, but she knew he did not trust her. Someone had to be on her tail. Probably Sniff. If she put on a good act and made it look as though she was doing as she had been told, she thought that Morlenni would be safe for the moment.

Lorin called out as she searched. 'Caryd!' she shouted so that Sniff could hear. 'Falryd!'

She searched in the direction of the park because that was the way she wanted to go. She guessed she would bump into some of the women eventually, but did so sooner than expected.

A terrified group were huddling behind a garden wall, clinging to each other in fright. None of them had ever been Topside before, and they were not only terrified but were also suffering from too much oxygen in the air. Consequently, they were feeling dizzy. When they heard Lorin calling, they let out a whoop of delight, broke cover and dashed towards her. Lorin knew about the Topside. She would tell them what to do.

Falryd and Falwyth talked noisily so that neither could be heard, and Dyran grumbled about how cold she was. It was only Caryd, holding tightly on to her daughter Gytha's hand, who explained to Lorin how the men had broken through and everyone had run away.

Lorin peered over her shoulder so that she could work out where Sniff was. Carefully positioning herself so that her back was towards him, she put her finger to her lips. 'Ssh.'

The women's talking died away.

'Us is going to have to be clever if us is going to beat the men,' Lorin said.

The women agreed noisily, but they simmered down when Lorin put her finger to her lips again.

'The men'll come Topside tonight.'

The women reacted badly to this, crying out and looking around.

'But do as I say,' Lorin quickly said, 'and they willn't come near you.'

They listened intently. They were used to being told what to do.

'If you keep going down this road, you'll come to a pond. Beyond it is a big stretch of grass. Cross that grass and you'll come to a tall wall with gates. Go through the gates and you'll be in the park.'

The women's eyes grew large with fright as they understood that Lorin was telling them to go into Guardian territory!

'You'll be safe in the park,' Lorin said. 'Once there, keep going until you find another pond just over that way,' she waved her right hand, 'and wait by it. Someone will come and keep you safe.'

'I's not going to the park!' Dyran exclaimed.

'Neither is I!' Falryd cried.

'Do you want to be taked by the men?' Lorin snapped.

They silently shook their heads.

'Then you has to do what I says.'

'B . . . but . . .' stammered Caryd, 'what about the Guardian People?'

'They willn't hurt you. They's got it in for the men, not the women.'

They did not believe her. The Guardian People were the enemy.

'They's got no quarrel with us,' Lorin continued.

'How does you know?'

'Cos I's been watching them for years. They's all right if you know how to handle them.'

'Handle them!' Dyran shouted. 'Does you think you can handle them?' She knew that the Guardian People were far too clever ever to be 'handled' by a Wrecca.

'It's not hard,' Lorin said. 'I know one of them.'

'Know one!' Dyran was appalled.

'Her name is Enderell,' Lorin spoke quickly, 'and her's a good'un. Us can trust her.'

'You can't trust none of them,' Dyran scoffed.

'That's not true!' Lorin said vehemently. 'Look, I know them better than you. Guardian women help other women, no matter if they's Wreccas or not. Her's my friend, and her'll be your friend too if you let her.'

They stared at her disbelievingly.

'Her'll feed you,' Lorin said temptingly.

'Ooh!' Gytha exclaimed. She was hungry. The women looked slightly interested. It was well known that the Guardian People ate well.

'What about Scratch and his men?' Dyran asked.

'They willn't dare come near, once you are with Enderell. You know they's scared of the Guardian People.'

'So am I,' Gytha said in a small voice.

'You doesn't have to be, little one,' Lorin said, gently touching her cheek. 'Enderell's really nice and her makes the best tea.'

'Has you drinked it?' Gytha asked excitedly.

'It was delicious.' She ran her tongue around her lips as if to emphasize the point.

Without knowing they were doing it, the women ran their tongues over their lips as if trying to imagine the taste.

'You has to tell every Wrecca woman you see that us is meeting by the pond,' Lorin pressed on. She was losing time.

'I'll tell them,' Caryd said.

Dyran looked up at her in disgust. 'Why's you helping her?'

'Cos them men taked my little Oryth. Him was only a little'un. This time they'll take my Gytha too.' She gripped her daughter's hand more tightly. 'I's not giving up another child, not to them, not to nobody.'

'They taked both my boys,' Dyran said resentfully. 'I never seed them again.' She looked at Caryd, and resolve settled across her face. 'I'll help.'

Then they looked at Falryd and Falwyth.

'All right, all right,' they said together. 'But you's better be right about this, Lorin.'

'I is,' Lorin replied. 'Now, spread out and tell everyone.'

'What about Berwyth?' Falryd asked. 'I's not doing all this so that she can come back afterwards and lord it over us again.'

Lorin knew what she was going to say but, if Berwyth ever found out, she would be in the worst trouble. It was time to risk everything.

'Berwyth's day is done.'

The women were stunned.

'In fact, the Committee's done too,' she expanded. 'When us is back in the Labyrinth, there'll be a new order.'

The women liked the sound of that.

'Now hurry.'

Caryd quickly started directing where they should go. Lorin watched, rather impressed by her efficiency, thinking that it was a pity that Berwyth had never invited her on to the Committee, but Berwyth only promoted flatterers.

Falryd and Falwyth darted off in one direction and Dyran in another. Caryd, still holding Gytha's hand, looked back at Lorin. 'What's you going to do?' she asked.

Lorin looked at Caryd. She was going to trust her with the truth.

'I's going to tell Sniff, who, by the way, is hiding over there, spying on us.'

Both Caryd and Gytha began turning their heads.

'Don't look!' Lorin quickly hissed.

They immediately stopped, resolutely holding their heads still. Lorin continued. 'I'll tell him that I's rounding all the women up. That'll get rid of him cos him'll want to report back to Scratch straight away. Then I has to find Enderell and tell her that the women'll be turning up.' She took a deep breath. 'And then I's going to the Underneath.'

Caryd was horrified. 'Why?'

'They's taked Morlenni. I has to rescue her.'

'Isn't that dangerous?' Caryd asked fearfully.

'I has to try.'

Old Father Tim passed Sofi a sandwich. Telling her grandfather that Tid and Sheldon had been drowned was the worst experience of her young life. She accepted the blame because she had been the one to insist that they cross the pool, and then she had persuaded Sheldon to go back to rescue Tid. She did not spare herself as she told her grandfather everything.

Old Father Tim heard her words with mounting anguish and hugged her close. For once, he had no words of comfort.

'Why was I not shown this book?' Aleyesu asked.

'It is only a children's book,' Wakaa explained.

'Any book could be important,' Aleyesu said.

'But now it's lost too,' Sofi said, trying to hold back her tears. 'I'm sorry, Grandfather.'

Old Father Tim said nothing but hugged her tighter. A tear seeped from his eye.

'Eat your food,' Aleyesu encouraged her.

Sofi took a bite but was too miserable to enjoy it.

'Do the Chronicles give us any more clues to the Gemetbur's whereabouts?' Wakaa asked.

Aleyesu shook his head. 'I stopped using it a while back. I was convinced that the route to the Gemetbur was within those pages, as well as instructions on how to get in, but it is simply not there. We are here by my calculations. Who wrote your book, Sofi?'

'Thadius Thead.'

'Interesting,' Aleyesu said.

'It says that the Gemetbur could only be entered in one special way, and if you try to do it the wrong way, then you will never see the light of day again.' She looked up at her grandfather. 'That's why we came, we had to tell you.'

'But it is only a storybook,' Wakaa said.

'Yes, but I had never read that bit before,' and then she quickly added, 'I mean, I had read it, lots of times, but . . .' this was a strange thing to have to say, '. . . I don't think it was there before. Somehow I had either not been reading it right or it just appeared out of the blue.' She looked at the Guardians. 'Does that sound crazy?'

'Not at all, young lady,' Aleyesu said. 'Does it tell us how to enter?'

'It says there's a key and only those with . . .' she tried to remember exactly, '. . . deep insight would able to find it and use it.'

'But it is just a children's story,' Wakaa reminded them again. 'You said yourself, Sofi, that it may have been there all along and you had read it incorrectly.'

'It told us the entrance was in Grandfather's workshop,' Sofi said boldly. 'Sheldon read the symbols in the border around the page. He said that they floated.'

'Floated?' Aleyesu was deeply interested.

'Yes, this far from the page,' and Sofi demonstrated. 'He sort of wiggles his fingers. That's how we found the trapdoor.'

'He read that from Thead's book?' Wakaa asked, amazed.

'I had no idea that he had the gift,' Aleyesu said. 'I should like to see this book.'

'But I think it may have been a trick,' Sofi said gloomily. 'Tid worked out that Thadius Thead is an anagram of "Thus aid death". Everything went wrong after that.'

'Are we are talking about Thadius Plemet-Thead?' Wakaa asked.

'That's what Enderell called him.'

'Then it is no trap. He was very well respected in my day. His writings have been around for a long time. I remember my grandfather reading them to me.'

'We must move on,' Aleyesu said, rising to his feet.

'Grandfather.' Sofi spoke softly to the old man.

Old Father Tim had not heard anything they had said. He just sat, staring into nothing.

'We must go,' she said gently.

Old Father Tim nodded. He stood with effort, leaning heavily on his staff.

Sofi thought he looked much older. She took hold of his hand.

Aleyesu led the way.

'How do you know which way to go?' Sofi asked.

'I have to trust my own judgement,' Aleyesu said.

The landscape changed once more. The glassy pools became less and less frequent and the ceilings were of a uniform height just above Aleyesu's head.

The light was good because the Guardians generated their own, but Sofi still clutched the wooden ruler in her hand. Every now and then, Aleyesu stopped and felt the wall with his hand, trying to read the signs.

They found they were constantly slowing down so that Old Father Tim could keep up. Sofi kept a firm grip on his hand and tried to pull him along.

Suddenly they heard movement from behind. It was hard to tell how far away it was because of the echoes, but it sounded like feet running towards them.

'The Wreccas!' Sofi gasped.

'Quick,' Aleyesu said.

Old Father Tim looked at Sofi and smiled. He kissed her on the forehead and put her hand into Aleyesu's.

'I cannot run,' he said. 'I am too tired.'

'No!' Sofi cried.

'I will hold them for as long as I can,' he said. 'You will have to go on without me.'

Sofi wriggled her fingers out of Aleyesu's grasp and threw her arms around her grandfather.

'Old Father,' Wakaa said, 'you can go faster. You must!'

Old Father Tim smiled at Wakaa and shook his head. Then he unfastened Sofi's hands, which were tightly clasped behind his back, and brought them round to the front. 'Sofi, I love you,' he said.

She stifled a sob.

'But you must prove your love for me by doing as I ask.'

Sofi nodded.

The sound of running feet was getting louder.

'There's no time for this,' Wakaa said in a voice full of concern.

Aleyesu took Sofi's hand. With a respectful nod to the Old Father, he started running.

Sofi stumbled along behind him, all the while looking back at Old Father Tim. Only when he was lost from sight did she face the front and run.

Old Father Tim gripped his staff and closed his eyes. He knew his magic would be of limited use down here, but he would do his best. The sound of running was louder. He was glad it was all over. It was a pity that he would not be there either to see Sofi grow up or to greet his son on his return, but it was a relief to know that he would not be the one to tell his son that *his* only son had died. Most of all, he was thankful that he would not have to return to his cottage without Tid. He did not think he would have the strength to do that.

He opened his eyes and walked a short distance back down the tunnel. The footsteps were coming closer. He gripped his staff in both hands. He believed he could call upon enough magic to hinder the Wreccas for a moment. Any delay could give the others the chance to escape.

The footsteps were almost upon him. It did not sound as if there were too many. Preparing himself, he took a deep breath.

He could see the glow from their torches. They were just round the bend.

Then suddenly they were upon him, except that it was only one person. Old Father Tim raised his staff and shouted, 'Geweald of lyfte!'

A blast of unseen power surged from his staff and blasted a figure off its feet. It sprawled backwards across the ground and lay prostrate on the floor.

Old Father Tim did not waste any time. He could hear someone else approaching. He knew that a second blast would not be so powerful; it took time for the magic to build up again. He brandished his staff in the direction of the prostrate body, ready for the next attacker, who sounded close. He drew breath to utter the incantation.

The body groaned. Old Father Tim's attention was momentarily taken by it. He thought he was seeing things. He lowered his staff and took a step towards it.

'Tid?'

It took a moment for him to believe his eyes.

'Tid!'

Tid lay unconscious on the ground.

Old Father Tim hurried to his side and knelt down. Unable to comprehend how this had happened, he tenderly took his grandson into his arms and held him close.

'No time for this,' Sheldon said, dashing past. 'They're right behind us.'

Old Father Tim looked up in astonishment. 'Sheldon?' he murmured, totally baffled.

Although surprised to see Old Father Tim, Sheldon knew how close the Wreccas were. He could see that Tid was out cold, and he expected the old man to pick him up and follow. When he did not, Sheldon rushed back, grabbed Tid out of the old man's arms and hoisted him on to his own shoulder. He pocketed Aleyesu's pencil that had fallen from Tid's hand. 'No time to hang about,' he said. 'It's just up here.'

Old Father Tim was still bewildered. What did Sheldon mean?

'You have to come now!' Sheldon yelled, totally disregarding the usual Guardian code of politeness. He tugged at Old Father Tim's sleeve. 'Wreccas are chasing us!'

Old Father Tim pulled himself together. Normally rational and dependable in an emergency, the old man had allowed personal emotion to cloud his mind. The mention of Wreccas brought him back to reality.

'I'm right behind you,' he said to Sheldon as he used his staff to help himself stand.

'There's a place we can hide, just round the corner.'

Old Father Tim looked questioningly at Sheldon.

'I have a map,' the youth added by way of explanation as he raced on with Tid over his shoulder.

Old Father Tim followed. He was not exactly running, but he was moving faster than he had in years.

Just around the bend, Sheldon stood back and pointed to an alcove. 'In there!' he yelled.

Old Father Tim hurried into the alcove and Sheldon followed him, pushing him to the back. 'We can't let them see your light,' he said, standing in front of the old man and pocketing the paperweight. It hung heavily there.

They waited.

'What the . . .?' Tid was beginning to come round.

'Sssh.'

Six or seven Wreccas hurtled around the corner. They were running flat out in hot pursuit. Two of them were holding flaming torches, and one a shovel. They did not expect Tid and Sheldon to be hiding, so they did not bother to look, and they rushed past the alcove without a thought and were quickly out of sight.

'Grandfather?' Tid said in a bewildered voice as Sheldon put him down. His legs were shaky.

Old Father Tim hugged his grandson tightly. 'I thought you were dead,' the old man murmured.

'Why?' Sheldon asked.

'Sofi said so.'

'Sofi?'

'You've seen her?' Tid asked. 'Is she all right?'

'She is fine.'

Ever since he had lost Sofi, Sheldon had had a knot of wretchedness deep in his stomach. To hear that she was alive and well brought a lump to his throat. He quickly looked away because he did not want the others to notice how he was feeling.

'Where is she?' Tid asked anxiously.

'Up ahead with the others,' Old Father Tim replied. Then, suddenly, he looked horror-struck. 'Oh no,' he gasped. 'Wreccas are heading straight for them!'

Enderell's Draught

Lorin did not stop to pound on the door; instead, she flung it open and dashed straight into Old Father Tim's kitchen. The Greenwich Guardian was sitting at the kitchen table, talking to Enderell, Ma Brownal and Ma Connal. They were discussing what food they could provide once the Wrecca women started arriving.

When Lorin burst into the room, the Guardian women looked up in stunned surprise.

'The men's breaked through and the women's runned away. They's all over the place. I telled them to meet at the pond in the park. I hope that's all right. I sayed that you,' she nodded to Enderell, 'will tell them what to do. I's sorry I didn't say you,' she now looked at the Greenwich Guardian, 'but I thinked they'd be too scared to meet up with a real Guardian.'

'The pond in the park?' the Greenwich Guardian asked.

'Yer. I's sorry to send them there, but Scratch wants them back and I thinked it best to get them as far away from him as possible.'

'You did right,' the Greenwich Guardian said.

'What are we to do with them?' Enderell asked, a little alarmed.

'I sayed you'll feed them,' Lorin said. 'I hope that's all right, too. They'll be scared of you, of course, but they love their food and I can't think of no better way to calm them down, specially the children. They's never tasted anything like the food you make. Then,' she paused to think what else she should say but realized she had told them everything, 'keep them here till I can work out what to do,' she finished lamely.

'I'll give them one of my draughts,' Enderell said. 'It will make them sleep. That will give us some time.'

'Good idea,' the Greenwich Guardian agreed.

'I'll go and fetch it now,' Enderell said, standing up.

'You has to meet the women by the pond,' Lorin reminded her.

'I cannot,' Enderell said. 'I must make haste to the Hither House.'

'I shall go for you,' the Greenwich Guardian offered.

'No, I will have to do some final mixing.'

'Us doesn't have time for mixing,' Lorin said anxiously.

'I shall be quick.'

The Greenwich Guardian took command. 'Lorin, you and I will have to go to the pond to talk to the women while we wait for Enderell to return with her draught.'

'Ner, I has to go to the Underneath.'

They all stared at her in disbelief. 'The Underneath?'

'Yer. Scratch has taked a friend of mine. Her's scared half to death. I has to get her out.'

'But how?' the Greenwich Guardian asked.

Lorin suddenly realized that she did not have the least idea. She lifted up her hands and let them fall in a gesture of hopelessness. 'I doesn't know.'

'Is it wise to be walking into the Underneath unprepared?'

Lorin was disappointed. She had thought that the Greenwich Guardian would understand. 'I has to try.'

'Of course you do,' the Greenwich Guardian agreed. 'But let us think for a moment. You cannot do this alone.'

'Does you want to come too?' Lorin asked drily.

'No, she doesn't,' Enderell answered quickly, afraid that the Greenwich Guardian might agree. 'Wait for me to prepare my draught. It will help there as well.'

'How?' both Lorin and the Greenwich Guardian asked together.

'If you slip it into their water, I guarantee that whoever drinks it will be asleep within minutes.'

'How can I get the men to do that?' Lorin questioned.

'We shall think about that in a minute,' the Greenwich Guardian said, anxious to send Enderell on her way. 'Meanwhile, Enderell, you go as fast as you can to the Hither House. Lycian,' she turned to Ma Brownal, 'you two will have to organize the food alone.'

'For how many?' Ma Brownal asked.

The Greenwich Guardian looked at Lorin questioningly.

'A lot,' Lorin said, not being able to count that far, 'and they'll all eat loads, specially the little'uns.'

Ma Brownal nodded. Then she and Ma Connal quickly left.

'Come on, Lorin,' the Greenwich Guardian said. 'You and I must go to the pond.'

'But I sayed that Enderell'll meet them there,' Lorin objected.

'You and I will do it instead,' the Greenwich Guardian explained, taking her staff and preparing to leave. 'You can tell them Enderell is delayed. They will believe you.'

Lorin hesitated. 'You can't come,' she said.

'Why not?'

'They willn't trust a Guardian.' She felt awkward saying this and quickly added, 'No offence.'

'They do not have to know that I am a Guardian,' the Greenwich Guardian explained. 'I shall leave my staff behind and you will introduce me as Grenya.'

Aleyesu skidded to a halt. Sofi could not stop in time and crashed into him. Wakaa brought up the rear and bumped into the pair of them. When they had steadied themselves, they stood looking at the wall that barred their way.

'A dead end,' Sofi said with rising panic.

'I am sorry,' Aleyesu apologized.

They fell silent. Each was thinking the same thing: how long until the Wreccas were upon them?

They did not have long to wait. Skidding round the corner came one, two, three, four Wreccas, who collided with the Guardians and Sofi and landed in a tangled mess on the floor.

Trying to seize the advantage, Aleyesu unscrambled himself from the Wrecca heap, grabbed Sofi and started to run back up the tunnel. Immediately they ran slap into two more Wreccas, who seemed more prepared and grabbed them both. Aleyesu was no match for them.

'Oh my!' Slime exclaimed, panting hard. 'A Guardian!' But as his eyes rested on Sofi, his face broke into a spiteful grin. 'Miss Topside!'

Sofi shrank back into the folds of Aleyesu's robes. He put his arms round her protectively.

The other Wreccas were pulling themselves together and scrambling to their feet, pulling Wakaa up with them.

'Doesn't you look different,' Slime said to Sofi. 'Wait till Offa Scratch claps eyes on you.' He moved towards her threateningly.

Aleyesu lifted his staff and drew breath to shout an incantation. He intended to hit Slime at point-blank range but, before he knew it, Slob and Stench had wrestled the staff out of his hands. At the same time, Wakaa's staff was wrenched from him.

Slime took hold of Sofi. Aleyesu tried to keep hold of her, but Spit roughly pinned Aleyesu's arms behind his back.

'How's you been, Snotty Snot?' Slime asked in a spiteful, sing-songy sort of voice.

Sofi stamped her heel as hard as she could on to Slime's foot. He cried out in pain and bent down to take hold of it.

Taking her advantage, Sofi ran for it, but she had taken no more than two steps before a pair of hands grabbed the tunic at the back of her neck and stopped her. She gulped as the material bit into her windpipe and made her cough.

'Not so fast,' Sick sneered.

While Sofi was making her bid for freedom, Aleyesu and Wakaa were slammed against the wall by triumphant Wreccas and pinned there. The Guardians could neither move nor attempt any magic.

'What is Offa Scratch going to say when I turn up with you?' Slime sneered at Sofi. 'It's been a while.'

'Ruckus,' Slob suggested.

This was a popular proposal and they enthusiastically agreed.

Sofi's stomach clenched with fear. The Ruckus! She would not last two minutes in a Ruckus.

'We'll give these two up to it first,' Slime guffawed.

'No!' Sofi cried. Slime looked down at her in surprise. 'What do you think Guardians would do to Wreccas who hurt other Guardians?' she asked spiritedly, staring at him hard. 'If you think that a Ruckus is scary, you should see what they can do!'

It was a bluff and one that the Wreccas nearly fell for. Momentarily Sofi thought she might have a glimmer of a chance, until Slime laughed. It was not the joyous sort of laugh that Sofi had come to know on the Topside. This was a cruel sort of laugh, one that she well remembered, and it made her sick with fear.

'Does you think you can threaten us?' Slime said, his lip curling cruelly. He grabbed hold of her hair, but only some of it. He knew it would be more painful if he lifted her off the ground by a small handful.

Sofi pressed her lips together, determined not to give him the satisfaction of crying out with the pain.

'Stop!' Wakaa cried, and immediately a filthy Wrecca hand was clapped over his mouth. Aleyesu was gagged in a similar way.

Tears of pain stung Sofi's eyes as the roots of her hair burned her scalp. Still, she would not cry out.

Slime did not mind. He knew he would make her cry in the end. Slowly he began to swing her to and fro. The watching Wreccas grinned inanely at the spectacle. Aleyesu and Wakaa stared in horror.

Sofi clenched her teeth tightly, her hands clutching at Slime.

He began to swing her more violently.

'Oi!'

Slime looked up, curious to know who had spoken.

Scamp who, until this moment, had been an onlooker stepped forward. On seeing it was only Scamp, Slime continued.

'I'd stop that if I was you,' Scamp said calmly.

'Eh?'

'Her's not done nothing to you. Put her down.'

Slime was so surprised, he stopped swinging and left Sofi dangling, painfully, in mid-air.

Scamp put his hands round her waist and lifted her up so that she was no longer hanging from her hair.

'Best leave the punishments to Offa Scratch,' Scamp said. 'Us doesn't want to deliver her damaged, do us?'

Slime thought about that for a moment and then let go, not sure if he agreed but unwilling to risk any chance of upsetting his leader.

'Best get them all back,' Scamp suggested as he lowered Sofi to the ground. He put his hand on her shoulder and his grip was tight.

Slime was furious that one of his juniors should be telling him what to do. 'I'll thank you to shut up!' he spat into Scamp's face. 'I give the orders.'

Scamp was not in the least intimidated. 'Course you does,' he said mildly, wiping his face with the back of his hand.

'Bring the prisoners!' Slime ordered.

Wakaa and Aleyesu were dragged roughly forward while Slime held the Guardians' staffs. Scamp gripped Sofi tightly. He was manoeuvring his way to the back of the party.

'Bring her up front,' Slime demanded before setting off.

Slime hoped that presenting his prisoners to Offa Scratch would go a long way towards making up for the failure of the troops. He planned to get back as quickly as possible, and so he kept the pace brisk. It was easy for him, walking alone, but those who held prisoners could not keep up.

'We're losing them!' Sofi exclaimed as they rounded a corner. She was anxious not to lose sight of her friends.

Slime looked behind him. 'Hurry up!' he yelled. 'Stop dawdling!'

There were calls of 'Us is coming!' but they did not appear.

'I'll go and see what's holding them up,' Scamp said, although Sofi got the impression that he did not intend going.

'Ner, I'll go,' Slime said irritably. He was in charge. 'You hang on to Miss Topside here.'

Slime started back down the tunnel.

Scamp casually watched him go, but as soon as he had disappeared round the corner, Scamp tightened his grip on Sofi and dashed off in the opposite direction, dragging her behind him.

'What are you doing?' she spluttered, trying to slow their pace.

Scamp hauled her round a couple more corners and suddenly released her.

Sofi struggled to find her balance.

Slime and his light were now far behind them. It was only at this moment that Sofi realized that she must have dropped her ruler. They were in the dark.

'Run for it,' Scamp instructed her.

'What?' Sofi did not trust him.

'Get out of here.'

'Why?' She would not allow herself to fall into his trap.

'Them Guardians'll get what's coming to them, but you's only a girl. Get lost!'

Sofi could not believe what she was hearing. A Wrecca was helping her to escape.

'Thank you,' she said, quietly. 'You're a good Wrecca.'

Scamp blinked at the suggestion but did not have time to protest because she had darted off before he could change his mind.

Sofi ran, bumping against the tunnel walls at the turnings. She was desperate to put as much ground between herself and the Wreccas as possible. She stumbled on and . . .

She thought she was seeing things. Up ahead she thought she saw her grandfather, standing majestically in the middle of the tunnel, staff aloft, ready to explode his meagre magic.

Fortunately, Old Father Tim was more alert this time. Seeing it was Sofi approaching, he held back his incantation.

Overwhelmed with joy, she ran straight into his arms. 'The Wreccas are right behind us,' she puffed. 'They've got Wakaa and Aleyesu.' She tried to run on, pulling Old Father Tim with her, but he kept hold of her and twisted her round so that she spun into the alcove.

It was dark in there, but not pitch black. Sofi could vaguely see outlines. She did not believe her eyes.

Tid was nearly as astonished to see her as she was to see him.

With a squeal of ecstatic delight, she threw her arms round his neck. 'I thought you were dead!'

They hugged each other and then Sofi let go and threw her arms round a very startled Sheldon. Unlike Tid, he did not respond by returning the hug. He kept his arms rigid at his sides. In the dark, she did not notice the tear in his eye.

'You're alive,' she breathed.

Old Father Tim put his head into the alcove. 'How far behind are they?'

'Not far.'

'Do Wakaa and Aleyesu have their staffs?'

'No, Slime does.'

Old Father Tim looked at the boys. 'You know what to do?'

They nodded.

Old Father Tim walked back out into the tunnel.

Sofi made as if to follow, but Tid pulled her back. 'We wait here,' he said.

'Have you got a plan?' Sofi whispered.

'Ssh!'

They did not have to wait long. Suddenly Old Father Tim's deep voice boomed, 'Geweald of lyfte!'

There was a noise that sounded like a small explosion. As soon as they heard it, Tid and Sheldon ran from their hideout. Sofi followed.

Old Father Tim's spell had blasted Slime and Scamp off their feet. Sheldon and Tid ran straight at Slob and Stench. They used their heads as battering rams and drove straight into the Wreccas' midriffs. This unexpected onslaught forced the Wreccas to slacken their grip on their prisoners.

Aleyesu was now only loosely held by one rather startled Wrecca, which gave him the chance to pull away. The Wrecca lunged for him. Aleyesu quickly stepped aside. As the Wrecca missed his target, Aleyesu pushed him hard, propelling the Wrecca straight into the wall with a loud thud. The Wrecca dropped to the floor like a stone.

Wakaa was also taking full advantage of the mayhem and dug his elbow hard into the stomach of his guard, who doubled up.

Meanwhile, Sofi had wrestled the staffs from a half-conscious Slime. 'Catch!' she shouted.

As Aleyesu looked up, she threw one to him and the other to Wakaa. Catching his, Wakaa used it to hit his captor hard on the back of the head. He crumpled to the ground. Aleyesu shouted, 'Geweald of lyfte,' a moment before Wakaa did the same. The Wreccas, who were recovering from the boys' attack, were now blasted off their feet by magic.

'Quick!' Aleyesu shouted as he started to run.

'No, this way,' Old Father Tim called back, turning to run in the direction from which Aleyesu had come.

Wakaa looked at the Old Father in confusion. 'That is a dead end.'

'No, it is not.'

Tid and Sheldon had already run off towards what Aleyesu and Wakaa believed to be a blind alley. 'Come,' Old Father Tim said urgently, taking Sofi's hand.

Confused, but unable to argue, the two Guardians followed. By the time they reached the dead end, Sheldon was already scratching at the wall.

'What are . . .?' Aleyesu began.

'Ssh,' Tid said. 'He's worked it out.' He was watching Sheldon very closely. Sheldon's fingers were frantically probing the wall in certain places, as if trying to dislodge years of grime.

They could hear noise coming from the recovering Wreccas.

'The spell won't hold them for long,' Wakaa warned.

'Ah!' Sheldon's voice sounded triumphant.

Aleyesu went to the bend in the tunnel and prepared to attack any Wreccas who should appear. Wakaa joined him. They knew they would not have enough power in their staffs yet, but they would try.

'Found it!' Sheldon's fingers were scratching away the dirt from a deep engraving in the middle of the wall. He was unearthing a sign that looked like an ornate hexagonal shape, inside which was a triangle.

Wrestling the paperweight from his pocket, Sheldon slipped the triangular base into the triangle shape on the wall and twisted.

Nothing happened.

They all watched anxiously.

Sheldon stared at the wall. Something should be happening. Had he got it wrong?

Then there was a soft *clunk!* and the wall slid slowly back, revealing a room.

'They are here!' Aleyesu suddenly shouted.

The Wreccas were in sight.

'Inside!' Sheldon yelled, grabbing the paperweight and running into the room. Tid and Sofi followed.

Scamp rounded the corner first. He was determined to capture at least one Guardian and did not seem to notice an open door that had not been there before.

Aleyesu and Wakaa ran towards the door.

'Hurry!' Tid cried.

They dashed over the threshold and immediately turned to encourage Old Father Tim to hasten. The old man was trying to evade Scamp, who had made a dive for him. Scamp fell heavily.

Old Father Tim stepped through the doorway.

'Shut the door!'

Scamp was rolling on the floor. Slime was closing in, and the other Wreccas were not far behind.

'Shut the door!'

Everyone looked frantically for some sort of a lever or button to push.

'Come on!' Wakaa shouted, putting his shoulder to the door. Aleyesu and Sheldon rushed to his aid.

The Wreccas were close. Scamp scrambled for the door.

The Guardians heaved, and slowly it started moving.

The Wreccas were almost upon them.

Sofi could see the effort Scamp and Slime were putting into reaching them before the door shut. She and Tid darted behind the others and leant their weight to the door.

It was closing . . . closing . . . closing . . .

Clunk.

It shut, but too late.

22

By the Pond

Lorin walked towards a small group of women who were huddled together by the pond. They were mightily relieved to see someone they knew and immediately started bombarding her with questions.

'What's us doing here?'

'What's you up to?'

'I's hungry!'

'Is the men in the Labyrinth?'

'Who's her?'

The last question was asked by a woman who jabbed her finger at the Greenwich Guardian, who was feeling mighty vulnerable without her staff. They stared at her distrustfully. She smiled graciously back at them, trying to look calm. This only made the women more suspicious.

'This is Grenya,' Lorin said. 'Her's going to help us.'

'Why?' a voice blurted out from the middle of the throng. 'What's in it for her?'

'Nothing,' the Greenwich Guardian said quickly.

Lorin winced. There was not a Wrecca woman present who would believe that.

'I's off,' one said, grabbing her child's hand.

'Me too,' said another, doing the same.

'It's a trap,' said a third.

This last comment fizzed through the gathered women as they started to leave.

'It's not a trap!' Lorin shouted above the din, jumping on to a Guardian park bench. 'Of course there's something in it for Grenya.'

The women came to a ragged halt.

'Grenya and her kind doesn't want us here. But us willn't go until them men has goed. And so if Grenya wants us out of her park, her has to help!'

'What's happening in the Labyrinth?' someone yelled out.

'The men's invaded,' Lorin said.

The women reacted to this noisily.

'Is they going to stay?' someone asked.

'They plan to, all right.'

There was uproar.

'But us is going to change their minds!' Lorin said, raising her voice above the hubbub.

'How?' a lone voice asked.

'Us can't fight them,' another said.

'Ner, fighting's no good,' Lorin said. 'Us has to be clever,' and as she said this, she tapped her forehead with a finger.

Total silence fell. The women knew they were not clever.

'That's where Grenya comes in. I know us doesn't like her kind. Her isn't all that keen on us, either. But us needs her brains and her needs us out of here.'

Lorin looked around. Women and children had been coming across the grass all the time she had been speaking; quite a crowd was gathering.

'Say something,' Lorin hissed as she jumped down from the bench.

The Greenwich Guardian felt alarmed but tried not to show it. The women were murmuring discontentedly. She stepped up on to the bench and said, 'We are all women.' Her voice sounded a little higher than usual. She cleared her throat and continued, 'We will not see you beaten by the men!' To her relief there were quiet murmurs of agreement. 'We shall win the day!'

She had hoped that they would like this too, but they fell quiet, as if not quite trusting her passion.

'In the meantime, you must stay here for your own safety. Food has been organized.'

This brought about satisfied mutterings.

'If you gather beneath those trees, someone will bring it to you shortly.'

Scamp stood in the Gemetbur, holding his shovel in front of him like a weapon. 'Stay where you is,' he said, watching carefully to see who was going to attack first.

'Now look here,' Old Father Tim said.

'Don't you try your magic on I!' Scamp yelled, threateningly thrusting his shovel towards the Old Father with one hand and running the other over the closed door behind him in an attempt to find a handle and a way back out.

'You won't open it without this,' Sheldon said, holding up the paperweight.

'Give it to I,' Scamp hissed, glancing towards Sheldon but quickly returning his eyes to Old Father Tim. Clearly, he thought the old man to be the most dangerous.

Sheldon put the paperweight behind his back. 'No way.'

Scamp put both hands back on his shovel. 'Your blasting magic willn't work again,' he said. 'I'll see it coming this time.'

'We won't have to use such primitive magic in here,' Old Father Tim said mildly. 'This is Guardian territory. Cannot you feel it? The air is pulsating with magic. One click of my fingers will stop you for good,' and he lifted his hand as if preparing to click.

'Nooo!' shouted Sofi, flinging herself in front of Scamp protectively. At once he grabbed hold of her round the neck and held her tightly.

Everyone froze.

'He won't hurt me,' Sofi said confidently, gulping.

'Says who?' Scamp growled.

Sofi did not answer him. Her eyes were on her grandfather. 'He rescued me from the others. He set me free.'

'I willn't make the same mistake twice,' Scamp snarled.

'It wasn't a mistake,' Sofi said, trying to twist her head so that she could look at him. 'You set me free because you're good. You won't hurt me now.'

All three Guardians were ready to unleash any

amount of unspeakable magic just as soon as Sofi was able to step aside, but Sofi had no intention of doing so.

'You rescued me from your friends and I will rescue you from mine.' Turning back, she said, 'Grandfather, he saved me. We can do the same for him, can't we?'

'Let go of her,' Old Father Tim said in a carefully controlled voice.

'Does you think I's a fool?'

'No, of course not,' Sofi answered, 'but you should release me. Grandfather and the others will promise not to hurt you if you do.' She turned to them and said, 'Won't you?'

No one answered.

'He's not like the other Wreccas,' Sofi pleaded. 'Please, Grandfather!'

Old Father Tim was not about to trust a Wrecca, but he would do anything that might help Sofi and so he said, 'If you release Sofi and sit quietly over there,' he pointed to a spot by the wall, 'and promise to be still, we shall not harm you.'

'And we'll help him to get out of here,' Sofi added, 'won't we?'

'Yes,' Old Father Tim said evenly, with eyes of steel boring into Scamp's.

There was something behind his eyes that surprised the old man. He had not expected to see honesty in a full-grown Wrecca.

'How does I know you'll do what you says?' Scamp demanded.

'Because he's a Guardian,' Sofi explained. 'Guardians never lie.'

'You can't trust a Wrecca,' Sheldon said, in a voice heavy with outrage. He knew from bitter experience that it was impossible to negotiate with them.

Scamp cast him a threatening look.

'You *can* trust him,' Sofi said, 'because he's not like the rest of them.' She looked back at Scamp. 'Are you?'

Scamp thought for a moment before saying, 'Yer, I is, Snotty Snot. I's a Wrecca. I'll never be nothing else and that one there is right.' He jerked his head towards Sheldon. 'You can't trust a Wrecca.'

'There you are,' Sheldon said. 'Blast him!'

'No!' Sofi cried, thrusting her arms out sideways in an attempt to make herself bigger and so offer Scamp greater protection.

No one moved. She looked warily around at them, just to make sure that no one was going to do any blasting, and then she spoke softly to Scamp. 'They will do as they say, so long as you don't do anything stupid. Sit quietly over there. It's your only chance.'

Scamp did not move.

'Look,' she continued. 'Whether you admit it or not, you are different from those Wreccas on the other side of the door. There is a decent streak in you that they don't have. Now, let go of me and sit over there like Grandfather says, and I'll give you a sandwich to eat.'

'Sandwich?' Tid and Sheldon said together. They had not realized there was food.

'Go on,' Sofi said softly, not taking her eyes off Scamp.

With measured movements Scamp slowly released his grip. Then, still holding the shovel like a defensive weapon, he edged to the place Old Father Tim had indicated at the side of the room.

Sofi took Old Father Tim's bag and pulled out a rather squashed sandwich. 'Sit down,' she said.

Scamp did so cautiously, still clutching his shovel. Sofi held out the sandwich towards him and he snatched it, before quickly sinking his teeth into it.

'Are there any more in there?' Tid asked, looking hungrily at the bag. Sofi pulled out a couple more and handed them over.

'Keep an eye on him, boys,' Wakaa said.

Tid and Sheldon nodded, their mouths too full of sandwich to reply.

'Well done, Sofi,' Old Father Tim said with a smile.

'Are you sure that door's secure?' Wakaa asked.

'So it would seem,' Old Father Tim said, eyeing it carefully.

Now there was time to look at the Gemetbur properly. It was not a particularly small room but, being filled, almost to capacity, with mechanisms and machines that whirred or buzzed or hummed, it was cramped, except for an open space in the centre, big enough for several people to stand. As one might expect from a room created by the esteemed Tempus, everything had been enchanted to glow. Even after several thousand years, it still radiated a bright and comforting orange light.

Sofi was struck by how much it looked like the picture in her book. Nothing was exactly the same, but the layout and proportions were similar. She found it hard to believe that the room was so old; it looked brand new. There was no dust or cobwebs that might show the passage of time. The room looked as if it had been sealed for no more than twenty minutes.

Old Father Tim and Wakaa moved towards a large, vertical, glass tube, domed at either end. It enclosed what looked like many silver plungers, all linked together, pulsating with magic, but none of the parts moved.

'This must be an Isochron,' Old Father Tim said.

'What's it for?' Sofi asked.

'It is a delicate instrument that keeps time balanced in the different time zones.'

'You mean, that is what keeps Human and Guardian time aligned?' she asked.

'It is.'

'It's wonderful, isn't it?' she said in awe. 'Is it working properly?'

'No, it should be moving,' Old Father Tim said. 'We must see what we can do about that.'

Aleyesu crossed to Sheldon, who was eating his third sandwich. 'How did you know that the paperweight was the key?' he asked.

'I wasn't certain,' Sheldon said, trying to speak respectfully although his mouth was full of sandwich. 'But there's a riddle in the book.' He started turning the pages and found the right one. 'Here it is,' and he read, '"Four has the compass." I reckoned that was the points of the compass.' He continued, '"Beneath me three."'

'That had to be the triangle,' Tid threw in.

'"Orb though I am" – that was the dome, "Beneath is the key."'

'It could only be the paperweight,' Tid said excitedly.

'Well done, boys, very well done indeed. I am impressed.'

Both boys glowed with pride.

Aleyesu continued, 'Sofi tells me that you, Sheldon, can translate the signs.'

'I don't know if I do it right,' Sheldon said, feeling a little self-conscious. After all, Aleyesu was the expert, and next to him any stumbling attempts at translation would look ridiculous.

'It got you here, did it not?' Aleyesu asked.

Sheldon nodded.

'You must have done something right.'

Embarrassed, Sheldon stammered something incoherent and gratefully accepted another sandwich from Tid.

'Give one to the Wrecca,' Aleyesu said. Tid reluctantly took one from the bag and held it out. Scamp did not give him a moment to change his mind and quickly snatched it out of his hand.

'May I see the book?' Aleyesu said.

Sheldon handed it over. It was still damp. 'It fell in the water,' he explained.

'How did you get out?' Sofi asked, as she joined them. 'I waited for ages. I thought you must be drowned,' and she felt a large lump in her throat as she remembered.

'Sheldon rescued me,' Tid said. 'Twice,' and he explained.

Old Father Tim and Wakaa had turned their attention to one large, slowly turning wooden wheel. Sharply chiselled cogs ran right round it. 'Ah yes,' the Old Father said to Wakaa, 'this is our problem.' He was pointing to another smaller wheel, also with cogs. Clearly this wheel was supposed to be linked to the turning wheel, and the two of them were supposed to be moving together. Now, however, they looked as if they had been well and truly bounced out of alignment.

'There must have been an almighty wobble to do that,' Wakaa said.

'Our job,' Old Father Tim said, rubbing his chin thoughtfully, 'is to try and move it back into position.'

'Will you use magic?' Tid asked, looking up. The sandwiches had taken the edge off his hunger and he was anxious to see some action.

'No,' Old Father Tim said. 'Not for this.'

'This will need man power,' Wakaa said.

Tid felt a twinge of disappointment.

'We shall have to lever it ourselves,' Old Father Tim said. 'Magic won't work on this. Still, I don't see that it will be a problem, not with the three of us.'

'What are you going to lever it with?' Tid asked.

'That is a good question,' Old Father Tim said. 'Look around for something.'

'What about a staff?' Sofi suggested.

'Too thick at the end,' Old Father Tim said. 'We need something flat so that it can slip between the two wheels.'

'But strong,' Wakaa added. 'It must be strong.'

'I don't see why you can't use magic,' Tid said.

'Magic is not the answer to everything, my boy,' Old Father Tim explained amiably. 'In fact, it is rarely the answer; but when it is, it can be most effective.'

'What about Scamp's shovel?' Sofi suggested brightly.

'Good idea,' Sheldon said, reaching out to take it.

Scamp gripped his shovel close to his chest.

'Give it here,' Sheldon snarled, trying to yank it out of Scamp's grip.

Scamp held it firmly, angrily jutting his face into Sheldon's.

'Leave it be, my boy,' Old Father Tim said soothingly, putting his hand on Sheldon's shoulder.

Sheldon relaxed.

Old Father Tim was preparing to say something but changed his mind. Instead, he turned to Sofi. She immediately understood.

'Scamp, please may we use your shovel?'

'Ner.'

'Grandfather, will we be able to do this without it?'

'I do not think so.'

Sofi turned back to Scamp. 'We need it.'

'So what?'

'It's really important.'

'Why?'

Sofi was not sure.

Her grandfather came to her rescue. 'Human time has bounced away from our own,' he said. 'It doesn't sound very important, does it?'

Scamp said nothing.

'But it is,' Old Father Tim continued. 'If our time is

not properly aligned with Human time, then it will completely split away. When that happens, everything will go horribly wrong. It will be the end of both our worlds.'

'Why are we wasting time?' Sheldon said. 'Why don't we just take it? There are more of us than him.'

'Because,' Aleyesu said, 'diplomacy is usually a much better option.'

Sheldon fell silent.

'What's that there?' Scamp asked suddenly, looking towards the Isochron.

In the Underneath, Scamp owned a screwdriver and a hammer and, with no teaching at all, he had fashioned some creative, yet simple machines that had never been of any interest to other Wreccas. Being interested in such things, he found the Gemetbur fascinating.

'I will show you if you like,' Old Father Tim said pleasantly.

Scamp tried not to look too interested.

'Come on,' Sofi said, not giving him the chance to refuse. Taking his hand and pulling him to his feet, she led him after Old Father Tim, who started explaining what some of the instruments were for.

Scamp gripped his shovel close. He was deeply interested in all he saw. 'I never knowed there was stuff like this. What's that?' he asked, pointing at a small, flat, gossamer-thin sheet that was held in its four corners by tiny silver fasteners that looked like butterflies.

'I would like to tell you,' Old Father Tim explained, 'but time is rather short. If you are interested in such things, when we get back home I will show you some of the instruments that I make.'

'What sort of things?'

'Well, I made the Timepiece. I will show you that if you like.'

Scamp had heard about the Timepiece.

'*If* we get back,' Aleyesu said from the edge of the room.

Old Father Tim glanced over. 'Is it going to be a problem?'

'It's not impossible,' Aleyesu said, 'but it might be difficult. You see, the Chronicle was a bit vague on the subject, but Sofi's book is far more forthcoming.'

'You can read it too?' Sofi asked, delighted.

'Absolutely. If I had seen this first, it would have saved a lot of trouble.'

'What does it say?'

'I am not sure as yet,' Aleyesu held the book out. 'Sheldon,' he said, 'would you give me your opinion about this?'

Sheldon felt very uncomfortable, but also thrilled, to be asked. Self-consciously, he took the book.

'Well?' Old Father Tim asked, turning back to Scamp. 'May we use your shovel?'

'You will show I the Timepiece and tell how it works?' Scamp asked.

'I most certainly will.'

Scamp thought for a moment.

'Go on,' Sofi encouraged him.

Scamp loosened his grip on the shovel. He then

extended his hand a short distance towards Old Father Tim, who put out his hand to take it. Scamp hesitated for a moment. Could he really do this? Could he offer help to the man he had always considered his enemy?

Old Father Tim saw something of the turmoil in Scamp's eyes, and he slowly wrapped his fingers round the handle of the shovel as if to take it.

For a moment, Sofi thought that Scamp would change his mind, but without any fuss it was done. Old Father Tim held the shovel and Scamp let his arm drop to his side. A lifetime of prejudice had been overcome.

23

An Enormous Wobble

The group of Wrecca women was growing so big that there were not enough trees to shade them all from the hot sun. Their grumpiness turned to delight, however, when Ma Brownal and Ma Connal appeared with the food, with Ma Lom bringing up the rear.

'I hope it is all right,' Ma Brownal said. 'There was not much time.'

However, she need not have worried. Every last crumb was enthusiastically swallowed and very much enjoyed by all the women and children.

As they were finishing, Enderell arrived and straight away handed a glass bottle to Lorin. 'Five drops into a large tub of water,' she indicated the size with her hands, 'will render the drinker asleep within minutes if they drink a small cup of it.'

Lorin nodded distractedly; she was anxious to be off.

'Have you got that?' Enderell asked.

Lorin nodded, holding up her hand and splaying her five fingers. 'Five drops, small cup.'

'Yes,' Enderell said with a warm smile. 'Good luck.'

With a brief word of goodbye, Lorin left.

'Have you got the draught?' Ma Brownal asked. 'The women are beginning to complain about the heat, and the children are uncontrollable. One has just fallen into the pond.'

Enderell poured the required number of drops into the large jugs of water that were standing ready, and it was quickly distributed. The women and children drank thirstily. It tasted utterly delectable and, as Enderell had predicted, they started falling asleep within minutes.

The Greenwich Guardian gave a sigh of relief as things began to quieten down. She hoped that everything was going as well for those below ground. Walking away from the trees, she enjoyed the calm that was spreading over the park. She saw Seth hurrying home from school and raised her hand in greeting. He did not see her.

'That seems to be working,' Enderell said as she joined the Greenwich Guardian. Some of the women were snoring loudly.

'Is there anything else I can do?' the Greenwich Guardian asked.

'No. They will all be flat out soon.'

The Greenwich Guardian looked back to Seth, but he had gone. Where was he? She had told him to go straight to Old Father Tim's cottage tonight. Why was he walking in the opposite direction?

She gave Enderell a distracted smile and walked a short way, just in time to catch a glimpse of Seth entering a secluded part of the park. She followed and watched him stop and lean against a tree. It looked as if he was waiting for someone.

This was an odd part of the park for him to be in. She drew breath to call his name but stopped abruptly because Seth was suddenly waving enthusiastically to someone. The Greenwich Guardian had seldom seen him so animated. She looked to see who he was waving at. It was a boy.

It was a Human boy!

The Greenwich Guardian stared in disbelief; finally the cause of all their troubles became clear to her.

Seth looked furtively around. The Greenwich Guardian instinctively shrank back behind a tree and he did not see her.

'Hey, Baz,' he called as he threw a football to the boy.

'Headers today!' Baz called back, throwing his bag on the ground, the proper distance from the tree to make a goal. He lobbed the ball towards Seth's head. Seth headed it straight into Baz's hands. 'Good one!' Baz shouted back. 'Now try and score!'

He lobbed the ball back and prepared himself for Seth's header. Seth jumped and headed the ball downwards. Baz dived to his side and saved it with ease.

'Not bad,' he said, standing up, 'but head it harder, next time.' He threw the ball back and prepared himself once more, but this time Seth caught the ball. His face was very serious. He was looking straight past Baz.

Baz wheeled around. The Greenwich Guardian was walking towards them. He knew who she was; Seth had described her accurately.

She reached them and smiled. 'Good afternoon, Seth.' The Human boy could see her; she was sure of it.

Seth did not reply.

'Are you going to introduce me to your friend?' She smiled at Baz, 'I am happy to mee–'

The Greenwich Guardian was not able to finish her greeting.

'What exactly does you need my shovel for?' Scamp asked.

Old Father Tim explained about the two wheels that needed realigning.

'That isn't ner bother,' Scamp said. All they had to do was slip the shovel's blade between the two wheels and lever the smaller wheel so that it flipped back into alignment. The principle was straightforward enough, but the reality was not so easy. Guardians are used to reading books. They understand theories. Old Father Tim could construct the most complex of mechanisms, and yet none of them was used to practical, physical labour.

Scamp could see they were hesitating and guessed they did not really know how to go about this operation. 'Let I do it,' he said.

Scamp could tell that they wanted to accept his help, but he was a Wrecca!

'Us does this sort of thing all the time when us is digging,' Scamp explained. 'Sometimes, there's things in the way and us has to prise them out. Other diggers doesn't like this sort of work, in case it goes wrong. I does it alone.'

Old Father Tim thought for a moment and then offered the shovel back to its owner. 'You do understand,' he said, before releasing it, 'that if either of the wheels is damaged, it could be very dangerous for us all.'

Scamp gave a nod. 'Stand back.'

They all moved a step backwards.

'Is this wise?' Tid asked, but was silenced by a look from his grandfather.

Carefully, Scamp slotted the blade between the two wheels. Then, putting his foot on the casing of the large wheel's axle, he eased himself up until he was resting on the shovel's handle with straight arms so that all his body weight could be used. He paused for a moment and then suddenly lunged at the handle. The spade sprang high in the air and Scamp fell on his back.

'Did it work?' he asked as the shovel clattered to the ground.

Everyone stared at the wheels.

'No,' Old Father Tim said.

Scamp scrambled to his feet and took a look. 'I see,' he said.

Sheldon and Tid exchanged nervous glances.

Once again Scamp slotted the blade in and climbed up. He concentrated on manipulating the shovel into exactly the right place at the correct angle. He balanced himself carefully.

He paused.

Everyone held their breath.

Then he lunged once more.

The result was the same. The spade somersaulted into the air and Scamp fell heavily.

He lay for a minute on the floor, then shook his head. He was not so sure he could do this.

'You did it!' Sofi suddenly cried.

Scamp leapt to his feet and joined the others as they stood staring at the two wheels. The cogs of the smaller one were neatly slotted between the cogs of the larger one. They all waited for the two wheels to start moving, but they did not. Instead of the larger wheel making the smaller one turn with it, the smaller one had made the bigger wheel stop.

'What's happening?' Sofi asked.

The three Guardians looked uneasily at one another. It was Old Father Tim who finally spoke. 'Guardian and Human time are once more aligned,' he said.

'Then it's worked!' Sofi cried, but no one else seemed pleased.

'It has worked *in a way*,' Old Father Tim said. 'But instead of Human time clicking into Guardian time, it has happened the other way round.'

'What does that mean?' Sofi asked.

'It means,' Wakaa explained, 'that Guardian time has stopped too.'

'So what's going to happen?' Tid asked apprehensively.

Old Father Tim and Wakaa exchanged worried looks. 'Time has to move forward,' the old man said. 'It cannot stand still.' He looked very grave. 'If time does not start working again very soon, then . . .' He did not continue.

'Then what?' Sofi asked, alarmed.

'Will it be the chaos?' Tid asked fearfully.

'No,' Old Father Tim said. 'It will be far beyond chaos. It will be total destruction for us all.'

*

The earth was struck by a wobble so powerful that people staggered, and some fell to the ground.

'What was that?' Baz asked.

'Another time wobble,' the Greenwich Guardian said, regaining her balance. 'Only that one was very serious.'

'How do you mean?' Seth asked.

'The wobbles are growing worse all the time,' she said. 'We are going to have to do something about you two.' She turned to Baz. 'I am Seth's grandmother.'

Baz twisted his fingers together behind his back.

'And you are?' the Greenwich Guardian asked.

'Baz,' Seth mumbled, looking down at the football in his hands.

'Hello, Baz.'

He did not answer.

'Seth,' the Greenwich Guardian said, 'how long has this been going on?'

'A few days,' Seth mumbled into his football.

'Since the wobbles started?' she asked.

He did not answer.

'Seth.' There was a warning note in her voice, and he knew that he must respond or be in even greater trouble. 'You realize that you two are the reason things are getting worse,' she continued.

'The first one came before Baz could see me,' Seth said defiantly.

'A time wobble is not unusual,' the Greenwich Guardian explained. 'They happen from time to time, but it is not important. But a friendship such as this, coming as it did on the back of a wobble, must be the reason why it stuck.' Her voice rose as her anger grew. 'Uncle Bryn has been to a lot of trouble because of you, and the Park Council has been up all hours, checking the time locators. No wonder they could not find a problem. I can't believe it was you all the time!'

Seth continued staring at his football.

'Do you not see how dangerous your behaviour has been?' the Greenwich Guardian continued. 'The Human and Guardian worlds are designed to be apart. Defying the laws, as you have, is catastrophic. If we do not realign our two time systems, we shall return to the chaos and turmoil of ancient times. Have you any idea how disastrous this would be?'

Seth said nothing but stubbornly continued looking at the football in his hands.

From the cradle, Guardian children learn the importance of not interacting with any Human. Walking through them was the most anyone would do, and they usually preferred not to. Having been born a Wrecca, Seth had missed out on much of this teaching and, because he had been so unhappy, he had never bothered to understand just how important it was.

The Greenwich Guardian realized that his ignorance was partly her fault. She took a deep breath and calmed down. When she next spoke, it was in her normal, calm manner. 'This cannot continue.'

Seth looked at her rebelliously.

'We are going to have to put it right,' she continued. 'If we cannot realign time quickly, we may never be able to. I am sorry, Seth, but this friendship has to stop now.'

'Why?' Seth asked angrily. 'Why do I have to lose everything? Why can't it be Tid or Sofi or someone else? Why me?'

The Greenwich Guardian put out her hand towards him, but he moved out of her reach.

She felt the rebuff, and it hurt. 'I know that Baz is a close friend of yours,' she said, 'but you still have the rest of us.'

'He's not *a* close friend,' Seth shouted. 'He's my *only* friend. Guardian boys don't like me. They know I'm a Wrecca and that I shouldn't be here. Baz doesn't care where I come from.'

'I do not care where you come from either,' the Greenwich Guardian said.

'You only took me in because you felt sorry for me,' Seth scowled. 'I'm not clever like Sofi. I bet you wish you had her instead.'

The Greenwich Guardian knelt down in front of him. 'No, Seth, that is not true. I do not want Sofi. I want you.'

Seth knew she had to say these things. In the Guardian world it was thought wrong to be unkind to children. He was not impressed, but he was suddenly taken aback when he saw tears in her eyes. He clamped his lips together to stop them from trembling.

'I love you,' she said, suddenly feeling very guilty that she had never told him this before.

Seth blinked.

'I am so sorry,' she added.

Seth pressed his lips even tighter together, but it did not work any more. His face crumpled, and soon he was sobbing in her arms.

Baz watched, finding it difficult not to cry too, not for Seth and his grandmother, but because he suddenly realized how much he wanted his own mother.

The Greenwich Guardian kissed the top of Seth's head. 'Seth, we *have* to do this.'

He nodded and sniffed.

The Greenwich Guardian turned to Baz. 'We have to put you back into your own time.'

'Will everything be all right then?' Baz asked in a curiously croaky voice.

'I cannot be certain, but we must try.'

Seth looked at his friend. 'We have to do this,' he said.

'I suppose so.'

'Very well, boys,' the Greenwich Guardian said, trying to sound matter-of-fact. 'Come with me.'

'Why can't we do it here?'

'Because I do not have my staff.'

Seth looked around. His grandmother never went anywhere without her staff.

'Where is it?'

'At Old Father Tim's house. Come.'

'Am I going to see inside a Guardian house?' Baz asked enthusiastically.

'Yes, but we must hurry,' the Greenwich Guardian said. Then she smiled and added, 'I think we may find some of Enderell's ginger biscuits there.'

*

Lorin stood by the Lower Topside door into the Underneath. She was feeling very nervous and took deep breaths in an attempt to calm herself. She had to do this.

She pushed the door open carefully, grateful that the Underneath doors were easy to open from the outside. How many times had she sneaked back into the Underneath as a child? She never thought she would be doing it again.

There was no guard. This did not surprise her; the men were too busy in the Labyrinth to think about guarding the Underneath doors.

Quickly, she ran down the dingy tunnels. She was making for the galley chamber. This was the Wrecca kitchen. No care went into cooking the food in the Underneath; it was just boiled up in one enormous greasy pot. Steam from it collected on the galley ceiling and dripped down the walls, making everything very wet, hot and sticky.

There were not many Wreccas about. It seemed that only the old ones had been left behind.

Suddenly she felt a bony finger poking her in the shoulder.

'What's you up to?'

24

The Cross-Back

Lorin's heart started thumping. Slowly she turned, fearing who might be standing there. To her relief, it was only an elderly Wrecca. He stood there with an unpleasant sneer on his lips, but he was too feeble and stupid to be a threat.

'Keep your nose out,' Lorin snarled. 'I's working for Scratch!'

There seemed to be only old men in the Underneath, and there was not much fight in them. No one bothered her after that.

She remembered the way without any difficulty, and it was not long before she was entering the galley. Clouds of steam wafted up from the enormous cooking pot. Squabble was bickering with Slop as usual. Lorin wrinkled up her nose in disgust. The smell of the Wreccas' food was revolting.

'What's you doing here?' Squabble asked as soon as he saw her, just like the old man had done. 'You isn't supposed to be here.'

'Hold your tongue!' she snapped back. 'I'm here on official business for Scratch. I work for him now.'

Slop eyed her suspiciously. She was not even calling their leader by his proper title. 'Offa Scratch willn't never have ner woman working for him.'

'That's all you know. I's the Tonic-Maker,' she said importantly. Then, seeing his lack of understanding, she explained, 'I mix tonics that make people better when they's ill.'

'I's not ill,' Squabble said.

'Oh, then you'll not want this,' she said, holding up the glass bottle that Enderell had given her.

'What's that?'

'It's a draught,' she said, using Enderell's word. 'It'll clear that headache of yours, but if you doesn't want it cured then that's up to you.'

'I doesn't have a headache,' Squabble said.

'Doesn't you?' She sounded surprised. 'I will have thinked that in this fug your head'll be bursting. It's all the steam, bungs up the cracks in your head and causes heaviness of the brain. Still, if you's all right,' she added, 'then that'll be one less person to treat.' She uncorked the bottle.

Squabble put his hand to his sweating forehead. Now he came to think of it, his head was hurting. 'It do hurt a bit,' he said, pressing his temples with his fists.

Lorin hid a smile. It was so easy to manipulate them. She tried to remember what Enderell had told her about the potion. Five drops into a large tub of water. Yes, that was it, but how many drops should she put in a sink this size? It was hard to tell. She decided it would be better to use too much rather than too little, and she poured about half of the amber contents into the enormous sink of slimy water before recorking the bottle.

'You can't do that!' Slop yelled, grabbing her wrist. She yanked herself out of his grasp and, picking up a large wooden stick, stirred the liquid into the water.

'Offa Scratch'll skin you for this,' Slop said, looking at the water. The amber liquid had given it a gentle, yellowish glow.

Then Lorin dipped her finger in and pretended to taste it, but she only put it to her lips. She could not risk feeling sleepy.

'Mmmm,' she said, closing her eyes and running her tongue over her lips. 'Delicious. It's a pity you two doesn't have a headache, it'd be worth having one just to taste this.'

'I does have one,' Squabble said, now feeling very sorry for himself. He scooped up a handful of water and put it to his lips. His expression was transformed into one of blissful joy.

This was too much for Slop. 'Ooh, I does have a bit of an ache,' he said, putting his hand to his forehead theatrically. He then scooped up some of the liquid and drank deeply.

Lorin gave a satisfied smile.

Both returned their hands to the water again.

'You can't have no more,' she said sharply.

'Why not?' they asked aggressively. 'Offa Scratch sayed it was for us.'

'For everyone,' she corrected. 'Only one drink per person. If you take more than one, you'll be for it.'

Both men hesitated. Nothing was worth incurring Offa Scratch's wrath.

'But,' she added with an inviting smile, 'if you help I take it around, then I'll tell Scratch. Him has more of this stuff, and him sayed him'll give it to anyone who helps.'

Squabble and Slop exchanged greedy looks. 'What does you want us to do?'

Lorin let them fill a couple of enormous chipped jugs, one of which no longer had a handle, and take a couple of grimy tankards. She filled a jug for herself to carry. Then she led them out into the tunnels. They distributed the water to everyone they met. There seemed to be no trouble in getting the men to drink. Her biggest problem was stopping them from taking more than one. Many times she had to threaten them with Scratch's displeasure if they were greedy. Squabble and Slop growled and spat at those whom she might have found hard to control by herself, but in no time at all they started yawning. Lorin suggested that they took a rest and let two others help. As soon as the last of the Wreccas was yawning contentedly, she hurried off to the chamber where Morlenni was being held.

The heavy old door was shut, but she pushed it open with her shoulder. Morlenni was on the ground in a corner, her knees pulled up to her chin, looking terrified. Her expression changed to one of desperate hope as soon as she saw her friend.

'Oi! What's you doing?' Stupid snarled. He had been left to guard Morlenni and was feeling very put out because of it. He had wanted to invade the Labyrinth with the others and now dearly wanted to hurt her to make up for it; but Scratch had warned him not to, and so he had had to amuse himself by terrifying her instead.

Lorin resisted the urge to hug her friend. Instead, she briskly said, 'Scratch says you's to have this,' and she picked up a dirty tankard from the table and poured Stupid a drink.

'What?' Stupid asked, his large, oafish face wearing an expression of bafflement.

'It's to make you feel better.'

'I doesn't feel bad.'

'What, no aches or pains?' she asked. Every Wrecca had some sort of problem, usually with their stomachs.

'Ner.'

'All right then, you willn't want none,' Lorin said. 'All the more for the others,' and she turned, pretending to leave.

'Don't go,' Morlenni breathed wretchedly.

'Shut up!' Stupid snarled.

'I'll give her some,' Lorin suggested.

'You're not to give her nothing,' he snarled. 'Offa Scratch never sayed nothing about giving her a drink.'

'I has the right number of draughts to give out. If you doesn't have one, then someone else will have to. I'll give it to her instead.' She smiled at Morlenni. 'You'll like it. It's delicious.'

'Give it here,' he said, snatching it. He was not going to stand by and allow a prisoner to have something that tasted delicious. He distrustfully dipped his long tongue into the golden liquid. His face lit up with pleasure and he gulped the rest down in one.

Lorin looked at Morlenni while Stupid was drinking. She risked a smile, trying to convey to her friend that everything was under control.

'I want more,' Stupid demanded.

Lorin knew he did not need more but, if he had extra, perhaps it would work faster. Morlenni looked as if she was about to die of fright.

Lorin filled the tankard to the brim once more and watched Stupid drink it down.

'More!' he demanded.

'You can't have ner more,' she said.

'Who says I can't?' he asked menacingly.

'Well, Scratch, actually,' she said, as casually as she could. 'If I tell him you had more than your share, you'll be for it.'

'Why does you call him that?' he asked but not harshly. He was suddenly feeling mellow.

Offa Scratch had been known simply as Scratch in Lorin's day, and she kept forgetting to use his new title.

'I call him Scratch cos him and I is . . .' she lowered her head as though slightly embarrassed, '. . . friends.'

Stupid looked puzzled. 'Ner way!' he exclaimed incredulously.

'Why not?' she asked.

Morlenni looked up at her friend, wide-eyed and totally confused.

Lorin waited. Stupid had to start yawning soon. He had had twice as much as everyone else.

'Offa Scratch don't want ner woman,' Stupid growled.

'That's all you know,' she said with a scowl. 'Him's going to rule the Underneath, and I's going to rule the Labyrinth.'

'Never!'

'With him as the leader,' she added.

Morlenni let out a stifled cry.

Stupid drew breath to say something but was suddenly overtaken by a yawn.

Relieved, Lorin said, 'Come,' holding out her hand to Morlenni.

'What's you up to?' Stupid asked, trying to sound fierce but not having the energy. 'I's guarding her.'

'Scratch wants to see her,' Lorin said.

'Then I's coming too.'

'All right,' Lorin said calmly.

Stupid yawned again.

Lorin took Morlenni's hand and pulled her up. Then she stood still and waited.

Morlenni was confused. Lorin had said that they should go, but now she was standing still and looking at Stupid.

Suddenly, his legs buckled beneath him and he crashed to the floor.

Lorin tugged at Morlenni, who was staring in amazement at the prostrate Stupid. He was already snoring loudly.

'Come on!' Lorin muttered urgently, dragging a confused Morlenni from the chamber.

*

'Who are they?' Seth asked as the Greenwich Guardian led him and Baz back past the sleeping Wrecca women.

'I shall tell you later,' his grandmother said.

Enderell stared at the Human boy who was following Seth. She was totally confused. 'What is going on?' she asked the Greenwich Guardian.

'Nothing. At least nothing that you can help me with. Come along, boys.'

Enderell watched them walk away and then gave a questioning look to Ma Brownal, Ma Connal and Ma Lom, but they shook their heads, totally at a loss.

Baz could not help feeling a tremor of excitement as he entered Old Father Tim's cottage. He stared around with bright, hopeful eyes. He had heard tales from Seth about how clever Old Father Tim was with magic, and yet, apart from a welcoming glow, there was nothing magical about his home. It was a little disappointing.

The Greenwich Guardian handed Baz a plateful of Enderell's ginger biscuits. 'You had better eat some quickly,' she suggested. 'You won't be able to taste them in your world.'

Still distracted by his surroundings, Baz absent-mindedly bit into the biscuit and suddenly all thoughts of the cottage disappeared. This biscuit was utterly, mouth-wateringly delicious.

'I am sorry to rush you,' the Greenwich Guardian said, picking up her staff, 'but I think we should do this right away. You will want to say goodbye to each other.'

There was so much that Seth wanted to say. Baz had

been the best friend ever, but all he could manage in a choked voice was, 'Goodbye.'

'Face each other,' the Greenwich Guardian said.

'Bye,' Baz said as he stood in front of Seth.

'Closer. You need to be nearly touching, but not quite.'

They edged towards each other so that the toes of their shoes were almost touching.

The Greenwich Guardian stood beside them, using both hands to hold her staff high above her head.

Suddenly Baz realized that this was the end. He was about to lose his one and only friend. 'I'll be under the tree every day after school,' he gabbled.

'Endebyrdnes is geniwad!' The Greenwich Guardian's voice filled the room. Suddenly her staff began to glow. She let it drop behind her, but before it reached the ground she stepped towards the boys and, with a hand on each of their heads, she pushed them forcibly together.

Both boys winced. Their heads were about to collide and they expected it to hurt, but there was no impact. They stumbled forward, straight through each other.

. . . Baz found himself standing alone in the park. Seth and his grandmother had disappeared. His brain could not quite take in the sudden change. He looked about him. He was not in a part of the park that he knew very well.

For a moment, Seth thought that his friend was going to turn around and say something, but he did not. Instead, Baz turned, thrust his hands deep into his pockets and, with head hanging low, slouched off.

Seth watched him disappear straight through the wall. He ran to the door and watched Baz walking away.

'Will he remember me?'

'I do not think so.'

Seth watched until Baz was out of sight. Then, with a deep sigh, he asked in a husky voice, 'Has it worked? Will time be all right now?'

'I hope so,' his grandmother said as she picked up her staff. 'You did the right thing, Seth. I'm proud of you,' and her voice trembled a little. 'Come,' she said, pulling herself together, 'there is still much we have to do. Will you help me?'

Seth slipped his hand into hers and they walked out of the cottage together.

25

Breaking Through the Fundament

Old Father Tim and the others were sitting on the floor of the Gemetbur. He was deep in conversation with Wakaa. Aleyesu and Sheldon had finished comparing Sofi's storybook with the two pages Aleyesu had ripped from the Guardian Chronicles; they could find nothing that would help with the realignment of time. A sense of hopelessness was overwhelming all those who understood what might soon happen to their world.

Sofi knew that her grandfather was having difficulty working out the time problem but, not knowing the consequences, she was not overly worried. She had every faith in the old man and thought that if they waited long enough he would come up with a solution. She read her storybook as she waited, and parts that she had never properly understood began to make sense to her now.

'". . . The secret of the Gemetbur is still with us hidden somewhere." It's hidden in the book,' she muttered to herself as she carried on reading. Then she nudged Tid. 'Hey, this bit is about you,' she said, pointing to the text. '"Only those with deep insight would ever be able to recognize it, find the key and use it." That's you,' she said. 'You found the key. If you hadn't brought the paperweight, we would never have got in. Do you think you knew when you picked it up?'

'All I knew was that I wanted to annoy you. That's why I brought it. I didn't have any insight.'

'We don't often argue,' Sofi said thoughtfully. 'Perhaps we had to, so that you would want to annoy me and therefore bring it. I never would have. I chose the ruler.' She looked back at the text. 'And the next bit is Sheldon. He worked out how to use the key. You must both have real insight.' She sounded impressed.

'What about you?' Tid asked. 'This first bit is you. You recognized what the book was saying. You knew there was something wrong. Without you, none of this would have happened. If anyone has insight, you do.'

'I suppose we all played our part,' Sofi said with a contented smile.

A sense of sleepiness pervaded the Gemetbur as each exhausted the possibilities of whatever thoughts they had. Even Aleyesu stopped trying to translate the Chronicles, although Sheldon kept going. Scamp dozed against the wall.

Suddenly, Sofi squealed.

Everyone jumped. Scamp woke up with a start and grabbed his shovel, instantly on guard.

'What is the matter?' her grandfather asked.

She was pointing at the wheels. 'Look!'

They were moving! Effortlessly and silently, their cogs were now interlinking as they turned in mechanical harmony.

The Guardians quickly got to their feet and scrutinized the Isochron closely. It was now beating rhythmically, like a heart. Relief flooded through them all. Both worlds were safe.

'How did that happen?' Sofi asked.

'Someone is giving us a helping hand above ground,' Old Father Tim replied.

'When did the Isochron start working?' Sheldon queried.

Sofi shook her head. She did not know.

'Probably when the wheels did,' Tid suggested.

Suddenly they were aware of chanting. The three Guardians were standing around the Isochron. Each held the end of his own staff in his left hand and his neighbour's in his right; the staffs formed a triangle at chest height, parallel to the ground.

Their voices were low and perfectly synchronized. It was something between a chant and a song. The children were enthralled, but none more so than Scamp. He stared open-mouthed as the three Guardians conjured up magic so powerful that the room started vibrating. Then everything started to glow, deep orange tinged with gold, not just the cogs and wheels, but the children too. Finally, Scamp began to glow.

'Quickly,' Old Father Tim said.

Without breaking the triangle or interrupting their chanting, the Guardians lifted their staffs high over the throbbing Isochron and moved away from it into the centre of the room. It was quite a squeeze. Each

Guardian stood at the point of the triangle, firmly holding the staffs.

'Each of you, come and hold the middle of a staff,' Old Father Tim instructed as the Guardians lowered their staffs again.

Tid picked up the paperweight and took hold of Old Father Tim's staff with his other hand. Sofi held Wakaa's staff and Sheldon grabbed Aleyesu's, the book firmly tucked under his arm.

'You will need to hold on with both hands,' Wakaa said.

'We'll use the bag,' Tid said, darting to fetch it. 'We can put the book and the paperweight inside.'

'No,' Old Father Tim said. 'This is a difficult enough journey. We cannot risk being slowed down by bags.'

'But we can't leave the book!' Sheldon exclaimed.

'You must leave not only that, but the paperweight too.'

'No, I can put that in my pocket.'

'Leave it, my boy.' Old Father Tim's voice was calm but stern, and Tid knew he must obey, but these things had brought them through a terrible ordeal. It felt wrong to leave them behind.

'Suppose we ever need to get back here?' Tid asked.

'The key will not work a second time, nor will the book. If Tempus ever needs us to return, he will find a way.'

The boys hesitated.

'These things are no good to us now,' the Old Father assured them.

Tid and Sheldon glanced at each other before reluctantly putting their treasured possessions back on the floor.

'Quickly,' Old Father Tim urged.

'What about Scamp?' Sofi asked, anxious that he should not be left behind.

'His is the most important place of all,' Old Father Tim said. 'Scamp, you are to stand in the middle. You are the drilling point of our exit plan.'

Scamp was a little surprised but did as he was told. He was learning to trust the old man.

'I suppose I's to leave this, too,' Scamp said, indicating his shovel.

'I am afraid so.'

He placed it respectfully with the bag, book, two pages from the Chronicles and the paperweight. Then he ducked under a staff so that he could stand in the middle of the triangle.

'Hold your hands up above your head,' Aleyesu instructed him, 'palms together. You are the one who has to break through the fundament. It is going to be a bumpy journey, so you will have to be strong.'

Scamp nodded and held his hands up high.

'Hold on, everyone,' Old Father Tim said. 'Remember that you must not let go. Whatever happens, hold on tight!' Then he joined in the chanting again.

They started rotating, slowly at first, except that they did not actually turn, but it felt as if they were. Sofi saw Tid close his eyes, and she thought this was a good idea and closed hers too.

Slowly the spinning grew faster and, as it did, Tid, Sofi and Sheldon found they had to grip the staffs tighter. The whirr of the turning became louder and drowned out the chanting. The spinning became more violent and the staffs vibrated alarmingly. Everyone held on desperately. Sofi thought the staff would be dragged from her grasp and she gritted her teeth and clung on with all her strength. Their knuckles turned white, as the blood drained from their fingers while they spun at top speed but, strangely enough, it felt that their feet were still standing on firm ground.

Then it started getting darker and darker, until through their closed eyelids there was no sign of light.

Scamp kept his hands tightly pressed together. He found remaining vertical almost impossible because of the wild vibrations. He was buffeted that way and this, and then the darkness was unexpectedly replaced by a blinding light.

Morlenni was not totally sure what was happening. All that had penetrated her confused brain was that Lorin was back and, for some bizarre reason, every Wrecca man seemed to be asleep.

'This way,' Lorin said as she nipped along a narrow tunnel. Morlenni dumbly followed.

They came to the hole in the wall that Scratch and his diggers had made. It appeared to be abandoned, the last of the troops having scrambled through some time ago.

'Here! What you up to?' came a gruff voice. A face

peeped through the hole. This Wrecca was not like the old men Lorin had encountered in the Underneath.

'What's you doing here?' Lorin asked curtly. This Wrecca was young and carried a wooden club. She thought he had to be one of Slime's crack troops.

'I's the one asking the questions,' he growled, climbing through the hole from the Labyrinth.

She lifted her chin and said self-importantly, 'I's here on official business. Offa Scratch put I in charge of this personally.'

His brow furrowed. She had used some mighty long words.

Lorin continued. 'You see,' she said, lowering her voice and glancing over her shoulder as if she was about to reveal a great secret, 'I need to get into the Labyrinth.'

'Ner one goes in or out. Offa Scratch, himself, telled me that,' he said, immensely proud of himself. 'I's on guard duty.' Then he added, shocked, 'You willn't believe it, but they's taking all Offa's Scratch's loot out of the Labyrinth here, and trying to get it back to the Underneath!' He stood back. 'Look!' and pointed through the hole.

Lorin peered through. To one side she saw a huge pile of the women's possessions and on the other side three bloodied Wrecca bodies. The Wrecca on guard duty had clearly stopped them with his club.

'Offa Scratch wants the women's stuff to stay here,' the guard said. 'He's going to live here and he don't want it empty.'

Lorin controlled her anger as she recognized some

of her own belongings in the heap. She wanted to drug this Wrecca and get him out of the way but knew that if he was drugged he would not be able to stop the Wreccas returning to the Underneath. Everyone in the Underneath was already asleep; no one in the Labyrinth was. She had to keep them separate. The best way of doing this would be to leave him in place, doing his job. He would have to be one of the last to be drugged. The problem would be to persuade him to allow her and Morlenni through. She stepped towards the hole.

'Oh ner you doesn't,' he said and then added by way of explanation, 'Orders.'

'Oh, I has to get to Offa Scratch at once. There's things he needs to know,' she said with a sweet smile. 'He has a reward for all the troops that doesn't fail him, unlike the dung-heads there,' and she motioned towards the small heap of bodies on the Labyrinth side of the hole.

'Reward?' the Wrecca said excitedly.

She nodded. 'A juicy, big, fat reward,' she said. 'I reckon you'll be in line for the best one of all.'

'What'll it be?' he asked greedily.

'I can't tell you that.'

He looked crestfallen and a touch suspicious.

'Let's just say,' Lorin said, leaning in close and lowering her voice, 'I heared that Sniff messed up big time and Offa Scratch is looking for,' she allowed her voice to trail away so that the last word was barely audible, 'a replacement.'

The Wrecca's eyes widened with amazement. Second-in-command! He had always dreamt of that but had never thought it could possibly happen.

It was enough of a bribe. 'All right,' he said, standing back.

Lorin grabbed Morlenni by the hand and pulled her towards the hole, but, before she could get through, the Wrecca put out his dirty hand and grabbed her. 'Don't you forget to tell him,' he said. 'I's stopping anyone taking his stuff away. You tell him!'

'I will,' she said. 'You's top of my list.'

The Wrecca released her, and the two young women scrambled through the hole and hurried off.

The Labyrinth was a sorry sight; everything was in total disorder.

'Oh my word!' Lorin suddenly exclaimed in shock.

Morlenni looked up fearfully and gasped in terror. She fell back against the wall. 'Don't hurt us,' she whimpered as she sank to the ground.

'What's you doing here?' Lorin asked.

'We came to see if we could find a way through,' Bryn answered. 'Tid and Sofi are missing.'

'Missing?' Lorin said. 'Why's you looking down here?'

'It's a long story,' Bryn replied, 'but we think they are in the Guardian tunnels. We hoped we might find a way through.'

'Oh, do get up, Morlenni,' Lorin said with an irritable sigh, 'they's not frightening.' She looked back at Bryn. 'I's heared of the Guardian tunnels, but I doesn't think there's a way through.'

'Then we'll just have to keep looking,' Bryn said,

glancing at the terrified young Wrecca woman on the ground.

'You can't do that alone,' Lorin said, concerned. 'Hasn't you noticed that it's dangerous around here?'

Bryn grinned. 'Just a little.'

Lorin pulled Morlenni to her feet. 'What *is* the matter with you?' she asked, 'It's only Bryn and Joss!'

This was of no comfort to Morlenni.

'I doesn't think it's a good idea, you two wandering about by yourselves,' Lorin said.

'We'll be all right,' Joss said confidently.

It was strange, but Lorin no longer felt awkward talking to him. Perhaps it was because she was below ground, on her own territory.

'You'll get lost,' she said bluntly. 'Everyone gets lost at some time or other, even Wreccas.'

'We have to try.'

She felt responsible for them. 'Look,' she said, 'if you two help us, then I'll help you find the Guardian tunnels.' They looked doubtful. 'You'll not find nothing down here without a guide. What good'll it do if you get lost? I'll help you, but I has to finish this first. I need some more water.'

Joss did not like the idea of delay, but Bryn saw the sense of it.

'What are you up to?' he asked, looking at the jug in her hand.

Lorin's face lit up as she said with a conspiratorial grin, 'Drugging the men.'

*

Seth was sitting in a tree. He had left his grandmother by the pond because he needed to be alone to think about all that had happened.

Whoosh!

The noise was not loud but the air swirled around the tree in one almighty gust. It forced Seth to cling on, desperately hoping that the tree would not be uprooted.

Then, as quickly as it had started, the wind died down. Everything was still once more.

Relaxing his grip, Seth spied a body lying on the grass. He was certain it had not been there a moment ago. It must have been brought by the wind.

He slid down from branch to branch until he was on the ground and ran towards it.

It was a Guardian youth. 'Are you all right?' Seth asked, kneeling by his side.

Sheldon groaned. His head was on fire. 'Where am I?'

'In the park. Where did you come from?'

Sheldon opened his eyes. For a moment they did not focus. He shook his head, and the movement made him wince. He would not do that again. 'I'm in the park?' he queried.

'Yes.'

'Where are the others?' he asked, putting up a hand to steady his bursting head.

Seth looked around. 'What others?' he asked, helping Sheldon to his feet.

'There!' Sheldon spied another body in the distance. He staggered over to it. Seth followed.

Breaking Through the Fundament

It was Sofi.

'Is she dead?' Seth asked.

'Sofi,' Sheldon said softly, kneeling by her side.

She did not move.

He touched her cheek. 'Wake up.'

She opened her eyes and then closed them again with a grimace. Clearly, her head was hurting as much as his.

'Are you all right?' Sheldon asked.

She tried to nod, but it hurt too much. 'Where are we?'

'In the park.'

'It worked,' she said, feeling too sick to show any pleasure. 'Where are the others?'

'I don't know,' Sheldon said, taking her hand and helping her to her feet.

'Sheldon Croe!' His name echoed across the park. 'Leave that child alone!'

Baffled, Sofi, Sheldon and Seth turned to see Conrad Lom running across the grass towards them.

'Conrad . . .' Sofi began but did not have time to finish, because when Conrad arrived he whacked Sheldon's arm so that he dropped Sofi's hand.

'I said, leave her alone,' Conrad said angrily.

'What's the matter?' Sofi asked.

Sheldon threw Conrad a contemptuous look and defiantly took Sofi's hand again.

Conrad shoved him roughly away. 'It's all right, Sofi,' he said. 'You're safe now.'

Sheldon staggered back a few paces. Although his

333

head pounded painfully, he squared up to Conrad. 'What's your problem?'

'Kidnapping is a serious offence,' Conrad snarled, 'especially the second time around.'

'I'm not kidnapped!' Sofi exclaimed.

The two youths faced each other, fists clenched.

'Sheldon!'

Wakaa was struggling across the grass as fast as he could manage, leaning heavily on his staff. 'What is the meaning of this?'

'That's right, blame me!' Sheldon retorted resentfully.

'He's not blaming anyone,' Sofi said reasonably.

Sheldon continued to feel aggrieved.

'It's Sheldon Croe,' Conrad explained. 'The kidnapper!'

'Don't be ridiculous,' Sofi said dismissively.

'But . . .' Conrad tried to protest, but Wakaa interrupted him.

'Sheldon is our friend,' Wakaa said quietly, wincing at the pain in his head.

To Conrad, Sheldon looked anything but friendly. 'But . . .'

'I saw you strike Sheldon,' Wakaa said sternly. 'I shall be taking this matter up with the Greenwich Guardian.'

'I was protecting Sofi,' Conrad said, offended. 'I thought he was hurting her. We were told that he had kidnapped Tid and Sofi.'

'Where are Tid and the others?' Sofi interrupted.

'I have no idea,' Wakaa confessed. 'Hopefully, they are together.'

Suddenly, there were people speeding towards them from all directions. They had been alerted by the rushing wind. Sofi found herself enveloped in Enderell's arms. 'Thank goodness you are safe,' she cried. 'Where is Tid?'

No one knew the answer and Enderell's joy subsided.

The Greenwich Guardian took Seth's hand in hers and held it tightly, grateful that the wind had not harmed him.

Sofi, Sheldon and Wakaa were taken back to Old Father Tim's cottage, where Enderell mixed restorative draughts for them and Wakaa began to explain what had happened.

'Sheldon was impressive,' he said, much to Sheldon's embarrassment. 'He translated the symbols in that book of Sofi's and risked his own life to rescue Tid.'

'Twice,' Sofi added with a smile.

Sheldon felt most awkward as everyone offered their congratulations and praised him.

'Conrad,' the Greenwich Guardian said, 'you must organize a search for the others.'

Anxious to make up for his mistake, Conrad left and started to gather a search party even before Wakaa had reached the part about entering the Gemetbur.

It was not long before Aleyesu was brought to the cottage. Enderell was scrambling eggs. 'Nothing like eggs after a long journey,' she said. 'But first, drink this,' and she handed him a glass. 'That will fix your head in no time.'

When Tid was brought in, Sofi flew across the room

and threw her arms round his neck. He pulled a face as he endured another long hug from Enderell. When they had released him, he asked Sheldon, 'Are you all right?'

Sheldon nodded. 'And you?'

'I will be when my head stops trying to explode.'

Enderell handed Tid a draught to drink.

'Where's Grandfather?' he asked.

From their silence, Tid knew that Old Father Tim had not been found.

26

Conrad's Second Mistake

Taking care to keep out of sight, Lorin found a couple of extra jugs, and Joss and Bryn helped her fill them as well as the one she had been carrying. Then she added the potion.

'Enderell is a marvel!' Bryn exclaimed appreciatively as she explained the plan.

'Now I has to get the men to drink it, and you can't help.'

'But you can't do it alone,' Joss said.

'I did the Underneath alone.'

'It would be quicker if we all lent a hand,' Joss tried again. He felt strangely uncomfortable at the thought of letting Lorin do this by herself.

'Oh yer, great idea,' Lorin said. 'How am I going to explain you two?'

'Tell them we are your prisoners.'

'You doesn't understand much about Wreccas, does you? They'll kill you without a second thought and then probably kill Morlenni and I for being with you. They's not going to ask questions, Wreccas doesn't.' She glanced at her friend, who was no longer trembling at

337

the sight of Bryn and Joss, but looked dazed. 'Actually, I think Morlenni will feel better if her was out of here.'

They tried to protest.

'You's not helping!' Lorin cried in frustration. 'The only way you can is to go Topside and take Morlenni with you. Us is running out of time!'

Finally they agreed to wait for her by the Topside door. Lorin had to bully Morlenni to go with them, but eventually the three left, leaving Lorin to get on with the job in hand.

She told every man she came across that she was giving him a potion from Offa Scratch himself. 'It'll make you stronger so you can fight even better.' They all liked this idea, and soon she had men pestering her for a drink. She worked her way systematically through the Labyrinth until she found herself back at the hole. The guard was standing there, alert, ready to prove that he was worthy of the job of second-in-command.

'Offa Scratch is so pleased that you's doing such a good job that he told I to give you this,' Lorin said, offering him a drink. 'It'll make you even stronger.'

He took the tankard she offered and drank greedily from it. Soon he was yawning.

Scratch and Sniff were her priority now.

Offa Scratch paced up and down the Committee Chamber. He had been enraged when Sniff had returned without Lorin. Sniff now cowered in the corner while his leader spent a long time brooding about where Lorin was and what she was planning. He did not know she was standing outside, trying to gather the courage to enter.

Lorin took a deep breath and, pushing the faded curtain to one side, finally stepped into the chamber, still clutching the jug.

'Where's you been?' Offa Scratch demanded as soon as he saw her.

Forcing herself to remain calm, she replied, 'Everything's in order. The women is gathering in a safe place. I's going to bring them back in one go. That way there'll be no stragglers.'

'I want them here now!' he roared.

Lorin thought he was behaving like a spoilt child. 'It'll be safer to bring them all together,' she said, as if talking to a small boy. Then she added confidentially, 'They's a bit dim. You know what women's like. They's happier if they stay in a group.'

'Who's guarding them?'

'Caryd. She's good at that sort of thing.'

'But can you trust her?'

'No,' Lorin said, as if this was a ridiculous question, 'but she has a daughter. I told her that if her don't do as I says, I'll take the girl.'

Offa Scratch visibly calmed down. He understood this kind of thinking. He gave Lorin an appraising look. So, Lorin was as tricky as some of the men. He liked that. Perhaps she would be a decent second-in-command after all. She could not be worse than that dung-brain, Sniff.

'What's you got there?' Offa Scratch asked, indicating the jug in her hand.

'Oh, this here's nothing,' she said in an offhand manner, hugging the jug.

'What is it?'

'A drink.'

'I didn't think it was a shovel,' Offa Scratch said, smirking at his own humour.

Lorin made herself laugh appreciatively. 'I doesn't think it'll be grand enough for you, Offa Scratch. I make this cos I like it. I never telled Berwyth about it.'

'What is it?' he repeated, this time trying to peer into the jug.

'Essence of marigold.' This was a flower that Lorin had overheard some of the Guardian People talking about while hiding in her tree. 'With a measure of morning dew.'

Offa Scratch had never heard of anything so exotic. He licked his lips. 'Give it here,' he said to her, and then yelled at Sniff, 'Get a cup!'

Sniff grabbed the nearest one and, bending low, handed it over. 'It's a pleasure to do your bidding, Your Mightyfulness.'

Offa Scratch grabbed it and held it towards Lorin.

She smiled at him very prettily as she filled it to the brim.

He tasted it and his eyes lit up with delight as he gulped the draught down. 'I want more.'

Lorin filled the beaker again.

He swallowed it in one, dribbling some down his chin.

She glanced at Sniff. He was looking enviously at the

jug in her hand. She knew it would not take much to persuade him to drink.

Offa Scratch wiped his chin with his filthy sleeve and thrust his beaker back at Lorin. 'More!' he demanded.

She took it from him and filled it once more. 'Why doesn't you sit down, Offa Scratch,' she said soothingly. 'It tastes so much better with the weight off your feet.'

Offa Scratch was feeling strangely mellow.

Lorin handed the full beaker to Sniff. 'Hold this,' she said and deliberately turned her back on him as she took Offa Scratch's elbow and helped him to Berwyth's couch. He flopped on to it; his legs were feeling unsteady. He yawned. 'More!'

Lorin turned and took the beaker from Sniff, pretending not to notice that it was now empty. Slowly she refilled it but, before she could hand it over, the chamber was echoing with Offa Scratch's snoring.

'Oh my,' she said, moving closer to Sniff. 'Him's tired from all that work, looking after us. I 'spect you's tired too, Sniff. Why doesn't you sit down on this bench here? Will you like a drink?' and she offered him the cup. He took it greedily and started drinking, but the beaker fell from his grip before he had finished and he fell into a deep sleep.

Conrad was scouring Blackheath. He was still smarting from the telling-off he had received from Wakaa. It was hard to believe that Sheldon was now considered not only a friend but a hero. He could not help but think that there must have been some sort of mistake. He remembered Sheldon Croe as the boy who had damaged the trees in the park, bullied younger children and terrorized the Bushytails. It was difficult to believe that, in less than two years, Sheldon had changed enough to save Tid's life, twice.

Still trying to reconcile the two Sheldons, Conrad caught a glimpse of someone in the distance. This person looked like a Wrecca, although it was hard to tell from so far away. The strange thing about it was that he was carrying something, or perhaps it was someone, across his back. Conrad looked more closely. Yes, it was someone. This Wrecca was carrying a person.

Conrad wondered what he should do. He had just decided to be Mindful to a friend, who he knew was not far away, when his jaw dropped in amazement. The Wrecca was carrying Old Father Tim!

A real kidnapping!

There was no mistake this time, and no time to call anyone. Running across Blackheath, Conrad started yelling long before he drew close. 'Put him down, you filthy scum!'

Scamp looked up painfully. He was trying to navigate through unknown territory while his head felt as if it was splitting apart. It took him a moment to take in the situation.

A young and athletic Guardian youth lacking the advantage of magic was no match for a full-grown Wrecca man, even one feeling as ill as Scamp did. Putting Old Father Tim down with as much care as he could manage in his weakened state, Scamp stood his ground.

As Conrad charged, Scamp stepped nimbly aside and tripped him with his foot. Conrad pitched forward with considerable force and landed, face first, on the ground. He lay still for a second, trying to work out how he had got there. When he tried to stand, a heavy foot pressed on the back of his neck, pushing his face into the hard earth. He feared his neck would break.

'Don't make this hard on yourself,' Scamp said wearily. 'I doesn't mean you no harm.'

Conrad tried to lift himself but was thudded down into the dirt again.

'This here is Old Father Tim,' Scamp continued, 'and him's not well. You need to take him to someone who can look after him.'

'What have you done to him?' Conrad snarled, trying to spit dirt out of his mouth.

'I hasn't done nothing.' Scamp felt very tired. An angry Guardian youth was the last thing he needed.

'If you've hurt him!'

'Oh, shut up!' Scamp exclaimed and then made a face. It felt as if his brain had exploded within his skull. 'The old man's ill. Is you going to help him?'

Conrad thought for a minute. Which was more important, teaching this Wrecca a lesson or taking Old Father Tim back to Enderell?

'Yes,' he said hoarsely.

'All right, then I's going to let you up,' Scamp said, but he did not lessen the pressure on the back of Conrad's neck. 'I's been told that the Guardian People doesn't lie. I's trusting you to do as you says, cos if you doesn't, you'll be eating more than dirt, boy.'

Conrad said nothing but felt the pressure slowly easing off the back of his neck. When Scamp had removed his foot, Conrad scrambled to his feet with as much dignity as possible, and stole a look at Old Father Tim. He looked very ill.

'What have you done to him?'

Scamp ignored the question. 'Can you take him back to the park by yourself?'

Conrad thought the Wrecca actually sounded concerned. 'If you help put him on my back.'

Scamp nodded, but had to stop as he winced with the pain of it. He thought his head might fall off if he did that again. Bending down carefully so as not to set his head pumping too violently, he hauled Old Father Tim up. Conrad knelt down on one knee to make it easier for Scamp to drag the old man across his back.

Conrad was not made for fighting, but he was strong. He stood up without difficulty.

'Is the others safe?' Scamp asked.

Conrad was puzzled. What others? Who was Scamp talking about?

'Them that was with him,' Scamp said, pointing to the Old Father. 'Has they made it back?'

'Yes,' Conrad answered, even more perplexed. Why would Scamp want to know about them?

'Good,' Scamp said. 'Get going.' He was grateful to relinquish the responsibility of getting Old Father Tim to safety. Now he could go home and nurse his sore head.

Conrad pushed his confusion to the back of his mind.

From the sound of Old Father Tim's breathing, he should bring him to Enderell and her healing herbs as quickly as possible. He trudged off with no thought of being Mindful.

When eventually he entered the cottage, the sight of the Old Father caused mixed reactions of relief that he had been found and concern that he was still unconscious. The old man was quickly taken to his room and put to bed. The Greenwich Guardian and Zeit muttered magical words over him and allowed him to sleep.

'He was being carried by a Wrecca!' Conrad exclaimed, appalled.

'Was he all right?' Sofi asked anxiously.

At first Conrad was perplexed by this question because he thought she was asking about Old Father Tim, who clearly was not all right. He was, however, even more baffled when he understood that not only she but also the boys were concerned about the Wrecca.

Lorin made her way to the Topside door. She was exhausted and did not relish the task of searching for Tid and Sofi. It was tempting to take a draught of the potion in the jug she was still clasping. How she longed to fall asleep!

She approached the door.

'There you are!' Joss exclaimed, relieved.

'Thank goodness,' Bryn said, hurrying towards her. 'I was not sure I was going to be able to keep Joss here much longer. He has been anxious to go back and search for you.'

'You were ages,' Joss said.

'I had a lot to do,' Lorin said wearily. 'And there's still more,' she added with a sigh.

'The only thing you are going to do, young lady,' Bryn said, taking the jug from her and giving it to Joss, 'is walk to Old Father Tim's cottage.'

'But what about Tid and Sofi?'

'Home,' Bryn said. 'Both of them, safe and sound.'

Lorin was too tired to ask how he knew this. She would have had difficulty understanding being Mindful even if Bryn had tried to explain it to her.

Lorin stifled a yawn. She noted with relief that Morlenni seemed used to the two men's presence now. 'How's your head?' she asked.

'Still hurts.'

'Come now,' Bryn said, offering his arm to Lorin. She took it gratefully. Morlenni looked alarmed, thinking that Joss might do the same for her, but he did not.

'I am certain that Enderell will have a restorative draught for us all,' Bryn said, and together they all walked back to the cottage.

Morlenni hesitated at the door. She was nervous about going into any sort of house, but especially one that she knew belonged to Old Father Tim. She did not want to cross the threshold, unsure what kind of magic he might have put on his own front door.

'Don't be so wet!' Lorin said, noticing her friend's hesitation. She shoved her in the back and Morlenni stumbled into the house. She spent the next few minutes trying to discover if she was turning into a frog.

They were warmly greeted by everyone. Enderell handed round drinks. Morlenni was hesitant about taking one; it did not seem safe to drink anything offered by one of the Guardian People, but Lorin was drinking hers down and so she took a nervous sip.

The sensation was something of a revelation to her. The delicious drink made Morlenni's lips tingle. Then her mouth was afire with pleasure. She took a larger sip, and her throat purred as the exquisite liquid slid down. Morlenni was so overwhelmed by the taste that she failed to notice her headache melting away.

'Where are the Old Father and Wakaa?' Bryn asked.

A silence fell upon the gathering.

'The Old Father is a little tired after his journey,' the Greenwich Guardian said, trying to not alarm anyone with the truth, 'and Wakaa is with him.'

'I'm not surprised the old man is worn out,' Bryn said. 'I'm exhausted! I wish I could be like the Wrecca men and take some of Enderell's sleeping draught.'

'Yer,' Lorin added happily. 'They's all drugged now. Every single one of them is snoring like anything, including Scratch!'

'How long will they sleep?' Joss asked Enderell.

'Did you use it as I directed?' she asked Lorin.

Lorin pulled a face. 'It's hard to tell,' she said. 'The sink was so big. I think I put in too much.'

'No harm done,' Enderell said. 'They will have a bit of a hangover when they wake up, that is all.'

'Serves them right!' Lorin declared.

'They should sleep for a few more hours.'

'Then we have time,' Bryn said, swallowing the eggs that Enderell had given him. 'We need every able-bodied man. The Wreccas must be taken back to the Underneath, and then we shall rebuild that wall.'

27

A New Day

Early next morning, as the sun was rising in the park, the Guardian People were already awake. Some sat by their front gates, some gathered together at the Line, others wanted to go out on to Blackheath. Excitedly they watched as Humans started their daily routine. It was different! Time had been bounced back into alignment.

The Bushytails slept late.

The weary adventurers in Old Father Tim's cottage also slept late. The Greenwich Guardian and Enderell had spent the night taking it in turns to watch over Old Father Tim. By the morning his condition had not changed. Lorin and Morlenni had slept on Sofi's floor and Seth on Tid's. Wakaa had spent the night at Bryn's cottage and Aleyesu had gone with Sheldon to the Loms.

By midday they were all back, eating a delicious meal of pancakes and syrup. There were too many to sit around the table, and so some sat on the floor and in Old Father Tim's comfy armchairs.

Then Bryn, Joss and Conrad returned with the work party. 'The Labyrinth is clear of Wreccas now,' Bryn said cheerfully. 'Any food going, Enderell? I could eat a horse!'

'Were there any problems?' The Greenwich Guardian asked.

'None at all,' Joss replied. 'They are all sleeping like babies. That draught of yours was pretty potent stuff, Enderell,' he added with admiration.

'I think Lorin made it up a little stronger than I intended.'

'I didn't want any mistakes,' Lorin said.

'Absolutely!' Bryn said jovially.

'And the wall?' the Greenwich Guardian asked.

'Conrad did a marvellous job,' Bryn told them. 'It looks better than the original. He's good at walls, Grenya. I'm thinking of letting him look at the one at the bottom of my garden.'

'I used fast-drying mortar,' Conrad explained. 'I hope the Wreccas will sleep long enough to let it set properly.'

'Even if they do not, I doubt they will be doing much when they wake up,' Enderell said. 'I added something extra to the bottle I gave Lorin.'

'What was it?' Lorin asked.

'I thought it might be helpful if they did not remember too much about what has happened in the last few weeks.'

'A forgetting draught!' Bryn exclaimed. 'Enderell, you are a star!'

She accepted everyone's congratulations with a serene nod of the head.

Then, more seriously, Bryn asked, 'How is the Old Father?'

'Still asleep,' the Greenwich Guardian said. She tried to sound light-hearted, but everyone knew that this was serious.

Enderell fed the work party, and then it was decided that they should go and get some sleep.

'Send word if the Old Father's condition alters,' Bryn said quietly to his sister. Then, quite suddenly, he drew in an enormous breath and let out a trumpet-like sneeze. 'Oh, no,' he moaned, 'I hope I am not starting a cold!'

The work party, except Joss, went to their beds, and everyone else left to tell the Wrecca women that they could return to the Labyrinth.

'Their draught was different to the men's,' Enderell explained. 'They won't have a headache when they wake up. In fact,' she added, 'they will probably be in a very good mood.'

'Any chance of using that draught regularly in the Labyrinth?' Lorin joked.

'I could teach you some basic herbal blends, if you like.'

'Really?' Lorin asked, hardly able to believe her ears. 'Will you really?'

'Of course.'

'I use soils, but they isn't very good.'

'Soils? I had read that some soils have healing qualities, but I have never used any. I think that my grandmother's grandmother did.'

'I doesn't know much,' Lorin said, 'but I'll show you what I does.'

As they walked towards the pond, the two women arranged when they should next meet.

Morlenni had now learnt not to fear the Guardian People, but she could not relax around them like Lorin did. She waited for her friend to stop talking to Enderell and then hurried to catch up with her. There was something they needed to talk about.

'Lorin.'

'Yer.'

Morlenni looked awkward, as if she had something difficult to say.

'Spit it out,' Lorin encouraged her.

'Well, it's not my business, really,' Morlenni began.

Lorin gave her a look that said, 'Get on with it.'

'Well . . . is you . . . is you really going out with Scratch?'

Lorin's reaction was not what Morlenni had expected. She threw back her head and roared with laughter. Then she put her arm round her friend's shoulders. 'Ner, Morlenni,' she said, 'I think I can promise you that will never happen.'

Sofi walked with Tid, but she kept an eye on Lorin. She had a question of her own. At the first opportunity, Sofi pulled her to one side.

'Lorin . . .' With her grandfather lying so ill in his bed at home, it seemed a terrible thing to be talking about, but Sofi had to know the answer.

'What's up, Sofe?'

'Is . . . is my mother with the women under the trees?'

Lorin's expression turned to one of the utmost seriousness. 'Ner,' she said gently. 'Her died, a while back.'

Sofi bit her lip hard to keep it from trembling.

'But I did know her.'

'Did you?'

'When I comed back from the Underneath, I was in a bit of state. She let I share her alcove. She was nice.'

Sofi's throat began to hurt as she tried to fight back tears.

'My own mother was dead,' Lorin continued, 'and so I always looked upon your mother as mine. She asked about you all the time, and I had to remember everything. I told her how you never telled when I went Topside. I told her you was a good'un.'

Tears filled Sofi's eyes. 'What was her name?'

Lorin smiled. 'When I getted back to the Labyrinth, no one remembered what my name was and so I taked your mother's name.'

'Lorin,' Sofi said softly.

Lorin nodded.

'What was my name before I was taken to the Underneath?'

Lorin smiled. 'You was Lorin, too.'

Sofi found herself smiling. 'We share the same name.'

'Us does.'

'Then we're like sisters.'

Lorin's face lit up. 'Us is.'

The smile faded from Sofi's lips. 'How did she die?'

'In her sleep, waiting for her daughter to come home.'

Sofi started to cry.

Lorin put her arms round her, and they hugged.

After the Wrecca women had eaten and Lorin had assured them that Scratch and the others had been taken back to the Underneath, they were anxious to go home. Lorin had half expected to see Berwyth among the women, but both she and her Committee had disappeared.

Lorin did not have much time to wonder about them, for she soon found herself trying to explain to the women the state the Labyrinth would be in when they returned. Bryn and the others had bundled most of the women's belongings in one enormous heap in the kitchen. Lorin knew it would take a great deal of organization to sort them all out. She suspected that she would spend much of her time in the next few days trying to keep the peace. However, for the moment, Enderell's draught had left the women in such good spirits that they listened to her with good humour and, while they did not exactly thank anyone for their kindness, they did leave happily.

Morlenni was relieved to be back with her own kind. Lorin hugged first Enderell and then Sofi once more. Quietly she whispered, 'I'll see you, Sofe,' and Sofi knew that she was not seeing the last of her new sister.

'Goodbye, Greenwich Guardian,' Lorin said, shaking her hand confidently.

'Come and see me any time.'

'Ner, I'll not be crossing Greenwich any time soon,'

Lorin said. 'Maybe I'll see you in the park sometime.'

Enderell and Sofi hugged Lorin once more at the park gate and then stood and watched as the Wrecca women started across Blackheath, before finally walking back to Old Father Tim's cottage, where Zeit and Wakaa were watching over the old man.

Halfway across Blackheath, Lorin heard someone calling her name. She turned and saw Joss running towards her, laden with something quite bulky. Her heart started thudding gently. What could he possibly want?

He quickly caught up with her and, slightly out of breath, offered her the wicker chair, neatly fitted with patchwork cushions, that she had sat on at the Hither House.

Lorin stepped back. 'N . . . no,' she stammered. It was far too beautiful for her to own.

Joss smiled kindly, as if he understood. 'The Greenwich Guardian says you are to have it. Chairs at the Hither House are made for those who sit on them. This is your chair. No one else will ever use it.' He held it out towards her again.

Lorin hesitated, before taking it with trembling hands. 'Thank you,' she said quietly.

The Old Father slept on. He was never alone; someone always sat with him. Enderell said it might help if he could hear voices, and so they all took turns to talk to him. Wakaa used deep magic, but even that could not wake the old man.

In the night, Tid found himself lying in bed, unable to sleep. He had been worrying that his grandfather might never wake up again. Softly, he crept to the old man's bedroom.

He peeped round the door, expecting to see one of the grown-ups sitting in the chair next to his grandfather's bed, but it was empty. Instead, Sofi sat on the bed, gently stroking Old Father Tim's silver hair and talking.

'My mother's name was Lorin,' she was explaining. 'That was my name, too, before I went to the Underneath. I'd like to use it again, not instead of Sofi, that's my Topside name. I thought I'd use it as a middle name. I shall be Sofi Lorin Mossel. Would you mind? I know it will be odd, having a Guardian and a Wrecca name but then, that is what I am, isn't it: a mixture, both Guardian and Wrecca,' and she suddenly realized that she did not mind; in fact, she was rather proud to have been born a Wrecca, like Lorin and her mother.

'I thought,' she continued, 'that my extra name would make it possible to make a good anagram, but all I came up with was "Noises fill rooms".'

Tid chuckled and Sofi, realizing he was there, beckoned him forward. He went and sat on the other side of the bed. Sofi began talking again and Tid took one of the old man's wrinkled hands in his and settled down to listen.

'It's quite sad, really,' Sofi was saying, 'because I wanted my own mother for as long as I can remember, and I'm sorry that she's dead; but if she had been alive,

I would not have wanted to go and live with her. It's not that I wouldn't have loved my mother, I would, I know it; but I also love living here. I love Tid.' She glanced up, a little self-consciously.

Tid gave her a supportive smile.

'But I love you most of all,' and suddenly her voice broke and she put her arms round the old man and buried her face in his neck.

Tid suddenly understood that Sofi shared his fear that their grandfather might never wake up. He wanted to say something reassuring but did not know what.

Then he felt a gentle pressure on his hand. He looked up hopefully. The old man's eyes were still closed, but a tear was trickling out of the corner of one, and his arm was round Sofi, hugging her.

'Grandfather!' Tid cried, letting go of his hand and throwing himself on the old man. Old Father Tim put his other arm round his grandson and held his grandchildren close.

Offa Scratch's mouth felt as if it was full of gravel. He licked his lips, but his tongue was dry. He opened his eyes and shut them again. Even the meagre light from the torch flickering on the wall was too bright for them.

He moved his head. 'Agghhh!' he cried, and that made his head hurt all the more. Where was he?

Opening his eyes a little, he squinted around. There were Wreccas in untidy heaps everywhere. Some were asleep. Those who were waking up looked to be in terrible pain.

'Getmeadrink,' Offa Scratch mumbled. The sound was too much for any of them. They all winced.

What had happened? He could not remember. He was certain he had done something very clever, but he could not remember what.

'Get me a drink!' he said in a hoarse whisper, but the only Wrecca response was a resonating snore.

28

Tempus Always Finds a Way

The next day, Tid and Sofi did not go to school. They had been given a couple of days at home to recover from their adventure.

Old Father Tim ate his breakfast in bed. Tid was cutting up his toast and handing him a slender, buttered oblong to dip into his soft-boiled egg.

'It was horrible while you were asleep,' Sofi was saying as she sat on the end of the bed. 'Everything is different without you here to love us.'

'And you to love me back.'

'Yes, one without the other wouldn't mean much, would it?' she said philosophically.

'My word, young Sofi Lorin Mossel,' the old man said with a grandfatherly smile, 'you have come a long way since you started living with us. I remember a lonely girl, newly out from the Underneath, who said she did not know how to love.'

Sofi smiled. 'It's easy here.'

'It's always easier to love where you are loved,' Old Father Tim said, squeezing her hand affectionately.

Sofi squeezed it back. 'What do you think happened

359

to the Wreccas who were locked out of the Gemetbur?' she asked.

'I suspect there may now be a few more shadows inhabiting those tunnels,' Old Father Tim said.

'Never to see the light of day again,' Sofi said darkly.

'So, the shadow of the Murky Deep will have some friends to keep it company. Doesn't bear thinking about, does it?' Tid said, pulling a face.

They sat, thinking about this for a moment. Then Old Father Tim fumbled in his bedside drawer and pulled out a scrap of paper that he handed to her. 'I wrote this out for you.'

On it was written, 'I, Tempus, halted death'.

Sofi looked at him questioningly.

'I could not sleep after you two had gone back to bed, and so I started playing with anagrams. That,' and the old man pointed to the piece of paper, 'is an anagram of Thadius Plemet-Thead.'

Sofi looked back at the paper and tried mentally to check off the letters. Tid hung over her shoulder and did it much more quickly.

'It's right!' he said, in delight. 'I, Tempus, halted death! Well done, Grandfather! It was a pity we didn't use the Plemet bit when we were in the tunnels. It might have cheered us up a bit.'

'It was a pity we had to leave my book behind,' Sofi said.

'When I am fit again, we shall go to the bookshop and buy you another copy.'

'Thank you, Grandfather,' Sofi said, with a smile. She loved going to the bookshop.

'Do you think we'll be able to find the same edition?'

'No, Sofi,' Old Father Tim said seriously, 'I do not think we will. Your book was an extra-special copy.'

'How did we get it?'

'Tempus finds a way,' Old Father Tim said.

'I wish we hadn't had to leave the paperweight behind,' Tid said. 'It could have been useful if anyone ever needed to get into the Gemetbur again.'

Old Father Tim smiled at his grandson. 'Tempus always finds a way.'

At midday there was a knock at the door. Enderell peered out of the window and gasped in fright. 'It's a Wrecca,' she hissed at the Greenwich Guardian. 'What do I do?'

Tid and Sofi looked out. 'Scamp!' they both shouted in delight and flung the door open.

Scamp was holding Old Father Tim's staff. 'I leaved it behind where I finded Old Father Tim,' he said. 'I fetched it this morning.'

Tid and Sofi insisted that Scamp go upstairs and give it to Old Father Tim himself. Comfortable in all surroundings, Scamp climbed the stairs and spent a relaxed hour talking with the old man. Old Father Tim promised that as soon as Enderell allowed him out of bed, he would show Scamp exactly how the Timepiece worked.

'How will I get in touch with you?' Old Father Tim asked.

'Ask Lorin,' Scamp said. 'The women has asked her to be their leader. Her's making all sorts of changes in the Labyrinth.'

'Wow!' Tid exclaimed, very impressed.

'What of Berwyth?' Old Father Tim asked.

'No one seed her. She runned away, I think. Lorin has choosed her Committee. From what I can make out, it's totally different from the last one. They's starting a school for the little'uns. Not that no one knows much to teach, but Lorin says us'll learn.'

'Us?' Old Father Tim asked.

'Yer,' Scamp said with a smile. 'I live in the Labyrinth now. Not all the women is keen on the idea, but Lorin says that Wrecca men who doesn't want to be nasty and mean deserve a chance, and so they's gived me an alcove. It's on its own, away from the women, but I doesn't mind. I's got a bench and I'll scavenge some tools so I can mend some of the furniture. Some of it's in a bit of a state.'

Tid suddenly remembered something and disappeared downstairs for a moment. When he returned he was holding a brand-new shovel. 'We thought,' he said, 'that is, all of us thought, that you might be able to find a use for this.'

'For me?'

'Yes,' Sofi said, grinning, 'because you had to leave your other one behind.'

Scamp took it and examined it carefully. 'Phew,' he said. 'It's a good'un.'

*

Seth strode through the park; he had something important to do. Baz had told him that he would be under his tree after school, and so that was where Seth was going. He did not, however, expect Baz to remember, and so when he arrived and saw his friend walking up and down under the tree he was pleased to see him. It was miserable, though, not to be able to talk to each other. Strangely, Baz seemed to be happy. Seth had thought that he might have felt bad.

'I don't know if you're here, Seth,' Baz began, 'but I said I'd be here and so I reckon you are. I have the best news. The results of Mum's tests are back, and she's OK. I mean, she'll still get tired and all that, but the cancer's gone. The doctors said so. She's going to be all right.' He spoke with such delight that Seth could not help but feel a little of his happiness. He did not know what cancer was, but it sounded serious.

'But the best thing is that Dad says that we're going to go back home so that we can all live together! Can you believe it? He says something about nearly losing Mum made him realize how much he misses her. Anyway, Dad's got his old job back and he's bought the plane tickets and everything.' His face suddenly lost some of its animation. 'And so I won't be around any more. I'm sorry, Seth. I know I can't see you or anything, but I had thought that I could hang out here a bit each day and it would be sort of like it was before, but I can't even do that now. Oh hell!' he suddenly exclaimed. 'I wish I knew if you were here.'

Seth wished he could tell him. Suddenly, he had an

idea. He paused. He had to be certain that he would not start the time wobble problems all over again. He thought carefully; no, this would be all right because he was not going to touch Baz. Throwing a stone would not cause any problems. Picking one up, he lobbed it towards his friend. The stone fell at his feet with a thud. Baz looked puzzled. Seth lobbed another one. This one fell on his shoe.

Baz's face lit up. 'You are here!' he exclaimed, looking around, wondering whether having a stone lobbed at him would make the time wobbles reappear. But nothing happened. The earth did not tremble beneath his feet. He could not see his friend.

'Look, Seth,' Baz said, 'I wanted to say that you were the best friend ever, and I'll never forget you.'

Seth picked up a handful of small stones and showered them at Baz's feet.

Baz understood.

29

The Time Apprentice

Everything returned to normal; it was as though nothing unusual had happened. Enderell only came during the day now to help Old Father Tim, and Sofi, Tid and Seth returned to school.

On the first day back, everyone in the playground was anxious to know what had happened, and soon a crowd of excited children gathered around Sofi and Tid. Seth hung his head and walked away. It was nice to know that his grandmother loved him, and it was good that Tid and Sofi were safe, but life at school was going to be the same lonely experience it had always been.

He was hanging around the edge of the playground when he heard an aeroplane overhead. He looked up, wondering whether Baz had already flown home to America. Suddenly, he heard his teacher.

'Seth!'

He looked towards her. She was approaching with a boy at her side. Seth did not recognize him. He looked nervous.

'Seth, this is Cory,' Ma Popple said. 'It is his first day

today and he does not know anyone. Please would you look after him?'

Seth looked at Cory. He was smaller than Seth, with mouse-coloured hair, and he looked scared stiff. Seth remembered how terrified he had been on his first day at school.

'Will you do that?' Ma Popple asked.

'Yes,' Seth said politely.

'Thank you.' And she left.

Cory looked ill at ease. There was an awkward silence.

'Where do you come from?' Seth asked, for the sake of something to say.

'America.'

Seth smiled. 'I know someone who lives there.'

'Whereabouts? Maybe I know him,' Cory said enthusiastically.

I doubt it,' Seth said with a wry smile, thinking briefly about Baz and wondering how he had settled into his Human world, back in America.

An uncomfortable silence fell between them again.

'Do you like football?' Seth asked.

'I didn't think you played it,' Cory said.

'Oh no, not American football, I mean soccer. That's what you call it, isn't it?'

'Yeah, I play it at home, but I'm not very good.'

'Neither am I,' Seth said, delighted to have found someone who might be as bad as he. 'We could practise together, if you like.'

'Great! I need all the help I can get!'

The bell went.

'Come on,' Seth said happily. 'I'll show you where to put your bag. You can sit next to me.'

It was time to choose the Time Apprentice. The Guardians and their apprentices were to gather at the Line, where Old Father Tim was to perform the official ceremony. Although still pale, he was recovering well.

'You, my boy,' he said to Tid, 'will be allowed to attend.'

'What about Sofi?'

Old Father Tim pulled a face. 'I know she will be disappointed, but you are the Old Father Grandson. You must be given the opportunity to attend such ceremonies. If you are diligent with your studies and work hard, it is probable that you will become the Old Father one day.'

'I know,' Tid replied. 'I remember Wakaa saying, ages ago, that it "is not written but it is usual practice", but it won't happen automatically. If I turn out to be useless and don't become the Old Father, is it possible that Sofi could?'

Old Father Tim thought about this. 'That is a very good question, my boy. There is no reason why she should not.'

'Then she should be allowed to come to the ceremony too.'

'If you put it like that,' Old Father Tim said, 'why do we not invite your whole school? After all, they all aspire to be apprentices.'

And so it was that the following afternoon, the entire school walked to the Line. They were very excited, never having been allowed to attend such an important occasion before. Many hoped to become apprentices when they left school. They sat in a circle at the Line and chatted away expectantly.

Wakaa, Vremya and Seegan sat with Kanika, Pasha, Sasha and Yu Yul. Zeit and Sheldon were also there.

Sheldon sat low in his chair and tried to look invisible. He looked across at Yu Yul, who sat nervously next to Seegan. Her glossy black hair shone in the afternoon sun. She smiled back at him.

The Greenwich Guardian stepped forward and helped Old Father Tim to stand up. He then walked to the middle and held up his staff. Everyone fell quiet and waited for him to speak.

'Welcome to you all,' he began. 'This is a very special occasion, as you know. We have five candidates who aspire to become the new Time Apprentice. This is an honour that will be bestowed on just one. It will give him or her spectacular opportunities for learning. In choosing this person – and any of the candidates would be worthy – we Guardians have to take into consideration many things. He or she must be reliable, hard-working and faithful, as well as showing outstanding ability.'

Sheldon looked across at Sofi and Tid, who were sitting with their friends, eagerly listening to the old man's words. Sheldon assumed that when Tid's turn came and he was old enough, he would become the Time Apprentice. Sheldon found that this idea did not anger him as it once would have done. In the past, he had resented Tid for being the Old Father Grandson, but not any more. Then he thought of Sofi and wondered if she might be a better choice. Tid was very good at what he did, but it struck Sheldon that in many ways Sofi was just as good and had had more to over- come. She glanced across at him and smiled. Sheldon looked away. Why did he always feel his face colour up when Sofi did something like that?

'So now we come to the part where I announce the new Time Apprentice,' Old Father Tim was saying.

Yu Yul sat a little straighter and looked apprehensive. Pasha's eyes were boring into the Old Father; Sasha looked nervously at his feet. Only Kanika appeared composed. She sat serenely, looking at Old Father Tim, waiting for his pronouncement.

'In my experience, this is the first time that the vote was unanimous. This Apprentice has proved worthy of such a title, not only in skills, but also in loyalty and steadfastness, which are qualities that he had to learn for himself. They did not come naturally.'

Yu Yul's shoulder's sagged a little. The Old Father had said 'he'. It would not be her. Pasha sat up eagerly. Sasha started biting his nails.

'I would like to ask our new Time Apprentice to come forward,' Old Father Tim said. He turned and called, 'Sheldon Croe!'

Momentarily there was a stunned silence. Although word of his recent exploits had been circulated, Sheldon was still regarded with suspicion. He was remembered by most people as a disaffected, unpleasant sort of boy who had been sent away to Reform School only eighteen months before.

Suddenly, a squeal of delight cut the air. Sofi, astonished by this announcement, was holding her hand in front of her mouth. No one had expected Sheldon to be chosen. Her eyes were full of joy. Next to her, Tid shouted, 'Good choice!'

Sheldon was no less shocked than the others. He sat as though glued to his chair, certain that there had been a mistake: a horrible, embarrassing mistake.

'Many of you seem surprised,' Old Father Tim said, looking around at the baffled faces. 'You remember Sheldon from his childhood.'

Sheldon gripped the sides of his seat tightly and looked into his lap. He knew he had been a nasty child. The thought of it made his insides squirm in shame.

'But I, for one,' Old Father Tim continued, 'would not like to live in a world that makes people pay for their mistakes forever. Sheldon did wrong in the past, there is no denying, but he has changed. Not only is this apparent from his time in Germany, where he worked with Zeit and attained the position of apprentice in record time, but also recently, here in Greenwich. Here in his home town Sheldon has shown courage, loyalty and strength that is second to none. However, I have to tell you that, in addition to this, Sheldon has shown a gifting in the field of ancient translations that has stunned us all.' He turned and looked at the youth sitting, slumped, in his chair. 'Please come up here, Sheldon!'

Sheldon did not move. He felt every eye upon him but kept his own on his lap.

Zeit nudged him. 'Go along.'

Sheldon did not move. He wanted to be anywhere but there. This was far too embarrassing. He knew what everyone was thinking: he had been an appalling boy. Everyone in Greenwich had hated him, and now he was being given this incredible honour. The other apprentices had far more right to it. They must all resent him so much.

Aleyesu approached. 'Sheldon Croe.' His voice was deep and commanding. 'I want you to study with me. You have an outstanding gift for translation. It would grieve me to see it wasted.'

Sheldon looked up. It would grieve him, too. He could think of nothing he wanted more than to be taught by Aleyesu.

'But you are Zeit's apprentice,' Aleyesu continued. 'You cannot be apprenticed to more than one Guardian unless you are the Time Apprentice.'

Sheldon took a deep breath. He wanted to study with Aleyesu so badly that he would do almost anything. Slowly releasing the sides of his seat, he stood up.

Aleyesu started clapping.

Tid stood up and cheered as he started clapping too. Sofi jumped up beside him and did the same. The Guardians joined in enthusiastically. Yu Yul smiled as she applauded. If she had not been chosen, she was glad that Sheldon had. Bryn stood up too. 'Well done, Sheldon!' he bellowed, clapping loudly.

Eventually everyone was applauding, although many

did so only half-heartedly. Sheldon was still disliked by the majority, and he knew that people would not change their minds overnight. This was something he was going to have to work at.

He walked awkwardly towards the Old Father, who shook his hand warmly. The applause died away.

'Congratulations, my boy,' Old Father Tim said cheerfully. 'I am delighted.'

Sheldon felt nervous, scared and excited all at once. He looked across at the faces of the children staring at him. Some seemed perplexed; they had expected one of the interesting apprentices from foreign lands to receive this honour.

There were two faces in the middle of the throng that were beaming: Sofi and Tid were thrilled. Sheldon found this encouraging. After all, they knew him better than anyone, and they seemed to think he was worthy.

'You have to tell us whether or not you accept,' Old Father Tim said quietly.

Sheldon's mouth had gone dry. He knew he had to say something. He wanted to accept. He desperately wanted to learn about translations. But how could he? He was just not good enough.

He looked across once more at Tid and Sofi, and it was Sofi's eyes, always so expressive, that held him. Although some distance away, he was caught by the look in them, and Sheldon suddenly realized that she was desperate for him to accept. At that moment, it seemed to him, this was the one thing she wanted most in all the world.

It was the one thing he wanted most in all the world, too. For the first time in his life he was being offered exactly what he most desired.

He had to speak.

Everyone was waiting.

'I am . . .' he thought carefully, wanting to say this correctly and not let anyone down, '. . . very happy to accept.'